Praise for the novels of Leonard Goldberg

Deadly Exposure

"Goldberg mines his considerable knowledge to create a story that will terrify his audience. This is the stuff of nightmares." —*Library Journal*

"Rushes along at a brisk clip." —*Chicago Tribune*

"Goldberg has created another exciting story." —*Booklist*

"A lethal microbe, a brutal murder, and a sentient iceberg menace coolly competent forensic pathologist Joanna Blalock . . . salty . . . zingy." —*Kirkus Reviews*

"Compelling." —*Publishers Weekly*

"A riveting biological thriller . . . a nonstop thrill ride of medical suspense." —*Lincoln Journal Star* (NE)

Deadly Harvest

"Diabolical . . . a first-rate medical thriller."
—*Virginian Pilot*

"Excellent . . . a tangled web of a case . . . Goldberg has the anatomy of ingenious murders down pat."
—*Kirkus Reviews*

"A page-turner with ample plot twists, medical realism, believable dialogue, and characters who command our sympathies." —*Charleston Post and Courier*

Continued . . .

A Deadly Practice

"Goldberg keeps Dr. Blalock in jeopardy and the culprit is well-concealed. . . . The sense of events happening in a real institution matches the work of other, longer-established doctors who write. The sights, sounds, smells and routines of a great hospital become a character in the story."   —*Los Angeles Times Book Review*

"Terrific! Guarantees medical authenticity, nonstop enjoyment. . . . Joanna Blalock is a great character. . . . This is truly a gripping mystery, well-written and altogether an extremely satisfying read."   —*Affaire de Coeur*

Deadly Medicine

"A shuddery venture, worthy of Robin Cook or Michael Crichton, into the cold gray corridors of a hospital that confirms our very worst fears."   —Donald Stanwood

"A terrific thriller, with unflagging pace, a driving sense of urgency that keeps the reader turning the pages, great characters (Joanna Blalock is especially good) and the kind of medical authenticity that really rings true."
                    —Francis Roe

ALSO BY LEONARD GOLDBERG

LETHAL MEASURES

Leonard Goldberg

AN ONYX BOOK

ONYX
Published by New American Library, a division of
Penguin Putnam Inc., 375 Hudson Street,
New York, New York 10014, U.S.A.
Penguin Books Ltd, 27 Wrights Lane,
London W8 5TZ, England
Penguin Books Australia Ltd, Ringwood,
Victoria, Australia
Penguin Books Canada Ltd, 10 Alcorn Avenue,
Toronto, Ontario, Canada M4V 3B2
Penguin Books (N.Z.) Ltd, 182–190 Wairau Road,
Auckland 10, New Zealand

Penguin Books Ltd. Registered Offices:
Harmondsworth, Middlesex, England

Published by Onyx, an imprint of New American Library,
a division of Penguin Putnam Inc. Originally published in a Dutton edition.

First Onyx Printing, November 2000
10 9 8 7 6 5 4 3 2 1

For Paige and Julie

There's no savagery of beasts
that's not infinitely outdone
by that of man.

—Herman Melville,
Moby-Dick

1

The Mardi Gras festival in West Hollywood brought out the cross-dressers in force. Most were men in cocktail dresses and evening gowns. A few had on Playboy bunny outfits despite the chilly night air. Onlookers lined the sidewalks, pointing and laughing as a pair in miniskirts and high heels blew kisses as they passed. A flasher in a raincoat quickly exposed and covered himself. The crowd roared. Two cops appeared out of nowhere and escorted the man away. The crowd booed.

Eva Reineke watched one of the policemen speak into a walkie-talkie. Her eyes went back to the crowd, trying to spot other cops listening with earpieces or talking into handheld transmitters. She didn't see any, but she knew they were there. She could sense their presence.

Someone bumped into her from behind and pushed her forward. She turned abruptly, her hand reaching instinctively for the semiautomatic weapon in her waistband.

"Sorry, little lady," the drunk slurred. He looked at her for a moment, then smiled crookedly. "Or are you a little boy?"

Eva tried to move around the drunk, who was wearing the uniform of an Air Force colonel. There were no ribbons or decorations on his chest. A fake, she thought. It was probably a costume.

The man grabbed her shoulders and pulled her close. His breath smelled like stale beer. "Let's take off that cap and see if you're a little boy."

Eva brought her knee up forcefully and slammed it into the drunk's crotch. The man dropped like a dead weight, gagging and groping for his testicles. Unhurriedly Eva walked away and waited a full ten seconds before glancing back. The drunk was still curled up on the sidewalk. No one had come to his assistance. The crowd was too busy watching the freak show.

Eva came to the window of a music store and stopped to study her reflection. She was wearing combat fatigues and a billed cap that was pulled down to the tip of her nose. The only exposed part of her face was her lips and chin. Her gaze went to the reflections of the people passing behind her. They were all civilians. No uniforms, no cops.

"Hey! This guy is hurt!" a voice cried out.

Eva walked into the store and browsed, occasionally glancing at the front window. People were hurrying by to see the new show. A sick man lying on the sidewalk. That would be more interesting than a bunch of loony transvestites. Fucking people, she thought disgustedly and wondered for the thousandth time what America was coming to.

"Can I help you?" asked a young clerk wearing jeans and a tank top with no bra.

"I'm looking for gospel," Eva said.

"In the back near the door," the clerk replied, pointing. "If you need any help, let me know."

"You bet."

"That's a cool outfit you've got on. Where did you get it?"

"Army-Navy store."

Eva strolled to the rear, and when the clerk wasn't looking she slipped out the back door. The parking lot was full, the attendant leaning against a wall, smoking a joint and listening to rap music on a boom box. Eva hurried across the dimly lighted lot, then stepped over a low cement wall and went down a narrow alley until she reached Fletcher Drive. She stopped, moved into the shadows and waited to see if anyone was following her. A dog barked. A television set up ahead was playing too loud. The alley remained deserted.

Eva walked up the street that led into the Hollywood Hills. It was after 10:00 P.M. and most of the houses were dark. Those few with their lights on had the living room drapes tightly closed. No doubt their doors were bolted and secured, Eva thought grimly. And some of the homeowners probably had loaded weapons because this was not a safe neighborhood. But the people on the block wouldn't have to worry about their safety much longer. Soon they'd be dead. The treacherous would die for sure, and so would some of the innocent. Eva had no regrets about that. When God wanted to stamp out evil, he frequently killed innocent people as well. He did it in Sodom and Gomorrah. He did it in Noah's time with the flood. It was God's way.

Eva glanced quickly up and down the street before she crossed over. There were a few cars parked along the curb, but she recognized them. They belonged to neighbors. She heard a rustling sound somewhere close by and stopped, all of her senses now alerted. Her eyes went to a nearby hedge as she reached for her weapon. Then she saw what it was. A neighbor's cat was stalking something in the bushes.

She moved quickly to the door and knocked once sharply. Then she knocked twice more.

"Who's there?" a male voice asked.

"One of the Righteous," Eva said.

The door opened and Eva entered a small living room. There was no furniture, not even a chair. The venetian blinds were old and yellow and drawn shut.

"Where are they?" Eva asked quietly.

"In the kitchen."

"Tell me everything that happened. I want the exact words that were spoken."

"Well, some of it was in Spanish, so I—"

"Just tell me what you remember." Eva cut him off. "I want it word for word."

Rudy Payte stroked his goatee as he thought back. He was stocky and well built, in his late twenties, with his hair shaved down to his scalp. "I went to take a leak, and when I came back I heard one of them speaking English."

"You were still in the hall outside the kitchen door. Right?"

"Right. They didn't know I was there," Rudy said, keeping his voice low. "Anyway, I thought it was kind of strange that the guy was speaking English. They always talk in Spanish when they're alone. "

"What was he saying?"

"He wanted to know how much the reward would be if he told them which bank was going to be robbed."

Eva's face hardened. "He had to be talking to the cops."

"Or the feds." Rudy nodded. "One of his friends said something in Spanish, and then the guy asked the cops how they could be sure they'd get the reward money."

"And then?"

"That's when I coughed real loud to let them know I was coming back into the kitchen."

"And he hung up?"

"Yeah. They went back to speaking Spanish real quick."

Eva moved over to the venetian blinds and cracked them apart to look out. The street was still quiet. An old man was walking his German shepherd. The dog was casually sniffing a tree. Eva turned back to Rudy. "Are you sure they used your cellular phone?"

"Positive," Rudy said at once. "It was still warm from

the guy's hand when I picked it up. And there ain't any other phones in the kitchen."

"Good," Eva said, frowning. "And we know there's no way they can trace your cell phone number to this address."

Rudy hesitated, unsure. "Maybe there's a way."

Eva shook her head. "The machine the cops have will only tell them the phone number that made the call, not the address."

"But they can look that up."

"And they'll find the phony Culver City address I gave when I got the phone."

She looked through the blinds once more, wondering if the cops had had the time to pinpoint the location of the cellular phone call. She knew it could be done by plotting the lines of transmissions as they bounced off the satellite orbiting high above the earth. That was how they'd located O.J. Simpson in his Bronco on the freeway. It could be done, she thought again, but it would take a fair amount of time to do it. Turning back to Rudy, she asked, "How long was he on the phone?"

"Not more than a few minutes."

"Be specific."

"Two minutes," Rudy estimated. "Three at the very most."

Eva nodded, but she thought he was lying. The Mexicans weren't stupid. They wouldn't have picked up the phone just because Rudy had gone to the bathroom. He had probably turned the shower on and stayed in there forever, like he usually did.

"What do you want to do?" Rudy broke into her thoughts.

"Make believe it didn't happen."

Rudy looked at her sharply. "What!"

"Just make believe everything is fine and follow my lead."

Eva walked down the hall and through swinging doors into the kitchen. Rudy was a step behind her, a fake grin on his face.

The four Hispanic men standing around the table waved and smiled at her.

"Evita!"

"Hola, Evita!"

"Buenas noches, Evita!"

The men knew her name was Eva, but they called her Evita after Evita Perón, about whom they had learned in the movies. The great Evita, who had worked so hard for the poor and downtrodden of her beloved Argentina. The great Evita, who had helped so many. And their Evita would help them as well. They would rob a bank for her, and she would make sure their families were financially secure. Each man would go to his grave knowing his family was looked after.

The men even thought she looked like Evita Perón, with her slim body and pretty face and green eyes and dark blond hair pulled back severely into a bun. They had argued about her age. Some believed she was in her early thirties. Others thought she was closer to forty. All agreed she would be heaven to sleep with.

"Evita, would it be possible for us to have some food?" the tallest of the Hispanic men asked. "We have not eaten all day."

"Of course." Eva smiled at the man, wondering if he was the betrayer, the one who had talked with the cops on the phone. "But first we must begin practicing for the bank robbery. Each of you has been given a protective vest, which you will wear at the time of the robbery. The vests are made of a special plastic material that will stop bullets in case of a gunfight. You must wear it under your coat to protect yourself. On the day of the holdup, you will have your body armor on for over two hours. That's a long time. We must make certain the vests will not cause any blisters or skin irritation, even after hours of wear. So tonight you will put the vests on and leave them on for a full hour to see if there is any reaction."

The tall man nodded his understanding.

"Please put them on now."

The vests were heavy sheets of bright orange plastic. They covered the chest and back and were held in place by Velcro straps. As the men put them on, they made brief eye contact with one another. All hoped that they would never have to wear the vests, that they could cut a deal with the police and collect a reward large enough to give their families security. All of the men had incurable diseases, all were certain to die within months. They were poor men whose deaths would leave their families destitute. But Evita had heard of their plight and approached them, offering a way out. The bank robbery would provide security for their wives and children.

"Good," Eva said, when they were finished. "For the next hour, I want you to walk around the house, wearing your vests at all times. Do not, under any circumstances, go outside. Understood?"

The men nodded.

"Good. We will return within the hour with food and drink for you."

"Gracias, Evita!"

"Gracias!"

Eva walked out of the kitchen, Rudy just behind her. Halfway down the hall, he grabbed her arm.

"You can't trust those bastards," he growled in a low voice. "They'll wait a few minutes and then they'll—"

Eva placed an index finger against his lips. "Shhh!"

They went out into the chilly night and scanned the neighborhood, looking for people or things that shouldn't have been there. The cat was still stalking something in the bushes. The old man and his dog were no longer in sight. Eva counted the cars parked at the curb, making certain their number hadn't changed while she was in the house. She signaled to Rudy, and they quickly crossed the street and got into their car.

Rudy turned the ignition key. "You're making a big mistake."

"Drive," Eva said tonelessly. "Keep the headlights off until we get to the big intersection."

Eva took off her cap and the dark blond wig she was wearing beneath it. She shook her red hair loose and fluffed it with her hands. Leaning forward, she wriggled out of the top of her combat fatigues.

Rudy watched out of the corner of his eye, admiring her breasts as she slipped into a football jersey with the number 32 on it. Then she reached into the glove compartment and took out a remote-control device that was the size of a pager. Rudy smiled, thinking he should have known better than to underestimate her. She was smart as hell, twice as smart as any man he'd ever met.

Now they were approaching the intersection.

"Switch your lights on," Eva told him.

"Which way do I turn?"

"Left. Away from the freak show."

At the intersection the light was red. They stopped and watched two transvestites stroll hand in hand across the crosswalk. One was wearing a miniskirt, the other a skintight unitard.

"This place is like Sodom and Gomorrah," Rudy grumbled. "I wish those two were in the house with the Mexicans."

"Their time will come too."

The light turned green.

Eva primed the remote control and pressed down on a red button.

In a fraction of a second an electrical impulse reached the detonator in the C-4 that was embedded in the orange vests the Mexicans had secured to their chests. There was a sudden flash, followed by a blast so powerful that it caused the pavement beneath the car to shake violently.

Rudy held on tightly to the steering wheel. "Whoa!"

Eva put her hand on the dashboard and braced herself. Car alarms were going off everywhere. People were running about, screaming and looking for cover. It took another few seconds for the car to stop vibrating. Eva put the remote-control device back into the glove compartment. "And that takes care of our friends."

"Jeez! How much C-four did you use?"

"Two bricks in each vest."

"Man, oh man! They won't find an intact toenail from those guys."

"That's the general idea," Eva said and pointed ahead. "The light is green. You can go now."

2

Simon Murdock stared at the television screen, shocked by the devastation he saw. The explosion had turned a half block of houses into rubble. Sixteen people had been killed, twenty-eight injured seriously enough to require hospitalization. And the numbers were rising. Now the television was showing a fireman as he emerged from a pile of bricks and wood. He was carrying a child, no more than three years old. The toddler with his nightie still on was obviously dead. Murdock winced and looked away, thinking that only a madman would do something like this. *A bomb! In the middle of Los Angeles! Jesus Christ!*

Murdock glanced around his office at Memorial Hospital. Potted plants and flowers were everywhere, gifts delivered yesterday to celebrate his twentieth year as dean of the medical center. They gave the room a cheerfulness that seemed extremely inappropriate at the moment. His gaze went back to the television set.

The intercom on Murdock's desk buzzed loudly. He quickly pushed a button and spoke to his secretary. "What?"

"Mr. Kitt from the Federal Bureau of Investigation is on line one."

Murdock used a remote control to turn off the television set and pushed another button on the intercom.

"Simon Murdock here," he said, reaching for a legal pad and a pen.

He listened to a perfunctory greeting, then began jotting down the instructions being given by William Kitt, the head of the FBI Domestic Terrorism Unit. The following needed to be done.

(1) All patients injured in the blast were to be hospitalized at Memorial; those now at other hospitals were to be transferred to Memorial if possible. (2) All autopsies were to be performed by Memorial's forensic pathologist, Dr. Joanna Blalock. (3) All clothing, jewelry and other objects found on the corpses were to be turned over to the FBI for analysis. (4) An area where bodies could be viewed for positive identification was to be set up. (5) Press releases were to be issued only after approval by the investigating agencies.

Next Kitt listed the units that would investigate the bombing and the names of those who would direct each unit. Murdock continued writing, unhappy that the casualties and autopsy work were not being spread out among other hospitals in the Los Angeles area. With everything coming to Memorial, its staff and resources would be severely strained. The surgery and orthopedic divisions, the ICU, the ER, radiology and pathology would all be stretched to their limits and beyond. But they would get the work done. Every request would be followed to the letter.

And not just because the FBI was calling. An hour earlier Murdock had received a call from a highly placed friend in Washington, D.C., who had served as special adviser to the presidents of four administrations and had enormous power. Over the years he had quietly seen to it that hundreds of millions of federal dollars were funneled to Memorial. Without his help Murdock could never have built all Memorial's institutes and research facilities. And now it was payback time.

"And of course," Kitt was saying, "the federal government will reimburse Memorial for expenses incurred."

"We have contingency funds to cover the costs," Murdock told him.

"We will require a full accounting of all monies spent."

"I understand," Murdock said, but he had already decided not to do it. He knew that any accounting of the expenses would be looked upon as a bill by the government and promptly paid. Murdock didn't want that. His friend had asked for a favor, and he would get it. In return Memorial would continue to receive more than its share of federal research dollars.

"We would like the accounting done on a weekly basis," Kitt said.

"It will be done in a manner satisfactory to all concerned," Murdock said firmly, closing the topic.

There was a pause. Murdock heard the FBI agent swallow.

"We appreciate your help, Dr. Murdock."

Murdock switched off the intercom and left his office. Passing his secretary, he said, "I'm not available."

He took the elevator to the B level and hurried down a long corridor, organizing his thoughts on how to carry out the FBI's instructions. Putting all the blast casualties into beds at Memorial shouldn't be a problem. Those already admitted were in either the orthopedic or the surgery ward. The new admissions should go there as well. It would be a tight squeeze, but it could be done. He'd call the nursing supervisors and have them begin rearranging beds. Then he would talk with the hospital spokespersonnel. No press releases unless cleared by the FBI or whoever took charge of the investigation. No press conferences on the victims until told otherwise. A goddamn bomb, he thought grimly. Something specially constructed to kill and maim. In his mind's eye he again saw the fireman carrying the dead child out of the rubble. With effort he pushed the picture away.

Murdock went through a set of double doors with a sign that read POSITIVELY NO ADMITTANCE EXCEPT AUTHORIZED PERSONNEL. A secretary talking on the phone looked up.

"Is the chief of pathology here?" Murdock asked.

"No, sir," the secretary said, her hand now over the mouthpiece.

"Do you know where he is?"

"In a meeting, I think."

"Call him and have him meet me in his office in ten minutes."

"May I tell him what it's about?"

Murdock ignored the question. "Is Dr. Blalock around?"

"In the back."

Murdock pushed through another set of swinging doors and entered the autopsy room. He quickly scanned the brightly lit area, with its eight stainless steel tables arranged in rows of two. His gaze went to the white-tiled wall at the rear. He counted the refrigerated units in the wall where the corpses were kept. There were ten of them, not nearly enough to hold the dead victims of the bombing. And besides, the autopsy room made a poor viewing area. They would need a large room to serve as a temporary morgue, a place where relatives and friends could come and view the bodies for positive identification.

Murdock stood on his tiptoes and saw Joanna Blalock at a far table. He moved around the periphery of the room, passing corpses waiting to be dissected. The bodies had bluish white skin and looked more like mannequins than humans. One had an apparent bullet wound in his chest that was large enough to put a fist through. Murdock tried to envision what kind of weapon could make a wound like that.

He stopped and stepped aside as two attendants removed a corpse from a wall unit and placed it atop a dissecting table. The corpse was an old man, gray and shriveled, mostly skin and bones. One attendant made an incision through the corpse's scalp line while the other uncoiled the wire of an electric saw.

Joanna Blalock's back was to Murdock, and she was speaking to Lori McKay, an assistant professor of forensic pathology. Both women looked so young, he thought, particularly Lori McKay. She could pass for a medical student with her long auburn hair, green eyes and scattered freckles across her cheeks. Murdock sighed wearily, wondering if she was really that young or if he was just getting old. Probably both, he decided.

"I'll be with you in a moment, Simon," Joanna called over to him.

Murdock nodded back, now studying Joanna's profile. She had hardly changed since he'd hired her ten years ago to head the Forensic Pathology Division. Her face was unlined, her patrician features striking. She still wore her sandy blond hair pulled back tightly and held in place by a simple barrette. And she still looked at least five years younger than her age. Nobody would guess that she was almost forty.

Murdock remembered his hesitation before hiring her, even though her letters of recommendation from Johns Hopkins were glowing. He couldn't believe someone so young and pretty could have that much brains. But he had been wrong. She had turned out to be an excellent addition to the staff. In only a few years she had become a nationally renowned forensic pathologist and was in constant demand to review outside cases.

And that had caused problems. She spent more and

more time away from Memorial as a highly paid consultant. When Murdock tried to limit her outside activities, she threatened to quit. And she would have if they hadn't reached a compromise. She would continue to run the division on a part-time basis, spending no more than a third of her time on outside projects. Despite their agreement, her independence remained a source of irritation between them. Over the past year Murdock had quietly interviewed two pathologists as possible replacements. One was from Harvard, the other from Duke. Neither could even approach Joanna Blalock's talents and experience. Murdock grumbled under his breath, still unhappy with the arrangement he and Joanna had, but knowing he was stuck with it. At least for now.

His gaze went to a piece of fleshy tissue Joanna was holding up to the light. The specimen was covered with skin and had two appendages hanging down. It took Murdock a moment to realize he was looking at part of a human hand.

He moved in for a closer took. "Accidental dismemberment?"

"That's one possibility," Joanna said.

Murdock glanced down at the clean stainless steel table. "Where is the rest of the body?"

"This was the only part found," Joanna said, now examining the fingers with a magnifying glass. "Some hikers stumbled on it in a secluded canyon in northern Los Angeles County."

Murdock rubbed his chin, thinking back. "Could it be a murder victim who was chopped into pieces to prevent positive identification?"

Joanna shook her head. "That's not what happened here. When a body is purposely chopped up, the perpetrator almost always uses a sharp instrument, like a hatchet or an ax, and that leaves a clean, even wound.

Here the wound edges are ragged and shredded, the bone splintered." She shook her head again. "This hand was ripped off by some very powerful force."

"Well, at least you have a few remaining fingers to give you some prints."

"Not really," Joanna said and pointed to the gnawed-off fingertips."You can see a number of bite marks here. I suspect the ends of the fingers were nibbled off by coyotes or other scavengers."

Murdock swallowed back his nausea, thinking that the dissecting tables at Memorial would soon be filled with dismembered body parts. "I need to talk with you about a matter of some importance."

"I'll be right with you," Joanna said. She examined the specimen once more, then gave it to Lori. "I'd like you to study the hand, paying particular attention to the skin. Then look at the X rays. When I come back I want you to tell me about the person this hand belonged to. You should be able to determine the victim's sex, age, size, marital status, ethnic origin, and his past and most recent occupations."

Murdock studied the third finger on the hand. He saw no wedding band. "Single," he guessed aloud.

"Married," Joanna told him. "You can see a distinct pale area on the third finger where the ring blocked out the sun's rays."

"Where's the ring?" Lori asked.

"Probably ripped off by the same force that tore off his hand," Joanna said. "Or perhaps nibbled away by a coyote. The finger has been gnawed down to its middle joint."

Lori looked at Joanna skeptically. "He could have been divorced a while back and removed his ring."

"Possible, but unlikely," Joanna said. "The sun would have retanned the area, and it would have done it quickly in Southern California. The man worked outdoors."

"Doing what?" Lori asked.

"You tell me," Joanna said and handed Lori the magnifying glass with a grin and a wink.

"Are you going to give me any clues?"

"I already have."

Joanna stripped off her latex gloves and went over to the wall of refrigerated units. She leaned back against the metal and felt its coolness come through her scrub suit. It was 8:20 A.M., and the autopsy room was warm and humid because the air-conditioning system was malfunctioning again.

At a nearby table a morgue attendant switched on an electric saw and began cutting through the skull of the corpse with the gunshot wound in his chest. A deafening high-pitched noise filled the air. Joanna glanced over at Murdock and wondered if he was ill. Her boss was aging so rapidly. His hair was now snow white, his face heavily lined and dotted with prominent age spots. And his posture had become stooped, like that of an old man. Joanna looked away and waited for the sound of the saw to stop.

Murdock said, "First, let me thank you for the plant."

"Let's hope for twenty more years," Joanna said and meant it. Simon Murdock had been an excellent dean at Memorial. He was a superb administrator and an outstanding fund-raiser, and he knew how to attract the very best staff. Almost single-handedly he had transformed Memorial into a leading medical center. It was now acknowledged to be among the top five in America. But Murdock had flaws too. Big ones. He could be cold and ruthless and manipulating. To him the ends always justified the means. Joanna neither liked nor trusted him.

"I need a large favor from you, Joanna."

"Fine," she said. "As long as I can do it between now and five o'clock tomorrow afternoon."

"What happens at five tomorrow afternoon?"

"I leave on a two-week vacation."

"I'm going to have to ask you to reschedule."

"No way," Joanna said at once. "My sister, whom I haven't seen in over two years, is flying in from Paris. And she's bringing her son, whom I've never seen."

"I think you'll change your mind when you hear the nature of the request."

"I doubt it, but go ahead."

Murdock took a deep breath, wishing it was twenty years ago, when deans gave orders that were never questioned. "This is not for me but for the FBI. They want you to perform the autopsies on the victims of the explosion that occurred last night."

"There are other forensics specialists who could—"

"They specifically asked for you," Murdock interrupted.

Joanna sighed weakly. "I'm not an expert in blast injuries."

Murdock shrugged. "They must have their reasons for requesting you."

Joanna looked over at Lori, who was now standing by the X-ray view box. "Damn it, Simon," she said softly. "I've never seen my little nephew. I've never seen the next generation of Blalocks."

"I know," Murdock said, thinking about the son he'd lost to drug addiction and all the times he should have spent with the boy and hadn't. He'd been too busy building Memorial into a world-class medical center. He brought his mind back to the problem at hand. "If you refuse, I'll have no choice but to bring in specialists who will take over your laboratory for as long as needed."

Joanna nodded slowly, understanding the subtle threat he was sending her. The outside people would covet her position at Memorial and do anything to get it. From among them Murdock could find a replacement for her if he wished. "Perhaps I could do it part-time for the first week," she suggested.

"It'll be a full-time job," Murdock said. "You'll be working sixteen hours a day on it. And even at that pace the FBI believes it will take months to get the work done."

Joanna nodded again. The autopsies would be straightforward and could be done in a matter of weeks. But examination and identification of the body parts would take months. She thought about resigning on the spot. But that would be stupid. She had the best of all worlds. She directed the division most of the time, but she also had her outside consulting practice, which allowed her to take whatever cases she wished. It gave her an independence few in academia had. It really would be stupid to resign, she thought again, but the urge to spend time with her sister and her nephew kept pulling at her. And so did the thought of missing a weekend in Montreal with Paul du Maurier, the new love in her life. It would have been so perfect. She and Paul in Montreal, then back to Los Angeles to see Kate and her little boy. Joanna quickly searched for a way out of her dilemma. She glanced over at Lori and wondered if her young assistant could lead the investigation, at least initially.

"I'm having trouble reading these X rays," Lori called from the view box. "There's mashed up bone all over the place."

Joanna walked to the view box, Murdock a step behind her. Lori was pointing to the metacarpal heads, which were larger than they should have been. And there was heavy calcification in the soft tissue around the shafts and heads of the metacarpal bones.

Joanna asked, "What do you make of that?"

"It looks like he broke his hands on more than a few occasions," Lori answered.

"And in what occupation do men repeatedly break their hands?"

Lori wrinkled her brow, concentrating. "Boxers!" she blurted out.

"Exactly," Joanna said. "And the extensive changes on the X ray tell us he had a lot of bouts, so he was probably a professional."

Lori's eyes suddenly narrowed. "How do you know he wasn't just some punk who was involved in numerous street fights?"

"That would account for the repeatedly broken bones perhaps, but not for the marked soft tissue calcification." Joanna used a red crayon to circle a dense calcium deposit. "This is the result of frequent continuous trauma, such as occurs when boxers hit punching bags over and over again."

Murdock listened attentively, his interest piqued. Boxing was the only sport he followed. In his teens he had been a Golden Gloves champion.

Lori stared at the X ray, unhappy with herself for not having deciphered the obvious clue. "So the victim was a male professional boxer who was married. And the color of his skin indicates he was probably Hispanic."

"Excellent," Joanna said. "What about his age?"

Lori went back to the dissecting table and pinched the skin on the dorsum of the hand, checking its elasticity. There were no lines or wrinkles. "I'd say late twenties or early thirties."

"And his size?"

"Small," Lori said promptly. "I'd guess he was just over five feet tall and weighed in the vicinity of a hundred and ten pounds. Those are just approximations based on the size of his hands and bones."

"You're getting pretty good at this," Joanna said.

Lori smiled widely, basking.

"Now tell me whether he spoke English and what his most recent job was."

Lori gave her a puzzled look. "We just determined he was a boxer."

"But not recently." Joanna used a tongue blade to turn the hand over, palm side up. She pointed to thick calluses. "Boxers don't have calluses on their palms. These are seen in men who do heavy manual labor."

"And you think he could speak English because he might have to in order to get such a job," Lori concluded. "You know, at a big construction site or someplace like that."

Joanna shook her head and turned the hand back over. "On the backs of the fingers are very pale tattoos."

Lori took a magnifying glass and carefully studied the bases of the fingers. "On the third finger I see a faded *V,* and on the fourth I believe I can make out the letter *E.*"

"Tell me what you think of that."

Lori thought for a moment, then shrugged. "I think I'm out of my depth."

"You should talk with Jake Sinclair about tattoos," Joanna said, her mind now on the homicide detective who had been her lover off and on for ten years. He was good-looking and fun to be with, but he was also a confirmed loner and always would be. He drifted away when he felt like it and came back when he felt like it. And she had put up with it. But no more.

Lori tried to read the expression on Joanna's face. "What would Lieutenant Sinclair tell me about the tattoos?"

Joanna brought her mind back to the hand. "He'd tell you that the most common tattoo seen on the hands of Hispanic males is the words *love* and *hate,* with one letter per finger. And most people won't have themselves tattooed with something they can't read. So it's fair to say this man could read and speak English."

"But why are the tattoos so faded?" Lori asked.

"Now I'm just guessing," Joanna said. "But I suspect he had the tattoo put on when he was a kid. And, as so often happens, he regretted it later on and wanted the tattoo removed."

Lori nodded. "Probably with a laser."

"And that's expensive to have done," Joanna went on, "so I would guess he was successful in the ring."

" But if that's true, why did he become a common laborer?"

"Maybe he came on hard times when he left the ring. That's the usual story with boxers."

Murdock nodded ever so slightly. That was the story with most boxers, even the great ones like Joe Louis and Sugar Ray Robinson. He continued listening to the interchange, amazed at how Joanna could make so much from so little. But then again, he reminded himself, that's what forensic pathologists do. No wonder the FBI wanted her.

"But we still have no idea what ripped his hand off," Lori was saying.

"Chances are, once we learn his identity the other things will begin to fall into place," Joanna told her. "So far, we're dealing with a young Hispanic, married, former boxer who was probably successful in the ring. We approximate his weight at a hundred ten to a hundred twenty pounds. He spoke English, so he'd lived in this country for a while. He may even be native-born. His last job involved heavy manual labor."

"Well, that narrows it down some," Lori said without enthusiasm.

"That narrows it down a lot," Joanna said. "And with some digging, you're going to find out who this fellow was."

"How do I go about doing that?"

"Through the boxing commission in California," Joanna explained.

Murdock interjected, "He'd be either a flyweight or a bantamweight."

"Are you sure?" Joanna asked.

"Positive," Murdock said.

"Good," Joanna said, but she made a mental note to look it up. "So he fought in the bantamweight or flyweight division some time during the past ten years. He had a fair number of fights, and I suspect he won more than he lost. And he had the words *love* and *hate* tattooed across his fingers."

Lori exhaled loudly. "You're talking about a lot of work. There could be hundreds of boxers who fit that description. Remember, his tattoo may have been for the most part removed when he was at the height of his success."

"Like I said, it's going to take some digging."

"If it's okay, I'd like the chief resident to help me with this project."

"Good idea," Joanna agreed. "But you do the questioning. You'll have to interview someone from the boxing commission and go over the fighters one by one."

"If only we had some distinguishing feature to go on."

"You do. He recently disappeared, and nobody knows where he is."

"His wife will be really worried," Lori added.

"She may have even filed a missing persons report," Joanna said. "Once you've narrowed your list down, we can cross-check it against the people reported as missing over the past week or two."

Lori scribbled a note. "Anything else?"

"That'll do for now." Joanna glanced at her watch. "Let's hustle down to radiology. If we get there before nine, they'll do a CT scan on the hand for us. Maybe there's something in the soft tissues that we missed."

Murdock looked up at the wall clock and cursed himself for wasting so much time. It was 8:55. He was late for his meeting with the chief of pathology to discuss a temporary morgue. There would be at least sixteen bodies. They would need a big room.

Murdock cleared his throat loudly and waited for the women to turn. "Joanna, I've got to run. Please carefully consider my request. I'll need your answer by noon, one way or the other."

Lori watched him leave, then said to Joanna, "What was that all about?"

"It's about being boxed in with no way out."

"By Murdock?"

Joanna nodded. "He's an expert at it."

3

Detective Lieutenant Jake Sinclair moved carefully amid the debris, avoiding the miniature flags that dotted the scene of the explosion. The color of the flag indicated the body part found. Red for head and neck, yellow for torso, green for arms and hands, blue for legs and feet. The largest part found so far was an intact shoulder blade.

Jake stepped over an oven door and onto the sidewalk. Just behind him was Lieutenant Dan Hurley from the Los Angeles Police Department's Criminal Conspiracy Division, a unit that dealt exclusively with bomb and arson cases.

"How many people were in the house?" Jake asked.

"It's impossible to tell." Hurley was a tall, lanky man with sharp features and a crew cut. His left hand was missing two fingers and the tip of a third. "We got nothing but bits and pieces. My guess is there had to be three in there, maybe more."

Jake scanned the devastation, now watching a medical examiner sifting through the rubble. "What kind of explosive caused this?"

"Our preliminary studies indicate it was C-four."

"Any idea how much?"

Hurley scratched at his ear. "A lot. These guys were major players."

"It looks like a damn war zone."

"Yeah," Hurley said flatly, his mind flashing back to

Vietnam, where his job had been to disarm land mines and unexploded shells. He had done it for over a year without so much as a scratch. He had been lucky. But his luck had run out eight years ago when a pipe bomb in downtown Los Angeles went off prematurely, taking two of his fingers with it. A careless mistake, he told himself for the thousandth time. Involuntarily, Hurley put his maimed hand into his coat pocket.

Jake asked, "Do we know who lived here?"

"Nope," Hurley said. "According to neighbors, it was recently rented out."

"Who owned the house?"

"The guy next door. He was killed in the explosion too. And so were his wife and baby daughter."

Jake sighed wearily. "This isn't going to be easy, is it?"

The men watched a plump medical examiner methodically push rubble aside. He extracted a heavy high-top work shoe. A human foot was still in it. The medical examiner put the shoe down and planted a blue flag.

Hurley unwrapped a stick of gum and placed it in his mouth, chewing slowly. "The FBI guy told me they're bringing a hotshot named Blalock to do the forensics."

"Joanna Blalock?" Jake asked.

Hurley made a guttural sound under his breath. "A woman, huh?"

"Have you got a problem with that?"

"Not really," Hurley said. But he did. "Is she any good?"

"Damn good," Jake said at once. "Do you remember that case a couple of years back of the faceless corpse with no fingertips? Well, she's the person who reconstructed the face and gave us his ID."

"But she had a whole body to work with. Now she'll have only bits and pieces, and that's a different ball game."

Jake smiled thinly. "You'll be making a mistake if you underestimate her."

"Uh-huh," Hurley said, unimpressed. He didn't have much confidence in women when it came to law enforcement. And it wasn't a matter of male chauvinism. Hurley had two daughters whom he loved more than heaven and earth, and he hoped that someday they would become doctors or lawyers or whatever they wanted. But that didn't change his conviction that when it came to criminal investigation, women simply could not perform as well as men.

The detectives moved aside as two federal agents hurried by them. The agents were wearing blue jackets with the yellow letters ATF inscribed on the backs.

"How many agencies are investigating this damn explosion?" Jake asked.

"Too many," Hurley told him. "For starters, there's the FBI, the ATF, and LAPD's Homicide and Criminal Conspiracy Units. And there's sure to be others we haven't heard about yet. Remember, this is a high-profile case. Everybody is going to try to get into the act."

"Christ." Jake groaned. "We're going to be tripping over one another."

"At first," Hurley agreed. "But once it's clear there is no easy solution and the trail runs cold, most of the units will start losing interest and begin distancing themselves from the investigation. They don't like to be associated with failure."

"And that'll leave you and me to do all the legwork," Jake said, thinking aloud.

"And to take all the heat if we don't catch the bastards behind this."

The men turned their attention to a medical examiner who was holding up another shoe. They could see a jagged bone sticking out of its top.

"I think we've got a match!" he called out.

"Two shoes, one left and one right, don't necessarily make a match," Hurley said quietly. "They could have come from different people."

"How do you know it's a match?" Jake called back to the examiner.

"Because the feet are wearing the very same type of sock," Girish Gupta answered. He was a pudgy, middle-aged man, born in New Delhi and trained in London, now a senior medical examiner for the county of Los Angeles. "I'll show you in a moment, after I finish up this area."

Out of the corner of his eye, Hurley saw a strikingly attractive woman ducking under the crime scene tape. A goddamn nosy reporter, he thought. "Hey, you! Get the hell back behind that tape!"

The woman ignored the order and walked over to them.

"Hi, Jake," Joanna said without smiling. "It's been a while."

"I've been busy," Jake said, stung by her coolness. "Real busy."

"Haven't we all?"

"I guess." Jake turned to Hurley. "Lieutenant Dan Hurley, meet Dr. Joanna Blalock."

"Jesus," Hurley hissed softly. "I'm sorry, Dr. Blalock. I thought you were a reporter."

"No problem," Joanna said, keeping her voice even to hide her irritation. His response was typical of many males. Women should be nurses and teachers and secretaries, but not forensic pathologists. It was something she'd had to put up with all of her professional life. She should have been used to it by now, but she wasn't.

Joanna glanced quickly around the area, appalled by the devastation. It looked like a tornado had touched down in the middle of the block. Houses were flattened, with only a few walls here and there still standing. Rubble covered everything. Just off the sidewalk was a Raggedy Ann doll, tattered and bloodstained.

"Oh, Lord!" Joanna said, moving the doll with her toe.

Hurley asked, "Have you worked bomb cases before?"

"Some," Joanna said.

Which meant damn little, Hurley thought unhappily. "Let me fill you in."

He told her about the explosion that had occurred at 10:40 the night before. In detail he described the type and makeup of the explosive used, and the most recent injury and body count. Twenty bodies had now been recovered. None of the nearby neighbors had survived. There was a possible witness, however—a man walking his dog a block away at the time the bomb detonated.

"What has the witness told you?" Joanna asked.

"Nothing so far," Hurley said. "He's got a bad concussion and he's still shocky. Also both of his eardrums are ruptured and he can't hear a damn thing. Maybe he saw something, maybe he didn't."

Joanna pointed to the pile of rubble in front of her. The only things standing were brick steps and a small cement porch. Metal pipes coming out of the ground were severely bent. "Is this the house where the explosion occurred?"

" Right."

"Where was the explosion center?"

"The kitchen, we think," Hurley said and gestured to the left of the steps. The explosion center was where the bomb was actually detonated. It was determined by two characteristics: it was where the maximum damage had occurred and where the highest concentration of explosive was found. The bomb squad had detected the greatest concentration of C-4 on various kitchen appliances.

Joanna pictured in her mind what an explosion would do to a kitchen. In most kitchens the refrigerator and sink were opposite each other. "I assume the sink went one way and the refrigerator another."

Hurley nodded. "The sink was blown forty yards south, the refrigerator twenty yards north. We located a piece of the stove a block east of here. We figured the explosion had to have occurred between the three objects."

"Please have the medical examiners carefully check each of the appliances."

Hurley thought for a moment. "Why?"

"Because some body parts may have been blown directly into those heavy appliances."

"Good point," Hurley conceded and took out a pen and notepad.

Joanna noticed the missing fingers on Hurley's hand and looked away. "Do you believe this was a work accident?"

Jake smiled wryly. "Work accident" sounded like such a benign term, but it referred to terrorists being blown up by one of their own bombs that detonated prematurely.

"I think a work accident is our most likely scenario for a number of reasons," Hurley said. "First, I can't think of any motive for blowing up a neighborhood with C-four. Can you?"

Joanna shrugged. "It could be a way to induce terror in the general population. People become frightened as hell when homes are being blown up."

"Nice try," Hurley said, "but no. Terrorists prefer crowded places, like planes and buses and buildings. They like to kill as many as possible. Had they put this much C-four in a shopping mall on a Saturday afternoon, they could have killed hundreds. And maimed God knows how many more."

"Maybe it was the work of some nut," Joanna guessed.

Hurley shook his head. "Nuts don't work in groups. And nuts don't use C-four. That's the mark of a terrorist." He shook his head again. "Naw. This wasn't done by a nut. A small group of terrorists in the kitchen were playing with C-four and it went boom."

"I'd feel more comfortable with your theory if we could find a nude body or two," Joanna said.

Jake asked, "What would a nude body tell us?"

"When terrorists construct bombs they frequently do it in the nude," Hurley explained. "Sometimes clothing produces enough static electricity to set off a bomb." He pointed with his thumb to the miniature flags, now waving in a soft breeze. "But all we've got is bits and pieces here. No intact bodies."

"But there'll be parts of torsos," Joanna countered. "And they can be examined for particles of clothing, or buttons, or zippers."

"And if you find those particles, so what?" Hurley asked. "They won't tell you much."

"Sure they will," Joanna said. "They'll tell me that at the moment of explosion there wasn't a group of nude terrorists sitting around a kitchen table constructing a bomb."

Hurley shrugged. "Sometimes bombers don't strip."

"But most engineers working with C-four do."

Hurley nodded, thinking that Joanna Blalock seemed to know her way around the bomb scene. She used the words that bomb experts used—terms like "work accident" and "explosion center." And she understood the significance of finding a nude body at a blast site. And she knew the word "engineer" referred to the terrorist who constructed the bomb. But that information was superficial. It could be obtained from newspapers or magazines or television documentaries. Hell, it was even on the Internet. Joanna Blalock talked a good game, he thought to himself. But he still wasn't sure of her.

"Hello, Dr. Blalock!" Girish Gupta called out as he walked over. He was wearing high black boots over his pants and thick rubber gloves up to his elbows. "It's been entirely too long since I saw you last."

"I agree," Joanna said, returning his smile. "I'm delighted to be working with you again."

"It's my pleasure." Gupta held up two heavy work shoes with feet still in them. "This is gruesome business, very gruesome business. But I think we are making progress. We may have a matched pair here. They have the exact same socks, you see."

Jake leaned forward and studied the backs of the shoes. "One heel is worn down a lot more than the other," he observed.

Gupta restudied the shoe, trying to come up with an explanation for the difference in heel size. "Perhaps our man had a limp or deformity of one leg."

Joanna carefully eyed the shoes, then pointed to the laces. "That wouldn't explain why the shoelaces on one shoe are tied differently than the laces on the other."

Gupta quickly looked at the laces. One pair had a double knot. He sighed loudly. "I've been out in the sun too long."

"It's tough when you're working in a field strewn with body parts," Joanna said. "It's easier when you're inside and have time to go over each piece carefully."

Gupta looked out across the crime scene and watched the miniature flags fluttering in the breeze. "I never thought I would see this in America," he said sadly. "I still can't believe this could happen here."

"Ever hear of Oklahoma City?" Hurley asked.

Gupta continued to stare at the flags. "But this happened here, in the city where I live."

"Which is the bomb capital of the world," Hurley said.

"What!" Joanna and Gupta spoke almost simultaneously.

"Oh, yeah," Hurley went on. "We're busier than Beirut

and Belfast put together. Our bomb squads respond to over a thousand calls a year."

Joanna was stunned by the numbers. That averaged out to almost three bomb threat calls a day. "Why so many?"

"Because Los Angeles is so volatile," Hurley explained. "We have every nationality on earth here, and every little country has its own axes to grind, its own hatred of other countries. And we also have the world's largest collection of crazies and nuts. So it was never a question in our minds of *if* a blast like this would occur in Los Angeles. It was only a question of *when*."

"And when is now," Joanna said sourly.

"And there's another reason for Los Angeles being the bomb capital of the world," Hurley told them. "Our nice weather."

"What the hell does the weather have to do with making bombs?" Jake asked.

"Before bombers explode something, they like to do practice runs," Hurley said grimly. "And our climate and great outdoors are perfect for that."

"Well, something went wrong with this little practice session," Jake said.

"Indeed." Gupta motioned to an assistant medical examiner and handed him the shoes with the blown-off feet, then turned back to Joanna. "As you can see, we've used small flags to indicate where the various body parts were found. We've uncovered eighteen pieces of human tissue so far and still have a lot of rubble to sift through."

"Could I make a suggestion or two?" Joanna offered.

"Of course," Gupta said, ears pricked.

"Do you know where the kitchen was located?"

Gupta hesitated. "I'm not sure."

"Lieutenant Hurley will show you," Joanna said. "I would like you to determine the exact center of the kitchen and let that be your reference point. Then measure the distances from that point to each of the planted flags. It would be very helpful if you could make a map showing the location of each flag and its distance from the center of the kitchen."

"Shall I wait until we've searched through all the rubble and uncovered every body part?" Gupta asked.

"No," Joanna said promptly. "Please do it now. And as you mark each flag on the map, take the body part and place it in a plastic container, then put the specimen in a refrigerated unit. Once you've—"

"Hold on a minute!" Hurley interrupted abruptly. "We don't move anything until it's cleared with central command. That way we don't do something we later wished we hadn't. Everything stays as is."

"That's not a good idea," Joanna said.

"Everything stays put," Hurley said firmly. "My orders are to freeze this crime scene, and that's what I plan to do."

Joanna's jaw tightened. "Well, while you're freezing the area, give your superiors a call and tell them we have pieces of human tissue lying out in the sun, rotting away by the minute. And remind them that the longer the tissues sit out there, the better the chance they'll become infected with worms and maggots, which will destroy what little evidence we have."

Hurley stared at her, trying to control his temper. He knew she was right, but he didn't like her condescending manner. He had the feeling she was going to end up being a real bitch. Slowly he turned to Gupta. "Come on. I'll show you where the center of the kitchen is."

Jake watched the men walk away. He could feel the lingering tension between Hurley and Joanna. "I don't think Hurley is accustomed to working with women."

"There are plenty of females in the LAPD," Joanna said.

"Not on the bomb squads, there aren't."

Joanna thought for a moment. "Why do you think that's so?"

Jake shrugged. "Probably because they have more sense and value their fingers more than men do."

Joanna's mind flashed back to Hurley's missing fingers, knowing that he had to be thinking about those fingers every time he got near a bomb site. She wondered what could induce a man to accept such hazardous duty. Did these men have exceptional courage? Or were they just big risk takers? Or maybe they had a secret death wish. Whatever it was, there was a long waiting list to join Los Angeles County's six full-time bomb squads.

"Hurley is a good guy." Jake broke into her thoughts. "We're going to need him if we ever hope to crack this case."

Joanna glanced out at Hurley, who was stepping into a crater in the cement slab where the house had once stood. "I sounded pretty hard a moment ago, huh?"

" Yeah."

She walked across the rubble, realizing it wasn't only Hurley who had set her off. It was a combination of things, like being pressured by Simon Murdock.

Joanna came to the cement slab and caught Hurley's eye. "Lieutenant, I could have phrased my response to you a moment ago a lot better."

"Forget it," he said evenly. "You made your point, and it was a good one."

Joanna moved back across the debris and stepped over a yellow flag. Next to it was a lemon-size piece of dark maroon tissue. It was probably liver or spleen, she guessed. She came to the sidewalk. "I apologized."

"Good," Jake said. "Now tell me what's bugging you."

"A lot of things," Joanna said evasively, watching two uniformed cops and a detective she didn't recognize pass by. "Where's your partner, Farelli?"

Jake took a deep breath and exhaled. "He got shot."

"What!" Joanna blurted out. "When?"

"Last month," Jake told her. "We were on a stakeout and some asshole appeared out of nowhere with a semi-automatic. Lou caught one in the leg. He lost a lot of blood, but he's okay now. He'll be back next week."

"You should have called me," Joanna said, upset. Farelli was a favorite of hers. "You could have picked up the damn phone."

"I know, I know," Jake said. "But I had my hands full. Between checking on Lou and talking with his wife and kids and a million other things." He let his voice trail off.

"You still should have called."

"Like I said, I had a lot on my mind."

Joanna gave him a long look, wondering how he could be so generous and considerate one moment, and so insensitive and oblivious to another person's feelings the next. It was like an intermittent blind spot in Jake. And it was becoming more noticeable and more irritating.

An assistant medical examiner called out. "I've found a digit!"

"Let's hope it's a thumb," Joanna said and stepped back into the rubble. Her heel caught in a cracked board, and she stumbled. Quickly she grabbed Jake's arm and steadied herself.

"Are you all right?" he asked, concerned.

"I'm fine," she said, cursing herself for wearing heels to a bomb site. She tested the heel, making sure it was intact, then pushed the board aside. Beneath it was a small piece of skin attached to a bit of shiny orange material.

Jake leaned down for a closer look. "What the hell is that?"

"Human skin with something attached to it."

"Do you think it's a body part?"

"No," Joanna said. "It looks like it's either plastic or ceramic."

Jake took a small white flag from his coat pocket and

planted it next to the unusual material. "A white flag means it's an unidentified body part."

They walked over to the western edge of the property, where Hurley, Gupta and the assistant medical examiner were standing.

"It's a toe," Gupta was saying. "A second or third toe."

"That's no damn help," Hurley grumbled. "A bucket of toes isn't going to help us here."

"Perhaps things will become clearer once we've uncovered all the body parts," Gupta commented. "Perhaps some of the vagueness will disappear."

Joanna shook her head. "I wish you were right, but I'm afraid it's going to take months and months to sort this out."

"We don't have months," Hurley said. "We have to come up with answers in a matter of weeks."

"There's no way we can do this in a matter of weeks," Joanna told him. "It's absolutely, positively impossible."

"Then do the impossible," Hurley said and walked away.

Joanna turned to Jake. "He's not serious, is he?"

"Oh, yeah," Jake said. "Hurley figures we've got a month at the most before it happens."

"Before what happens?"

Jake gestured with his hand to the giant mounds of rubble. "Somebody was playing around with a lot of C-four here last night. And you don't need that kind of power to blow up a stucco house. With this much C-four, I think it's safe to say these guys were planning on blowing up something big."

" Like what?"

"That's what we have to find out," Jake said. "And we've got to find out before the bastards actually do it."

Joanna looked at him strangely. "Weren't all the terrorists killed in the explosion?"

"We don't think so," Jake said. "At about ten-forty last

night a man who lives a block and a half away from here was letting his cat out of the house. He saw a car drive by with its lights off. Now this street is poorly lit. You can barely see unless your lights are on. Twenty seconds after the car passed, the bomb went off."

"Suspicious," Joanna said. "But not very solid."

"There's more," Jake went on. "At eight o'clock last night a woman who lives directly across the street from the house that exploded saw a car pull up to the curb. A man got out and went into that house. The woman is a nurse and works the graveyard shift at a nearby hospital. When she left her home at ten-thirty, the car was still there."

"So?"

"That car is no longer here," Jake said. "Sometime between ten-thirty and ten-forty p.m. somebody moved it."

"Which means some of them are still out there," Joanna said quietly.

" Oh, they're out there all right." Jake nodded slowly and again glanced around at the devastation and the miniature flags marking the body parts. "And what we're looking at now is just a preview of things to come."

4

Eva Reineke looked like a tourist. She was wearing
faded jeans, a dark sweatshirt and a New York Yan-
kees baseball cap with a fake blond ponytail attached to
it. A camera was draped around her neck. She fitted right
in with the crowd of tourists behind the crime scene tape
at the explosion site. To the rear a food vendor was hawk-
ing hot dogs and soft drinks.

Eva brought her camera up and scanned the area
through the viewfinder. Cops and medical examiners
were carefully sifting through the rubble. Specially
trained dogs were sniffing around in collapsed houses,
looking for the bodies of those still unaccounted for. An
ambulance waited off to the side just in case someone
was found alive.

Eva moved her camera back to the center of activity,
estimating the killing radius of the blast. It had to be at
least a hundred feet. And that was with the bombs clus-
tered together. If the men carrying the explosives had
been appropriately spaced, the killing radius could have
easily been doubled. And that would have been more than
enough for the target she had in mind. Too bad her original plan had had to be discarded. But she wasn't overly
concerned. She had a backup plan that was just as good.
Maybe even better.

A fat woman holding a hot dog elbowed her way
through the crowd and came up to the tape. She stood
next to Eva and stared out at the destruction.

"Holy shit!" the woman said, chewing away on her hot dog. "Look what some son of a bitch did."

"Terrible," Eva said quietly.

"I hear twenty people were killed."

"Terrible," Eva said again.

"I'll bet it was some damn foreigner who did it."

"Probably," Eva agreed. She had considered planting evidence in the house that would have pointed to some foreign fanatical group, but she hadn't had the time to think it through. And she hadn't wanted to make a mistake. Sometimes bogus clues boomeranged, particularly if the group being falsely accused found out about them.

A search dog began barking loudly.

The crowd grew silent and watched. The dog frantically tried to paw its way through a mound of brick-covered rubble. Rescue workers rushed in with pickaxes and power saws. Moments later they uncovered the body of a teenage boy wearing a UCLA football jersey.

"That makes twenty-one," the fat woman said somberly.

"I hope they catch the bastards," a man behind them muttered.

"Oh, they will," the woman said. "I heard on the radio that they've got an eyewitness."

Eva stiffened. Quickly she brought the camera up to her eye to cover any change in her expression. She stayed close to the fat woman, not wanting to miss a word.

News of the eyewitness spread through the crowd and started a buzz of conversations.

"Did you hear that?"

"Yeah, an eyewitness who saw everything."

"How close was he?"

"I don't know, but he saw it happen."

Eva cleared her throat and moved even closer to the fat woman. "Has he given the police any descriptions?"

"I don't think so," the woman reported. "He's in pretty

bad shape over at Memorial. But if he survives, the police have got themselves an eyewitness."

"Let's hope he makes it," Eva said evenly.

"Damn right." The woman nodded as she chewed the last of her hot dog.

"That hot dog looks pretty good. Where'd you get it?" Eva asked.

The woman pointed to the rear with her thumb. "There's a vendor back there. And tell him to double up on the mustard. It's really tasty."

Eva moved through the crowd, pulling the bill of her baseball cap over her brow to cover most of her face. She walked around the vendor, then past two vacated police cars. Keeping her head down, she opened her camera and appeared to be checking the film. *An eyewitness! A damn eyewitness! Who was he and where was he standing and what did he see?* A streak of fear went through her, but she pushed it aside and concentrated. The witness couldn't have been very close and survived. And it was dark and the street was poorly lighted and they had kept the headlights of their car turned off. But apparently he had seen something.

Eva stopped to close the camera, then bent over to tie her shoe. With her peripheral vision she looked up the street to make certain no one was following her. The sidewalk was clear, but a cop was approaching one of the police cars, his partner right behind him. Eva watched them get into the car, then quickly began retying the laces on her other shoe. Out of the corner of her eye, she continued watching them. The car didn't move. The cops were just getting out of the sun, she decided.

Eva strolled away, her pace slow and even, like a person in no rush. Now the street was curving and widening, the crowd and police cars no longer in sight. Ahead Eva could see the intersecting boulevard. She came to an alleyway and waited for a truck to back out before hurrying down it. Glancing over her shoulder, she entered the rear of a music store.

At the rock and roll section she paused to browse through the new CDs. She stayed there a full minute, peeking at the rear door every ten seconds. Again satisfied no one was following her, she left the store via the front door and went to a nearby public phone. She dialed the number of a cellular phone.

"Yeah?" Rudy answered.

"We have a problem."

"I heard."

"Fix it," Eva said and hung up.

5

"Mr. du Maurier has been delayed but will arrive shortly," the maître d' told Joanna. "Would you prefer to wait at the bar or at your table?"

"The table, please," Joanna said.

She followed the maître d' across the beautifully appointed restaurant. Everything was done in white except for the sparkling crystal chandelier, which gave off a pleasantly muted light. The tables were spaced generously, giving the patrons a sense of privacy. Off to the side, waiters stood silently and watched for anything the diners might require.

As Joanna was being seated, the sommelier appeared and uncorked a bottle of Dom Pérignon 1983. He waited for Joanna to taste the champagne and nod her approval. Then he placed the bottle in a bucket of ice and disappeared.

Joanna sipped her drink and glanced around at the others dining at Le Chateau. The crowd seemed more European than American, with their dark, conservative attire and quiet manners. They looked like old money, people accustomed to wealth and everything it brought. Old money, she thought again, and plenty of it.

Her mind went back to her childhood in the San Francisco Bay Area and the privileged life her family had lived. They had big homes and luxury cars and belonged to the best country club and vacationed in Aspen and Maui. It was an existence most people could only dream of. Then her father died in a plane crash and left a mountain of debts. Suddenly her world was turned upside down and life became a struggle. She needed scholarships and loans to finish her college education and more loans to get through medical school. And even more loans to see her sister, Kate, through college and graduate school. The big houses, the luxury cars, the country clubs—all gone in the blink of an eye. Joanna knew what it was like to have real money, and she knew what it was like to lose it.

Her gaze went back to the decor of the restaurant. Everything about it had elegance and style and understated richness. Those were the qualities she so admired in places and people. And those qualities pretty much summed up Paul du Maurier, she thought.

She had met Paul three months earlier, at a cocktail party in Bel Air. She had glanced across the room at him, wondering who he was and whether he was married. A moment later he caught her eye and walked over, saying, "I wasn't planning on coming tonight, but now I'm glad I did." He was an investment banker who commuted between Santa Barbara and Los Angeles, and he was handsome, charming and bright. And his timing was perfect. She had just parted from Jake Sinclair for the umpteenth time, vowing never to go back but knowing deep down she eventually would. He was like a bad habit she couldn't break. Then Paul showed up and swept her off her feet, and Jake faded. She had to admit that she still thought about him now and then. And when she saw Jake at the crime scene, she'd gotten that funny hollow feeling. But she had quickly pushed it aside. Jake was no longer the main man in her life.

God! How long had it been since she started up with Jake Sinclair? In over ten years nothing had changed, not a damn thing. And like an idiot she had stuck around, hoping he would. Not that it was all bad. Jake could be fun and exciting and sexy as hell. But with the right man she could have been married with children by now. It was time for a sea change, she told herself, time to let go of the old and move on.

The couple at the table next to her turned their heads toward the door. Joanna followed their line of vision and saw Paul du Maurier being greeted by the maître d'. As he walked across the room a dozen pairs of eyes watched him. He had that effect on people. Something about the tall, debonair man drew their attention. He was very good-looking, with sharp features, a firm jaw and wavy grayish blond hair. His gait was even and unhurried, like that of a man accustomed to setting his own pace.

Paul reached for her hand and kissed it. "You look beautiful in that dress. I don't think I've ever seen it before."

Joanna smiled. The black cocktail dress was new, and so were her black shoes and purse. The only thing old was the strand of Mikimoto pearls around her neck.

Paul leaned away as the waiter poured from the bottle of Dom Pérignon. He raised his glass to Joanna. "To us."

"To us," Joanna toasted him back and sipped the champagne, now studying Paul's clothes. He was wearing a dark blue Armani suit with a pale blue shirt and subdued red tie. He looked like a model for *Gentlemen's Quarterly.*

"I'm sorry I was delayed," Paul said, squeezing her hand gently. "I hope you didn't have to wait long."

"I just arrived," she said. "Was there a problem at your meeting?"

Paul sighed wearily. "The Japanese don't seem to realize that the wheel has turned and their country is mired in a sea of red ink."

"Is it that bad?"

"Worse than anybody thinks," Paul said gravely. "To

begin with, their banks are holding a trillion dollars in bad paper, mainly from bad real estate loans."

Joanna's brow went up. "A trillion?"

"A trillion, with a capital T." Paul continued, "On top of that, some of their giant corporations and trading houses are teetering on the brink of bankruptcy and are being propped up by the Japanese government, and of course that can't go on forever. To make matters even worse, their Asian markets are drying up, and the value of the yen is dropping like a rock. Put this all together and you have an economy that is floundering in the water like a ship without a rudder."

Joanna looked at him seriously. "Are they going to go belly up?"

Paul grinned. "Are you worried about them?"

Joanna shrugged. "Not really. They didn't give a damn when America was in trouble. I remember one of their ministers telling America to get its house in order. That would be my advice to them."

Paul's grin turned into a wide smile. "You sound like a banker."

"Is that good?"

"For me, it's perfect."

They both chuckled. Paul brought Joanna's hands up to his lips and kissed them. "Don't concern yourself about the Japanese. Eventually they'll make the necessary reforms. But until then, foreign capital will stay away."

"And you're certain they'll make these reforms?"

"They won't have any choice," Paul said hoarsely. "No choice at all."

"Are you saying they'll be dictated to?"

"I'm saying they'll receive an offer they can't refuse."

"That sounds like a line from *The Godfather*."

Paul smiled thinly. "It's used in banking too."

The change in his expression and tone of voice told

Joanna that international pressure was already being applied and that reforms in the Japanese financial systems were not far off. And Paul du Maurier would know these things firsthand. He was a senior executive with a Los Angeles investment bank that did business all over the world. It had branch offices in New York, London, Paris, Singapore and Tokyo.

"Enough about business," Paul said, signaling for more champagne. "Let's talk about you and our trip to Montreal. Are you all packed?"

Joanna smiled unhappily. "I'm afraid I can't go. I'm sorry."

Paul's eyes narrowed. "Why not?"

"You heard about the bomb explosion in West Hollywood last night?" she asked. "Well, I'm the forensic pathologist assigned to the case."

"Can't they get somebody else to do it?"

Joanna shook her head. "I'm the one they want."

"Damn it," Paul grumbled. "I had everything planned so well for us. It would have been perfect." He strummed his fingers on the tabletop, his gaze still on Joanna. "Are you sure there's no way for you to get out of this?"

"Believe me, I tried," Joanna said. "We'll just have to do it later on."

"Do you have any idea how long this project will take?" Paul asked. "Are we talking weeks or what?"

"Months," Joanna said, thinking about the body parts at the bomb site. A total of twenty-eight had been uncovered, the largest being a scapula and two blown-off feet. The C-4 blast had virtually vaporized its victims, leaving behind only scraps of tissue. There was no way she could make a positive ID from them. She would need something more to go on. Clothing or jewelry or something else that was distinctive to a given individual.

"My daughter, Sasha, will be very disappointed." Paul

broke into her thoughts. "She was really looking forward to meeting you."

"And I her," Joanna said. "Please tell her we'll meet soon."

Paul sighed loudly. "I'll call Sasha's mother in the morning and tell her about the change in plans."

"You make it sound as if that will be a very unpleasant task."

"Any conversation with my ex-wife is unpleasant," Paul said. "It becomes impossible when I have to ask her for a favor."

"But surely she'll understand when you explain why—"

Paul flicked his hand disdainfully. "You don't know Catherine."

The waiter came over to refill their wineglasses. Paul watched, keeping his expression even. To himself he seethed, remembering the bitter divorce five years ago. Catherine had tried to break their prenuptial agreement, despite its generous terms. And when the court ruled against her, she demanded full custody of their daughter, claiming that Paul had an explosive temper and had emotionally abused the child. That was absolute bullshit. When Sasha misbehaved he raised his voice and corrected her. That was discipline, not abuse. But Catherine's lawyers made it sound as if he yelled at the child constantly. The embarrassment—Paul bristled inwardly—the utter embarrassment when the judge warned him to control his temper when he visited his daughter in Montreal. And Catherine, who loved her daughter so dearly, couldn't wait to hire a full-time nanny so she could travel and play on the Montreal social circuit. Son of a bitch! He hated even the thought of talking to his ex-wife.

Joanna noted the faraway look on Paul's face and

guessed that he was thinking about his daughter. "How old is Sasha now?"

"Twelve."

"So she's a young lady."

"Absolutely," Paul said. "And she becomes more beautiful by the day."

"Damn it," Joanna cursed softly. "I should be with you on that plane to Montreal tomorrow."

"Yes, you should," Paul said and sipped champagne, his mind going back to his ex-wife. Catherine had been a clinical psychologist when he married her. She had a big practice that always seemed to be interfering with their family life. At times her patients appeared to be more important to Catherine than her husband and daughter. The female judge in their custody fight didn't allow that to be entered as evidence. Irrelevant, she said.

Joanna studied Paul's expression. "Your mind is somewhere else."

"I was thinking that all too often events dictate our lives," Paul lied.

"I guess," Joanna said resignedly. "It just would have been so great for us to get away together."

"And we still will," Paul said. "In six weeks there's a bankers' conference in Bermuda. It will take up very little of my time, and the island will be perfect for us. How does that sound?"

"Like paradise," Joanna cooed.

"Great! I'll make all the arrangements." Paul waved a finger at her playfully. "And I won't accept any excuses this time. You must clear your calendar for the third week in April."

Joanna took a date book from her purse and flipped through the pages. Her smile suddenly faded. " Oh, no!"

"Don't tell me you can't make it."

She sighed dejectedly. "I'm scheduled to receive the

Medal of Freedom from the President on April nineteenth."

Paul's eyebrows went up. "From the President of the United States?"

Joanna nodded.

"Tell me why they're giving you the medal," Paul said, interested. "I want all the details."

Joanna told him about the scientific expedition to the waters off Alaska where a toxic iceberg was killing people and sea life. "We were able to locate the iceberg and identify the toxin and eventually destroy it. All the scientists involved are receiving the medal."

"What was the toxin?"

"It was biologic," Joanna said evasively. "But it's no longer a problem."

"I think you're downplaying the importance of this scientific mission," Paul said. "They are very particular when it comes to awarding the Presidential Medal of Freedom. I know that for a fact."

"It was dangerous," Joanna admitted, thinking about all the people who had died in those icy waters. "I was lucky to survive."

"I thought the medal was usually presented in Washington, D.C."

"It is," Joanna told him. "But the President will be out here to dedicate a new research institute. And since the three scientists who will receive the award are from western universities, they decided to make the presentation in Los Angeles."

"May I come?"

"Of course," Joanna said, pleased. "But what about your bankers' conference in Bermuda?"

"You're more important to me than they are," Paul said, his eyes twinkling. "Way more important."

" Damn! I want so much to be with you in Montreal tomorrow."

"Well, that's not possible," Paul said and leaned over, his lips brushing over hers. "So we'll just have to make the most of tonight."

Saturday, March 13, 6:48 A.M.

From the balcony of the penthouse suite at the Beverly Wilshire Hotel, Joanna watched the dawn breaking. The sky was overcast and gloomy, matching her mood. She had spent the night in the lap of luxury, making love to Paul du Maurier. But soon they would part and she would return to the world of bombs and terrorists and rotting scraps of human tissue. It was like going from heaven to hell.

A chilly breeze blew in, and Joanna snuggled up in her thick terry-cloth bathrobe, wondering what it would have been like if there had been no bomb. They would have had a leisurely breakfast, then dressed and taken a limousine to the airport and boarded an Air Canada jet to Montreal. And there she would have met Sasha and gotten to know Paul even better. It would have been perfect.

Again she thought about calling Simon Murdock and removing herself from the case. Let somebody else take on the impossible task. But she knew she'd never make that call. Once she started something she never backed out. Tenacity was a trait in the Blalock family. Her father and sister had it, and so did she. It ran in their genes and drove them to succeed. But at times it could be a curse. Like now.

Behind her Joanna heard a shower being turned off. Moments later she heard Paul walking into the living room and switching on the television set. The announcer was talking about early morning drizzle that was already causing slow-ups on all the freeways. Who cares? Joanna asked herself. And it surely wouldn't have mattered if she was in the backseat of a limousine listening to Mozart while she nibbled on fresh strawberries and washed them down with a nice Blanc de Blanc. Now the announcer was talking about the bomb explosion in West Hollywood.

"Joanna," Paul called out. "You may wish to listen to this."

Not really, Joanna told herself, but she went and sat next to Paul on a large, soft sofa. "They won't say anything."

"You never know," Paul said, his eyes glued to the television screen.

"They'll say nothing that might aid the remaining terrorists," Joanna said evenly.

Paul looked at her oddly. "The newspaper said that all the terrorists were killed in the blast."

Joanna gestured, not wanting to go into any detail. "There could still be one or two out there."

"Will you be in any danger?" Paul asked.

"None whatsoever," Joanna said, touched by his concern. "I'll be working inside my laboratory at Memorial."

The television screen was now showing a live aerial shot of the explosion site. Giant floodlights illuminated the crime scene and the people working on it. Joanna could make out several ATF agents with their distinctive jackets. They appeared to be moving toward a truck.

"Something is going on down there," the Channel 4 helicopter pilot reported. "I think they've found something important."

"Any idea what it is?" the studio announcer asked.

"I can't be sure," the pilot answered.

Joanna watched as the ATF truck sped away with several police cars right behind it. Then she noticed others running from the bomb site, heading down the winding street. "They're clearing the area," she said quietly.

"Why?" Paul asked.

"They must have come across something dangerous."

"Like another bomb?"

"That's possible," Joanna said, wondering if the terrorists had left behind some type of booby trap.

The helicopter reporter blurted out, "They're clearing the area! We've been instructed to leave immediately."

"Then get out of there!" the studio announcer said urgently.

Now the television showed the devastated block of houses from a distance. The floodlights remained on and caused the mounds of rubble to glow eerily in the early dawn darkness.

Paul lit a cigarette, thinking for a moment. "Didn't you tell me you had investigated the bomb site yesterday?

"Yes."

"And didn't you just tell me there was absolutely no danger for you?"

"There's always some risk," Joanna said, still wondering what could have made the ATF agents run for their lives. It had to have been a bomb or at least something that could have exploded. And it had to have been there yesterday and the day before. She shuddered, wondering how close she and Jake and Dan Hurley had been to the device. Probably close enough to blow them all to kingdom come.

Paul reached over and gently rubbed the back of her neck. "You must promise me you'll be careful."

"I promise."

"I don't think I could stand it if I lost you," Paul said softly.

"I plan to be around for a while," Joanna said and hugged him. But she was still thinking about the device that had caused the ATF agents to scatter and wondering how close she might have been to it.

6

Joanna and Lori McKay were at the rear of the forensics laboratory, standing in front of a giant map of the blast scene. A solid red circle indicated the explosion center. It was surrounded by twenty-eight numbered squares. Each square represented a body part.

Lori carefully studied the distance between the explosion center and the square most distant from it. Forty feet. The blast had torn off a man's arm and blown a piece of it forty feet away. She wondered if the man had felt anything at the instant he was being atomized. "Well, so far we can say there were at least two victims, since we found two different shoes that probably had two different feet in them. But I'd guess there were three, maybe four blast victims in that house."

"Based on what?" Joanna asked.

"A very preliminary scan of the body parts and where each was found."

Joanna nodded, agreeing with Lori's assessment. Her gaze went back to the explosion center. She envisioned the victims gathered around the kitchen table, where the bomb lay. Then the sudden detonation that blew everyone to smithereens. Now Joanna envisioned body parts flying through the air before they landed in a distribution pattern that could be predicted. It was all based on something called blast force, which Joanna had spent the morning reading about. From a forensics viewpoint, all bombs explode upward and outward, sending a giant, powerful wave of pressure. If the victims were huddled around the bomb, as Joanna and Lori assumed, the direction the blast force carried an individual's body parts would have depended on where he was standing at the time of detonation.

Joanna stepped away from the map. "My guess is that there were four victims in that house. Now we have to prove it."

"DNA typing of the tissue parts would help here," Lori suggested. "It would tell us beyond any doubt what part belonged to whom."

"It sure would," Joanna agreed. "But it's going to take weeks to get those results back. In the meantime, it would be a good idea to have every blood specimen typed for all twenty-three antigens. That will serve as a double check in case there are any gray areas with the DNA typing."

Lori reached for a legal pad and pencil and began scribbling notes. "How do you want to examine the individual pieces? Shall you and I study them together?"

"No," Joanna said at once. "We'll study them apart. You'll be in one room, I in another. Write down everything you uncover, even the smallest, most seemingly insignificant finding. If you have to guess, guess. If you have to assume, assume. But make the most of everything you see. Then we'll compare notes."

Lori smiled thinly. "I have the feeling you're going to see a lot more than I do."

"You're probably right," Joanna said. "But you just might see something I missed. And that something could turn out to be something very important."

That'll be the day, Lori thought, wondering if she'd ever measure up to Joanna Blalock. Joanna was so quick and sharp, and she had the ability to make so much from so little. She could detect the smallest clue that somehow always turned out to be crucial. And at crime scenes Joanna's talents really sparkled. She seemed to have a sixth sense for reconstructing events. That was why they called her in on the toughest cases. Lori sighed, wishing she had half of Joanna's expertise and reputation. "Is there anything in particular we should concentrate on?"

"We're searching for distinguishing features," Joanna told her. "Look for pieces of clothing or belts or buckles that the terrorists may have been wearing. Check the skin for color, scars and tattoos. Search for pieces of metal that could have been rings or pieces of a watch."

Lori looked up from her legal pad. "What would the metal tell us?"

"If it's part of a ring, maybe it has something inscribed on it," Joanna said. "Remember James Robert Butler?"

Lori nodded, recalling the skeletal remains found in a washed-away grave in the Santa Monica Mountains. The skeleton had had a wedding band on its ring finger with the letters *J.R.* inscribed on the inner surface. It was a major clue in helping them uncover the man's identity. "Something could be on the back of a watch, too, right?"

"You never know."

Lori hurriedly jotted down another note. She tapped her pencil against the table, thinking. "Is there anything special we should get set up for?"

"Let's see how the preliminary studies go," Joanna told her. "We'll do the gross examination of the tissues and then study the microscopic slides. After that, we'll have a better idea of what direction to take."

"What in the world would microscopic slides of the tissue tell us that we don't already know?" Lori asked. "I mean, it's just going to show blast injury to a given tissue."

"And a lot more if we're lucky."

"Can you give me an example?"

"Let's say one of the tissue specimens is a piece of liver," Joanna said, thinking aloud. "And on microscopic examination we discovered it was infested with the liver fluke *Schistosoma haematobium.* What would you make of that?"

Lori hesitated. "Well, I know that fluke is found throughout Africa. But the skin on our specimens doesn't appear to be Negroid."

"*Schistosoma haematobium* also occurs in North African countries, like Egypt and Algeria," Joanna explained. "And it's endemic in Iraq, Iran, Syria and Yemen."

"You think we're dealing with Middle Eastern terrorists?"

Joanna shrugged. "They're as good candidates as anyone. Maybe even better."

The women walked over to a large blackboard that listed the two forensic projects currently in progress. Number one was the West Hollywood bomb explosion. Number two was the dismembered hand discovered in a secluded canyon in northern Los Angeles County. Under the latter were the subsections (A) MRI and (B) Boxing Commission.

"Let's spend a little time on the hand," Joanna said, checking her watch.

Lori groaned under her breath. "I feel like I'm in the Laboratory of Bits and Pieces."

"You are."

Joanna studied the blackboard at length, then picked up a piece of chalk and added another subsection: (C) DNA typing.

"How will the DNA typing on the hand help us?" Lori asked.

"In California, it's mandatory that boxers have their blood tested for HIV and their urine for drugs before a bout. Maybe those specimens are still frozen away somewhere. And if they are, we can compare the DNA of the specimens with that of the hand."

"But it's serum, not whole blood, that's frozen," Lori argued. "You can't do DNA typing on serum or urine."

"You can if there are some white blood cells left in the specimens."

Lori grumbled to herself, thinking she should have thought of that. In urine and serum samples white blood cells were occasionally present; all you had to do was spin the specimen down to obtain them.

Joanna continued to concentrate on the blackboard, sensing she'd forgotten something. Something about the calluses on the hand. They were already being analyzed to determine what substances were ground into them. If cement or concrete was present, it would suggest the victim worked at a construction site. If the calluses were the result of landscaping, they might contain compost or some other fertilizer. But it wasn't the chemical analysis of the calluses she was overlooking. What the hell was it? It was right on the tip of her tongue, but she couldn't come up with it. She reached for the chalk and wrote in another subsection: (D)—with a big question mark after it.

Lori's gaze went from the blackboard to the charm bracelet on Joanna's wrist. "That's a beautiful bracelet," she commented.

"It was a gift," Joanna said as a picture of Paul du Maurier flashed into her mind. His Air Canada jet was somewhere over the Midwest by now, no more than a few hours from Montreal. She peeked down at the bracelet. A trinket, Paul had called it. It was eighteen-carat gold with small diamonds around the edges. Joanna brought her attention back to the blackboard. "Did the MRI of the hand show anything?"

"Yeah, but nobody knows what to make of it." Lori walked over to a stack of X rays and began putting them up on a viewbox. "There is something in the soft tissue that shouldn't be there."

Joanna carefully studied the films. In the soft tissue of the palm were splinterlike objects. "Are they metallic?"

Lori shrugged. "The radiologists aren't sure, but they don't think so. The fragments weren't radio-opaque on routine X ray."

Joanna saw a triangular-shaped fragment near the base of the thumb. It was the largest piece, over four millimeters in width. She drew a circle around it with a red crayon. "I'd like you to dissect out this fragment and have it analyzed. Let's find out what it is."

Lori took out a small notepad and jotted down the instructions. "By the way, I'm having trouble with the Boxing Commission. They claim the records are confidential."

"What kind of nonsense is that?" Joanna asked, irritated.

"They say their records contain medical reports and information on drug use and things of that sort. We apparently need some kind of special permission to open those files."

"Did you tell them this was a criminal investigation?"

"I'm not certain I used those exact words."

"Well, call them back and use those exact words, and tell them you represent the coroner's office. If they still refuse to cooperate, tell them we'll obtain a court order and confiscate all of their files. And if necessary, we'll have the court issue a subpoena for the entire Boxing Commission so they can help us sort through the records."

"Can we really do that?"

"In a New York minute."

There was a knock at the door. The women turned and watched Jake Sinclair enter the laboratory. He was carrying two plastic containers under his arms.

"More body parts," Jake said and placed the containers on a countertop.

Joanna asked, "What are they?"

"Number twenty-nine is a piece of skull with hair on one side and brain stuck on the other."

"What color is the hair?" Joanna asked.

"Black," Jake reported.

"Kinky?"

Jake shook his head. "Straight with medium thickness. It could be American or Mediterranean."

"Or Mexican," Joanna suggested. "What did his scalp look like?"

"Dark tan."

"Any thinning?"

"Nope. It was full. No graying."

"Good luster?"

"Oh, yeah. He was young," Jake said. "And his hair smelled kind of sweet."

Joanna smiled to herself. Jake had an incredible sense of smell. He was able to detect and discern odors that most people didn't even notice. "We'll analyze it and check it against samples from Mexican and Middle Eastern barbershops."

Lori listened, mouth agape, Joanna and Jake Sinclair had gotten so much from so little. They seemed to feed off each other, as if each knew what the other was thinking. So far they had deduced that one of the terrorists was young, probably under thirty-five, dark-complected and most likely of Latin or Mediterranean descent. And analysis of the hair tonic might narrow down the man's nationality even more.

"What's in the second container?" Joanna asked.

"We're not sure," Jake said, removing the lid. "It looks like a piece of plastic foot."

"Like an insert?"

"No. It's more than that."

Joanna put on a pair of latex gloves and lifted the object from the container. It was cream colored and appeared to be the heel and plantar surface of a foot. The material was either plastic or ceramic.

"Strange," Joanna said, perplexed. "Maybe it's part of a mannequin."

"What the hell would they be doing with a mannequin?"

Joanna shrugged, then examined both sides of the heel with a magnifying glass. "There's some blood and tissue stuck to the inner surface. And that indicates somebody was wearing it."

"Maybe it's some kind of insert," Jake guessed.

Joanna studied the width and texture of the heel. "It's too thick for that."

"Could it be a piece of a plastic shoe?" Lori asked.

"Now that's a possibility," Joanna said and gave Lori a big nod. "Nice thinking."

"How can we check that out?" Lori wondered.

"Maybe the bioengineers can help us." Joanna placed the plastic heel back in the container and handed it to Lori. "First, let's examine it carefully for fingerprints and remove the blood and tissue for study. Then I'd like you to take it down to the Bioengineering Department and see if they can identify the material and tell us where it came from."

"I'll get right on it," Lori said. "Then I'll see if I can get things sorted out with the Boxing Commission."

Jake watched the young pathologist sling a knapsack over her shoulder and bounce out of the laboratory. She had her auburn hair in a ponytail, which made her seem even younger than she was. He thought she looked like a college coed. He turned to Joanna. "You got problems with the Boxing Commission?"

"They're being a little obstinate." Joanna told him about the dismembered hand and the findings that made her believe it belonged to a boxer. "The size of his metacarpal bones suggests he weighed between a hundred and ten and a hundred and twenty."

"He might weigh less than that," Jake said at once.

"Why?"

"Because some boxers have really big hands, much bigger than you'd expect," he explained. "Hell, I once knew a welterweight whose hands were larger than mine. He told me they started growing that way when he was a teenager."

Joanna thought about mechanisms that might account for boxers having large hands. She knew that bones in males continued to grow until the age of eighteen. Maybe the repeated trauma to the hands of boxers in their adolescence stimulated bone growth. She made a mental note to check with the representative of the Boxing Commission about the size of boxers' hands.

"So you could be dealing with a featherweight here," Jake told her.

"Are you a boxing fan?"

"A long time ago," he said and sat down wearily. He lit an unfiltered Greek cigarette, inhaling deeply.

"I thought you were going to quit."

"One of these days."

Joanna studied Jake briefly. He was so damn good-looking, with his high cheekbones and gray-blue eyes. And his swept-back brown hair now had more gray in it, and that made him even better looking. But the lines in his face seemed deeper and he looked very tired.

"I had an early wake-up call from Dan Hurley," Jake said. "They had some trouble at the bomb site."

"I saw it on television this morning," Joanna said, nodding. "What was all the commotion about?"

"A pipe in the ground started hissing natural gas. Apparently the pipe was bent shut by the explosion, and it became unplugged when somebody started moving rubble around."

"Don't tell me they forgot to cut off the gas lines."

"Oh, they were closed off all right," Jake said. "But there was still a fair amount of gas trapped in a feeder pipe."

Joanna shivered. "Was it dangerous to the people working at the site?"

"It could have blown sky high." Jake remembered the day before, when he was about to light a cigarette at the bomb site and Hurley had stopped him. He wondered if natural gas had been leaking then and what would have happened if he'd lit that cigarette.

"Have the federal people got any insight into who was responsible for the bomb?" Joanna asked.

"They've got nothing," Jake said. "According to their informants, it wasn't any of the known terrorist or paramilitary groups. They think it was one of those phantom cells that consist of five or six people, none of whom anyone has ever heard of or knows about."

"This gets worse by the minute."

"Tell me about it!" Jake pushed himself up from his seat and crushed out his cigarette. "I've got to go." He turned to leave, then glanced at Joanna. A half smile came across his face. "You look happy."

"That's because I am."

"It suits you," Jake said, his voice husky. " You look great."

"Thanks," Joanna said, feeling herself blush. She quickly turned back to the blackboard and wondered for the hundredth time if she would ever get Jake Sinclair completely out of her system.

7

Artificial light streamed in through stained-glass windows, giving the hospital chapel a reverence that neither Eva nor Rudy felt. They were sitting in the front row, staring straight ahead at the empty pulpit.

"What are we waiting for?" Rudy asked.

"For eight forty-five," Eva said. "It's near the end of visiting hours," she explained. "There'll still be people in the halls and elevators. We'll blend right in. Nobody will notice us."

"Yeah. I guess," Rudy said, then squinted an eye. "But what if the old man has got a visitor?"

"Then we'll wait for the visitor to leave." Eva handed him a white plastic cap and a pair of thick glasses. "Put these on."

They were wearing white shirts and pants, the mandatory uniform for the cleaning crews at Memorial Hospital. The caps were optional, but Eva thought they helped their disguises. Caps cover hair and alter the way people look. The idea for Rudy to wear glasses came from an article published by a paramilitary commander on the Internet. If the glasses were thick enough, the commander had written, they became the dominant feature people would remember about the individual who had them on. Rudy's glasses were made of clear plastic, but they appeared thick enough to be magnifying glasses.

"How much longer?" he asked impatiently.

"About five minutes."

"Maybe now would be a good time for you to lead us in prayer."

Eva nodded and lowered her head. "O Lord, guide us through this mission and let us complete it successfully. Keep us safe as we destroy your enemies, in thy name. Thank you for—"

Rudy nudged her with his elbow and gestured with his head to the rear of the chapel. An elderly woman was slowly walking down the center aisle. She sat across from them, then stared up at the stained-glass window and fingered her rosary beads.

"—for your help and mercy. Amen," Eva quickly finished.

"Amen," Rudy added solemnly.

In his peripheral vision Rudy studied the woman. She was very dark, and he could hear her praying in a foreign language that he didn't recognize. She knelt and started crying, her soft sobs clearly audible. Then her voice became louder and high pitched and began to grate on Rudy's nerves. He wished she'd do her crying somewhere else.

Rudy glanced up at the beautiful stained-glass window. A white archangel looked down at him. Their eyes met and held. Rudy felt the power flowing through him. He was being blessed.

Eva stood, her back to the woman. "Keep your head down," she said in a whisper.

They left the chapel and walked over to a bank of elevators. The corridor was deserted except for a young woman pushing a stroller with a sleeping child. A nearby information desk was empty.

"I thought you said there'd be people in the halls," Rudy said, concerned.

"On the ward there will be," Eva told him and pushed the up button.

"How can you be so sure?"

"Because our friend at Memorial said there would be."

Rudy didn't trust their contact at Memorial Hospital. The guy always stayed in the background and never got his hands dirty or did any of the killing. And if the contact was ever caught, Rudy had the feeling he would snitch on the others to save himself. But Eva had vouched for him.

"We leave by the fire escape, right?" Rudy asked, thinking ahead.

"Right."

Eva checked their appearance in the mirrored wall adjacent to the elevators. With their white clothes and caps, they looked like cleaners down to the smallest detail. Even their ID badges seemed real. And the commander on the Internet was correct about the thick glasses. Rudy now looked like a studious nerd. Eva tucked a red curl of hair under her cap as the elevator door opened.

At the back of the elevator was a teenage girl in a wheelchair, an IV running in her arm. A big, heavyset man in working clothes stood beside her, his hand on her shoulder. There was the distinct scent of an air deodorizer in the elevator. It was not a fresh aroma but a sickly sweet one. Eva noticed that the floor was damp, as if it had just been mopped. She thought she could detect an underlying odor of vomit.

"Working late, huh?" the man asked.

"Yeah," Eva said, keeping her head turned away from the man. "But we're almost done."

Rudy looked over at the girl in the wheelchair. She was a pretty little thing, he thought, no more than fourteen or fifteen. Then he saw the rash on her arms, red and angry with blisters and scabs. Even her feet and legs were affected. And now she was scratching at the sores on her neck. Rudy pushed himself against the wall, putting as much distance as possible between himself and the girl. He hoped that whatever the hell she had couldn't be spread through the air.

The elevator jerked to a stop, and the door opened. Eva and Rudy got out on the sixth floor and went directly to a cleaning closet at the end of the corridor. After obtaining a bucket on wheels and two mops, they headed back for Room 602.

There were only a few people in the hall: an old man helping an old woman walk, a young man strolling along next to his mobile IV pole. Eva and Rudy stepped aside as a technician pushing an EKG machine hurried by.

"Perfect," Rudy said under his breath.

"Not so perfect," Eva said, pointing with her mop. "There's a chair outside the old man's room."

"So?"

"Look down at the nurses' station."

Rudy squeezed water from his mop and glanced over his shoulder. A cop was standing at the station chatting with a nurse. They were laughing, making small talk.

"Shit," he growled. "What now?"

Eva sized up the situation, weighing the chance of getting caught. So what if the cop walked in? she asked herself. So what? He could be killed quickly and silently. With her foot she felt the Beretta with its silencer that was taped to her leg.

"Well?" Rudy asked, his eyes fixed on the policeman. Now the cop was drinking coffee, still laughing with the nurse.

"We go for it."

They moved quickly into the room, leaving the door open. An old man was lying in bed, his eyes bandaged. On a movable table beside him was a half-eaten dish of vanilla ice cream. As Rudy moved toward the old man, he bumped into the table, pushing it against the bed.

"Is that you, Lieutenant Sinclair?" the old man asked loudly.

"Yeah," Rudy grunted.

"I'm glad you came back," the man said. "I just remembered something else. Two of the men I saw going into the house were speaking Spanish. I'm sure they were Mexican. And one of the white guys had a mustache and goatee. Funny how this stuff comes back to you, isn't it?"

"Yeah. Real funny." Rudy clamped a hand over the old man's mouth and reached for the pillow. The man tried to twist away, but Rudy pinned him to the mattress with his weight. Quickly he placed the pillow over the old man's face.

Eva peeked out the door and down the corridor. The cop was still at the nurses' station. But he was standing away from the counter now, and held his head back as he drank from the coffee cup. His break was almost over. She looked back at Rudy and the old man. "Hurry it up!" she urged.

"The old bastard doesn't want to die."

The old man was stronger than Rudy had anticipated. He was clawing at Rudy's arms, breaking skin and drawing blood. Rudy pushed down on the pillow even harder.

Now the old man was kicking and making a muffled sound beneath the pillow. Suddenly he stiffened and retched and retched again. Then he was still.

Rudy removed the pillow and studied the man's face. There was spittle and vomit all about the man's nose and mouth, but Rudy saw no bubbles. No air was moving. He felt for a carotid pulse. Nothing. Rudy placed the pillow under the man's head and said, "Let's move it."

They went back into the corridor, swishing at the floor with their mops. Out of the corners of their eyes they watched the cop heading toward them.

Rudy leaned down and reached for the pistol inside his sock.

"Cool it," Eva said evenly. "Let's mop our way down the corridor, nice and easy."

"I think he saw us coming out of the room."

"If he comes over to question us, kill him." Eva put a

fake smile on her face, nodding as if Rudy had just said something funny. "One shot to the head."

They swished their mops back and forth, moving slowly away from Room 602, never looking up but keeping the cop in their peripheral vision.

The cop had his hands on his hips, studying them now.

"What do you think?" Rudy asked, his voice barely above a whisper.

"I think he's going to sit down."

A moment later the cop sat in his chair and stretched out his legs.

"Good boy," Eva said, pushing the bucket down the corridor toward the fire escape.

8

Joanna stared at the ringing phone, knowing it was bringing bad news. Early morning calls always did. It was 7:30, and Joanna was just starting her second cup of coffee. She pushed away from the breakfast and picked up the phone.

"Yes?"

"Good morning," Paul said. "I hope I didn't wake you."

"I've been up," Joanna said softly.

"And by now you're on your second cup of coffee."

"Exactly right." Joanna glanced up at the wall clock. "Is anything wrong?"

"Everything is fine in Montreal," Paul said. "Except for Sasha's disappointment at not being able to meet you."

"You tell her we'll do it soon, and that's a promise."

"I'll try, but she may not believe it. You see, her mother is using this as an example of Sasha not being able to depend on me and what I say."

Joanna could sense the bitterness in Paul's voice. "Lord! Your ex-wife sounds awful."

"That may be the understatement of the year." Paul lit a cigarette and blew smoke into the receiver. "And to make matters worse, I was supposed to have dinner with Sasha tonight, but I have to fly to New York for an important meeting."

Joanna wondered what it would feel like to be an only

child pulled in opposite directions by divorced, feuding parents. It had to leave emotional scars. "I'm certain that Sasha will understand that because of business—"

"Children do not understand business," Paul interrupted. "Not when it takes a parent away."

"Is your business that important?"

"It's top priority," Paul said, his voice now very serious. "We're trying to take over an investment bank in New York, and there are problems."

"Well, solve the problems as quickly as possible and return to Montreal," Joanna said. "And bring Sasha a surprise present from New York."

Paul sighed deeply. "I wish it were that easy. But there's going to be a series of meetings in New York; it could go on for a week or more. I'm afraid we'll have to cancel our dinner plans this weekend."

"Events dictate our lives," Joanna muttered under her breath.

"What?"

"Nothing."

"When I get back to Los Angeles we'll have one of our special dinners. How does that sound?"

"Great," Joanna said, trying to sound enthusiastic.

"I miss you," Paul said warmly. "I really miss you."

"I miss—" Joanna heard a series of clicks, then Paul's voice came back on.

"I've got an urgent call on another line," he said quickly. "Can I call you back later?"

"Of course."

"Stay sweet and gorgeous."

Joanna stared at the phone for a moment before putting it down. She wondered if she had just gotten a glimpse of the future. Up until now all of her dates and meetings with Paul had been carefully planned. Everything had been moonlight and wine and roses. But their professional lives were coming into play and interfering with their plans. She couldn't go to Montreal because of her involvement in the West Hollywood bombing, he couldn't return to Los Angeles because of a bank takeover in New York. And then there were his ex-wife and daughter, who would undoubtedly be mixed into their relationship. Jesus! Joanna groaned. Why couldn't her life be smooth and uncomplicated, just for once?

The phone rang loudly, breaking into her thoughts. Joanna smiled. It was Paul. She could feel it in her bones. He probably wanted to tell her how he missed her again. Or maybe the meeting in New York was canceled and he was back on his way to Los Angeles.

Joanna reached for the phone. "Yes?"

"We've got a problem," Jake Sinclair said.

"What?"

"Our only witness to the bombing was found dead in his bed at Memorial this morning."

Joanna quickly refocused her mind. "Any evidence of foul play?"

"Maybe, maybe not," Jake said. "You'd better take a look."

Joanna edged her way through the crowd of doctors and nurses gathered at the sixth-floor nurses' station. She ducked under the crime scene tape and walked down the quiet corridor. Most of the doors were closed, but a few were cracked open with curious eyes peeking out. A policeman standing outside Room 602 recognized her and gave her a half salute.

On entering the room, Joanna first noticed the strong stench of vomit. She glanced at the floor and bed, searching unsuccessfully for the source of the odor. She noted that the furniture was in place, the bedcovers unwrinkled. Nothing was askew. If there had been a struggle, Joanna saw no evidence for it.

Jake came over to her. "There's strange business here."

"What have you got?" Joanna asked.

"I've got a dead man," Jake said. "And there's a smudge of blood on his pillow I can't explain."

"Does he have a shaving cut?" Joanna inquired.

"None that I could find."

"Or maybe a nosebleed."

"Possible," Jake said. "But there's no crusted blood around his nostrils."

"Or he could have coughed it up," Joanna suggested. "People with blast injuries sometimes have hemorrhaging into their airways."

"So it may be nothing after all," Simon Murdock said, worriedly pacing the floor by a large window. The morning light streamed in and seemed to magnify the lines in his face. "The diagnosis here may well be the one made by the attending physician."

"Which is?" Joanna asked.

"Regurgitation and aspiration with acute airway obstruction."

Joanna nodded, now knowing the source of the stench. "And perhaps he coughed so hard trying to clear his airway he ruptured a small blood vessel."

"That would explain everything," Murdock agreed eagerly.

"Un-huh," Jake said, unconvinced, as he lifted up the corpse's head to examine the nape of the neck.

"Now look, Lieutenant," Murdock said, a noticeable edge to his voice. "I know it's your job to investigate, but the evidence here seems quite clear, and I don't see the need—"

"Nothing is clear here," Jake cut him off. "A man who survived a bomb blast and was recovering is suddenly dead and nobody knows why. And he just happened to be the only eyewitness to the bombing."

"But a diagnosis of regurgitation and aspiration seems obvious, don't you agree?"

"I'll agree when I see the autopsy that shows his lungs filled with vomit," Jake said, making no effort to hide his dislike for the dean of the medical school. "And I'll believe the blood on this pillowcase belongs to this guy when we match it against his blood type."

Murdock stared back for a moment, then looked away and began pacing again.

Joanna could sense the lingering tension as well as the mounting mutual dislike between the two men. Whenever they were together it required effort by both to remain civil. And she understood why. Their meetings always involved a criminal investigation at Memorial Hospital. And it was Murdock's job to protect Memorial's image at all costs. Nothing was worse for a medical center's reputation than a blatant crime, and Memorial had had more than its share. Drugs, sex scandals, even murder. Just like the outside world, Joanna thought grimly. And each year seemed to bring a new scandal and a new threat to Memorial's reputation. To Murdock, Jake Sinclair wasn't just a detective, he was an adversary who could do real damage to Memorial Hospital.

And Jake couldn't have cared less. All he saw was a crime that needed to be solved and its perpetrators punished. Joanna wondered if there really was a crime here. Nothing so far suggested it, but, then again, Jake had a sixth sense when it came to murder. He could feel it, and he was rarely wrong.

Joanna studied Jake as he threw the bedcover and sheet back to expose the corpse's body. Jake was so damn good-looking, with those gray-blue eyes that could peer down into the pit of your soul. Your nerves tingled while he was doing it, and you didn't want him to stop. Too bad he was a confirmed loner, incapable of living with another person for any length of time. Jake was meant to be single. She sighed, wondering when would be a good time to tell him about her relationship with Paul du Maurier. And she wondered how he'd deal with the news. He would probably just walk off into the night, a loner alone again.

"Do you want to take a look?" Jake asked.

Joanna came over to the bedside and studied the nude corpse. She started at his feet and worked her way up. His toenails were yellowed and misshapen, from a chronic fungal infection. The musculature of his lower extremities was surprisingly well developed for a man who appeared to be in his seventies. He had been a jogger or a walker, Joanna guessed. His genitals were shriveled and barely visible in a mound of gray hair. There was a well-healed appendectomy scar and a few large nevi on his chest. The closer she got to his head, the stronger was the stench of vomit.

Joanna's gaze went to the man's arms. The musculature was good there too, but not as well developed as that of his legs. There were venipuncture marks on one forearm, but none of them was bleeding. Next she carefully examined the dead man's fingers. She reached for the magnifying glass in the pocket of her white coat and studied the corpse's fingertips and fingernails. "He put up a fight," she said.

Jake hurried over. "Do you see skin under his nails?"

Joanna nodded. "And blood. It's under the index and third finger on the right."

"Son of a bitch!" Jake said hoarsely. "I knew it."

Murdock moved closer to the bed, trying to overhear. "What? What?"

"We got murder," Jake said. "That's what."

Murdock swallowed audibly. "How can you be sure?"

Joanna told the dean about the bits of skin and blood beneath the corpse's fingernails. They were reliable signs of a man fighting for his life, clawing at the face and arms of his assailant. The manicured nail on his index finger was also chipped, adding more weight to the evidence. "We'll type the blood under his nails against the blood on the pillow and against his own, and that will clearly establish that the man was attacked. And we'll use the bits of skin to do a DNA type. If we ever catch the killer, the DNA type will give us a positive ID."

"So you have absolutely no doubt?" Murdock asked nervously.

"None." Joanna sniffed the air near the head of the bed. "Why is the smell of vomit so strong here?"

"I noticed it too, and it's coming from the back of his head or neck." Jake leaned down and looked under the bed. "Or from the floor."

Joanna lifted the corpse's head and examined the occiput and neck. They were clean, but the smell was even stronger. She stared down at the pillow briefly, then turned it over and saw the dried vomitus. "Was anything on the bed moved after they found him dead this morning?"

"The cop on guard didn't let them move anything," Jake answered. "Why?"

Joanna pointed to the dried vomitus on the back of the pillowcase.

"The bastards suffocated him," Jake said, his jaws tightly clenched. "And the poor guy had his eyes bandaged. He didn't even see them coming."

Joanna looked to the door. "Did you say you had a guard posted outside?"

"Around the clock."

"Then how did the killers get in here?"

Jake thought for a moment, wondering if it could have been a doctor or nurse who did the killing. No, he quickly decided. The cop on duty had told him that no one had entered the room after 8:00 P.M. No one. But maybe he was talking about visitors and not hospital staff, like doctors and nurses and technicians. "Gorman! Come in here for a minute."

The tall, broad-shouldered cop hurried in. "Yes, sir?"

"Did anyone enter this room after you last saw the patient at eight o'clock?"

"No, sir."

"I'm talking about anybody. Doctors, nurses, orderlies, technicians."

"Not a soul."

Jake rubbed at his chin, knowing that somehow the killer had gotten by the policeman. He wondered if the cop had dozed off briefly. "Did you leave your post for any reason?"

"No, sir."

"To take a pee?"

The cop nodded slowly. "Twice. But I used the head in the room, and I left the door open."

"Did you walk around any? You know, to stretch your legs?"

The cop thought for a moment. "I went to the nurses' station for a cup of coffee at eight-thirty or so. But I stayed in the corridor and kept my eye on the door."

"How far do you figure you were from the door?"

"Thirty-five feet, maybe forty."

"And you saw nobody in the corridor?"

"Nobody," the cop said, then squinted as he remembered back. "Except for a cleaning crew."

Jake's eyes narrowed. "Are you sure they were cleaners?"

"Yeah. I guess," the cop said. "They were dressed in white and had on ID badges. And I can tell you for damn sure they didn't come into this room."

No, you can't, Jake wanted to say. You were forty feet away, and one of the cleaners could have slipped into the room while you were reaching for a cup of coffee. "That was between eight-thirty and nine o'clock, right?"

"Correct."

Jake took out his notepad and jotted down a reminder to check with the hospital officials and see if a cleaning crew was scheduled to be on the sixth floor at that time. Even if they were, he'd want to talk with them. They might have seen something. "Can you describe the cleaners?"

The cop hesitated, thinking back again. "Two white guys. Young, in their late twenties. One of them had a goatee."

"Good," Jake said. "Thanks for your help."

Joanna watched the policeman leave, then turned to Jake. "You think the cleaning crew were murderers?"

"Could be," he said. "White uniforms and fake ID badges are easy to come by."

Murdock shook his head disgustedly. "And they just walked right in and killed a patient, then walked out."

"They didn't just walk in," Jake said, wondering what thoughts had been going through the old man's mind while he was being suffocated. He probably thought he was having a nightmare. "If it was the cleaners, they had inside help."

"You have no way of knowing that," Murdock said defensively.

"Sure I do," Jake told him. "They knew all about the correct uniform and ID badge to wear. They knew where the cleaning closet was. And, most important, they knew the room the witness was in. Keep in mind that the witness's name wasn't even listed with hospital information. Somebody would have to supply those details to the killers. And that somebody had to know Memorial Hospital."

"You're still guessing," Murdock said. "There is no evidence whatsoever that someone on staff here was involved. It's all circumstantial."

"Uh-huh," Jake said, disliking Murdock even more

than before. He put his notepad away. "I want to check the nurses' station. Let's see how good the officer's view was. Maybe there was a blind spot."

He led the way out past the policeman, who was standing guard at the door. Jake stopped and looked down the corridor as the door to the fire escape opened. A tall black man wearing a white uniform and ID badge came out and walked toward them, cursing under his breath. He was pushing a bucket on wheels and carrying two mops over his shoulder.

"What's the problem?" Jake asked him.

"I'll tell you what the problem is," the custodian said, his voice raspy. "The help you hire today ain't worth a damn. They want good pay, but they're lazy. Just plain lazy. Left their mops and bucket in the fire escape instead of putting them away in the closet."

Jake's eyes suddenly narrowed. "Where's the cleaning closet?"

The black man pointed down the corridor. "Halfway between here and the nurses' station. Hell, they had to pass it on their way back to the elevator."

Jake and Joanna followed the man's line of vision. In their minds' eyes they both saw the cleaning crew mopping their way away from the room and away from the cop at the nurses' station. They nodded to each other and said almost simultaneously, "Inside job."

"What?" Murdock asked. He watched Jake take the mop and bucket from the janitor and tag them as evidence. He still didn't understand their significance.

Jake waited for the man to walk out of hearing distance, then said, "Somebody at Memorial is involved in murder."

Murdock gulped. "Are you saying someone on staff actually did the killing?"

"I'm saying someone on staff helped plan it," Jake said. "And in the state of California that's murder one."

9

"Are you okay?" Jake asked.

"I'm fine," Sergeant Lou Farelli said.

"You look a little peaked."

"That's what sitting on a couch watching TV for a month will do to you."

Jake studied his partner's face, wondering if Farelli had come back on duty too soon. His color wasn't good, and there was no bounce to his step. But the doctor had cleared him, said he had recovered from his bullet wounds. In his mind's eye Jake could still see the blood gushing out of Farelli's leg onto the sidewalk. "If you get tired, you let me know."

Farelli shaded his eyes from the bright sun and glanced around at the mounds of rubble that had once been homes. "Un-fucking-believable."

"It hits you a lot harder when you see it up close, doesn't it?"

"One moment it was a neighborhood, the next a pile of nothing."

"With twenty-two people dead," Jake added.

Farelli watched the miniature flags scattered about the bomb site fluttering in the breeze. "Do you think the doc will ever be able to put the body parts back together again?"

Jake shook his head. "Only God could do that."

"Yeah," Farelli said. "But he ain't working this case."

A loud engine roared to life. A tractorlike earthmover

began pushing aside the rubble from a collapsed chimney and fireplace. An ATF agent gave hand signals to the driver, motioning him to come forward a little more, then a little more. A stone slab split into two pieces, sending up a cloud of dust and debris. Abruptly the agent held up his palms, waving them, and the earthmover came to a stop. An assistant coroner appeared and climbed over the pile of bricks, then reached in with a pair of tongs. Jake and Farelli stood on their tiptoes and tried to see into the rubble but couldn't.

Moments later an ATF agent hurried by them, carrying a small plastic crate with a biohazard label attached to it. Dan Hurley was a step behind the agent. He saw the two homicide detectives and came over.

"Glad to see you back," Hurley said to Farelli, noting his color. The whole department knew how close Farelli had come to bleeding to death. A friend of Hurley's had told him that Farelli lost a quart of blood on that damn sidewalk. "Kellerman says you'll be a better cop now that you've got some of his blood in you."

Farelli grinned, nodding. Bo Kellerman was a member of the vice squad and had donated a unit of hard-to-find AB negative blood for Farelli. "You thank him again for me."

The engine of the earthmover came to life once more, louder now. It backed away from the collapsed chimney. More dust went up into the air and gradually settled. The earthmover backed up farther, and the noise from its engine faded.

"Still finding bits and pieces, huh?" Jake asked.

"This time I think we found a real body part," Hurley said. "It looks like an elbow with a nice section of upper arm still attached."

Farelli shrugged. "Hard to make an ID with that."

Hurley smiled thinly. "And it looks like there's a tattoo on that arm."

"What kind of tattoo?" Jake asked, his ears pricked.

"It's hard to say," Hurley said and rubbed at his chin with the hand that was missing two fingers. "But it appears to be some type of flower."

"Is it a good tattoo or a cheap one?" Jake asked.

"It looked pretty good to me," Hurley said thoughtfully. "You know, the color and details were really nice and clear."

Jake nodded. Excellent tattoos could be traced, particularly if they had unusual features. Some tattoos were so distinctive and intricate that they could be attributed to only a few artists. Jake jotted down a note, reminding himself to study it carefully later. "Have the feds heard anything?"

"Not a peep," Hurley said. "The group that did it isn't talking."

"Not even the usual nut calls?" Jake asked.

"LAPD got one late last night," Hurley said disdainfully. "A real fruitcake. He claimed the explosive he used was a special type of TNT that was made by Pontius Pilate."

"So it's looking more and more like a work accident, isn't it?"

"I guess so," Hurley said, not really convinced. "But I'll tell you this. These guys weren't amateurs, and their bomb wasn't homemade. It was a special type of C-four." He reached into his coat and handed Jake a lab report.

Jake held the paper so Farelli could read it as well. It was from the ATF Explosives Laboratory in Rockville, Maryland. The C-4 used in the bomb was a mixture of RDX and PETN, both very high-grade explosives. The ratio of RDX to PETN was not usually seen in C-4 preparations.

"The RDX and PETN were pure, virtually no contaminants," Hurley explained. "That tells us the C-four wasn't homemade. It was manufactured under strict quality control."

"Where did they get it?" Jake asked.

"They probably stole it from some military facility or maybe bought it on the black market," Hurley said. "There's plenty of it around. But it's the proportions of RDX and PETN that tell us the most. These ingredients were mixed in a precise ratio that assured them they'd get the biggest bang for their buck. It was done by somebody with expertise in explosives. It was done by a pro."

"If they were such pros, how come they blew themselves up?" Farelli asked.

"It happens." Hurley's mind flashed back to the pipe bomb that had blown away two of his fingers. He had been careful, so very careful, but the bomb had exploded anyway. He could still remember the puff of smoke just before he heard the boom. And he still had nightmares about it, but not as frequently as before. Hurley brought his mind back to the present. "I heard we lost our witness."

"Yeah," Jake said sourly.

"Did he die from his injuries?"

Jake shook his head. "They got to him. It looks like they suffocated the poor bastard."

"Shit," Hurley grumbled.

"Now we got no eyewitness."

"And now we *know* they're going to blow up whatever the hell they were planning to blow up in the first place."

"How do you figure that?"

"Because most bombers would have run like hell and disappeared in the woods," Hurley said. "You don't hang around when there are twenty-two counts of murder staring you in the face. But these guys did. They're sticking around to clean up all the loose ends so they can get on with their business. I'll bet they've got a specific target set for a specific date. And they're not going to let anything or anybody get in their way."

Jake ran a hand through his hair, trying to follow Hurley's line of reasoning. "But their chances of getting caught are now so much greater."

"They don't give a damn about that. Fanatics only care about their mission."

The cellular phone inside Hurley's coat pocket sounded. He reached for it and spoke briefly, then put the phone away. "Got to go. I'll check with you later."

Farelli watched the bomb squad detective hurry away. "Probably another bomb threat."

"Hurley told me that the bomb squads in Los Angeles get over a thousand calls a year," Jake said. "We make Belfast look like a safe playground."

"This city is turning into a real shithole," Farelli growled. "And now we've got some terrorists to add a little flavor to it."

"And not a clue as to who they are."

Farelli pulled his loose-fitting trousers up over his waist. Despite his inactivity during the past month, he had lost ten pounds since the shooting. "Did the witness tell you anything before he was iced?"

"Not much," Jake said. "He was still having a hell of a headache from his concussion."

"He saw nothing at all?"

"He saw a couple of guys go into the house, but he couldn't remember what they looked like. And he had no recollection of the blast itself. He was walking his German shepherd, and the dog stopped to take a leak. That's the last thing the old guy recalled."

Farelli thought for a moment. "How many times a day did the guy walk his dog?"

"Twice," Jake said. "Morning and night."

"And where did he live?"

Jake pointed with his thumb. "A block and a half up that way."

"Did he live by himself?"

"With his wife, but she's got bad eyesight and doesn't walk with him. According to neighbors, she usually sits in the swing on the front porch and waits for him to return from walking the dog."

"She can't see, huh?"

"Cataracts."

Farelli smiled, his eyes lighting up. "Do you think that maybe when he came back from his walks he described to her what he had seen while he was away?"

Jake slapped an open palm against his forehead. "I've got my head up my ass."

"Let's go see her."

They walked up the winding street past houses leveled by the blast, then past houses that were badly damaged, with windows blown out and siding split by the force of the explosion. Even the trees had been hard hit. Branches and limbs were strewn about the sidewalk and on front lawns.

Jake glanced over at Farelli, glad to have his partner back. Farelli's strong points were tracking down and questioning witnesses. He knew how to find them, and he knew how to extract information from them. People seemed almost happy to give him the information he wanted. Jake thought that was because of Farelli's appearance. He was a short, stocky man, heavily bearded, with a quick smile. A lot of people believed he looked like a waiter in an Italian restaurant. But he was really tough as nails and, in a fight, he was the man you wanted by your side.

"I'd guess all the body parts are going to the doc's laboratory at Memorial." Farelli broke the silence.

"Yeah."

The sergeant nodded. "So that's why you didn't want to examine the tattooed piece of arm back at the site."

"I'm not following you."

"You just wanted another excuse to visit Joanna Blalock."

Jake shrugged. "I don't need an excuse."

"Sure you do," Farelli said at once. "You two have split again and you don't know how to get back together."

Jake sighed heavily, knowing Farelli was right. The more he and Joanna were apart, the more he thought about her. Particularly at night, when he was alone in the silence. "It'll happen when it happens."

"She's a special woman, Jake," Farelli went on. "Like one in a million. She's pretty and smart and sexy as hell. And you're taking her for granted."

Jake shrugged again.

"You want some advice?"

"I guess so."

"Stop screwing around," Farelli said earnestly. "Or one day you'll go by there and Joanna Blalock will be gone."

"What the hell brought all this on?"

"Getting shot and watching yourself damn near bleed to death," Farelli answered. "It focuses your mind on the important things in life."

Jake stopped in front of a single-story house with white asbestos siding. There was a front porch with an empty swing on it. "Here we are," he said.

"How do you want to handle it?"

"I'll start."

They walked up the steps and rang the bell. A plump woman in her midsixties with gray-brown hair came to the door. The detectives showed their badges and introduced themselves to the widow's sister. They followed her down a hallway into a small living room. In the background Jake heard music playing softly. It was Frank Sinatra singing "I'll Be Seeing You."

"Claire," the sister said quietly. "These two gentlemen are detectives. They'd like to ask you some questions. Do you feel up to it?"

Claire Stonehauser nodded slowly and pointed to a sofa covered with a well-worn tan fabric. "Please have a seat."

The detectives sat across from the widow and studied her briefly. She was a small, frail woman with short white hair that was neatly combed. Her rocking chair squeaked against the hardwood floor as she gently rocked back and forth.

"We're sorry about your husband, ma'am," Jake began.

"We were married almost fifty-eight years," she said, her voice just above a whisper.

Jake leaned forward to hear better. The music in the background seemed louder.

"Does the song bother you?" Mrs. Stonehauser asked.

Jake shook his head. "Not at all."

"This song is very important to me," she said. "They were playing it the night I met my husband." She rocked back as a faint smile crossed her face. "It's a wonderful story. Would you like to hear it?"

"Yes, I would." Jake really didn't want to listen to the story, but he knew that witnesses who were at ease talked more and remembered more.

"My husband was a senior at West Point in nineteen forty-one," she reminisced, "and my brother Phillip was his roommate. Phillip fixed me up with Art, and we went to the prom together. The Tommy Dorsey Orchestra was playing, and Frank Sinatra was their lead singer. Art and I fell in love to Mr. Sinatra singing 'I'll Be Seeing You.' Eight months later Art and Phillip were in Europe fighting the Nazis. I didn't see Art for four years, but every day I listened to this song on my phonograph. And every time I heard Mr. Sinatra sing 'I'll Be Seeing You,' I could see Art's face and feel his touch and hear his voice. It brought him back to me, just like it's doing now. That's why this song is so important to me."

Jake asked, "You married him after the war?"

Mrs. Stonehauser nodded. "A month after he returned."

"And Phil should have been his best man," the sister added sadly.

The widow continued to nod. "Our brother Phillip was killed at the battle for Bastogne. He died in Art's arms." She reached for a Kleenex and sniffed back tears. "At our wedding there was no best man, just an empty space where Phillip should have been standing."

Farelli stared ahead expressionless, but he swallowed hard.

With effort Mrs. Stonehauser took a deep breath. "So tell me, Lieutenant, how can I help you?"

"I've got just a few questions, ma'am," Jake said, taking out his notepad. "Your husband told me that he usually went for a walk with the dog a couple of times a day."

"Sometimes more," she said. "Whenever Ralphie wanted to go, Art would take him."

The German shepherd looked up with sad eyes at the mention of his name. He studied Jake briefly, then put his head down next to a pair of brown slippers tucked under an empty overstuffed chair.

"Did he ever mention the house that was blown up?" Jake asked.

"He thought it might have been used as a drug house."

Jake's brow went up. "Why?"

"Because of the people who rented it," she said. "They were young and not too friendly and came and went mainly at night. And they always kept the blinds drawn, day or night."

"Did he ever see them dealing drugs?"

"No. But there were a lot of them for a single small house. Maybe six or seven of them, white and Mexican, and definitely lower-class."

"What made him think they were lower-class?"

"The way they dressed, and a couple of them had tattoos."

Jake leaned forward. "Was there anything unusual about the tattoos?"

"My husband didn't say."

Jake jotted down a note, thinking about the piece of upper arm that had just been uncovered at the bomb site. "Did he mention anything about the guys who had the tattoos?"

"Only that they were Mexican."

"Based on what?"

"The Spanish they spoke."

Jake sighed. The men could have come from anywhere in Central or South America. "But he really couldn't be sure they were Mexican."

"Oh, yes, he could," the widow said firmly. "My husband was a linguist, Lieutenant. He spoke five languages fluently, including Spanish. According to my husband, Mexicans speak a distinct type of Spanish—at least it was distinctive to his ears. He believed the two men he heard talking came originally from Northern Mexico."

"He couldn't by chance narrow it down to a city," Jake said, half in jest.

"He thought the Monterrey area," she said promptly.

"Could he be that precise?" Jake asked, not convinced.

Mrs. Stonehauser smiled thinly. "If I put you in a room with two Americans, one from New York City and the other from Atlanta, could you tell me the area they came from?"

"You've got a point." Jake wrote down the information, now wishing even more that the old man had survived. Art Stonehauser would have been a hell of a
witness once his senses returned. "Did these people at the
house have a car?"

"My husband never mentioned it."

Jake leaned back and studied his notepad, then began
flipping pages. It was a signal to Farelli.

"Just one or two more questions, ma'am," the sergeant
said. "Your husband stated there were six or seven people
coming out of that house. Right?"

"Right."

"And a couple of them were white guys," he went on,
watching her nod. "Was there anything unusual about the
white guys? Did they have any distinguishing features?"

The widow thought back, concentrating hard. Her lips
began to move as if the answer was on the tip of her
tongue.

Jake smiled. Farelli hadn't lost his touch. Of course,
the old man would have focused in on the white guys.
Stonehauser came from a generation that didn't believe in
racial mixing, and when they saw it they zeroed in on the
whites, giving them a long, hard look.

"Now that I think about it," Mrs. Stonehauser was saying, "I remember one afternoon after he'd returned from
his walk, we were watching television and one of those
boys with the shaved heads came on. You know, they call
them skin—ah—skin something or other."

"Skinheads?" Farelli asked.

"Yes. Skinheads," she said, nodding. "The fellow on
TV had all of his hair shaved off with just a little stubble
on his chin. My husband said one of those people looked
like that."

Jake leaned forward, eyes narrowed. "By stubble, do
you mean a short beard? Like a goatee?"

"Yes."

Jake wondered if the man she was describing was the cleaning man with the goatee who had killed her husband. It had to be. The skinhead had probably seen the old man getting a good look at him. When the news broke about the eyewitness who was walking his dog, they knew who it was and had to kill him. They couldn't take a chance.

Jake was about to ask another question, but the woman had her face turned toward the phonograph. The record was beginning again. Mrs. Stonehauser started softly singing along.

Jake got to his feet and handed her a card. "If you can think of anything else, please give us a call."

She nodded absently, her mind going back sixty years to a prom at West Point. She was dancing with a handsome cadet captain, the most handsome man she had ever seen. His name was Art Stonehauser.

She didn't hear the detectives say good-bye.

10

Maxie Birnbaum was giving Joanna and Lori McKay a boxing lesson in the forensics laboratory.

He crouched down and moved gracefully in a counterclockwise circle, his eyes riveted on an imaginary opponent. "You've got to stay low and keep away from the other guy's power."

"And make him reach for you," Lori added.

"You got it, kiddo. If a guy has to reach for you, he can't hurt you."

Joanna smiled at the man, liking him more and more. He was an old-time boxer, now seventy-six years old, with broad shoulders and a firm body. He looked as if he could still handle himself in a fight. "What weight class did you fight in?"

"I was a welterweight."

"Any good?"

Maxie's eyes sparkled. "At one time I was ranked sixth in the world."

"Did you ever fight for the title?"

"Once, against Sugar Ray Robinson," Maxie said, now standing a little taller. He was wearing an old dark suit, shiny in places but clean and neatly pressed. "He took me out in ten rounds, but he knew he'd been in a fight."

"So you've been around the boxing game for a long while."

"Longer than most."

"And you work for the Boxing Commission?"

"I'm a consultant," Maxie said unimportantly. "That means I do part-time work for them."

"In their archives section," Lori said.

"Archives." Maxie scoffed. "When I first heard the word I thought it was something you put in a salad."

Joanna grinned. "I think you just might be the man who can help us."

"I think I can point you in the right direction." Maxie took a neatly folded piece of paper from his coat pocket. "As I understand it, you're interested in a fighter that weighed between a hundred ten and a hundred twenty pounds."

"He may have weighed a little less." Joanna told him how they'd approximated the fighter's weight from the size of the hand bones and how she had learned from a friend that boxers often have larger hands than one would expect.

"Your friend is right," Maxie said. "Boxers' hands are big, probably from all the hitting they do. But that's not important here, and I'll tell you why. The smaller boxers—the featherweights, the flyweights, the bantamweights—are like peas in a pod. They can go from one weight class to another by sitting in a sweatbox and skipping a few meals. So to make sure I didn't miss anyone I included everybody who weighed between a hundred and a hundred and twenty pounds. They must have fought sometime in the past ten years or so. And they now must be retired."

"Your list must be a mile long."

"And some," Maxie went on. "But I was able to whittle it down for you. First, you got to understand that at these lighter weights almost all of the fighters are foreigners. Since you're looking for a Mexican American, I could cross out the Koreans, the Japanese, the Thais, the

Filipinos, and what have you." Maxie nodded, obviously pleased with his performance. "How am I doing so far?"

"Great," Lori said. "You'd have made a pretty good detective."

Maxie thought about that for a moment, then dismissed the idea with a shake of his head. "Anyhow, I came up with twenty-two Mexican American fighters who fit the bill. And then I started tracking them down."

"How did you do that?" Joanna asked. "Does the Boxing Commission keep files on retired fighters?"

"They don't give a damn about old fighters," Maxie said bitterly. His face hardened briefly, then he came back to the sheet of paper and the question Joanna had asked. "I tracked the guys by asking around. Some of the old boxers stay in the game as trainers and cut men and things like that. And they keep in touch with their old buddies one way or another, or maybe see each other at the fights. The guys in the same weight class tend to stick together, kind of like the old fraternities. So, if you ask around you can pick up a lot of information. Here's what I found out. Of the twenty-two Mexican American fighters I started with, there are two that died, six who live in Arizona or Texas, and four nobody knows anything about. That leaves us ten possibilities, and only one of those had the tattoos *Love* and *Hate* on his fingers. His name is José Hernandez."

It can't be this easy, Joanna thought. It just can't. "Were you able to find out Mr. Hernandez's whereabouts?"

"His friend says that José dropped out of sight about three weeks ago," Maxie said. "The friend thinks he went back to Mexico to die."

Joanna nodded, thinking the time frame was right. The hand was about three weeks old. "Why would he go back to Mexico to die? He was still a young man."

"A young man with a bad cancer," Maxie said. "He didn't have too long to live."

Joanna asked quickly, "Do you have an address or phone number for him?"

"Not yet," Maxie said. "But I'm working on it."

"It would really be important."

Maxie folded the sheet of paper carefully and placed it back in his coat pocket. "Do you think he's the guy in the morgue?"

"Could be," Joanna said. They had told Maxie Birnbaum that they had a body with a disfigured face at Memorial. They didn't want to give him the details of the dismembered hand. "For now, I think it's best not to mention that the corpse might be José Hernandez. We should wait until we're absolutely positive."

"Not a word from me," Maxie said and made the gesture of zipping his lips shut. "Let me go do a little digging and see if I can get you the information you need."

"We really appreciate your help." Joanna watched the boxer leave. He had a lively step, an old man suddenly useful again, back in the flow of life.

"I think we're about to get lucky," Lori said quietly.

"I hope so," Joanna said, returning Maxie's wave as he went out the door. "I'd like you to do me a favor."

"Sure."

"Find out when the next important boxing match is in Los Angeles and get Maxie Birnbaum a ringside seat. Use money from the miscellaneous account to pay for it."

"He'd love it," Lori said, then grinned up at Joanna. "It'd be a nice touch to hire a limo to take him there."

"Do it."

Joanna's gaze went over to the blackboard where the projects under investigation were listed. The mystery of the dismembered hand was about to be solved. But she'd need proof beyond any doubt. And that would require DNA testing. She hoped José Hernandez had children, because she wanted to type their DNA as well as the mother's and match them against the DNA from José's hand. That would give her proof positive. The question of how and why José was killed would have to be answered by the LAPD's Homicide Division.

Joanna moved to the blackboard and circled the subsection DNA under the category Hand. One project would be out of the way, she was thinking, and there would only be one remaining. The bomb and its victims. And once that was over, she'd be free to start her new life with Paul du Maurier. She glanced down at the gold bracelet he'd given her, then at her ring finger, where she was certain a diamond would soon be sitting.

There was a sharp knock at the door. A young technician entered and hurried over to Lori.

"This fax just came in for you, Dr. McKay," he said and handed Lori a sheet.

Lori read it quickly, then reread it. "Son of a bitch," she said under her breath.

"What?" Joanna asked.

"Remember that orange, triangular-shaped fragment I dug out of the dismembered hand and sent for analysis?" she asked, reading the report a third time. "It's made out of a plastic material."

"So?"

"It's loaded with C-four. That hand was blown off by a plastic explosive."

11

Rudy Payte splashed water on his face and removed the remaining shaving cream, then studied himself in the bathroom mirror. Without the goatee his entire facial contour changed, just as Eva said it would. His jutting jaw seemed far more prominent, his lips closed and serious. The overall effect was older, much older. Rudy smiled at himself, pleased with his new image. Carefully he dried the water from the top of his head and put on the wig, with its brown hair swept back and covering the tips of his ears. He studied himself in the mirror once more. Now he thought he looked handsome.

Rudy wrapped a towel around his waist and walked into the motel room, still dripping water from his shower. "Well, what do you think?"

Eva looked up from the Gideon Bible she was reading. "Your wig is on crooked."

"I'll fix it later," Rudy said and reached for a cigarette.

"Do it now," Eva said curtly. "And get used to doing it. A crooked wig is a sure sign you're wearing one."

Rudy went back into the bathroom and returned a moment later. "How is it now?"

Eva glanced up briefly and nodded. "Good."

"You want to tell me about the trip I'm going on?"

"In a minute. Let me just finish this passage." Eva was mulling over the story of David and Bathsheba. Both were adulterers, she thought, yet neither had been punished by God. As far as she could see he had actually blessed them. After all, their son, Solomon, became the wisest and best of all the kings of Israel. He should have punished them, Eva told herself. Particularly David, who had sent Bathsheba's husband, Uriah, into battle to die so he could marry her.

But then again, God hadn't punished the federal agents who had killed her brother Samuel. The government devils came to her family's compound in the wilderness and demanded taxes and public access on the roads that went through their property. When the family refused, the agents opened fire and killed innocent men and women who were only fighting to protect their land and rights. Then a blaze started and children died too, like in Waco. And the agents kept on firing and firing. She could still see Samuel's body, riddled with bullets, his face almost unrecognizable.

Eva's jaw tightened. She would avenge her brother's death and the deaths of all the others. She would make the federal devils pay in a way they never thought possible. Oh, how they would pay!

She brought her attention back to the Bible and again read the passage about David sending Uriah into battle to die.

Rudy sat on the edge of the bed next to Eva and studied her out of the corner of his eye. She was really pretty, with a nice body and long, graceful legs. His gaze went to her thighs. She was wearing pink panties and a football jersey that barely covered the panties' lace. Rudy leaned forward to steal a better look between her legs. He saw her silk-covered pubic mound and felt himself stir.

Eva closed the Bible with a loud thud. "I just don't understand it."

"Understand what?" Rudy asked, quickly hiding the bulge in his towel with his hands.

"How God let David get away with it."

"Get away with what?"

"I'll explain it to you later."

Eva left the bed and went over to the window of the motel room. She cracked the drapes and peeked out at the noisy traffic on Sunset Boulevard. In the distance she could see the skyscrapers of downtown Los Angeles shrouded in smog. The patio outside the room was deserted except for a cleaning man near the pool. She checked the patio once more, then closed the drapes and turned on the television set loudly just in case the sound of their voices carried through the flimsy walls to the adjoining rooms.

Eva came back to the bed and sat next to Rudy, her lips close to his ear. "Listen carefully," she said in a low voice, "and do exactly as you're told. You leave here in thirty minutes and drive to Las Vegas. Don't speed. Keep it at an even sixty-five miles per hour. At six o'clock sharp you go to the front entrance of the Golden Nugget and wait. A man in a cowboy hat smoking a cigar will come over and ask if you're one of the Righteous. Your response will be, 'There's only a few of us.' You follow him and make the exchange." She reached under the pillow and took out a thick manila envelope. "You give him this, and he will give you the C-four."

"How much C-four?" Rudy asked.

"Four bricks."

"Is that enough for what we have to do?"

"More than enough," Eva assured him. "Remember, we're talking about detonation at close quarters now."

Rudy thought for a moment, dreading the five-hour drive to Las Vegas. And five hours back. "Why don't I just take a plane?"

"Too risky," Eva said, her voice even lower. "You'll be carrying it by hand, and they'll check it when you go through the metal detector."

"But C-four is not metal," Rudy argued. "The alarm won't go off, so they won't open the container."

"Suppose the alarm goes off for some reason?" Eva snapped. "Or suppose they've got police dogs sniffing around the airport? What then?"

"I hadn't thought of that," Rudy conceded.

Not very smart, Eva was thinking, but he had other talents that were useful. "Just follow the instructions and things will work out fine."

"Where should I put the C-four?"

"Under the backseat."

Rudy rubbed at his chin where the goatee used to be. "What if a cop stops me?"

"Why would he do that?"

"Maybe he's some asshole looking to write another ticket," Rudy said. "Or maybe one of my taillights goes out."

"Then let him write the ticket."

"What if he wants to search the car?"

"Then kill him."

Eva lay back in bed and reached for the Bible. Her legs were bent at the knees, the football jersey now up to her navel. Rudy stared at her smooth thighs and flat stomach and at the space in between. He felt himself stirring again.

"What?" Eva asked, peering over the top of the Bible on her chest.

"Nothing," Rudy said and hurried into the bathroom.

12

"Here's the original specimen." Lori McKay inserted the slide into the projector, and the image of a dismembered upper arm appeared on the screen. Its tattoo was partially obscured by dirt and grime. "And here's the tattoo after it's been cleaned up."

Jake leaned forward to get a better look. The skin was wrinkled and torn and in some places missing altogether. The tattoo seemed to consist of flower petals. Beneath it were indistinct letters, an *M* and an *O* and maybe a *T*.

"Next we dissected off the skin and flattened it out on an adhesive surface," Lori said and went to the next slide. "Our photography department touched it up to restore some of its original color."

Jake turned his eyes away quickly. "You got an untouched photo of the cleaned-up tattoo?"

"Of course," Lori said indignantly, as if only a fool wouldn't. "But this one really shows the details."

"Just put the damn untouched one up," Jake said sharply, still averting his gaze from the image on the screen.

"Why don't you take a look before you—?"

"For Chrissakes!" Jake growled. "I don't want the Walt Disney version. I want to see the tattoo the way everybody else saw it."

Lori glared at the detective, hating his rudeness and bossiness and wishing he'd stay the hell out of the forensics laboratory.

Joanna tilted back in her chair next to Jake, wondering why he and Lori were always at each other's throats. It was probably an age or generational thing, or maybe Lori's need to rebel against authority. Whatever it was, they just didn't get along. "Lori, indulge the lieutenant and put up the untouched photo, please," she said.

Lori removed the slide from the projector, and the screen went blank. She cursed under her breath while she searched for the slide of the untouched photograph.

Joanna leaned over and whispered to Jake. "Being nice works better with Lori."

"Right," he said, still trying to erase the image of the bright red flower petals from his mind. It was so stupid to let photographers touch up the picture of the tattoo. They added a little here and took away a little there and before long they ended up with a tattoo that even the guy who had it wouldn't recognize.

The next slide came onto the screen. Jake studied it carefully. It showed a tattoo with pink petals on one flower and parts of petals on two others. The details were fair, the coloring mediocre. It was an inexpensive tattoo.

"It looks like a rose," Farelli said.

"Yeah," Jake agreed. "You can see the petals within the petals arranged in circles."

"A lot of blossoming flowers can give that appearance," Lori argued. "You can't be sure it's a rose."

Jake ignored her comment. "Can you focus it a little more? I'm interested in what looks like a stem at the bottom of the flower."

Lori slowly adjusted the lens, sharpening the stem's image. Then she saw what Jake was after. The stem had thorns on it. "It's a rose," she conceded.

Jake's attention was now on the letters beneath the petals. There was a distinct *M* and *O,* then a space, then a blurred *T,* then parts of letters that were indecipherable because of ground-in dirt. In some places the skin was abraded down to the dermis. "Okay," he said. "Let's move on to the touched-up photograph."

Lori pressed a button on the projector, and an image of the touched-up tattoo appeared on the screen. The petals were now distinct and bright red. The letters beneath the flower spelled out *MONTANA*.

"How did they figure out it was 'Montana'?" Jake asked.

"They did some photographic tricks and were able to decipher 'Mont,'" Lori explained. "They guessed it was 'Montana.'"

Jake counted the letters in the tattoo, including the parts of letters he couldn't make out. "It looks as if it has more than seven letters to me."

Lori shrugged. "Like I just said, it's a guess."

Jake pondered, knowing the word wasn't *Montana*. And finding out what word was written was every bit as important as identifying the floral part of the tattoo. The word was almost always somebody or something the person loved dearly. *Mother*. The name of a girlfriend. Some organization or unit the person belonged to, like the Marines. "Tell me about the adhesive surface you stuck the tattoo onto. Is it transparent?"

"It has the consistency of white putty," Lori told him. "You can't see through it."

"Can we stick the tattoo onto a transparent surface?"

"I'm not sure," Lori answered. "I'll check it out with our senior technician later."

Jake got to his feet. "Let's do it now."

Lori took a deep breath, wondering if Jake Sinclair ever used the word please. "She might be tied up."

"Then get her untied," Jake said.

"I'm not going to take any orders from you," Lori snapped. "Not now and not in the future. If you want something, make a request and I'll consider it."

"Well, consider this," Jake said, his eyes boring into

hers. "We've got a bunch of goddamn terrorists out there, and they've already set off one bomb that's killed twenty-two people. And unless we find out who, what and why real quick, they're going to set off another bomb and kill maybe even more. Now I don't have time for the usual niceties or for much of anything else except tracking down the terrorists. So let's you and I cut out the bullshit and do our jobs. That being understood, where's your senior technician?"

Lori stared back at Jake, but only for a moment. His eyes were so piercing and cold they frightened her. "Don't worry about me doing my job. I'll hold up my end and then some. But I'd appreciate a little civility while I'm doing it."

"You don't get it, do you?" Jake asked stonily. "You keep wasting time while the terrorists are busy setting up their next bomb. And all because you think your feelings have been hurt."

"You don't seem to see—"

Jake held up his hand, palm out. "Oh, I see just fine. And my eyesight was really good at the blast site the morning after the bomb went off. I watched a fireman climb out of that rubble carrying a little child. I thought it was a doll at first—the way its tiny arms were dangling. I swear to God I thought it was a doll. But then I saw its eyes and I knew it was a dead little baby. So, young lady, I can tell you I see really well. Sometimes too well. Now let's go find your head technician."

Lori swallowed, caught off guard by the emotion in the lieutenant's voice. Like half the world, she had seen pictures of the fireman carrying the dead toddler. "The technician is in the front lab."

Farelli watched the two leave the laboratory, then turned to Joanna. He slowly stretched out his leg, its quadriceps still sore from the gunshot wound. "Your Dr. McKay has got some growing up to do."

"I know," Joanna said. "But she's bright and eager, and someday she'll be a very fine forensic pathologist."

"Maybe she's just supersensitive because she looks so young," Farelli said thoughtfully. "Maybe she feels like we're coming down on her and not taking her seriously, if you know what I mean."

"Could be," Joanna said, nodding. "But Jake can be a little rough on people. He's not exactly Mr. Tactful, you know."

Farelli rubbed at his beard, heavy and dark though he had shaved only four hours ago. "I think he's kind of mellowed since the shooting."

Joanna looked at him oddly. "You're the one who got shot, not him."

"We both got shot," Farelli said evenly.

"What!"

"He didn't tell you, huh?"

"No," Joanna said quietly.

"He probably didn't want to worry you. You know how Jake is."

"Yeah, I know."

Farelli stood and walked around in a circle, trying to get the circulation going in his leg. He rubbed at his thigh and wondered why the pain was lasting so long.

"Is your leg still bothering you?"

"It's getting better," Farelli lied.

"Tell me about the shooting."

Farelli shrugged, not really wanting to talk about it. He could still see his blood streaming onto the sidewalk. "We were on a stakeout when a pickup truck pulled up in front of us in a no parking zone. Some girl was driving. I got out to tell her to move it. Suddenly a guy stood up in the truck bed with an AK-47."

"Oh, Lord!" Joanna shivered. The AK-47 could fire a hundred rounds in seconds and at close range cut a man in half.

"I went down, and Jake came out firing," Farelli continued. "Before Jake got hit he fired off a couple of rounds. He caught the guy just above the eye and blew his goddamn head off."

"Good," Joanna said and meant it. "Where did Jake get hit?"

"Shoulder," Farelli said. "Six inches lower and he would have been dead. Anyhow, the guy with no head falls off the truck, and his girlfriend speeds away. We're still looking for her."

Joanna shuddered. "You two were very fortunate."

"You'll never know how lucky we were," Farelli said somberly. "There were thirty bullet holes in our car and double that number of shell casings on the ground. How all those slugs missed us I'll never know. We should have been dead ten times over."

"Did you require surgery?"

"We both did," Farelli told her. "I was in the hospital for over a week, Jake a few days less. His slug didn't hit a big artery, like mine did."

"Were you at Memorial?"

Farelli shook his head. "Over at Mercy."

Joanna sighed deeply. "Jake should still have called me," she said, more to herself than to Farelli.

"I think he tried, but you were away up in San Francisco."

Joanna thought back to the Friday before Valentine's Day. On the spur of the moment she and Paul had decided to spend a long weekend in San Francisco. She glanced over at Farelli and studied his grave expression. "You really thought you were dying, huh?"

"Both of us did," Farelli said. "We were laying in the ambulance covered with blood and had those damn IV's running in our arms. I really believed it was checkout time. I even told Jake what to tell my Angela if I didn't make it. And he told me what to tell you."

"What did he say?"

Farelli hesitated. "You'll have to ask him."

The door opened without a knock. Jake and Lori came back into the laboratory, still arguing loudly.

"You're impossible," Lori was saying, her voice high-pitched. "Absolutely impossible."

"You talk too much and listen too little," Jake said.

Lori stopped and stared at him, her face turning beet red. "Jesus," she hissed. "You just don't stop, do you?"

Joanna asked, "What's the problem?"

"Now Lieutenant Sinclair is telling me how to mount our tattoo," Lori called over. "He wants it done on a rounded surface, not a flat one."

"And why do you think he wants that?"

Lori paused, her brow wrinkling as she concentrated. "I'm not sure."

"Consider the anatomical location of the tattoo," Joanna hinted.

Lori's eyes brightened. "It's from the upper arm. And a rounded surface would show us how the tattoo looked in its natural setting."

"So Jake's idea wasn't so bad after all, was it?"

Lori nodded firmly and looked up at Jake. "Your suggestion was a damn good one, and I thank you for it," she said, totally disarming him.

"Any time," Jake said. "Now let's shine that baby up on the screen."

Joanna watched Lori, who was setting up the projector so it would show the tattoo now mounted on a transparent surface. She would have to talk with Lori about her temper, although she doubted it would do much good.

"Here we go," Lori said.

Everyone leaned forward and studied the tattoo. The letters *MONT* were now clearly visible. The other letters appeared badly faded and out of focus.

"Somebody get the lights," Jake said.

The room went dark.

Lori refocused the projector, and the other letters sharpened. Under the tattoo was the word *MONTERREY.*

"I'll be damned," Lori said, impressed. "How did you know that would bring those letters out?"

"Tattoos can go fairly deep beneath the skin surface," Jake explained. "So even when the top layer of skin is abraded away, the letters may still be faintly imprinted on the bottom layer. But you can only see the bottom letters when you shine a bright light through them."

"You think he's from Monterey, California?" Lori asked.

"Monterrey, Mexico. It's spelled with two *r*'s." Jake told them about the interview with the widow of the eyewitness. He detailed how Stonehauser believed one of the Mexicans was from Monterrey based on the man's Spanish dialect. "So, according to Mrs. Stonehauser, the terrorist group consisted of two Caucasians, both of whom we think got away, and four or five Mexicans."

"There were four Mexicans," Joanna said.

"Are you positive?"

"Pretty much so," Joanna said. "Come along and I'll show you why."

She led the way out of the laboratory and down a wide corridor. They came to a large metal door with a pull-down handle. Joanna used a key to open the locked door. The group entered and immediately felt the cold air.

"This is a cold storage room that we used as a temporary morgue for the blast victims," Joanna told them. "The victims have all been identified and removed, so I converted the room into a model of the blast site."

The room was twenty-five by twenty-five feet and had no furniture. The floor was cement, the walls stainless steel, with a walk-in freezer at the rear. In the middle was a red-and-white-striped pole with a sign attached that read EXPLOSION CENTER. It was surrounded by wooden stands, each with a photograph of the body part that was discovered at that location. It reminded Jake of the bomb site with its fluttering miniature flags.

"According to the various body parts, we can safely say there were at least two people in that house," Joanna said, breaking the silence. "When we did blood types on the parts, we found four distinct types. And that told us there were four people."

Jake asked, "What about DNA typing?"

"That will take another week to complete," Joanna replied. "But I think it will only confirm what we already know."

"And we're still no closer to knowing who the hell they were," Jake said sourly.

"Well, we know one of them was very sick," Joanna said, and she walked over to a stand directly west of the explosion center. "We found a piece of torso with liver stuck to it at this location. The liver was studded with nodules of adenocarcinoma."

Jake's eyes narrowed. "What does that mean?"

"That means he probably had less than six months to live."

Farelli made a guttural sound as he thought about the new evidence. "Maybe the guy figured, 'What the hell! I'm as good as dead. I may as well blow up something.'"

"Could be," Jake said, confused by the myriad of unrelated clues. Nothing fit together. Nothing. He looked down at the wooden stand next to him. It showed a photograph of the plastic heel found under the debris at the bomb site. "What about the heel insert or whatever it is?"

"I sent it over to our Bioengineering Department," Joanna said, reaching into her pocket for a small book of phone numbers. "Let me give them a call and see if they've made anything of it."

She went to a nearby wall phone and punched in numbers. While she waited, she stretched her back and neck, relaxing tense muscles. She did it again, and her vertebrae began to crack pleasantly.

Jake watched her, thinking she was getting even more beautiful. And she just didn't seem to age, not even a little. There wasn't a single sag or unsightly bulge on her body. Her form-fitting silk blouse accentuated her bust and narrow waist.

With effort Jake pried his eyes away. Next week, he decided, he'd call and take her to dinner. Maybe they'd go to their favorite Greek restaurant in Long Beach and drink wine and throw dishes and start again. And maybe this time he'd get it right.

Joanna came back to the group, shaking her head. "It gets stranger and stranger."

"What?" Jake asked, quickly clearing his mind.

"That plastic heel was part of a prosthesis," Joanna said. "One of those terrorists had an artificial leg."

"Are they sure?" Jake asked, wondering how many places in the Los Angeles area made or sold prosthetic legs.

"Beyond any doubt," Joanna said. "And they detected a small trademark under the bloodstain. It was made here at Memorial Hospital."

"Well, well," Jake said, rubbing his hands together. "Now we've got an artificial leg made at Memorial. That narrows it down a lot."

"Not as much as you'd think," Joanna told him. "The prosthetics unit at Memorial is the biggest and best in California, and they get referrals from everywhere. I'll bet they've made thousands of artificial legs over the years."

Jake began pacing the floor, hands clasped behind him. "So one of our guys has got an artificial leg? Do we know if he's Mexican or not?"

Joanna came over to the wooden stand and studied the information listed under the photograph of the plastic heel. "We typed the blood on the heel and compared it with the blood type of the tanned scalp with black hair attached. They were identical. Same blood, same guy. The man was Mexican."

Jake nodded and continued. "So we've got a Mexican with an artificial leg. Can the type of prosthesis tell us how he lost his leg?"

"Not really," Joanna said after thinking for a moment. "He could have lost it in an accident or had some congenital abnormality, and the prosthesis would have been the same."

"Maybe he lost his real leg in an earlier explosion," Lori suggested.

Jake stopped and stared at her. "Good idea," he said and nodded approvingly. "But no. Bombers lose hands and fingers, not legs."

"Maybe he lost a hand too," Lori countered.

"You've got a point," Jake said and started pacing again, concentrating on the prosthesis and what information it might yield. He needed an expert on artificial limbs.

Turning to Joanna, he asked, "Was the plastic leg actually manufactured here at Memorial?"

Joanna nodded. "By our prosthetics unit."

"Let's go see if they can help us find our way."

13

Joanna and Jake walked out into a gray, overcast day and crossed Wilshire Boulevard. A block away from Memorial they turned onto a smaller street and came to a Bank of America branch office. They stopped near the drive-through teller's window to let a car exit, then moved on.

"Why is the prosthetics unit separate from the rest of the hospital?" Jake asked.

"Because it's so big," Joanna said. "It's not only a prosthetics unit, it's the entire Institute for Rehabilitation. It could easily take up several floors at Memorial."

Ahead Jake saw a large, newly constructed building, three stories high, with a polished granite exterior. Steps and broad ramps led up to closed black-glass doors. He slowed to look at the bold letters engraved in stone just above the entrance. It read JOHN EDGAR WALES INSTITUTE FOR REHABILITATION. "Here?"

"No," Joanna said. "This will be the home of the new rehab institute. It's supposed to open in another month or so."

"Who is John Edgar Wales?" Jake asked, wondering how many millions the building had cost and why they'd wasted so much money on polished granite when brick would have done equally well.

"Wales was a bomber pilot who got shot down over Hanoi and lost an arm while imprisoned there."

"So he was a Vietnam war hero, huh?"

"No more than a lot of others."

"Then what makes him so special?"

"His brother, Josiah Wales, is the director of the institute."

"What's the brother like?"

"A real handful."

They came to an old two-story building with a green plaster exterior that was cracked and peeling. It had steep steps with no railing and a narrow entranceway. A sign read, HANDICAPPED ACCESS AND RAMP IN REAR.

"This place can make you cry," Joanna said. "Particularly the children."

They entered a large reception area that was crowded with patients, standing and sitting. Most were Caucasian or Hispanic, a few Asian, all missing one limb or another. A baby cried out from somewhere, but Jake couldn't see it.

He followed Joanna past the receptionist and into a huge clinic area. People were milling about on a linoleum floor, some walking cautiously on new prosthetic legs, others attaching lifelike artificial arms to their stumps. Their ages ranged from preschool children to bent old men. No one was smiling.

Across the room a burly man in a white coat waved to Joanna and held up a finger, indicating he'd be with them in a moment. He was talking to a woman holding a toddler in her arms.

"That's Josiah Wales," Joanna said quietly.

"Jesus," Jake hissed. "He's as big as a mountain."

"And twice as strong-willed."

Jake studied the mother and child next to Wales, looking for a deformity or missing limb but not seeing it. His gaze went to Wales and the long, white laboratory coat he was wearing. A small American flag was sewn on the sleeve. "He's a real patriot, huh?"

"He wakes up singing 'The Star-Spangled Banner,'"

Joanna said, her tone hardening. "And he makes sure everybody hears him."

Jake detected the hostility in her voice. "I take it you two aren't exactly friends."

"We've had our differences."

"Over what?"

"Assault weapons and Saturday night specials."

"What!"

Joanna stared at Wales, remembering their vehement argument a few years back. "Some time ago the faculty members at Memorial, me included, tried to pass a resolution that would ban the sale of all assault weapons and Saturday night specials. The resolution was going to be sent to Congress and to the State Assembly in Sacramento. That sounds reasonable and civic minded, doesn't it?"

"So far," Jake agreed. Saturday night specials were used in most holdups. Assault weapons were meant to kill people; they had no other purpose. "But Wales didn't go for it. Right?"

"That's the understatement of the year," Joanna said, still remembering the harsh words Wales had for her and anybody else who opposed him. "He stood up before the entire faculty, ranting and raving about our constitutional right to bear arms and protect ourselves. And then he looked me straight in the eye and said—and I swear to you these were his exact words: 'Anyone who favored the resolution is an enemy of the Constitution and is trying to unravel the fabric of America.'"

"You've got to be kidding."

Joanna shook her head. "And the scariest part was that he meant every word of it."

"Did the resolution pass?"

"No way," Joanna said disgustedly. "Murdock jumped in and squashed it. Wales, you see, comes from a very wealthy family, and he and his friends contribute heavily to Memorial. They and the federal government put up equal amounts of money to build the new institute."

"Sounds to me like Wales may have bought his way onto the faculty at Memorial."

"No, no," Joanna corrected him hastily. "He's very good at what he does. That I can tell you for sure."

"I can tell you something else about him for sure," Jake said hoarsely.

"What's that?"

"He's never been shot with an AK-forty-seven."

Jake watched Wales, who was patting the shoulder of the woman holding the toddler. The doctor stepped away, and now Jake had a good view of the mother and child. The little boy had one real leg, one artificial. Jake swallowed hard and looked down at the linoleum floor.

Involuntarily Joanna straightened the front of her white coat as Wales approached them. She forced herself to make and keep eye contact with him.

"Well, Joanna," Wales said without warmth. "What brings you to the low-rent district?"

"We need your help," she said, skipping the amenities. "This is Lieutenant Sinclair from the LAPD."

The men sized each other up for a moment, then nodded briefly.

"What can I do for you?" Wales asked, his face closing slightly.

Joanna reached into her pocket for the broken plastic heel and handed it to Wales. "What can you tell us about this piece of prosthetic foot?"

Wales examined the piece carefully and handed it back. "It's part of a heel, and the circled M trademark means it was made here."

"Is there any way to determine who it belonged to?"

"No," Wales said at once. "We'd need a serial number for that. And the number is imprinted higher up on the prosthesis, not on the heel."

Jake made a mental note to take a team to the bomb site and go through the rubble again with a fine-tooth comb, searching for a piece of plastic with a number on it. "Is this number stamped on or what?"

"It's engraved, just like the trademark," Wales said. "You can see it with the naked eye."

"How high do the serial numbers go?" Jake asked.

"We're somewhere in the twenty thousands," Wales answered, then squinted an eye. "What's all this about?"

"The piece of heel was found at the bomb site in West Hollywood," Joanna told him.

Wales thought for a moment before asking, "Do you think this prosthesis belonged to a victim or one of the terrorists?"

"That's what we're trying to determine," Jake lied.

"Well, that's all I can tell you," Wales said, glancing at his watch. "Now we're all busy, so I—"

"We're going to need a little more of your time," Jake interrupted.

"I'm very, very busy," Wales said, his voice deep and controlled.

"I'll keep that in mind," Jake said, taking out his notepad and flipping pages until he came to the one he wanted. He looked up at Wales, staring back at the man who was trying to stare him down. Wales was at least six-five, with broad shoulders, a massive head and thin lips that seemed pasted together. He was probably damn good at scaring the bejesus out of people.

"We think the guy with the artificial leg was Mexican or Mexican American. Would that help you narrow down the number of people that leg could have belonged to?"

"Ha!" Wales forced a laugh. "California has a population of over thirty million, and a third of it is Mexican. That's ten million people, Lieutenant. Does that narrow it down for you?"

"Not much," Jake admitted.

"And that's not counting the two million illegals that are here," Wales added disapprovingly. "Our borders are like a sieve, and the federal government does nothing about it."

"Ah-huh," Jake said, now envisioning Wales on a hill-top at the border, armed with a high-powered rifle and shooting at anything that moved. Jake quickly cleared his mind. "Do you keep computerized records of all your patients?"

"Of course."

"Do you record the patient's race?"

"No," Wales said promptly, again glancing at his watch. "Just age, sex, diagnosis, and prosthetic device."

"Is there any other medical information?" Joanna asked. "Things like distinguishing features, such as scars or tattoos—"

Wales shook his massive head. "This is not a diagnostic clinic, Joanna. We do rehabilitation here."

"So," Jake said, thinking aloud, "the only way to find out who is Mexican is to go through all of your records and pick out the Mexican-sounding names."

"Correct," Wales said.

"Then we'll do it."

"Whoa!" Wales held up a hand that looked as if it could grasp a watermelon. "You can't just go through our medical records. They're strictly confidential."

"That's no problem," Jake said easily. "I'll have a search warrant within an hour."

"And I'll have an attorney get a restraining order until a judge can properly sort everything out," Wales countered.

"Fine," Jake said, unperturbed. "Of course, I'll have to red-tape every office and door in this building and put a cop by each of them to make sure no chart or record leaves that shouldn't leave. And it will stay that way—until some judge sorts everything out for us."

Wales's jaw tightened. A vein on his forehead bulged.

"There's an easier way," Jake went on. "You could set aside a room and let a team of detectives go through your computer records and make a list of all patients with Mexican names who have leg prostheses. One of your doctors will have to be available to help us with the medical mumbo jumbo."

Wales gave the detective a long look, wondering how far he could push him and whether a call to the mayor's office would help. Not much was the answer to both questions. "I want as little disruption as possible."

"No one will know they're here."

"Timothy Bremmer is the man who will assist your officers," Wales said, the vein on his forehead less obvious now. "He's the person who set up our current computer system."

"Is he a doctor?" Joanna asked quickly.

"A very good one," Wales said. "He's also a wizard at biomechanics."

Wales spun around and walked away with giant steps. It took Jake and Joanna a few seconds to realize they were supposed to follow him.

Joanna moved in closer to Jake as they hurried along. "He's a real cutie, isn't he?"

Wales led the way through the clinic and into a large workshop. Technicians wearing pale green smocks sat at benches inspecting and repairing prostheses of every imaginable type. There were artificial hands and forearms and complete arms as well as feet and legs and entire lower extremities. Some of the hands were mechanized and moved silently, their fingers making a grasping motion.

As they passed a Plexiglas window, Jake looked in. A robot fitted with prosthetic legs was stomping up and down, testing the plastic's strength and durability. Jake felt as if he were in some futuristic world.

They went through a wide set of doors and entered a large room filled with heavy machinery that made a soft, whining sound. Off to the side, a man in a white coat leaned over a console and carefully adjusted several dials. The whining noise increased briefly, then almost disappeared.

"Tim," Wales called out. "Can I see you for a moment?"

"Sure," the man said and walked over. "Boy! That new lamination process is working well. When I double the number of layers, I triple the prostheses' strength. Amazing." He nodded, obviously pleased with the results. Then he saw the puzzled look on the visitors' faces. "Our prostheses are constructed of laminated strips," he explained. "The more strips you laminate together, the greater the strength of the end product."

"Doesn't that substantially increase the weight of the prosthesis?" Joanna asked.

"Not if you thin out the strips," the man answered. "But it's a good question. Weight is very important to the people who have to use the prosthesis every day of their lives."

Wales glanced at his watch impatiently. "Dr. Timothy Bremmer, meet Dr. Joanna Blalock and Detective Lieutenant Sinclair."

Bremmer nodded to Joanna. "It's a pleasure, Dr. Blalock. I keep hearing good things about your work in forensics."

"Thank you," Joanna said, thinking she'd seen Bremmer in the hospital before but not remembering where.

Bremmer turned to Jake Sinclair and shook his hand firmly. "Is there something I can do for you?"

"We need your help in compiling a list." Jake quickly summarized the details on the piece of plastic heel found at the bomb site. "We have to use your computer records to obtain the names of all Mexican American patients who were fitted with leg prostheses."

Bremmer rubbed at his chin. He was a slender man, shorter than Joanna, with a broad forehead and straight blond hair. His boyish face was unlined. "Just by using their surnames, huh?"

"Right."

"That's going to be a lot of work," Bremmer said thoughtfully.

"How many patients will we have to sort through?" Jake asked.

Bremmer shrugged. "Somewhere around eight thousand. Maybe more."

"Too many," Jake grumbled under his breath, then asked, "Is there any way to shorten the list?"

Bremmer looked over at the machinery, now making a more noticeable whining sound. He studied it for a moment, lost in concentration, then turned back to the others. "Do you have that piece of heel with you?"

"Here you are," Joanna said and handed him the broken piece of plastic.

Bremmer carefully studied the plastic heel, holding it up to the light. "Did you determine how many layers of plastic were used to make this prosthesis?"

Joanna shook her head. "Is that important?"

"It could be," Bremmer said, now running his finger along the jagged edge of plastic. "When I joined the staff six years ago, we installed this new machinery to manufacture our prostheses. It uses a different lamination process than the old one did. The newer products have more layers."

Jake asked, "If the plastic heel was made by the new machine, how many patients are we talking about?"

"Around four thousand."

"That's better," Jake said, nodding.

"You'll still be facing a mountain of work," Bremmer

cautioned. "Getting the list together will be the easy part. Tracking down four thousand patients will take months, and there'll be a fair number we never find."

"Don't they come back for periodic follow-up visits?" Joanna asked.

"Most do," Bremmer answered. "But some, like Mexicans who may be here illegally, come once and never show up again. I guess they return to Mexico."

Jake sighed heavily. One step forward, he thought, then two steps back. "We'd appreciate your finding out whether this plastic heel was made by your newer machinery."

"No problem," Bremmer said, holding the piece up to the light again. "I'll have the answer for you tomorrow."

Jake studied the plastic's shiny surface, now noticing its neutral color. "Are all prostheses painted that cream color?"

"Just about," Bremmer said. "Although we had one patient who insisted his leg be painted purple."

Bremmer and Wales grinned briefly at each other, sharing a private joke.

The whirring sound from the machines suddenly intensified, then gears shifted and the noise began to fade.

"The prosthesis is going through the finishing stage," Bremmer told them. "Then we put the padding and holding straps on by hand."

Something kept gnawing at Joanna, something that was obvious yet being overlooked. What was it? A light on the console blinked red, then turned green.

"And that tells us that the measurements of the finished prosthesis are identical to those programmed in by the computer," Bremmer went on. "Each prosthesis is, of course, custom-tailored to the individual patient."

"These measurements are critically important," Wales added authoritatively. "If you're off a few millimeters here or there, you can end up with a poorly functioning prosthesis."

Joanna's eyes brightened. Somebody with expertise had to take those measurements. Somebody had to examine those patients before a prosthesis could be made. "Who does the actual measurements?"

"I do," Bremmer said matter-of-factly. "I get the dimensions of the stump and the contralateral limb, then feed the numbers into a computer. The computer shows what a model should be like and, if everything is in order, it gives our machines the exact specifications for the new limb. Everything is fully automated."

"So you see every patient?" Joanna asked.

"Yes."

"Do you take pictures of the patients with their new prostheses?"

"That wouldn't be of any help," Bremmer said, shaking his head. "Still photographs would be useless. We take videos. That way we can see the prosthetic limbs in motion and determine how well they function."

"What are the male patients with leg prostheses wearing when the videos are being shot?" Joanna asked.

"Bathing suits or walking shorts."

"So we could see their arms well?"

"I would think so," Bremmer said, wondering why she was so interested in the arms of a patient with a leg prosthesis. "But, of course, with a leg prosthesis, our camera would focus in on the lower extremity."

"So one may or may not see multiple views of the patient's arms?"

"That's correct."

"Where are these videos stored?"

"In our new building," Bremmer replied.

Jake asked, "Have you got a video viewing room there?"

Bremmer nodded, grinning. "Lieutenant, our new institute is one of the most advanced in the world. Not just in America," he emphasized, "but in the entire world. Our new viewing room has four screens that simultaneously show the patient from four different angles."

"Nice," Jake said, as he envisioned excellent views of the upper arm where the tattoo was located.

"Better than nice," Bremmer said. "The new institute will be the envy of the medical world." He glanced over at Josiah Wales. "For once, the federal government did something right."

"With a lot of help from the Wales family," Wales added.

"Absolutely right," Bremmer agreed. "And the end result is a sparkling gem that everybody wants to be associated with. The dignitaries are already lined up to attend the grand opening on April nineteenth. Congressmen, senators, the governor. Even the President."

Jake squinted an eye, wondering why a new institute would attract the nation's leaders. "What's the big attraction?"

"Votes," Wales growled. "They figure that between the Vietnam veterans and the disabled there must be a couple of million votes."

"But it's quite an honor having the President here," Joanna said, thinking about the Medal of Freedom the President would present to her. She decided to make only a brief statement at the ceremony, thanking the President and asking him and the others not to forget those who died aboard the *Global Explorer II*. "Quite an honor," she said again.

Wales shrugged. "I didn't vote for him."

"Me neither," Bremmer chimed in.

I did, Jake wanted to say, but he held his tongue. "Can we start the search first thing in the morning?"

"Fine," Bremmer said. "Have your team meet me here

at eight o'clock. It'll help if they have expertise in com-
puters."

"Oh, they will," Jake said, smiling thinly. "You can
bank on that."

"Eight sharp, then."

Joanna and Jake walked out into a light drizzle. The
sky was darkening with the promise of more rain to
come.

"Finding out about the video was a nice touch," Jake
said. "What made you think of that?"

"It was luck," Joanna admitted. "I was thinking more
of photographs, which are usually taken to show how
well a prosthesis fits."

"Well, thinking of the photographs led to the videos."

"I guess."

"And if by chance one of those videos shows a Mexican American with a rose tattoo on his arm—well, we've
got our man."

"It's a long shot."

"Not really," Jake said. "There were four terrorists in
that house. That means that the chances are one in four
that the guy with the tattoo had an artificial leg."

"That's not the long shot," Joanna told him. "The long
shot is finding a video of a leg amputee that happens to
show a side view of an arm that happens to have a rose
tattoo on it. And you may have to go through as many as
eight thousand videos to look for that tattoo."

"Are you saying our chances of finding that tattoo are
one in eight thousand?"

"Something like that," Joanna said. "Unless you get
very, very lucky."

"Shit!" Jake grumbled.

They hurried along, the rain now falling harder.

14

"Look at this," Lori said, moving her chair aside. Joanna leaned in and studied the slide under the microscope. It showed clusters of malignant bone cells. "It's a clear-cut osteogenic sarcoma. So what?"

"This section of bone comes from a blown-apart leg found at the bomb site," Lori said, busily chewing on a piece of gum. "Which means two of the four terrorists had malignancies."

Joanna quickly restudied the slide. There was no question about the diagnosis. The osteoid cells appeared wild and bizarre, indicating a high degree of malignancy. "Do you think this guy had symptoms from his bone tumor?"

Lori shrugged. "You can't tell from a slide."

"But you might from an X ray."

"I've got X rays and photographs of the gross specimen," Lori said. "But they don't give any clues as to whether he was symptomatic."

"Let's take a look."

They walked over to a row of view boxes on the far wall of the lab. Using a magnifying glass, Joanna examined the enlarged photographs of the specimen. It appeared to be a chunk of thigh with a splintered femur protruding at a sharp angle. The tissue around the bone was burned and shredded. Next she went to the X rays. They showed a quarter-size invasive tumor of the femoral shaft.

"He felt pain," Joanna said, pointing to a destroyed

area of the femur. "The tumor eroded right through the cortical bone and into the soft tissues. He had plenty of pain."

"So now we've got two terrorists dying of cancer, and both probably knew they had it," Lori said. "They had to be suicide bombers. There's no other explanation."

"Maybe," Joanna said dubiously. "But why commit suicide when you know you're going to die in a matter of months?"

"Maybe the pain was so bad they couldn't stand it," Lori suggested. "You know, they killed themselves to stop the pain."

"People don't use C-four to commit suicide." Joanna studied the X rays once more, wondering about the relationship between the two terrorists. They had to be connected, but she couldn't find the thread. Even their malignancies were different. One was an adenocarcinoma metastatic to the liver, the other a vicious osteogenic sarcoma. There didn't seem to be any common denominator.

Joanna's eyes suddenly narrowed. She turned to Lori. "Did you do blood types on the two specimens that showed malignancy?"

Lori opened a laboratory data book and flipped through it. "We couldn't get a blood type on the liver. It was partially fried."

Joanna sighed wearily. "Damn it."

"What's so important about the blood types on these specimens?"

"We're assuming that there are two patients with malignancies and there may be only one," Joanna explained. "Sometimes one patient will have multiple malignancies. It's not common, but it happens. And if we have only one patient with a cancer, it's less likely to have any significance here."

"Well, the blood types aren't going to help us here."

"But DNA typing will," Joanna said at once. "Let me know the results the moment they come back."

"You of course realize that it's almost certain we're dealing with two individuals who have two different cancers."

"I know," Joanna said. "But let's prove it so we don't waste time chasing a false lead."

"Strange business," Lori said and turned to another page. "You want to talk about the dismembered hand?"

"Only if you've got good news."

"I don't," Lori told her. "Our friend Maxie Birnbaum isn't making any progress finding José Hernandez. Nobody knows where he is. But Maxie says he knows a friend of a friend of José's who might have some information."

"Which means he's stumped."

"Yeah," Lori said. "But he keeps plowing ahead."

"Just like the rest of us."

"We've got a little more information on the C-four found in the hand," Lori went on. "It's made of two separate explosives, each with a name a mile long. It contained no traceable material, of course."

"Of course," Joanna said sourly. A few years before Congress had tried to pass a bill that would have required all explosives manufacturers to include a traceable substance in their products. This would have allowed investigators to trace any explosive made in America to its point of origin. The powerful gun lobby made certain the proposal was voted down.

"Our outside lab says the combination of ingredients in our C-four is somewhat unusual, so they're going to send a sample to the ATF Explosives Lab for further study."

"How long before we get those results back?"

"They put a rush order on it, so we should hear in a few days."

"Good."

Lori closed her data book. "Well, now I can get back to the other thousand things I have to do."

"If you've got a minute," Joanna said, "there's something we have to talk about."

"Sure," Lori said, a cold sensation running down her back. The words 'we have to talk' always meant bad news. "Is anything wrong?"

"Your temper," Joanna said straightforwardly. "It's going to get you into trouble, particularly when you're dealing with people like Jake Sinclair. He won't stand for it."

"I know," Lori said quietly. "I try to control myself, but that damn Sinclair always seems to set me off."

"Do you think he does it intentionally?"

Lori shrugged. "Sometimes it seems that way. Christ! He can be so abrupt and rude. He never considers the other person's feelings."

"That's Jake," Joanna had to admit. "But don't take it personally."

"How else should I take it?"

"Professionally," Joanna said at once. "Jake is a tough cop who solves murders. He doesn't want to be your pal. He just wants you to answer his questions because that will help him solve his murders. And being nice and polite and tactful is not part of his makeup."

"So you want me just to put up with his boorishness?"

"If you want to learn from him, you will," Joanna told her. "He can teach you every bit as much as I can. Maybe even more, when it comes to murder."

Lori slowly nodded. "He is sharp. You have to give him that."

"Oh, I do."

"So what you're telling me to do is cool it."

"That's the smart move."

"Can I tell him to go to hell every now and then?"

"I guess." Joanna grinned. "But pick your spots carefully."

Lori turned to leave, then stopped and turned back. "I could use a little advice on how to handle something else."

"What?"

"The news media," Lori said. "They've gotten my home number, and I swear the damn phone hasn't stopped ringing. They want to know all about the bomb and the victims and the body parts."

"What do you tell them?"

"I don't. I just hang up. But the calls keep coming, even in the middle of the night."

"I'd advise you to take your phone off the hook when you go to bed and go to sleep with your beeper."

"Then I'll probably end up getting beeped," Lori said. "Are you getting the same kinds of calls?"

"Constantly," Joanna replied. "Yesterday I got a call from a tabloid offering me two hundred and fifty thousand dollars for an interview. And another two hundred thousand for some photographs of body parts."

"Jesus! The media will do anything for information."

"They're just responding to public pressure," Joanna said. "The newspapers and TV news programs make this their lead story every day and every night. Remember, people are scared, particularly since the bomb went off in a residential neighborhood. Everybody wants to know who and why and how close we are to solving this crime. And those are the major questions the press has."

"The answers are really simple."

"Oh?"

Lori hung a knapsack over her shoulder. "The answers are as follows—we don't know who and we don't know why and we're still a million miles away from solving this case."

15

The television screen showed Simon Murdock mounting the podium for a press conference at Memorial Hospital. His expression was somber, his face closed and lips tight.

"He ain't too happy," Farelli commented.

Jake watched the screen, thinking that Murdock in his dark pinstriped suit had the warmth of an undertaker. "I'll bet he screws things up."

"I thought he was supposed to be so smart."

"He's one of those people who can be smart and stupid at the same time."

The detectives were seated at the counter in a luncheonette having coffee and donuts. It was 11:00 a.m., and lunchtime customers were starting to drift in. Outside the day was humid and hazy, the sun barely visible.

"Why have a press conference at all?" Farelli asked.

"It beats me," Jake said absently. He reached for a napkin and began writing down numbers: 5 X 10 = 60.

"Five times ten is fifty," Farelli said, glancing over Jake's arm.

"I'm just rounding off numbers," Jake said, continuing the calculations on the napkin. "I've got four men in the screening room at the rehab institute. The room has four screens, so each man will be watching a different view as a video comes up. An individual video lasts five minutes. So, if you wanted to see ten videos, it would take five times ten, or fifty minutes. Right?"

"Right," Farelli agreed. "But you've got sixty written down."

"You have to allow ten minutes each hour for loading the camera and focusing and that kind of thing," Jake explained. "So the actual viewing time per hour is fifty minutes. That means you can look at ten videos per hour. That's eighty a day, or around five hundred a week." He restudied the numbers and sighed heavily. "That means it'll take over two months to get through all the videos."

"And by then, your bombers will have done their deed and be long gone."

"Tell me about it."

The detectives turned their attention back to the television screen.

"And, of course," Murdock was saying, "there are some matters which I cannot comment on at this time. That being understood, I will now take your questions."

A female reporter with blond-streaked hair quickly got to her feet. "The only eyewitness to the bombing has died suddenly and unexpectedly at Memorial," she said in a nasal tone. "There are reports he was murdered. True or false?"

"The patient died from aspiration with airway blockage," Murdock answered promptly. "Some unusual findings were discovered, and these are being investigated."

"So you're saying there was no evidence of wrongdoing?" the reporter persisted.

"I've answered your question," Murdock said evasively. "Let's move on."

A local television anchorman, recently demoted to roving reporter, stood. "Is it true that the widow of the eyewitness has filed a wrongful death suit against your hospital?"

Murdock swallowed, his Adam's apple bobbing noticeably. "I can't comment on that."

"To the tune of ten million dollars?" the reporter followed up.

"No comment."

Farelli whistled softly. "That's a lot of money."

"A person's got to live," Jake said.

A black reporter in a smartly tailored suit raised her hand. She identified herself as being from *Time* magazine. "Did the eyewitness describe any of the terrorists before he died?"

"No comment," Murdock said.

"We have two independent sources who say he did," the reporter went on. "The terrorists involved were described as Caucasians and Mexicans. And some other identifying features were given as well. We believe the story to be true, and we're going to run it. If you want to deny it, now is your chance."

There was an awkward silence as Murdock put a finger inside his collar and stretched it.

Jake leaned forward. "Say something, you dumb son of a bitch," he urged quietly.

"You'll have to ask the police about those matters," Murdock said finally.

"One of our sources is associated with the police," the reporter pressed on.

Bullshit, Jake thought. The story most likely came from Claire Stonehauser or her sister or both. That was where a reporter with a good nose would go to sniff out information.

Farelli asked worriedly, "You think we got a leak?"

"I doubt it."

"But that's a reporter from a national magazine saying the cops gave her the information."

"She said the source was *associated* with the police," Jake corrected him. "The reporter got the story from the widow or her sister. And since the widow discussed everything with two homicide dicks, that means the source had exchanged information with the police. That's a form of association."

"Give me a break," Farelli said, hating the play on words. "Doesn't anybody speak English anymore?"

"Not on television."

Murdock was still dancing around the subject, trying to evade the direct questions.

The *Time* reporter asked pointedly, "Did one of the terrorists have a goatee or a shaved head?"

Oh, shit, Jake groaned to himself.

"I have no knowledge of that," Murdock said.

"Exactly what knowledge do you have?" the reporter asked curtly.

Murdock stared at the woman, fighting a losing battle to control his temper. "I have knowledge of a forensics laboratory at Memorial that's filled with body parts from that explosion. And in that laboratory is a very fine forensic pathologist who is going to put those body parts back together and tell us exactly who those terrorists were."

"And that could lead to the murderers of your eyewitness?"

"It very well cou—" Murdock caught himself, but too late.

Farelli slapped an open palm against his forehead. "Christ! He is dumb."

The reporter smiled thinly. "How many body parts do you have, and how close are you to putting them back together?"

Murdock cleared his throat quickly. "That subject is no longer open to discussion."

The reporters jumped to their feet and yelled questions at Murdock. The clamor was so great that the individual questions couldn't be heard. Murdock held up his hands and tried to restore order. The reporters raised their voices even more.

"What do you think?" Farelli asked.

"I think anybody who knows anything about those ter-rorists is going into deep cover," Jake said. "If they're Mexican they're running for the border. If they're Caucasian they're heading for the woods."

Farelli nodded. "I'll bet our guy with the goatee is shaving it off right now."

"Damn right," Jake agreed. "And he's going to let his hair grow too."

"Think this will be enough to scare away the bombers?"

"Hell, no," Jake said at once. "They'll stick around until they finish what they set out to do."

"They're not going to like what Murdock just told them," Farelli said. "They won't like it a damn bit."

"And they know how to get into Memorial Hospital," Jake said darkly. "They've done it once before."

"My thoughts exactly." Farelli finished his donut and got off his stool. "We need a cop outside that cold storage room where the body parts are kept."

"Make it two cops," Jake said. "Have the other one standing outside Joanna's office, around the clock."

16

Maxie Birnbaum led the way up the stairs of the four-story apartment building. Joanna and Lori were just behind him, hurrying to keep pace. At the third-floor landing they stopped to catch their breath.

"Isn't there a city ordinance that says you've got to have elevators in these buildings?" Lori bitched.

"Not in East Los Angeles, there ain't," Maxie said. "If the landlords thought they could get away with it, they wouldn't have stairs either."

The stairwell was narrow and poorly lighted. The dull gray paint on the walls was cracked and peeling, exposing plaster held together with chicken wire. There were water stains everywhere.

"Are you sure José Hernandez lives here?" Joanna asked.

"That's what a friend told me," Maxie answered. "He lives in an apartment with his wife and mother-in-law."

"Did you call to see if they're still here?"

"I called, but the phone had been disconnected."

"Great," Joanna muttered and reached for the railing to pull herself up the steep steps.

Maxie sprinted ahead, his powerful legs taking the stairs two at a time. They came to the corridor on the fourth floor. All of the doors were closed with noises coming from behind them. A television set on too loud, children screaming and crying, adults arguing in Spanish. The smell of spicy food permeated the air.

Maxie knocked sharply on the door and stepped back, waiting. A dead bolt lock turned, then another lock turned. Slowly the door cracked open, its chain still in place.

A middle-aged Mexican woman with a lined face looked out. "*Qué?*"

"We're here to talk with José Hernandez," Maxie said in an official-sounding voice.

"He's not here," the woman said, eyeing the group suspiciously. "You bill collectors?"

"No," Joanna said quickly. "We're from Memorial Hospital."

"Oh," the woman said, nodding. "You here about his cancer?"

"Could we speak with you for a moment?" Joanna asked. "It's very important."

The woman unchained the door and opened it widely, then stepped aside. There was no furniture in the small living room. No chairs, no couch, no lamps. Light came in through a closed window, one of its panes missing. Against the wall were big cardboard packing boxes.

"You are his mother-in-law?" Joanna asked.

"*Sí,*" the woman said. "Why has José not called?"

"We think he was involved in a very bad accident," Joanna said quietly.

"Is he dead?"

"We think so."

The woman's expression didn't change. She made the sign of the cross and murmured a prayer in Spanish. "We knew death was always close by. The cancer was bad."

"What did José tell you about his illness?" Joanna prompted.

"That he had a bad cancer in his intestines and that it had spread to other places in his body."

"Did the treatment help at all?"

The woman shook her head. "Even when they removed his tumor at Memorial Hospital he did not improve. Then they gave him drugs by vein, but that too did not help. His tiredness grew worse. He could no longer work as a gardener."

Joanna nodded to Lori, both remembering the calluses on the dismembered hand. "Was he still involved with boxing?"

"He only watched on television."

"And when was his last fight?"

"More than five years ago." The woman stared at Joanna for a moment, her dark eyes narrowing noticeably. "What does this have to do with José's illness?"

"The accident was very bad," Joanna told her. "We're trying to make an accurate identification of the person."

"His face . . ." The woman's voice trailed off.

"Destroyed," Joanna said truthfully.

The woman crossed herself again. "God will restore it."

"Did he have a tattoo?" Lori asked softly.

The woman nodded. "On his fingers were the words *Love* and *Hate*. He had tried to have them taken off, but you could still see traces of the letters." She smiled faintly. "My daughter was so pleased that he had the tattoos removed. He did this for her."

"So they were very much in love?"

"They have been close since childhood," the woman said. "And with his illness she has been very worried about him."

"Where is José's wife?" Lori asked.

"She has returned to our home in Guadalajara," the mother-in-law said.

"If we wanted to speak with her, how—?"

"Hold on a moment," Joanna interrupted, thinking something was wrong. A wife who was worried about a sick, missing husband wouldn't move back to Mexico without him. "She had no hesitation about leaving without José?"

"It was José's wish," the woman said. "We were to

take the five thousand dollars and make our home in Mexico beautiful. He told us he would join us later."

"To die in Mexico?" Joanna concluded.

"That was his plan, I believe." The woman shifted on her feet, taking some of the pressure off. "He was so proud to give her the money. It was everything he had left in the world."

"All of his savings, huh?" Maxie inquired.

"Oh, no, *señor*. There were no savings left. Everything had been used up long ago. The money came from a modeling job José had obtained last month."

"Modeling what?" Joanna asked quickly.

"Clothing that one wears to go hunting."

That didn't make any sense, Joanna thought. A man wasting away with widespread cancer wouldn't be a good model for anything but death. "Who gave him this job?"

"Two crazy gringos," the woman said matter-of-factly, then realized her inadvertent rudeness. "I meant no offense, *señora*."

"None taken," Joanna said, concentrating on the hunting apparel José was supposed to model and wondering if that was what he was doing in the rugged terrain where he was blown apart. "Did he describe the two gringos?"

"Only that they were young Americans."

"Did one have a short beard or a goatee?"

The woman shrugged. "José made no mention of that."

"Will you ask his wife this question when you see her next?"

"Of course," the woman said, then took a deep breath. "What shall I tell my daughter about her husband?"

"Tell her the truth," Joanna advised. "The dead man is almost certainly her husband. We'll have a positive identification within a few weeks."

The woman opened her purse and reached for a small card with handwriting on it. "This is my address and phone number in Guadalajara. Please notify us when you know for sure."

"Thank you for your time, *señora*."

Outside the afternoon sun was setting, the temperature starting to drop. The street was congested with rush-hour traffic. It was so noisy Maxie had to raise his voice to be heard. "How much you figure it'll cost to send José's remains back to Mexico?" he asked.

"It could be expensive," Joanna said. "He'll need a sealed casket, so I guess it would cost at least two thousand dollars."

"I'll call around and see if I can get a collection going," Maxie said thoughtfully. "A man should be buried in his home country, close to the people who love him."

Joanna watched Maxie walk away. A little man, broad-shouldered, tough as nails, with a gentle heart. "He reminds me of the world my parents used to live in."

"It's a world I'll never see," Lori said half to herself as she unwrapped a stick of gum. "You know, those ringside seats and the limo rental to take Maxie to the fights will cost us over five hundred dollars. We could contribute that to his donation plate."

"I think Maxie would like that a lot better than the fights."

"Me too," Lori said and reached for the car door. "But the reality is we may never be a hundred percent positive that the hand belonged to José Hernandez."

"Oh, I think we'll know for sure," Joanna said. "Remember that José had his cancer removed at Memorial Hospital. They've probably got his tissue stored away somewhere in pathology. All we have to do is check the specimen's DNA type against the DNA type in the dismembered hand. If it's a match, we have our man."

"And then we'll have three Mexicans with cancer who were blown apart by C-four," Lori said, shaking her head in puzzlement. "Two at the bomb site and a third somewhere out in the woods of northern Los Angeles County. What do you make of that?"

"They're connected to one another."

"How?"

"I'm not sure," Joanna said, getting into her car. "But these cases are all interconnected. You can bet your house on that."

17

Jean-Claude Fonteneau was running around in circles in Joanna's living room. The little boy had his arms spread out wide, making believe he was an airplane. He hummed loudly as he zoomed by his mother.

"He looks just like Daddy," Joanna said.

Kate Blalock Fonteneau nodded. "He even has some of Daddy's mannerisms. The same walk, the same smile."

"It's the Blalock genes," Joanna said, watching her nephew stumble onto the carpet and pick himself up and start running again. The two-year-old was already handsome, with sandy blond hair, high-set cheekbones and dark, mischievous eyes. All Blalock, Joanna thought, now wondering what her children would look like and whether the Blalock genes would predominate.

She glanced over at Kate, tempted to tell her about Paul du Maurier but deciding to wait. With any luck, Paul would be back in Los Angeles next week and they could all have dinner together. That would be the time to—

"What?" Kate asked, breaking into Joanna's thoughts.

Joanna shrugged. "Nothing."

"Come on," Kate urged. "I can tell when there's something on your mind. The little lines at the bridge of your nose start to bunch up."

Joanna grinned. "I think I've found my man."

"Get out of here!"

"Finally," Joanna said softly.

"What's his name?"

"Paul du Maurier."

Kate moved in closer on the sofa. "Tell me all about him. I want details."

"He's tall and gorgeous with tons of money," Joanna said dreamily. "He's an investment banker who loves me to death."

Kate reached over and hugged Joanna tightly. "I'm so happy for you, Sis. And you deserve it more than anybody else in the whole world. I know it wasn't easy for you all these years, looking out for the family."

"It wasn't that difficult," Joanna said modestly.

"Oh, yes, it was," Kate said, nodding firmly. "When Daddy died you had to take care of the financial mess he left behind. And you had to make sure Mom and I were all right, and you did it so well. You were only a junior in college, but you took control of things without missing a beat. I marveled at that."

"I missed plenty of beats," Joanna muttered, more to herself than to Kate.

"No, you didn't," Kate told her. "Even when Mom got sick you saw to it she was always comfortable and well cared for. And while you were doing that you paid my way through college and graduate school and supported me until I could earn a living as an archaeologist. You put everybody before yourself, and we all knew it."

"It was my pleasure to do it," Joanna said, a picture of her dead parents flashing in her mind. Her father had been gone over twenty years, her mother almost ten.

"Lord! The debts you must have accumulated," Kate went on. "Did you finally get them paid off?"

"Four years ago," Joanna said. "And now there's not a piece of paper on the face of the earth that says a Blalock owes anybody anything."

"And now you're free, Joanna. It's your time to fly."

Joanna smiled broadly. "It's my time to fly."

The doorbell rang, then rang again.

Joanna glanced at her watch. It was almost 9:00 P.M. With effort she pushed herself up from the sofa, wondering who it was. It couldn't be the pizza man, she told herself. They never delivered that fast.

She hurried across the living room and looked through the peephole. Jake Sinclair was standing in a light drizzle, his coat spotted with rain.

Joanna cursed softly under her breath and opened the door. "Jake, you've got to call before you come over."

"I tried, but the line was busy."

Joanna shook her head. "That's impossible. Nobody has been on the phone for the past hour."

"Then it must have been off the hook."

"I hope this visit is professional."

"It is."

Joanna studied Jake's face, still not sure he was telling the truth. "And it's important enough for this late at night, huh?"

"If you want to discuss it in the doorway, fine," Jake said hoarsely. He reached into his coat pocket for an envelope.

Joanna sighed deeply and stepped aside. "Come in."

"Jake!" Kate jumped to her feet and ran over, hugging him with all her might. "I've missed you."

He hugged her back, then held her out at arm's length and carefully inspected her. "You look great, kiddo."

"Somewhat better than the last time you saw me, I would hope."

"Those were bad days," Jake said, remembering her life-threatening illness five years ago. Kate had been infected with an Ebola-like virus while on a dig in Guatemala. She was airlifted back to Memorial Hospital near death, her liver almost destroyed by the virus. No one, including Joanna, had expected her to live. But an experimental treatment with plasma had turned the tide and Kate made a complete recovery. It had been a very close call.

Jake felt something tugging on his pants leg. He looked down and saw a little boy smiling up at him. Quickly he picked the toddler up and held him high. "Do you have a name?"

"Jean-Claude," the little boy said immediately.

"*Bon soir,* Jean-Claude," Jake said, his French accent passable. "My name is Jake."

The little boy looked over to his mother, unsure of the name he'd just heard.

"He is called Jacques," Kate explained.

"Jacques," Jean-Claude repeated, then leaned forward and kissed Jake's cheek.

"*Merci,*" Jake said and put the boy down.

Kate looked at Jake admiringly. "He really likes you. Do you always do this well with children?"

"I guess."

"And puppies," Joanna added. "Little children and puppies are his favorites."

"Why little children and puppies, Jake?" Kate asked.

"Because they love unconditionally and don't make any demands."

Joanna felt her face color, knowing the barb was meant for her. "I knew I shouldn't have let you in," she said, half-meaning it.

Jake walked over to the wet bar and replaced the phone on its hook. "Just in case somebody needs to reach you."

"That's Jean-Claude's doing," Kate explained, then waved a finger at her son. "Do not do that again unless Aunt Joanna tells you to. Do you understand?"

Jean-Claude went over to Joanna and opened his arms wide.

Kate said, "That's his way of asking you to forgive him."

Joanna knelt down and ran her hand through the little boy's hair. "Would you like to go watch television?"

Jean-Claude nodded and looked up to his mother for approval.

"All right, but keep the sound low." Kate watched her son scamper away, then turned to Jake. "That's a habit I must break him of. You see, when Jean-Claude's father comes home, the first thing he does is take the phone off the hook so he can play and talk with his son. Thus, Jean-Claude associates removing the phone from its hook with happiness."

Jake smiled thinly. "So do I."

"Well, I know you two have things to discuss, so I'll—"

"No, no," Jake said quickly. "We might need the expertise of an archaeologist."

Kate rubbed her hands together gleefully. "Is it murder?"

"For sure."

"I'd better get us some cold beers," she said and hurried over to the bar.

Joanna moved closer to Jake, unable to contain her interest. "Did you find something new?"

He nodded. "We found something new in something old."

"What was the something old?"

"The dismembered hand."

"And what was the something new?"

"I'll tell you in a minute."

Jake glanced around the living room, with its French antique furniture covered with royal blue silk. There was a fire going in the fireplace, the logs red hot and crackling softly. Jake's gaze stayed on the fireplace and the bearskin rug in front of it, where he and Joanna had spent so many nights together. He wondered for the hundredth time if they would ever get things right. Jake vowed to try harder the next time.

Kate came back with three bottles of beer and frosted mugs. They sat around a coffee table, Jake in a highback chair, Joanna and Kate on the sofa. Carefully they poured their beers to minimize the foam.

Jake took a large swallow of his beer, delicious and cold as ice. "You've heard about the bomb explosion in West Hollywood?" he asked Kate.

"I think the whole world has," she said.

"Well, here are some things the whole world doesn't know." Jake told her the particulars about the plastic explosive that was used and the terrorists who were involved. "And two of the four terrorists had cancer."

Kate looked over at Joanna. "Cancer? What the hell does that mean?"

Joanna shrugged. "Don't ask me."

"Anyhow," Jake went on, "the C-four explosive used in the West Hollywood bomb was not the run-of-the-mill C-four. It contained an unusual mixture of RDX and PETN, which were its two major ingredients. The mix was so unusual that the people at the ATF laboratory believe it was custom-made."

"So?" Joanna asked, hearing nothing new thus far.

"So that same C-four was recently used in another crime."

"What crime?" Joanna leaned forward, her ears pricked.

"To blow off the dismembered hand you have in your lab," Jake said. "The piece of plastic from that hand contained the exact same C-four ingredients as the West Hollywood bomb."

"Jesus," Joanna hissed softly. "I knew they were connected. I knew it."

"How did you know?" Jake asked.

"Let me fill Kate in." Joanna told her sister about the

dismembered hand found in a secluded wooded area and the small fragments of plastic in it. Then she related the details of the visit to José Hernandez's apartment. "That hand almost certainly belonged to José Hernandez. And he too had widespread cancer."

Jake groaned; now the case was even murkier. "Why are Mexicans dying with cancer involved?"

Joanna shrugged again. "I'm not sure, but I have the feeling if we can answer that question, everything else will fall into place."

Jake nodded. That was the key question, but he didn't have a clue about the answer. He finished his beer and lit a Greek cigarette, then turned to Kate. "For a minute, I want you to forget everything I've told you about this case. Just concentrate on the dismembered hand. What would you think if you came upon an isolated hand while you were out on one of your archaeological digs?"

Kate gave the matter thought, moving her head one way, then another, as if excluding or including possibilities. "You understand I would be dealing with bones. There'd be no soft tissues remaining."

"Right," Jake said. "Then just from his bones, tell me how you'd determine who the guy was."

"Are there any rings or jewelry?"

"Only bones."

"Well, we could distinguish children from adults by bone size and whether the epiphyses had fused. And if it was an adult we could approximate the age from the degree of degenerative changes around the joints. If his hand showed evidence of old fractures, we would assume he was a warrior or athlete." Kate considered another idea but shook her head at it. "Of course, where we found it could help. For example, if we found a hand with old fractures in a palace, that would suggest it belonged to a warrior-guard or a high-ranking officer."

"Suppose you found it out in the woods?"

"Without anything else?"

"Just a hand."

Kate shook her head again. "The possibilities are too numerous to count."

Jake decided to try another tack. "Could you determine how the guy lost his hand?"

"Maybe," Kate said, thinking back to the skeletal remains of a leg she'd uncovered in Guatemala. "If the bones were cleanly severed, it would indicate the amputation was done with a sword or ax. That would suggest the hand belonged to a warrior or soldier. Less likely possibilities are that the hand was surgically removed or amputated as a form of punishment."

Joanna said, "The big bones in our hand were ragged and splintered."

"Then it was crushed or ripped off."

"By C-four," Jake said, coming to another dead end.

"But where's the rest of him?" Kate asked.

Jake gestured. "Blown to bits, I guess."

"Wait a minute," Kate said quickly. "You found a lot of body parts at the Hollywood bomb site, along with some clothes and shoes. Yet you find only a hand here. That doesn't make sense."

Jake smiled. "No, it doesn't."

"So you think there's more?" Joanna asked at once.

"There's got to be," Jake said. "There's got to be something left out there."

"But I was told the area where the hand was discovered had been gone over with a fine-tooth comb."

"And they didn't find a damn thing," Jake grumbled. "They came up with zilch. Not a shred of clothing, not even a fragment of another body part."

"We're running around in circles," Joanna said.

Kate sipped her beer, absently licking the foam from her lips. "Did you look underground?"

Jake thought for a moment.."Why under the ground?"

"Why not?" Kate asked. "When we find an isolated part of a skeleton in the field, the first thing we do is dig around and look for the remaining pieces. We usually find something."

"But why would—" Jake stopped in midsentence and slammed his fist into his open palm. "Son of a bitch! They blew him up and buried what was left."

"And that hand had animal chew marks on it," Joanna recalled. "I'll bet a coyote or some other scavenger dug it up."

"You'd better get out your shovels," Kate advised.

Jake got up and started pacing from front door to wet bar, mumbling under his breath. "We've been going down the wrong track, chasing our own tails. We've been working under the assumption that the West Hollywood blast was a work accident, an unintentional detonation. Now I'm not so sure. The guy in the woods wasn't blown up by some work accident, I'll tell you that. Somebody blew him up with the same C-four that was used to blow up those Mexicans in that West Hollywood house."

Joanna gave Jake a puzzled look. "Are you saying those Mexicans weren't terrorists?"

"I'm saying I'm not sure."

Joanna's eyes suddenly narrowed. "I didn't tell you about the job José Hernandez was given just before he disappeared."

"I thought he was dying from widespread cancer," Jake said.

"He was," Joanna continued. "And that's what makes the story so screwy. According to his mother-in-law, two young Americans offered José a job modeling hunting clothes."

"Get real," Jake growled.

"I'm telling you what she told me."

Jake stopped and spun around. "Did one of the Americans have a goatee?"

"The mother-in-law didn't know," Joanna answered. "She didn't see them. But what she did see was the five thousand dollars paid to José in advance. His wife used the money to fix up their home in Mexico."

Jake's face hardened. "They bought those Mexicans to use them. That modeling job was a load of crap. They had something else in mind for those Mexicans."

"Like what?"

Jake shrugged. "Who the hell knows?"

"And why pick men with cancer?" Joanna asked. "And why pay someone five thousand dollars only to blow him into smithereens with C-four?"

"I don't have a clue," Jake said, scratching at the back of his head. "Maybe we'll get some answers when we find the rest of José Hernandez."

"How will you do that?"

"With dogs," Jake told her. "Which brings me to the purpose of my visit. I'm going to need a piece of that hand to give the dogs a scent to track. I'll need it first thing in the morning."

Joanna hesitated. "I'd use dogs that can sniff out C-four. The remaining parts of José Hernandez should be loaded with it."

Jake nodded. "Good idea. But I'll still want them to take a sniff of that hand."

"What time will you stop by tomorrow?"

"How does eight o'clock sound?"

"Early. But I'll have the tissue ready."

"Good," Jake said, checking his watch. "I've got to run." He waved to Kate, glad to have seen her again, gladder yet that life seemed to be going well for her. "You look super, kiddo. Say good night to Jean-Claude for me."

"Once we're settled I hope you'll join us for dinner," Kate said. "It'll be like old times."

"Just let me know when," Jake said and reached for the door.

Joanna came over and took his arm. "I'll walk you to your car."

Outside the drizzle had stopped, but the air was still heavy with humidity. The moon was a blur in the cloud-filled sky.

Jake said, "Are you going to apologize for being so bitchy when I first walked in?"

Joanna smiled at his directness. "That's not what I had in mind." She took a deep breath and tried to think of the best way to tell him about Paul du Maurier. Jake had been an important part of her life, the closest thing she had to family besides Kate. And the last thing she wanted to do was hurt him. "Jake, there's something you should know."

"I'm all ears."

Christ! Joanna moaned to herself. *How do I do this?*

"Well?" Jake prompted her.

"Jake!" Kate called from the doorway. "Jean-Claude insists on saying good night to you."

The little boy ran over to Jake and hugged him. "Good night, Jacques."

"Good night, Jean-Claude," Jake said, patting the boy on his backside and sending him back to his mother.

At the door Jean-Claude waved good-bye with both hands.

Jake took Joanna's arm and headed for his car. "He's a great kid."

"He's all Blalock." Joanna grinned. "Every stitch of him."

"So what was it you wanted to tell me?"

Joanna's smile faded as she again struggled to find the right words. To hell with it. She'd tell him another time. "It's a long story. I'll save it for tomorrow."

18

"I gave Lieutenant Sinclair a piece of the dismembered hand," Lori said, closing the freezer door in the cold storage room.

"Was it as putrid as I thought it would be?" Joanna asked.

"Worse," Lori said, wrinkling her nose. "It smelled awful, even the frozen part. I doubt those dogs will be able to do much with it."

"You'd be surprised," Joanna told her. "Not only do those dogs have a remarkable sense of smell, they also have an incredible ability to discriminate between odors."

"But won't the terrible smell of rotting tissue throw them off?"

"Not really. Those dogs are trained to detect C-four, and they're rewarded every time they are successful. Somehow they're able to zero in on small traces of C-four regardless of what other odors are present."

"But even if they uncover more body parts now, the tissue will be so decayed it won't be of any use to us."

"It's not so much the tissue we're interested in," Joanna said. "It's other things that might give us a clue to who the terrorists are and what they plan to blow up."

Lori squinted, not following Joanna's line of reasoning. "Give me an example."

"A piece of paper in a pocket that contains a telephone number we can trace."

They left the cold storage room and passed the guard

posted at the door. Ahead another policeman was standing outside the door to the forensics laboratory. He eyed the approaching women carefully, then returned to the military position of parade rest.

"What the hell is the world coming to?" Lori asked sourly.

"What do you mean?"

"When you have to have policemen guarding laboratories in a hospital," Lori said, keeping her voice low as they walked by the second police officer. "And their presence is really scaring the technicians."

"The police are there to protect them from harm."

"That's what's so scary," Lori said. "Every time a door opens, everyone in the lab jumps. They're really uptight. Maybe you should have a little talk with them and try to calm things down."

Joanna nodded. "I'll do it right after lunch."

They came to a bank of elevators. Joanna pushed the up button, now wondering what she could say to her technicians to allay their fears. Nothing came to mind. They had every reason to be on edge, just like everyone else in the hospital. It was now common knowledge that the patient who was an eyewitness to the bombing had been murdered in his bed at Memorial by the terrorists. Even with a policeman posted outside his room.

"Have you ever thought about leaving this madhouse?" Lori asked.

"On occasion," Joanna admitted.

The door to the elevator opened. Joanna and Lori stepped aside to let an attractive young woman dressed in a blue blazer and white silk blouse pass by. Her dark blond hair was pulled back into a tight bun. There was a large diamond on her ring finger.

The women exchanged glances and half smiles.

"This is the Department of Pathology," Joanna told her. "Is that what you're looking for?"

"Yes," the woman said, studying Joanna's face and name tag briefly. "I'm trying to find the director's office."

"It's to your left halfway down the corridor."

"Thank you," Eva Reineke said and walked away.

19

The two police officers assigned to guard the forensics laboratories had the same name, Michael Murphy. Both were well-built and broad-shouldered with auburn hair and green eyes. Although unrelated, they could pass for brothers and were often mistaken for each other. Their colleagues had nicknamed them Big Murph and Little Murph because of a four-inch difference in their heights.

"Hey," Big Murph called out to his partner who was stationed outside the cold storage room. "I've got to make a run to the john."

"You'd better pack a lunch for the trip," Little Murph called back.

The nearest public bathroom on the B level was at the far end of the corridor, the equivalent of a city block away. Some of the laboratories had private bathrooms, but all doors had been locked for the night, and only a short list of medical personnel was allowed entry. Little Murph studied the list of names on his clipboard. Dr. Joanna Blalock, Dr. Lori McKay, Marci Wetterman, Cathy Grimes and Mary Chen. A photograph was next to each person's name.

"Anybody still in your lab?" Little Murph asked.

"Two," Big Murph said. "If they leave before I return, doublecheck to make sure the door is locked."

"You got it."

Little Murph leaned back against the cool metal door and listened to his partner's footsteps echoing down the corridor. The B level was actually underground and had no windows or doors leading directly to the outside world. It had a closed-in feeling to it, like that of a dungeon. Little Murph yawned loudly, his gaze going to the wall clock. It was 9:55 P.M. In two hours he could go home to his wife and his baby girl, whom he called Sunshine because sunlight turned her hair a golden blond. He'd kiss both of them, then sleep like a log and wake up and return to Memorial Hospital at noon so he could guard the place against a bunch of goddamn terrorists. He couldn't believe they'd bomb a hospital. But then again, he wouldn't have believed they'd bomb a residential neighborhood either.

Little Murph thought he heard a door opening and quickly looked down the corridor. He saw nothing, but the light was dim in the distance. Turning on his flashlight, he moved forward slowly, again searching the hallway and again seeing nothing.

He unfastened the strap on his holstered pistol, still staring down the corridor and listening intently. Except for the sound of his own breathing, there was only silence. Then he heard a cabinet door close and a woman's laughter coming from within the forensics laboratory. He switched off his flashlight and returned to his station outside the cold storage room.

He refastened the strap across his pistol, wondering if the terrorists would be stupid enough to try something inside a hospital with policemen everywhere. They just might. Little Murph nodded, remembering the terrorists had killed the eyewitness with a cop sitting right outside the door. The bastards had disguised themselves as a cleaning crew. Well, if they try that again they'll wish to God they hadn't. Little Murph's gaze went back to the clipboard. There were no cleaning crews or maintenance men or anybody else scheduled to be on the B level after 8:00 P.M.

Again Little Murph heard a woman's laughter from inside the forensics lab. He wondered what could be so amusing about sorting through body parts and trying to put them back together. He wouldn't do it for all the money in the world. Little Murph hated the sight of blood, and viewing mangled bodies gave him the jitters for days, sometimes even caused nightmares. And it was getting worse. That's why he'd decided to go to night school for his law degree. Three more years and he'd have it. Then he would move up the coast to someplace where Sunshine could have pets and a big backyard, to someplace where the air didn't choke you and the schools weren't filled with drugs. Three more years, Little Murph thought again.

The wall clock struck ten, emitting a click as its hands moved. From down the corridor came another clicking sound, louder and moving toward Murphy. He spun around, concentrating his sight and hearing, trying to see who or what was making the sound. Then he saw a woman approaching, her high heels clicking against the linoleum floor.

He unfastened the strap over his pistol.

"Oh, Officer! Thank goodness!" Eva Reineke gushed. "I thought I was doomed to stay down here forever."

"What's the problem?" Little Murph asked, studying the smartly dressed woman. She was wearing a gray woolen skirt and white silk blouse with a blue blazer. A large diamond sparkled on her ring finger.

"I was in the ICU waiting for my husband and took the elevator down," Eva said. "And now I can't find my way to the front lobby."

"That's because you're on the B level," Little Murph told her, now seeing she was young—no more than thirty—and very pretty. "You've got to go back up to the main floor."

Eva sighed wearily. "I'd be grateful if you could show me where the elevators are."

"I can't leave my post, ma'am," Little Murph said. "But I can give you directions."

Too bad, Eva thought. It would have been easier to shoot him in the back of the head as he walked away. "Thank you," she said warmly and slowly reached for the semiautomatic Beretta inside her blazer.

The door to the forensics laboratory opened abruptly. A middle-aged technician with Asian features looked out and called over to Little Murph. "We're having trouble unscrewing a plastic top. Could you help us?"

"Sure," Little Murph said, then turned to Eva. "You stay here, ma'am. I'll be right back to give you directions."

"You're very kind," Eva said.

Little Murph walked over to the doorway where the technician stood. Following her, Little Murph kept his head down, not wanting to see any blood or guts or body parts. Off to the side, giant centrifuges were humming, and racks of test tubes were being rocked back and forth in a water bath. Little Murph didn't look up even when a timer sounded at the rear of the room.

"Here you go," the technician said and handed him a small bottle with a plastic screw top. "Please be careful. It contains radioactive material."

The top was stuck fast. It took Little Murph two tries to loosen it. "Anything else?" he asked.

"That'll do," the technician said. "Thanks."

Little Murph turned and walked back through the doorway, still keeping his head down. He closed the door after him, making certain it was locked. In the hall he took a deep breath.

He looked down the corridor to the door of the cold storage room. The woman was no longer there. Christ, he growled under his breath. She was probably wandering around, searching for the elevators. In the distance he heard an elevator open, then close. He nodded. She'd found it.

Little Murph walked back to the cold storage room. At the bottom of the metal door he noticed a small, odd-shaped pile of puttylike material. His first thought was that something was leaking out of the room. He knelt down to examine it more closely.

The C-four detonated, giving off an intense yellow flash. Little Murph saw the brilliant color coming at him and, for a fraction of a second, it reminded him of his daughter's blond hair and how it glowed in the sun.

20

The policeman lifted up the crime scene tape for Joanna. She ducked under it and hurried down the corridor on the B level, wondering if the forensics laboratory had been completely destroyed. She kept thinking about the bomb in West Hollywood and how it had wiped out a row of houses. Her laboratories had to be gone, she thought dejectedly, and ten years of work gone with them.

At the bank of elevators she saw Jake and Farelli with Dan Hurley and two ATF agents, all standing behind a second yellow tape. Inside the opened elevators members of the Crime Scene Unit were dusting for fingerprints.

"Welcome to the Late Late Show," Jake said humorlessly.

"What have we got?" Joanna asked.

"A bomb went off and a cop was killed," Jake said, thinking about the cop's young widow. She hadn't been notified yet because they hadn't found enough of Michael Murphy to make a positive ID. "That's all we got."

"Why are we waiting here?"

"We have to make sure there's not a second bomb," Hurley told her.

Joanna looked at him quizzically. "Why would they leave a second bomb behind?"

"As a booby trap," Hurley explained. "That way they can kill more cops."

"Bastards," Farelli muttered. "What the hell kind of people are we dealing with?"

"Ordinary-looking people," Hurley said flatly. "Your usual bomber is white, middle-class and between the ages of twenty and forty. And every damn one of them believes in some cause or other. The scariest part is that they're all convinced God is on their side."

"What about the innocent people they blow up?" Joanna asked bitterly.

Hurley shrugged. "They couldn't care less."

The group turned as an ATF agent approached. His blue jacket was covered with grime and a white powder-like substance. He waved them in. "It's all clear, but watch out for hanging wires."

Hurley led the way down the quiet corridor. The air was murky with particles of dust and debris still suspended in the draftless hall. They kept their eyes on the ceiling and walls, looking for any objects that might be dangling or protruding. They crossed an intersecting corridor, and the damage became more obvious. Now the walls were badly cracked, the ceiling buckled upward. Light fixtures were shattered, and in their place were large, powerful spotlights.

Nearing the door to the main forensics laboratory, Joanna held her breath and hoped that at least part of her lab was still standing. The ceiling above her was gone, and she could see exposed pipes and wires. The smell of something electrical burning permeated the air.

Joanna stopped and looked in. The door was hanging by a single hinge, its glass pane blown out. The floor was littered with broken glass and overturned instruments, but the large centrifuges were still upright and running. And the cabinet doors were still closed, their contents secure.

"Were any of my technicians here at the time of the explosion?" Joanna asked.

"Two," Hurley answered. "They got bounced around pretty good. One may have a broken arm."

"Where are they?"

"In the ER."

They walked on through the debris and came to where the cold storage room should have been. The entire wall was blown away, without a trace of the large metal door. Part of the opposite wall still stood, but it was covered with fissures and craters. In some places there were jagged slivers of metal sticking out, like darts in a dartboard.

"Wait a minute," Jake said, now studying a badly pitted section of the wall. "There's something shiny in here."

Using a pocketknife, he carefully pried the piece of glistening metal out of the plaster. It appeared to be gold and appeared to be twisted back on itself. Then Jake saw the letters *LOS A* and the numbers 214, and he immediately knew what it was. "It's Murphy's shield," he reported grimly.

"Jesus." Farelli winced, thinking they weren't going to find enough of Murphy to bury.

They entered the space where the cold storage room used to be. Nothing was recognizable. A portion of the rear wall remained, but where the freezer once stood was a gaping hole. The force of the blast had ripped open the ceiling, leaving only the edges intact.

Joanna waded through the debris, ankle deep in splintered wood and broken glass. Everything had been smashed into small pieces. Her gaze went back to the freezer area and the blown-out wall around it. Two nights ago she and Lori had worked late in that area, no more than five feet from the freezer. Had the bomb gone off then, they would both have been blown to kingdom come.

"Were all the specimens stored in here?" Jake broke into her thoughts.

"Every one of them."

"Is anything retrievable?"

Joanna moved some rubble and debris around with her foot and saw a broken test tube. "I doubt it."

"But you've already done most of the important studies," Hurley said hopefully. "Right?"

Joanna shrugged. "Maybe, maybe not."

Jake took out his notepad and flipped through pages. "You've done the microscopic studies and the blood typing, and the DNA profiles are now in the works. What else is there to do?"

"At this point, nothing." Joanna unintentionally stepped on broken glass and heard it crunch. "But as new clues and findings are uncovered, we'll think of plenty of other things to do. Only now we won't have the tissues to do them with."

"I'll have my men sift through everything," Hurley said. "Maybe they'll be able to recover some of the specimens."

"Good luck," Joanna said. She walked slowly around the perimeter of the room, looking for anything salvageable, anything that might have been left intact. There was nothing but bits and pieces. She came to a glossy photograph. It too was shredded apart. At the freezer area Joanna stopped and peered through the large hole in the wall. All she saw were dangling wires and pipes. She again thought about the force of the explosion and what would have happened to her had the terrorists come two evenings earlier.

Joanna glanced over at Jake. "How in the world did those terrorists get in here with two policemen guarding the doors?"

"We don't know," Jake said, "One of the officers took a bathroom break. He was gone ten minutes at the most.

When the bomb exploded he was on his way back, just past the elevators."

"Is he all right?"

"He's got a bad concussion and a ruptured eardrum," Jake told her, unhappy that the cop hadn't used a private john in one of the labs rather than walk to the end of the corridor. He would have been back at his post at least five minutes earlier. "He'll be okay."

Joanna walked on, coming to the side wall that had held shelves and cabinets. The wall was ballooned out, the rear section missing altogether. Using her foot, Joanna pushed aside chunks of plaster and broken glass and a metal plate that was bent out of shape. Then she saw what appeared to be a dust-covered test tube. With the toe of her shoe she turned the object over. It was a finger with a piece of hand attached to it. Joanna quickly leaned over and removed the dust from the finger with a Kleenex. Now she could see the letter *E* tattooed on it. It was José Hernandez's hand. Joanna stepped back and surveyed the immediate area. To her left she recognized a workman's shoe and next to it a piece of scapula, both from the West Hollywood bomb site.

She looked over at the blown-out freezer and restudied its structure. The side wall of the freezer nearest her was gone. The side wall farthest away was badly buckled but intact. She nodded, understanding why the specimens had ended up where they did. They had followed the path of least resistance, exiting the freezer where there was no wall to stop them.

Joanna picked up a small stick and wrapped the Kleenex around its tip. Then she stuck the stick in the shoe to mark its location.

"What did you find?" Jake called over.

"José Hernandez's hand."

"What kind of condition is it in?"

"Good enough for your dogs to sniff again, if need be."

Jake checked his watch. It was 2:00 A.M. There would be no sleep tonight. At first light he'd take the hand, let the dogs sniff it again and see if the scent would lead them to the remains of José Hernandez. They had turned up nothing in their initial run.

Joanna walked back to the detectives. "I also found a workman's shoe and a piece of scapula. Both I think come from the West Hollywood bomb site."

"So that's three out of thirty something specimens found on the first go-round," Hurley said. "That's not half bad."

"It'll do for starters." Joanna pointed to the area she had just searched. "Have your men concentrate their search efforts near the wall. And in the blown-out wall at the rear of the freezer. That's where they're most likely to find specimens."

Hurley asked, "What should we do with the specimens we find?"

"Refrigerate them," Joanna answered, "but don't freeze them."

A uniformed policeman appeared at the entrance to the cold storage room and signaled to Farelli.

As Farelli turned, a dangling wire above him suddenly made a crackling noise and gave off a shower of sparks. Then it went dead again. Farelli looked up at the blackness where the ceiling had been. "Is anything flammable in here? Natural gas? Oil?"

"Nothing," Joanna assured him. "Everything in here runs on electricity."

"Ah-huh," Farelli said, wondering about the solvents and cleaning fluids that were present in most laboratories. He walked over to the policeman, giving the dangling wire a wide berth. They spoke briefly, and Farelli returned.

"One of the technicians just got back from the ER," Farelli reported. "They put her in the doc's office."

"Where's the other technician?" Joanna asked at once.

"Still in the ER," Farelli said. "She's got a fractured arm. They're calling in a specialist to set it."

Joanna sighed, feeling partially responsible for what had happened to her staff. She should never have allowed them to work late when the danger was the greatest. From now on everybody, herself included, would be out of the laboratory by 6:00 P.M.

They followed the policeman down the corridor and into the forensics lab. Someone had swept a path through the broken glass that littered the floor. The ceiling and walls had large cracks but otherwise were intact. Joanna glanced over at the heavy equipment off to the side. The centrifuges and the gas chromatograph setup were still standing, with no outward evidence of damage. Lucky, she thought, very lucky. She could have the lab up and running in a matter of days if the structural engineers gave their approval.

They entered the rear laboratory, which appeared untouched by the explosion. The only thing out of place was the hanging skeleton that had come off its hook and fallen to the floor.

Mary Chen, the senior forensics technician, was seated at a small desk staring straight ahead. There was a large bruise on her forehead and deep abrasions on her hands and arms. The front of her scrub suit was spotted with blood.

Joanna sat next to her and gently squeezed her shoulder. "Are you all right?"

"I'm okay," Mary said in a monotone. She was a petite, middle-aged woman with prematurely gray hair and delicate Asian features. "Poor Cathy broke her arm."

"I heard," Joanna said softly. "Once we're finished

here, I'll go down to the ER and make sure everything goes smoothly for her."

A faint smile came to Mary's face. "Good."

"Do you feel up to talking with the detectives?" Joanna asked.

Mary nodded, the smile now gone. "I don't think I'll be of much help to them."

"Just tell them what you know."

Jake pulled up a chair and briefly studied the woman. Her face was calm and expressionless, but her hands were balled up into tight fists. "I only have a few questions," he began in a quiet voice. "Where were you when the explosion went off?"

"In the front lab," Mary said. "We were pipetting saline into test tubes to use as experimental controls. Then suddenly there was a loud boom and the whole lab seemed to shake. The next thing I knew I was on the floor, covered with glass. Everything went dark, and I could hear Cathy screaming. Then the lights came back on and I saw Cathy holding her wrist." Mary swallowed audibly. "You could see it was broken."

Jake nodded, pleased with the technician's eye for detail. "Did either of you leave the lab for any reason between six p.m. and the time the bomb went off?"

Mary thought for a moment. "We went to the cafeteria and had dinner around seven."

"What time did you return?"

"About eight."

"Did you see both policemen in the corridor when you left and came back?"

"Both were there," Mary recalled. "The larger one was by our door, the smaller officer near the cold storage room."

"And you didn't leave the laboratory after that?"

"Neither of us did."

Jake leaned back in his chair, sensing he was coming

to a dead end. There was a bathroom in the laboratory, so they wouldn't have left for that. And during their stay in the lab the door should have remained closed and locked. "You kept the door closed at all times?"

Mary shrugged. "There was no reason to open it."

"Did you—"

Mary held up an index finger. "Now that I think about it, I did open the door once."

"For what?"

"We couldn't unscrew the top off a bottle, so I asked the officer if he'd help."

"Did he?"

Mary nodded. "He stepped inside the doorway to the lab and opened the bottle on the second try."

"When did this happen?"

"A couple of minutes before the explosion."

That's when the bomb was placed, Jake told himself. Big Murph was a block away taking a pee, and Little Murph was inside the lab unscrewing a bottle top. The corridor was unguarded for at least a minute. That was plenty of time for a pro to set the bomb and get the hell out. "Other than the policeman, did you see anyone else in the corridor?"

"Just the woman."

Jake jerked his head forward. "What woman?"

"I think she was a visitor," Mary said, remembering. "I think she was lost, because the policeman said something to her like, 'When I return I'll show you the way.'"

Farelli reached for his notepad as Jake was saying, "Describe the woman for us."

"She was young, in her mid- to late twenties, and very smartly dressed," Mary told them. "She had on a blue blazer."

"Did you get a good look at her face?"

"Not so good."

"Tell us what she looked like."

"Well, she was Caucasian and very fair, with blond hair that was pulled back." Mary tried to remember more, then shook her head. "That's about it. I only saw her in profile and only for a second."

Joanna quickly held up a hand. "I think I saw her too."

"When?" Jake asked.

"Yesterday afternoon," Joanna said at once. "She was getting off the elevator down here."

So she could scout things out, Jake was thinking. "Can you add anything to Mary's description?"

"Not really," Joanna said, concentrating and trying to recall details. "I only got a glimpse of her. But I'd recognize her if I saw her again."

Jake turned back to Mary. "What about the woman's features?"

Mary shrugged.

"Big nose or little nose?" Jake coaxed her. "Overbite or underbite? Can you recall any distinguishing features?"

"Nothing out of the ordinary."

"From your description, she sounds Anglo-Saxon," Jake said, thinking aloud.

"Beyond any doubt."

"And nothing else about her comes to mind?"

"I'm afraid not."

Farelli closed his notepad. "If you feel up to it tomorrow, would you talk with our sketch artist and help him come up with a picture of this woman?"

"I'll try," Mary said. Then her eyes narrowed suddenly. "Do you think this woman did it?"

"Maybe," Jake said tonelessly.

Mary sighed softly. "What is happening to America? Have we lost all civility?"

Just about, Jake wanted to say. It's now a country filled with nuts and crazies and murderers and rapists who don't give a damn about anything or anybody. At this very moment a smartly dressed terrorist was probably having a beer and relaxing, pleased with what she'd done and eager to do it again.

"May I go?" Mary asked, pushing herself up. "My family will be worried about me."

Jake nodded. "Do you have a way home?"

"My car is in the lot."

Jake signaled to the uniformed policeman. "Officer, make sure the lady gets to her car all right."

Mary asked, "Would you like me to meet your sketch artist here?"

"I think the station would be better," Jake said.

"You'll contact me then?"

"Yes."

Jake watched the technician and policeman walk out and waited for the door to close. "Son of a bitch! A woman! A woman!"

"And a man," Farelli added. "Don't forget Mr. Skinhead with his goatee."

"So we've got us a couple," Jake said. "Maybe they're married."

Hurley shook his head. "Probably not. Terrorists don't like to use people close to them. It tends to complicate things."

Right, Jake thought sourly. The bastards didn't want to worry about someone close to them getting killed. They didn't want any distractions while they were blowing things up and murdering innocent people. Like Little Murph. A good cop, just standing watch and dead because of it. Of course, the department would give him a big funeral and half the force would turn out for it. And every one of them would strain to hold it together as the flag was taken off Murph's coffin and folded and handed to his grieving widow and his little daughter, who was too young to understand what was happening.

Jake took a deep breath and brought his mind back to

the present. "At least now we might end up with a halfway decent picture of the female terrorist."

Hurley said, "Assuming what the technician saw and what she said she saw are the same."

Jake squinted an eye. "Why wouldn't they be?"

"Bomb victims are usually badly shaken and don't have good recall," Hurley explained. "They tend to fill in the blank spaces with what they think should have been there."

"She looked pretty calm to me," Farelli commented.

"Outwardly, yeah," Hurley agreed. "But inside her head things had to be scrambled."

"You don't know Mary Chen," Joanna said.

"But I know blast victims."

"Let me tell you about Mary's background," Joanna went on, "then you can tell me how tough she is, or isn't. Mary was born in a small village south of Shanghai when China was ruled by Mao and the Red Guards. When she was a child, her family commandeered an old steam-driven ferryboat. The entire village, all two hundred of them, piled on that boat and sailed for Hong Kong. They had virtually no chance to succeed. They had to navigate along a rugged coastline for several hundred miles while being hounded by Red Chinese patrol boats. Do you want to guess what Mary's job was?"

The men slowly shook their heads, engrossed in the story.

"She was the lookout," Joanna continued. "Because of her exceptional vision, they asked her to be the lookout. She agreed. So they strapped her in a chair at the bow of the boat to be their warning system. She was their radar."

Farelli thought about his grandfather who had come to America on a ship in steerage. That was a joyride compared with the story he was hearing now.

"The patrol boats caught them once and nearly blew them out of the water, killing half the passengers in the process. Mary stayed at the bow and directed them into a fogbank, where they lost their pursuers. A week later they limped into Hong Kong harbor. When all this happened Mary Chen was ten years old."

Joanna looked over at Hurley and smiled thinly. "Now, do you really think a bomb blast down the hall is going to scramble her brains?"

"You've got a point," Hurley conceded, then shook his head in admiration. "She went through all that, huh?"

"And more."

"I'll bet we end up with a pretty accurate picture," Jake predicted.

"But only in profile," Hurley reminded him.

"That's better than nothing," Jake said, wishing he had a clear frontal picture of the female terrorist.

Farelli asked, "Do you think she was in a big enough hurry to leave some prints in the elevator?"

"My guess is she took the stairs," Hurley said. "The timer on that bomb was set for only a few minutes."

Farelli nodded. "You're probably right. The last place you want to be when a bomb goes off is in an elevator."

Jake made a mental note to have the railing on the stairs checked for prints. They'd also have to check the doorknob to the stairwell, both on the B level and in the lobby. And the people sitting in the lobby at the time of the explosion would have to be questioned. Maybe they saw a young blonde wearing a blue blazer. Maybe somebody got a good look at her face. "They're taking bigger and bigger chances now. And this bombing was the riskiest of all."

"They don't think in terms of risk," Hurley told him. "All they care about is their target. Everything else is incidental."

"That's my point," Jake said, walking over to the skeleton on the floor. He picked it up and hung it back on its hook. "These are very clever people. They could have bombed their target a dozen times over by now. Yet they risk everything to blow up a pathology laboratory that's heavily guarded. Why? Why not just do the target and get the hell out?"

"Like I told you before," Hurley said, "they are probably waiting for a specific date. And it's not far off."

Jake rubbed his chin. "What's so important about a date in April? Is there some major event that occurs during April?"

"Easter? Passover?" Farelli guessed.

"What about Tax Day?" Joanna asked. "Income taxes have to be paid by April fifteenth."

"No," Hurley said, his face losing color for a moment. "The nineteenth. Domestic terror day in America."

The group stared at one another in silence.

Hurley quickly regained his composure, then continued. "The first shots of the Revolutionary War were fired at Lexington and Concord on April nineteenth. You remember, the so-called shot heard round the world. Well, our modern-day domestic terrorists consider themselves patriots, and they commit their very worst acts on April nineteenth."

Jake nodded slowly. "Like the bombing of the federal building in Oklahoma City."

Hurley nodded back. "And the firefight at the Branch Davidian compound outside Waco."

"What could they go after in Los Angeles that could compare to those?" Jake asked. After a pause he said, "Nothing could be worse than the Oklahoma City bombing."

"Don't bet on it," Hurley said darkly.

21

Joanna twisted and turned in her sleep, trying to escape from a nightmare. She was back in the forensics laboratory, desperately pulling on the locked door. A plastic bomb was on the countertop, a timer next to it clicking off the seconds. Joanna jerked at the door with all her might. It didn't even budge. Through the glass pane she saw a policeman talking to a smartly dressed woman. Joanna rapped on the glass and screamed at the top of her lungs—but they ignored her and walked away. *Oh, God! Oh, God!* Frantically Joanna grabbed a metal stool and threw it at the window, smashing out the pane. The seconds were ticking off, louder and louder. Five seconds. Four seconds. Joanna dove for the bomb. *Oh, God! Oh, God!* Two seconds. Now she had the bomb, ready to throw it. One sec—

Joanna jerked out of her sleep, the bedside phone clutched tightly in her hand. It took her a moment to realize she was at home in her bed. She took a deep breath and looked over at the clock on the night table. It was 7:15 A.M. She lay back and tried to collect herself. Jesus, she thought, now feeling the perspiration soaking through her nightgown. Everything had seemed so real, particularly the bomb and its timer and the terrorist wearing the blue blazer. Joanna glanced over at the ticking clock. That sound had probably set off her subliminal imagination and started the nightmare. She decided to buy a new clock, a digital one that didn't tick.

The phone rang, startling her. Bad news, she told herself. Early morning calls were always bad news. She picked up the phone on the third ring.

Quickly she cleared the sleep out of her throat and brought the receiver to her ear. "Yes?"

"Joanna?"

"Hi," she said, recognizing Paul's voice. "How are things going?"

"Not very well," he responded, lighting a cigarette and coughing into the phone. "The meetings seem to go on and on, and we don't make any progress. We've suspended our talks until next Monday."

"That doesn't sound good," Joanna said, propping herself up in bed.

"And to make matters worse, one of our competitors has entered the bidding for the bank we're trying to acquire. And we may not be able to match their bid."

"It looks like you're in a tight spot."

"And it's getting tighter," Paul said. "Hold on for a moment, will you?"

Joanna heard him barking out orders to someone. In the background was the sound of a door closing loudly.

"Sorry about that." Paul came back on the line. "Anyhow, this could take a lot longer than I had anticipated."

"How long?"

"Weeks."

"That'll be the most time we've ever been apart."

"Unless we do something about it."

Joanna smiled and curled up in her blanket. "What did you have in mind?"

"You flying into New York for the weekend."

"Oh, I wish I could," Joanna said.

"Don't wish," Paul said seductively. "Just do it."

"It's not possible," she told him. "The bomb case I'm working on is getting worse by the minute. You wouldn't believe what we're up against."

"I'm talking about you flying out Friday and returning Sunday," he said, his voice firmer now. "Are you telling me they can't spare you for two days?"

"We're working day and night on this case," she said. "Nobody is sleeping very much because we know it's just a matter of time before—" She caught herself before she gave out information she didn't want to.

"Before what?"

"I can't talk about it."

Paul puffed on his cigarette. "Why not fly Saturday and return the next day? You'll only be away a day."

"That's a day I can't afford."

"Can't or won't?"

"Both."

There was a long, awkward pause.

Joanna could hear Paul lighting another cigarette.

"I need you right now," he said finally.

She hesitated, wanting to fly to New York but knowing she couldn't. Not with April nineteenth so close. "Why don't you fly out to Los Angeles? You don't have any meetings until Monday."

"Oh, I have meetings all right," Paul said quickly. "We'll be planning our strategy all weekend. So why don't you get your beautiful body on that plane and fly to New York?"

"I just can't."

"So when I really need you, you just can't make it. Right?"

Joanna took a deep breath, trying to control her temper. "At this point in time, it's a matter of priorities."

"Yours or mine?"

"Look," Joanna said, raising her voice, "when you told me you had to cancel a dinner date with your daughter to fly to New York for an urgent meeting, I understood. That was a major priority for you. It didn't mean that you loved your daughter less. It meant that at that moment your meeting had priority over a dinner with your daughter. I'd like you to understand that I have priorities too."

"You're comparing apples and oranges," Paul countered.

"No, I'm not. I'm telling you that my priorities are as important to me as yours are to you."

There was a clicking sound on the phone.

"I've got a call on another line," Paul said hurriedly. "Hold on."

Joanna sat up, hating the position she was being put in. It was as if Paul was asking her to choose between him and her career. And she detected a dictatorial tone in his voice, something she hadn't heard before. He seemed to be demanding that she put him and his plans ahead of her career. He expected his priorities to take precedence.

Paul came back on. "Well, have you changed your mind?"

"I can't, I just can't fly out. Not now."

Paul took a deep breath and exhaled loudly. "We're going to have to sort out this priority business."

"I think we already have."

There was another awkward silence, longer this time.

"I think we should stay apart for a while," Paul said.

"A long while," Joanna said and hung up.

She lay back in bed and stared up at the ceiling, wondering if she would ever get things right. Or would she always have to make the choice between career and relationships and even marriage? Damn! Damn! A picture of Paul came into her mind. He was rubbing her neck and telling her how important she was to him.

Joanna pulled the covers up over her head just as the tears started.

22

Jake hurried up the steps to the John Edgar Wales Institute for Rehabilitation. Lou Farelli stood at the entranceway, waiting for him.

"How many have you got?" Jake asked.

"Three videos of amputees with red tattoos above their elbows," Farelli said.

"With writing beneath?"

"Two for sure. One maybe."

They went through the black glass doors that opened automatically and entered a beautifully appointed reception area. The floor was made of polished granite, the dome-shaped ceiling painted with murals of doctors and nurses helping patients. In the center of the deserted room was a raised information desk made of mahogany. It reminded Jake of a judge's bench.

"They didn't spare any expense, did they?" he asked.

Farelli shrugged. "The federal government never does. It ain't their money."

Jake glanced up at the murals. "I feel like I'm in a damn museum."

"It'll look better once they get all the fixtures and furniture set up."

"When will that be?"

"In a few weeks," Farelli said and punched the elevator button. "That's when they're having their grand opening."

They took the elevator to the second floor and walked

down a broad, empty corridor. The walls were covered with lime-colored grass cloth, the floor with a deep brown linoleum. An overhead air-conditioning system switched on, and the air began to stir.

"This place gives the guys the creeps," Farelli said. "Particularly at night, when it's like a dungeon up here."

"How many teams do you have working the videos?" Jake asked.

"Three," Farelli told him. "They rotate every eight hours around the clock."

Jake did rapid calculations in his mind. "They still couldn't have gotten through all those videos."

"They're further along than you think." Farelli explained how Dan Hurley had helped narrow the list down. Anyone over the age of fifty or under the age of fifteen was excluded. Those age ranges didn't fit the terrorist profile, nor did they match the descriptions given by Stonehauser's widow. "That left us with eight hundred possibilities. Thus far, our guys have viewed just over six hundred. So we've only two hundred to go."

"With our luck the perp will be number eight hundred," Jake said.

"Tell me about it."

They quietly entered a darkened room. The camera was on and projecting images onto four separate screens. Jake leaned against the wall and watched the film. A double amputee was trying to walk on artificial legs with the help of canes. There were no tattoos on his arms.

"That's sure as hell not him," a voice in the darkness spoke out.

The camera was switched off and the lights came on. The air had a gray haze and smelled of stale cigarette smoke. Four detectives were seated around a table that was littered with empty pizza cartons and overflowing ashtrays.

"That's number sixteen on your scorecard," said Del

Harriman, a twenty-year veteran in the Homicide Division. He knew more about films and cameras than most of the so-called experts and had been doing double shifts in the viewing room. "When this shit is over, I'm going to need a week to recover."

"You got it," Jake said, liking the hawk-faced detective who would soon retire to open a camera shop somewhere in Arizona. "Tell me, how good is their video setup?"

"The best in the world," Harriman said. "It's a Sony that does everything except go to the bathroom for you."

"Let's look at tattoos."

Harriman began pushing buttons on a handheld remote control. The room went dark, and a new video appeared on the screen.

All eyes moved to a young Mexican walking on an artificial leg with an obvious limp. His jaw appeared tightly clenched, because of either the effort he was making or some pain he was experiencing. On his right upper arm was a tattoo with an indistinct red design.

Harriman stopped the film, then pushed more buttons on the remote control. The frozen frame on the screen suddenly enlarged and came into focus. The tattoo was a flower but not a rose. If anything, it was an orange-colored sunflower. There was a long stem with a looped pattern beneath the tattoo, but no writing.

"That's not our boy," Jake said, looking at the screen to his right, which showed a profile view. "Let's move on."

Harriman punched in new numbers. The screen went blank for a moment, then zigzag lines appeared, then another video came up. Again the subject was Mexican, but he seemed older than the first. Mid- or late forties, Jake guessed, seeing the loose skin at the base of the man's neck.

The second patient seemed much more comfortable

with his prosthesis and walked with a barely noticeable limp. A profile view showed a tattoo of red roses on his right upper arm. There was writing beneath it.

"Freeze it!" Jake said quickly.

The film stopped, and the still frame was slowly magnified. Jake thought he could make out the first letter. An *M.* Gradually the whole word came into focus. *MACHO.*

"Shit," Jake grumbled. "Go to the next guy."

The third patient appeared younger than the others. He was in his mid- to late twenties, with a carefully trimmed mustache and slick black hair. Jake studied the man's hair, now remembering the piece of scalp found at the West Hollywood bomb site. It was laden with some type of hair lotion.

Jake's gaze went to the man's arm and the red rose tattoo on it. Beneath the tattoo was writing, but it blurred as the man stumbled and righted himself. His arms were still moving when the profile faded.

"Can you back it up?" Jake asked at once.

Harriman pushed a button on the remote control, and the frames flashed by in reverse. He stopped the film at the place just before the patient began to stumble. Everything was in very slow motion now, going frame by frame. The tattoo came into view, but the patient's arm was rotated, and only the last part of the writing under the tattoo was visible. The letters *EY* could be clearly seen.

"Could be the last letters of Monterrey," Farelli suggested.

"It could be a lot of things," Jake said. Turning to Harriman he asked, "Can we get a better look at the first part of the writing?"

"Not with the equipment we have here," Harriman said. "We only got a couple of frames of it, and he was twisting his arm away from the camera at the time."

"Can the individual frames be broken down and reconstructed to bring out the lettering?"

"It might be possible," Harriman said dubiously. "Let me check with my friends over at the FBI." He slowly stretched his back and neck, listening to his vertebrae crack. "Lord! I hope this guy is our perp. If I look at much more film, I'm going to go blind."

"I want every one of the remaining two hundred videos screened and examined," Jake said firmly. "No exceptions."

The detectives sitting at the table groaned loudly. One lit a cigarette and started coughing.

Harriman asked, "But what if this guy's tattoo reads 'Monterrey'?"

"Then maybe we'll have our man. But keep in mind, there's no law that says the same tattoo can't be present on more than one guy." Jake thought about the quality of the tattoo on the dismembered arm. It was mediocre, probably done by a south-of-the-border tattooist who could churn out a dozen a day. "Do you have any information on this guy?"

Harriman pressed a button on the remote control. The screen went blank, then a black-and-white insert appeared that read

RAMÓN GONZALEZ
CASE: 8422
DOB: 5/4/70
DIAGNOSIS: OSTEOGENIC SARCOMA

Jake took out his notepad and carefully wrote the information down.

Farelli asked, "What the hell is osteogenic sarcoma?"

"I don't know," Jake said, closing his notepad. "But it sounds like something you don't want to have."

They left the viewing room and took the elevator down. Outside the day was gray and muggy, the air still and very warm. Farelli put his finger inside his collar and pulled at it as he glanced at the flashing neon sign atop the Bank of America building. It said the time was 2:40 P.M., the temperature eighty-two degrees.

"We've got to give those guys upstairs a break," Farelli said. "Otherwise they'll go stir-crazy."

"Can't," Jake said. "Time is running out."

"Hurley is sure it's going to happen on the nineteenth, huh?"

"Positive." Jake's gaze went to the neon sign above the bank. Now it was flashing the date, April 6. "We've got thirteen days."

"That ain't enough time," Farelli said honestly. "It'll take a lot longer than that to track these bastards down."

"We've got to get them before that bomb goes off or they'll disappear forever."

Farelli looked at him oddly. "You mean, like vanish in thin air?"

"It happens more times than not," Jake said. "The really smart ones are never found. They never use credit cards or a social security number, so they never leave a trail you can track. They never write checks, never have bank accounts. And when they want to vanish altogether, they go into some isolated wilderness and nobody ever sees them again."

Farelli gave the matter thought, still not convinced. "Hell, the Unabomber—Ted whatever the hell his name is—did everything you just said and they still managed to catch him."

"They didn't actually *catch* him," Jake said. "The FBI tracked him for years and never even came close until his brother turned him in. If his brother hadn't squealed, that crazy bastard would still be sending bombs in the mail." Jake used a finger to wipe perspiration from his brow. "And there are a dozen other examples I could give you."

"Shit," Farelli said disgustedly. "Are you saying either we get them now or we don't get them at all?"

"That's what I'm saying."

Jake could sense something wrong the moment he entered Joanna's office. She was staring into space, her mind a million miles away. On her desk was an ashtray brimming with cigarette butts, one of them still smoldering.

"You don't look so good," he said, remembering the last time he saw Joanna smoke. Kate had been deathly ill with the Ebola-like virus. "What's wrong?"

Joanna reached for a Kleenex and dabbed her eyes. "A man."

"Who?"

"Somebody I thought was wonderful and turned out to be not so great."

"Anything I can do?"

"Yeah. Don't ask me what happened." Joanna crushed out her cigarette, now remembering her last phone conversation with Paul. He had called back ten minutes after his earlier call. At first she thought he was going to try to make up. But he didn't. It was better to end it cleanly, he had told her. It made no sense to just hang on and wait to see what happened. Better to get on with their lives. And then he said good-bye.

"Jake, let me ask you something. It's a hypothetical question."

Jake leaned back against a countertop. "I'm listening."

"Someone you really care about needs you. But you're tied up with something very important. You can't go."

"So?"

"How would you feel?"

"Like I'd better do the best I could without her."

"No hard feelings?"

Jake shrugged. "No. Why should there be?"

Joanna nodded. That was the answer she had expected. That was Jake. He understood priorities.

Jake studied Joanna's face briefly. She looked tired and drawn, and her eyes were red and puffy. But she was still so damn pretty. She had the kind of beauty that wouldn't fade with the years. It would last a lifetime. "Are you going to be okay?"

"No," Joanna said honestly. "But I'll get by."

"If you need anything, you call."

"Thanks, Jake."

He shrugged again. "I haven't done anything."

"Yes, you have."

Joanna's stomach growled loudly, then made another rumbling sound. "I forgot lunch," she said and walked over to her desk, where she took out a candy bar and unwrapped it. "Want some?"

"No, thanks," Jake answered, glad to see some of the sadness gone from her face. He reached for a cigarette but decided against it. "If you've got a minute, I could use some help with medical terminology."

"Fire away," Joanna said, licking chocolate off her fingers.

Jake read from his notepad. "What the hell is an osteogenic sarcoma?"

"It's a rare type of bone cancer. Why?"

"Because I just saw a video of a Mexican with a prosthetic leg and a red rose tattoo on his arm."

"Was the word 'Monterrey' written under it?"

"That I can't be sure of," Jake said. "But his diagnosis was osteogenic sarcoma."

Joanna's eyes narrowed as the pieces began to fall into place. "One of the bones we found at the West Hollywood bomb site had an invasive osteogenic sarcoma."

Jake nodded slowly. "And that piece of bone could have come from the guy with the rose tattoo."

"There's one way to find out for certain."

Joanna led the way toward the rear laboratory. The floor was now cleared. Plasterers were repairing the cracks in the walls, carpenters putting safety latches on all the cabinets and drawers. Off to the side Mary Chen was checking out an ultracentrifuge machine. Jake waved to her.

"How did the picture turn out?" Mary called over.

"Pretty good," Jake called back. "It's going to be a big help."

Joanna said quietly, "But it's only a profile view, right?"

"One of the cops in the lobby thinks he saw her," Jake said. "We may end up with a full face yet. And if we do I'll want you to look at it and see if it's the same woman you saw getting off the elevator."

They walked over to Lori McKay, who was busily working at a computer. She had cherry lollipop in her mouth.

Joanna asked, "Do you have the DNA tissue types from the West Hollywood explosion logged into the computer?"

"Sure do," Lori slurred, moving the lollipop around with her tongue. "I entered all that data yesterday."

"Let's see the DNA type of the tissue from the osteogenic sarcoma," Joanna requested. "Then let's determine if it matched up with any of the other tissues."

Lori punched buttons on the keyboard. Then she sat back and waited. In seconds a DNA tissue type was on the screen. Under it was listed SCALP, BONE (SARCOMA) and TATTOO. "The tattoo and piece of scalp came from the guy with the osteogenic sarcoma."

"Are you absolutely positive?" Jake asked.

"The chances of my being wrong are about one in five billion."

"Well, well!" Jake said, rubbing his hands together. "It looks like we've got our man."

23

The receptionist spoke briefly into the phone, then looked up at Joanna and Jake. "Dr. Wales is tied up in a conference."

"We'll wait," Jake said.

"It could be a while." The receptionist glanced over at the wall clock. It was 4:40 P.M. "And we close the building and leave at five sharp."

"Not tonight you don't," Jake told her. "Everybody stays until I say otherwise. That includes Dr. Wales and Dr. Bremmer and anyone else who sees or talks to patients or handles their charts."

"But—but some of the staff have already gone."

"If we need them I'll send a black-and-white to pick them up and bring them back." Jake put his knuckles on the desktop and leaned forward, giving the young woman a long stare. "You might want to pass that information on to Dr. Wales."

The receptionist spoke into the phone again, her eyes avoiding Jake's. She waited for a response, hoping she wouldn't have to stay late. A handsome intern had asked her out to dinner, her first date in six months. She had to get her hair done and a million other things. "Lieutenant, will I be able to leave by six?"

"You got something important to do?"

"Real important." The receptionist pressed the phone to her ear and listened intently, then nodded to Jake. "Dr. Wales can see you now."

Jake took Joanna's arm and guided her around the information desk.

"Lieutenant," the receptionist called after them, "will I—"

"You'll make it," Jake said.

They entered a large clinic area that was deserted except for two patients using parallel bars to support themselves as they tried to walk on artificial legs. Perspiration was pouring off their faces, every step a struggle. A black therapist stood between them, coaxing them on.

"Doing good, doing good," the therapist encouraged them. "Looking like a champ."

Jake could feel the patients' eyes on him, watching him walk with no effort. And no doubt envying his legs.

Joanna led the way into a spacious workshop. Equipment and tools were neatly stacked atop the vacated benches. All of the technicians were gone, their green smocks hanging loosely on wall hooks. At the far end of the room Jake saw Josiah Wales sitting in an elevated chair. One of his pants legs was rolled up, exposing a stump just below the knee. Timothy Bremmer was seated on a metal stool, measuring the diameter of Wales's stump.

Jake slowed and quietly asked Joanna, "Do you think we should come back a little later?"

"Nope," Joanna said. "They're working on his leg, not his larynx."

As they approached, Jake studied Wales's stump. It was fleshy and reddened and resembled an overstuffed sock. "We appreciate your taking the time to see us."

"This better be good," Wales said gruffly.

"We think we know the guy whose prosthesis was found at the West Hollywood bomb site." Jake kept his voice even, trying not to show his dislike for Wales. "We need to look at his medical record."

"What's his name?"

"Gonzalez."

Wales shrugged. "We've got dozens of Gonzalezes in our files."

"This one's first name is Ramón, and he has a rose tattoo on his arm," Jake said, watching for a reaction. "It had the word 'Monterrey' written underneath it."

Wales shrugged again.

Bremmer looked up. "So that's why you were so interested in seeing those videos?"

"Right," Jake said. "Does a red rose tattoo ring any bells with you?"

"Not offhand," Bremmer said and turned his attention back to Wales's stump.

Wales shifted in his chair, repositioning his large frame. "Give us a few more minutes here, and we'll pull the records on this patient for you."

Jake leaned back against a workbench and glanced over at a side wall. There were hands and feet coming out of the plaster, and in the dim light they all seemed so real. It took him a moment to realize they were artificial hands and feet that were set on pegs.

Wales followed Jake's line of vision. "Those are reconditioned prostheses."

Jake asked, "How long do the new ones usually last?"

"That depends on how active the wearer is," Wales said. "Mine lasted six years before the damn thing cracked. At first there was only a little fissure near the heel, but it kept getting bigger and bigger."

"That happens with the older models," Bremmer explained, now using calipers to take more measurements. "They don't hold up nearly as well as our newer designs."

"I hate to change over to a new prosthesis," Wales complained. "They never fit the same, no matter how carefully you do the measurements. You have to break the damn thing in until it gets comfortable. And that takes a while."

"Why not just patch up the old one?" Joanna asked.

"Oh, we tried," Wales said, nodding. "Like a half dozen times over the past month. But it didn't hold up."

"The newer ones will," Bremmer assured him, writing the measurements on a legal pad. "The laminated models will last at least twice as long."

"Just make sure it's ready by the time we open the new institute," Wales said. "I want my prosthesis to be the first one fitted and worn in the new building."

"No problem," Bremmer said. "You'll be the first director and the first patient at the John Edgar Wales Institute."

Wales flexed and extended his stump, studying it and the empty space just beyond. "You know, I can still feel my foot, which of course isn't there."

Jake gave Wales a puzzled look.

"It's called the phantom limb syndrome, Lieutenant," Wales told him. "People who have lost a limb sometimes still sense its presence. It's believed that the nerves in the stump send back information which the brain misinterprets."

"Is it painful?" Jake asked.

"Only when you look down and see that your foot is still missing," Wales said, staring out into space. "Sometimes you forget that, even after being without it for forty years."

Wales shifted in his chair again, his face now hardening. "But there's one thing I never forget, Lieutenant. That's the son of a bitch who cost me my leg." He spat angrily at the floor. "He was driving drunk when he hit my bicycle and crushed my leg. He got a year in jail, I lost a foot. A goddamn drunk . . ." Wales let his voice trail off.

Jake glanced at the doctor's reddened stump once again, thinking he'd have felt the same way if some drunk bastard had cost him his leg. And made him limp for the rest of his life.

"Well, enough of that," Wales said. He reached down and strapped on his old prosthesis. "What was that patient's name again?"

"Ramón Gonzalez."

They walked into a nearby glass-enclosed office that was packed with files and journals and books. On the wall behind the desk was a large framed black-and-white photograph. It showed a fighter pilot climbing out of his jet plane. The inscription read: "To my little brother. Much love, John Edgar."

Bremmer sat at the computer and punched buttons on the keyboard. A moment later two names appeared on the screen.

"We've got two patients named Ramón Gonzalez," he said and pushed more keys. The first Ramón Gonzalez died in 1996. The second was still alive.

"It's got to be the second guy," Jake said.

Bremmer typed in the information and sat back as the others leaned forward. In an instant the patient's medical history appeared on the screen.

RAMÓN GONZALEZ
2801 ESCONDIDO STREET—APT. 26
LOS ANGELES, CA 90038
AGE—28
RACE—HISPANIC
BIRTHPLACE—COLIMA, MEXICO
DIAGNOSIS: OSTEOGENIC SARCOMA—LEFT
FEMUR
SURGICAL AMPUTATION IN MEXICO, 1998
RECURRENCE OF TUMOR, 1999
PROSTHESIS FITTED—MARCH 2, 1999

"I wonder why they amputated his leg," Joanna asked, more to herself than to the others.

"Because he had a bone malignancy," Bremmer said, pushing more buttons to see if there was additional information on Ramón Gonzalez. There wasn't.

Joanna shook her head. "They don't do amputations for osteogenic sarcoma of the femur nowadays. They resect out the tumor and put in titanium rods."

"Well," Bremmer said thoughtfully, "maybe they believed that was their best chance for a cure."

Joanna shook her head again. "There's a high rate of recurrence with amputation, even when you add radiation. That's why they've gone to the new procedure. His surgeons should have known better."

Wales asked derisively, "What do you expect from a south-of-the-border hospital?"

"Some of their doctors are very good," Joanna said.

"Well, Ramón didn't get one of those, now, did he?"

"I guess not." They probably did the best they could, Joanna was thinking. Mexico didn't have the wealth to set up a good health care system. The Mexican rich came to America for their medical needs while the lower class had to make do with second-rate facilities. The poor always caught hell, Joanna thought. "Do we have any of his sarcoma frozen here at Memorial?"

"Not that I know of," Wales said. "Why?"

"Because one of the bones found at the West Hollywood bomb site contained an osteogenic sarcoma. If its DNA type matched that in Ramón Gonzalez's leg, we'd know for certain he was in the house that blew up."

Bremmer asked, "So you're not sure Ramón Gonzalez was in the explosion?"

"Not absolutely," Joanna answered. "There's a slim possibility that there is more than one Mexican with a rose tattoo and an osteogenic sarcoma."

"But you also found a prosthesis at the bomb site," Bremmer said, thinking aloud.

"Which may or may not belong to Ramón Gonzalez," Joanna countered. "The only surefire proof would be the DNA testing."

"Well," Wales said, "you can forget about getting any of that osteogenic sarcoma from a Mexican hospital. That leg is long gone."

"Maybe, maybe not," Joanna said. "I'd like to look at his complete medical records. I want all the information you have on Ramón Gonzalez."

Wales hesitated. "It's not going to be that much. Remember, we don't do extensive work-ups on our patients."

Joanna pointed to the computer screen. "It says he had a recurrence of his sarcoma in nineteen ninety-nine. How do you know that?"

Wales gestured with his hands. "I guess he told us."

"And if that were the case, you would have referred him to Memorial to have the diagnosis verified. He would have had X rays taken. He would have been seen by an oncologist. And just maybe the oncologist would have requested a specimen of Ramón Gonzalez's osteogenic sarcoma from the Mexican hospital where the leg was amputated."

Wales made a mocking sound. "That's a real stretch, isn't it?"

"We'll find that out when we see the chart, won't we?"

Wales slowly reached for the phone. "The people in our records room may have left for the day."

Jake smiled thinly. "That's no problem. We can have them picked up and brought back."

Wales's eyes narrowed, his dislike for Jake obvious. He was about to say something, then changed his mind. Picking up the phone, he turned his back to the others.

Jake looked over at Joanna admiringly, impressed with

the way she'd handled the arrogant physician. And even more impressed with her medical insight. Jake had just assumed that all the information on Ramón Gonzalez was stored in the computer. Joanna knew otherwise. She knew there had to be a larger chart somewhere. And the more comprehensive chart might tell them a lot of important things. Like where he worked and what his occupation was and whether it involved the use of explosives and on and on. All of that information could be on a chart that Jake had overlooked. In the field he knew his way around. In the hospital he needed a Joanna Blalock.

Wales placed the phone down. "They're pulling his chart now. You, of course, realize that the chart can't leave this building."

"But a photocopy of it can," Joanna said promptly. "We'll need two copies."

"Is that an order?" Wales asked curtly.

"It's a request," Joanna said evenly. "But if you like, we can get a court order."

Wales grumbled something unintelligible under his breath, but the last word sounded like *bitch*.

Jake gave the doctor an icy stare. "Would you like to repeat what you just said?"

Wales stared back, but only for a moment. Then he turned away.

"Must not have been too important," Jake muttered as he took out his notepad and began flipping pages back to his earlier interview with the rehabilitation doctors.

He looked down at Bremmer. "So you do all the measurements for the prostheses, right?"

"Just about."

"So you'd see all the patients referred here for artificial limbs?"

"That's right."

"And every one of the patients would first be seen by the receptionist?"

Bremmer nodded. "That's where they check in."

"And then they see the therapist?"

"Correct."

"Do you see them every visit?"

"No, but the therapist does."

"How many therapists do you have here?"

"Four."

"I'll need their names," Jake said.

A pudgy, middle-aged woman came to the door and cleared her throat audibly. "Here's the chart you wanted, Dr. Wales."

Wales pointed to Joanna. "Give it to her."

Joanna placed the chart on top of the computer and quickly thumbed through it. The medical record of Ramón Gonzalez was thin, consisting of only twelve pages. The information in it matched the data stored in the computer. Gonzalez's leg had been amputated because of an osteogenic sarcoma, and the disease had recurred a year later. He was fitted for a prosthesis by Dr. Timothy Bremmer.

Joanna glanced up at Jake. "Gonzalez was seen in the clinic here on a regular basis. His last visit was six weeks ago."

"Who did he see on those visits?" Jake asked.

"It doesn't say."

"It was probably a therapist," Bremmer informed them.

Joanna asked, "Does the same therapist always see the patient?"

Bremmer nodded. "Always."

Joanna went back to the chart. Gonzalez had been seen by an oncology specialist at Memorial. His malignancy had recurred and spread. There were now pulmonary metastases. The oncologist had suggested a biopsy be taken to confirm the diagnosis. Gonzalez had refused, not wanting further treatment. He was told his life expectancy was less than a year.

Joanna turned back to the front sheet of the chart and studied Ramón Gonzalez's personal history. He was twenty-eight years old, a part-time gardener, married, his spouse's name Maria. He lived at—Joanna quickly looked up. "Do we know whether he had children?"

"If it was listed anywhere, it'd be on the front sheet," Bremmer said.

"I don't see it."

The pudgy woman at the door said, "We don't require that information. The front sheet is primarily for billing purposes."

Right, Jake thought sourly. No need to list kids. They couldn't pay the bill. "Why are Ramón Gonzalez's children important here?"

"Because they can tell us whether the osteogenic sarcoma found at the bomb site belonged to their father," Joanna answered.

Jake squinted an eye. "You've got to explain that one to me."

"It would work like a paternity blood test," Joanna explained. "If you know the DNA types of the parents and children, you can state for certain who the father was. So it would just be a matter of doing DNA typing on the mother and children and comparing it with the DNA type of the osteogenic sarcoma. If it fits, Ramón Gonzalez is our man. No ifs, ands or buts."

Jake made a note in his pad and placed a big asterisk by it. "Let's hope he has kids."

Joanna handed the chart to the woman at the door. "We'll need two copies of this."

The woman glanced over to Wales, who hesitated briefly before nodding.

Joanna watched the woman leave, her mind concentrating on the evidence that indicated Ramón Gonzalez was in the West Hollywood explosion. The osteogenic sarcoma and the prosthesis found at the bomb site were probably his, as well as the rose tattoo. But the writing underneath the tattoo may or may not have read "Monterrey." Although he was in all likelihood their man, they didn't have absolute proof.

Joanna sighed wearily and turned to Bremmer. "Did the studies on the piece of prosthesis we gave you reveal anything?"

"Only that it was made here sometime over the past three years."

"How did you determine that?"

"We changed to our current model three years ago," Bremmer explained. "It's an acrylic that is less likely to chip and crack." He rubbed at his chin thoughtfully. "Maybe you should send a piece of it over to Bioengineering to see if they find anything unusual."

"There's no more left," Joanna said. "The remaining fragment was destroyed when they bombed my laboratory."

Bremmer shook his head. "What kinds of animals bomb a hospital?"

Jake said, "The same ones who would bomb a federal building in Oklahoma City."

"But this is a hospital filled with sick people," Bremmer told him. "That makes it somewhat different."

"No, it doesn't," Jake said hoarsely. "Premeditated murder is premeditated murder, no matter where you do it or who you do it to."

"Of course," Bremmer said defensively. "I was just thinking that a hospital would be more of a sanctuary."

"Not to terrorists," Jake said. "They couldn't give a damn less." He took Joanna's arm and turned away. "Let's get those photocopies."

They left the office and walked across the workshop. Behind them they could hear Wales and Bremmer arguing in low voices. Jake slowed and concentrated, trying to overhear. He couldn't make out anything. "I wonder what they're squabbling about."

"Whatever it is, you can bet Bremmer is on the short end of it," Joanna said.

Now they could hear Wales yelling a profanity.

"They don't get along too well, do they?" Jake asked.

"Can you imagine anybody getting along with Wales?"

"You got a point."

They entered a large clinic area. There was only one patient remaining, and he was heading out the door, limping badly on his artificial leg.

"Muy bien, Miguel," the black therapist called after him. *"Hasta la vista."*

"Buenas noches." The Mexican waved back.

Joanna stopped in her tracks.

"What?" Jake asked.

"The therapist speaks Spanish."

"So?"

"Let's see if he treats all the Spanish-speaking patients."

Joanna strolled over to the therapist, Jake a step behind. The name tag on the man's scrub suit read LUCAS. "How are you doing, Lucas?"

"Real good." Lucas was a big, mustached man with a square jaw and hands the size of hams. "I'm a little tired now though."

"I'm Dr. Blalock, and this is Lieutenant Sinclair from the LAPD," Joanna said. "Do you have time to answer a few questions for us?"

"Sure," Lucas said pleasantly. If he was intimidated by them, he didn't show it.

"Do you speak Spanish well?" Joanna asked.

"I get by."

"Well enough to converse with the Mexican patients."

"Oh, yeah," Lucas said easily. "It makes them more comfortable when we talk in their native tongue. You know, they can express themselves better."

"So you look after the Spanish-speaking patients?"

"Most of them."

"Do you know Ramón Gonzalez?"

"Yeah," Lucas said, then wrinkled his brow in thought. "But I haven't seen him for a good six weeks. Is he okay?"

"We're trying to find him," Joanna lied. "Do you recall if he had a tattoo?"

"He had a big one. On his arm," Lucas said promptly, narrowing his eyes as he tried to envision it. "I think it was red roses."

"Was there any writing on it?"

Lucas nodded. "The word 'Monterrey.' It was his hometown, you see. He talked about it all the time."

Joanna and Jake exchanged knowing glances.

Lucas tried to read their expressions but couldn't. "I hope Ramón is all right. I know he was really worried about his cancer coming back."

Jake moved in closer. "Did he talk to you a lot about his illness?"

Lucas nodded again. "He was plenty worried, knowing he was going to leave a young wife behind and all. But he told me he planned to leave her well off."

"How was he going to do that?"

"He was going to strike it rich," Lucas said. "His exact words were, 'There'll be enough money to last her a lifetime.'"

"And where was this money coming from?"

Lucas shrugged. "He didn't say."

"You figure he was telling the truth?"

Lucas nodded a third time. "A man don't lie about things like that."

24

Joanna hurried into her condominium and checked her answering machine for phone messages. There was one call. A new bank wanted to send her a credit card. She switched on her computer to see if there was any E-mail. Nothing.

She kicked off her shoes, reminding herself that it was 9:30 P.M. in New York and that Paul might still be in a meeting. She again wondered if she should try to reach him. No, she quickly decided.

"Long day, huh?" Kate asked, walking into the library.

"Too long," Joanna said and slumped down onto a sofa beside the desk. "Were there any calls?"

"Not while I was here." Kate studied her sister's face, seeing the sadness and knowing there was nothing she could do about it. "I guess he's not going to call."

"I guess," Joanna said quietly.

"Jean-Claude insisted on having chili dogs for dinner. Would you like to join us?"

"I really don't have much appetite."

"Starving yourself isn't going to help."

"I know," Joanna said. "I'll get something later."

Jean-Claude burst into the library, riding a broomstick for a horse. He had on cowboy boots and a toy pistol in a holster.

"Hello, Jean-Claude," Joanna said and reached out to him. "May I have a kiss?"

The little boy carefully placed the broom against the

wall in the far corner of the library. He came over to Joanna and kissed her on both cheeks.

Kate said, "Jean-Claude thinks America is full of cowboys, and he wants to be one."

Joanna kissed her nephew on the nose, again struck by his resemblance to her father. The face. The eyes. All Blalock. "I think you'd be a fine cowboy."

Jean-Claude smiled broadly.

"Okay, my little buckaroo," Kate said, turning her son toward the door and playfully patting his behind, "go watch television until I call you for dinner."

Jean-Claude hesitated, glancing at his broom against the wall.

"I think you'd better let your horse rest for the night," Kate said.

Jean-Claude was almost to the door when he turned and waved to Joanna and threw her a kiss. Then he galloped out of the room.

Joanna began crying the moment the library door closed. She tried to sniff the tears back, but they kept coming. Kate rushed over and held her close.

"I can't stop thinking about him." Joanna sobbed.

Kate hugged her closer. "Time will take care of it."

"I know. But I keep remembering the good things and the wonderful moments."

"Have you thought about calling him back?"

"A thousand times. I even dialed the New York number a few times, but hung up before there was an answer." Joanna reached for a Kleenex and blew her nose. "It's over. Deep down I know it's over."

"Maybe you should give it another chance," Kate suggested. "Maybe he acted so abruptly and coldly because he was in a very difficult situation."

"That's when you find out about a person," Joanna told her. "All the facades and pretenses come down during tough times. That's when you find out what someone is really made of."

"So there's no hope?"

"Not after the second phone call," Joanna said. "His voice was so cold and unforgiving. It was all business, like I was some deal that didn't come through for him."

"He sounds like a first-class bastard to me."

"That's how he turned out. It's too bad I didn't find out sooner."

"So it's over and done?"

"Absolutely."

"Then don't waste your tears over him." Kate grinned.

Joanna smiled back. That was something their father used to tell them when they cried unnecessarily.

"That's better," Kate said, giving Joanna a wink and heading for the door. "Now you fix your face while I see how our chili dogs supreme are doing."

Joanna tilted her head back on the sofa, wondering if her luck with men would ever change. She always seemed to involve herself in no-win relationships. The men were usually good-looking and bright and exciting, but they never lasted over the long term. She considered the possibility that the flaw was really hers, that she subconsciously searched for men she would eventually clash with. Or maybe it was her profession. Maybe she was not capable of putting her career on hold for men or anything else. Hell, she decided finally, we're all flawed one way or another. A picture of Paul du Maurier came into her mind. He was smiling at her. With effort she pushed the image aside.

Joanna walked over to the computer and checked her E-mail again. There were still no messages. Using an index finger, she typed a message to herself that appeared on the screen.

DON'T WASTE YOUR TEARS

Joanna smiled, remembering her father's face and voice and wishing he was still here. He was so wise and kind and patient. Not a day went by that she didn't think about him and the things he used to tell her. But she hadn't thought about his instructions on tears for a long time. And there was more to it than what Kate had just said. What else did he say about tears? What else? Slowly it came to her, and her smile faded. She typed in the last part of her father's words.

DON'T WASTE YOUR TEARS
YOU WILL NEED THEM LATER

25

Eva and Rudy wore Los Angeles Dodgers baseball caps with the bills pulled over their brows. They were sitting in a parked car directly across the street from the apartment building where Maria Gonzalez lived. The sun visors in the car were both pulled down so that pedestrians passing by couldn't see their faces.

"Are all the others accounted for?" Eva asked.

"Yeah," Rudy said, keeping his hands under the dashboard while he inserted a clip of ammunition into his semiautomatic pistol. "The Hernandez and Espinoza families are somewhere down in Mexico. The Reyes have disappeared. According to neighbors, they're headed for southern Arizona."

"So the cops can't get to them, right?"

"Not unless they're magicians."

"What about the fifth guy?" Eva asked, snapping her fingers as she tried to remember his name. "You know, the guy who spoke English so well."

"Alvarez," Rudy said. "His wife moved. Nobody knows where to, although the people I talked to still think she's in East Los Angeles."

"Keep tracking her," Eva ordered. "And when you find her, *kill* her."

"What makes you so sure these guys blabbed everything to their wives?"

"I'm not sure, but we're going to assume they did,"

Eva told him. "We're not going to take any chances. We don't want them talking to the cops."

Rudy shrugged and placed his weapon in the inner pocket of his leather coat. "Hell, the wives won't know anything more than their husbands did. They all thought they were going to rob a bank and leave their families rich. That's all the wives will know."

Eva took a deep breath, wishing Rudy was smarter. He'd be less likely to make mistakes. "But the cops won't buy that story. Not with C-four explosives going off all over Los Angeles."

"Yeah," Rudy conceded. "I guess you're right."

"Cops aren't stupid," Eva reminded him. "And the ones we're up against are plenty smart."

"But not smart enough to figure out that we're going to kill the—"

Eva gave him a hard look. "Keep your mouth shut. You've been told a dozen times never to mention that."

"But there's nobody here but you and me."

"What about the people passing by on the sidewalk who might overhear through your open window?"

Rudy scanned the sidewalk to make certain no one was close, then quickly rolled up the window.

Eva's gaze went to the apartment building across the street. The women who had been sitting on the steps gossiping were disbanding, some moving inside, others walking away. "Go take care of business."

Eva watched Rudy leave the car and stroll to the corner, where he waited for the light to change. Eleven days, she thought, and their target would be dead and meeting his judgment before being sent to eternal hell, where he belonged. He and others like him had ruined the country, opening the gates and letting immigrants flood in from everywhere. No whites, of course. But plenty of blacks and browns and mixed breeds who immediately went on welfare and then bitched that the government wasn't doing more for them. And of course no school prayer and no ownership of guns for citizens to defend themselves with. But the FBI and DEA were allowed plenty of weapons so they could shoot innocent people at will, like they did at Ruby Ridge and Waco and a dozen other places. And don't forget the U.S. marshals, she thought bitterly. They had murdered her family and walked away as if nothing had happened. She would make them pay. She would destroy their very center. She would cut off the serpent's head.

Her eyes went back to the apartment building. A black car pulled up in front of the steps in a no parking zone. Two people exited, a man and a woman. Their backs were to Eva, but she could sense they didn't belong in the neighborhood. They were too well dressed, and their car was too new. She glanced over to the crosswalk. Rudy was on the other side of the street now, no more than twenty yards from the black car.

The man and woman turned to talk, and Eva immediately recognized their faces. *Oh, Christ! Oh, Christ!* It was the detective she'd seen at the West Hollywood bomb site, and next to him was Joanna Blalock, the doctor she'd passed in the corridor while scouting the Pathology Department. Eva stared at Joanna. She looked different without her white coat on, but there was no question it was the same woman.

Now Rudy was only ten yards away from the black car. *Get out of there! Get out of there!* Eva wanted to yell. She saw Rudy reaching inside his coat and knew what was going to happen next. Quickly, Eva turned on the ignition and reached for the gearshift.

Less than five yards away from the detective, Rudy stopped and gestured as if he had forgotten something. He did a casual about-face and returned to the corner, where he patiently waited for the light to change. Then he crossed the street and came back to the car.

Eva's heart was still pounding in her chest. She took a deep breath and tried to calm herself. "Man! That was a cool move."

"What move?" Rudy asked.

"The way you turned around and walked back to the car."

Rudy looked at her oddly. "I came back because I forgot the silencer for my gun."

"You mean you didn't see them?"

"See who?"

"The detective who got out of the black car as you approached the apartment building."

Rudy's eyes almost popped out of his head. "That was a *cop*?"

"The head cop."

"And who was the woman next to him?"

"Joanna Blalock," Eva told him. "She's the forensic pathologist whose lab I blew up."

"Jesus," Rudy muttered, now wiping his forehead with his sleeve. "I was near enough to touch them."

"They're getting too close," Eva said, thinking aloud. She now wished she had used a bigger charge of C-4 on the laboratory. Not only would it have destroyed all the evidence but it would have killed all the witnesses. Stupid, she thought, again wondering why she had underestimated the amount of C-4 needed. "We're only one dumb move away from getting caught."

"That big guy is the head cop, huh?"

"That's right."

"Maybe we should take care of him."

"He's not our major problem," Eva said. "The woman is."

"How do you figure that?"

"Without her the investigation would be nowhere," Eva said, unwrapping a stick of gum and placing it in her mouth. "She's the one putting all the body pieces back together for them. She's the one identifying the victims and pointing the cops in the right direction."

"Do you want me to kill her?"

Eva thought for a moment. The woman would be easier to kill than the cop, and that would make one less headache. But that too could be dangerous. The last thing she wanted was more cops chasing them. What Eva needed more than anything was accurate information. If the cops were too close, she would have to consider calling off the assassination. No, she quickly decided. That was not an option. The setup was so perfect. They'd never get another opportunity like this. She refocused her mind on the two questions she needed answered. What did the cops know? And how close were they to discovering the assassination plan? There were only two people who were privy to that information. Joanna Blalock and the cop with her.

"Do you want me to kill the Blalock woman or not?" Rudy asked again.

"Let's find out what she knows first."

"How do we do that?"

"There are ways," Eva said and drove away from the curb.

Maria Gonzalez stared at the small crucifix in her hands. "My husband is dead, isn't he?"

"I'm afraid so," Joanna said.

Maria nodded slowly. "I knew it. I felt it deep in my bones." She ran a hand through her hair and patted it in place. She was young and pretty, with straight black hair and doelike eyes. "His cancer had returned and was spreading. The doctors told him there was no hope."

"He didn't die from his cancer," Joanna told her. "We think he was killed in an explosion."

Maria furrowed her forehead, not understanding. "At the hospital?"

"No. It was some blocks away," Joanna said vaguely. "Did your husband ever mention explosives or dynamite to you?"

Maria shook her head firmly. "Never."

Joanna studied the young widow's face briefly. There was no expression, no sign of real grief. Maria was nervously twisting the small crucifix.

Outside the apartment a jackhammer started drilling the pavement. The deafening noise came into the living room through a half-open window.

"Excuse me," Maria said and hurried across the room to close the window.

Joanna quickly leaned over to Jake and whispered in his ear. "She's not exactly broken up over the news, is she?"

"You noticed, huh?"

Maria shut the window, and the noise faded. She came back and sat on the edge of her sofa. "There is a leak in one of the big water pipes. The drilling has been going on all week. At times you cannot hear yourself think."

"We won't be much longer," Joanna said, glancing at the widow's wristwatch. It was expensive, with a gold-link band. "So you are certain your husband never mentioned explosives?"

"Not to me."

"And you can't think of any reason why he would be around explosives?"

"No," Maria said at once. "He did not like—" She stopped in midsentence, her eyes suddenly widening. "Did they try to blow up the bank?"

"What bank?" Joanna and Jake blurted out almost simultaneously.

Maria hesitated, not sure how much to confide. Perhaps Ramón was not dead, she thought quickly. Perhaps he'd been caught and was being held by the police. Or maybe he was dead and the other robbers had gotten away. If that was the case, she would still receive

Ramón's share of the money. "He—he talked of robbing a bank. But I never took him seriously."

"Tell me about the bank," Jake said, sensing that she was lying.

"It was only foolish talk," Maria insisted.

"I see," Jake said evenly, nodding as if her answer was satisfactory. He watched her involuntarily breathe a sigh of relief. "By the way, are you a citizen?"

"I have a green card," Maria said, a hint of defiance in her voice.

Jake stared at her, again sensing that she was lying. Green cards were the prize possessions of all aliens. They allowed them to work and live in America with all its privileges.

"Good," Jake said neutrally. "That card gives you a lot of rights, including the right to have an attorney." He gave Maria a long, cold look. "And if you're lying to me, you're going to need an attorney. A real good one."

"But I haven't done anything," Maria protested.

"Withholding evidence in a murder case is a crime," Jake said, now seeing fear in the woman's eyes. "All we want from you is the truth. You give us the facts, and we'll walk out of here."

Maria glanced down at the crucifix. "Nothing will happen to me?"

"Nothing," Jake assured her.

There was an awkward silence. The noise from the jackhammer faded.

"I didn't know he was really going to do it," Maria said softly. "I swear I didn't."

Jake took out his notepad. "Did your husband plan to rob the bank by himself?"

"No. There were others."

"Who?"

"Some people approached Ramón and some of his

friends to rob a bank," Maria said. "Each person would receive a hundred thousand dollars on the day the bank was robbed and an additional hundred thousand a month later. If anyone was caught or got killed, their families would receive the money."

"As long as they didn't talk?"

Maria nodded. "That is correct."

Jake asked, "Did your husband say anything about the people who hired him to rob the bank?"

"He would tell me very little about them," Maria said. "He was warned that if he did they would kill him."

Joanna remembered her conversation with the mother-in-law of José Hernandez and the description she gave of the two who had hired him to pose in hunting attire. The police had tried to reach Hernandez's widow in Guadalajara to corroborate the description, but she had disappeared without a trace. "Were these people gringos?"

Maria nodded again. "Young gringos."

"Was one a woman?"

"Sí. A pretty woman."

"Did she ever speak her name?"

Maria thought back, vaguely recalling a female name Ramón had mentioned once. The only name that came to her now was Evie or something like that. Or was it Ava or Etta? She couldn't be sure. Better not to mention it and cause trouble. If she gave them the wrong name and they thought she was lying, they would make trouble for her, particularly when they found out she didn't have a green card. No. Better not to mention it.

"Well?" Joanna pressed. "Did the gringo woman ever speak her name?"

"I do not think so," Maria said. "But Ramón once heard them talk of an organization they belonged to. It was a name that didn't fit them—like the name of a church group."

"We need that name," Jake urged.

Maria's lips began to move, then stopped and started again. "There was a number that went with it. Ten something."

"An address?" Jake guessed.

"No," Maria said, still concentrating. "It was religious. This was a religious group, I remember thinking." Her eyes suddenly brightened. "The Righteous! The Ten Righteous. That was their name."

· Jake and Joanna exchanged puzzled looks, both unfamiliar with the phrase or organization. Jake flipped a page in his notepad and jotted the information down. "Did they tell your husband the name of their group?"

"No. He overheard one of the gringos speaking on the phone."

Jake asked, "Where did he hear the phone conversation?"

"At their meeting place in West Hollywood."

"Did he give you the address?"

Maria shook her head. "He said only that it was a house."

Yeah, Jake thought sourly. It was only a house that was loaded with enough C-4 to level a row of homes and kill over twenty people. "Was the bank they planned to rob near the house?"

"No, no," Maria said promptly. "Ramón said it was close to Memorial Hospital."

Jake asked, "Was it a Bank of America?"

"He did not say."

Jake turned to Joanna. "Are there any other banks in that area?"

"Not really. There's a Western Federal branch in a supermarket six blocks away."

Too far, Jake thought. Besides, banks in supermarkets never carried that much cash. It had to be the Bank of America he and Joanna had passed walking from Memorial Hospital to the rehab institute. "Did your husband tell you why they picked a bank close to Memorial?"

Maria squinted an eye and thought back before shaking her head. "All he said was that it was the one the gringos and their friend at Memorial wanted to rob."

"What friend at Memorial?" Jake asked quickly.

Maria shrugged. "I do not know. The gringos must have had some friend at the hospital."

The door to the bedroom opened. A handsome, well-built Latino man looked over at Maria. He was bare-chested with a small tattoo just above his nipple. "Is anything wrong, Maria?"

"There is no problem," she told him. "These people need some information on Ramón."

The man's eyes narrowed suspiciously. "Oh?"

"Please close the door. I'll only be a few minutes more."

The man hesitated, then did as he was told.

"A cousin," Maria explained.

"Ah-huh," Jake said, smiling to himself and wondering how long Ramón had been the odd man out. "You said that Ramón and some of his friends were approached to rob the bank. How many men were involved altogether?"

"Four including Ramón."

Jake nodded over to Joanna. That was the number of bodies she had determined were in the house at the time of the explosion. He turned back to Maria. "Do you know the names of the others?"

"No."

"They never visited here?"

"Not that I know of," Maria said. "They were people he only saw at Memorial Hospital."

"I see," Jake said, not seeing at all. Why were the people involved from Memorial? And why did they select a bank near Memorial to rob? The only common denominator was Memorial Hospital, and that made no sense. Jake wrote down the questions and turned a page in his notepad. "So we have four people from Memorial that—"

Joanna held up an index finger, interrupting him. She asked Maria, "Who were these friends of Ramón? Were they patients at Memorial?"

"Yes. In the clinic."

Joanna leaned forward. "At the rehabilitation institute?"

"No. He told me he met them in the cancer clinic."

"So they all had cancer?"

Maria nodded. "All with less than a year to live." With effort she took a deep breath and exhaled. "These men were not thieves. They were just trying to find a way to provide for their families before they died."

Joanna leaned back and let the new information sink in. Now she knew why the tissues found at the West Hollywood bomb site contained malignancies. She also knew how and why the poor Mexican men were selected to participate in the bank robbery. But who was behind all this craziness? And why?

Jake asked, "How many times did Ramón meet with the others in West Hollywood?"

Maria shrugged. "Three or four times, I think."

"What did they do at these meetings?"

"They practiced the robbery, Ramón told me. They rehearsed where their positions outside the bank would be and what to do and when to do it. And they had to learn how to wear their protective vests."

Jake's eyes narrowed as he thought about a Bank of America robbery a few years back in which the two robbers had armed themselves with AK-47 assault rifles and worn body armor. Both were killed by head shots from a police marksman. "Did he tell you what the vest looked like?"

"Ramón said it was made of a thin plastic that had a bright orange color. It didn't feel very heavy."

"Light, huh?"

Maria nodded. "That's what Ramón told me. It was easy to put on and take off."

That didn't sound like body armor, Jake was thinking. Most body armor was heavy and cumbersome and would never be bright orange. That would give a shooter a target to aim at. "Did he ever bring the vest home?"

"No."

Joanna reached for her pen and scribbled a note on Jake's notepad. *Ask me about the orange color later.*

"Right," Jake said, underlining the word *orange*. His gaze went back to Maria. "Did your husband know the date the bank was to be robbed?"

"The nineteenth of April," Maria said without hesitation. "Ramón circled the date on our calendar."

"Show me the calendar," Jake said, closing his notepad.

They walked into a small kitchen, the air heavy with the aroma of spicy food. On the door of a cabinet was a large calendar. April 19 was circled in red crayon. Several other dates had red checkmarks by them.

Jake pointed to the checkmarks. "What are these for?"

"Those are the dates he met with the people in West Hollywood."

Jake put his finger on the last checkmark on the calendar. It was the day the West Hollywood bomb detonated. "Did you see your husband after this date?"

Maria sighed sadly. "That was the last date."

Jake took out one of his cards and stuck it next to the calendar with a thumbtack. "If you remember anything else, you call me at this number. We want names. Names of people. Do you understand?"

Maria nodded nervously, intimidated by the detective's stare.

Jake studied her eyes. "Is there something else you want to tell us?"

"No, *señor.*"

They went back to the living room and headed for the front door. On a side wall was a large painting of Jesus smiling benignly down at them. The portrait was tilted. Jake studied it for a moment before straightening it.

"I have told you everything I know," Maria said. "Please do not make trouble for me."

"If you've told us the truth, you've got nothing to worry about." Jake glanced around the living room once more, feeling that he had overlooked something. "But if you've lied to us, you'll wish to God you hadn't."

"There were no lies."

At the door Joanna stopped and turned back to Maria. "Just one more question. Do you have children?"

Maria's face suddenly closed. "Why is that important?"

"Because your husband was badly mangled in the explosion," Joanna explained. "We are almost certain it was him because of his tattoo and the type of cancer the body had. But to be a hundred percent sure we require DNA studies. Samples of blood from your children would help us with that."

"There are no children," Maria said. "We were married only a short time before Ramón lost his leg. After that he could not—" Maria stopped abruptly and flicked her hand, closing the subject. "There were no children."

Outside the afternoon sun was setting, the sky red and blue and gray. The city workers were loading their jack-hammers into a utility truck.

"Hurley was right," Jake said. "April nineteenth is the day the bombers are waiting for. They're going to blow up something big in Los Angeles on that date, and it sure as hell isn't going to be some bank."

"They might be planning to use the bank bombing as a diversion," Joanna suggested.

Jake considered the possibility. "Maybe," he said. "But a diversion from what?"

"That I can't tell you."

"Crazy, crazy," Jake said, shaking his head. "All that damn C-four couldn't have been just for a bank. And those plastic vests they were supposed to wear were no more body armor than the sports coat I've got on."

"Those orange vests were filled with explosives," Joanna told him. "We found slivers of orange plastic embedded in José Hernandez's hand and in some of the body parts uncovered at the West Hollywood bomb site. We wondered what they were and how they got there. Now I know."

"How can you be so sure?"

"Because the levels of C-four in those plastic bits were sky-high," Joanna said. "My guess is they were wearing explosives-filled vests at the time of the explosion. That's why there were only scraps and shreds of the victims at the bomb site."

Jake's brow went up. "Are you saying they were going to be used as suicide bombers?"

"That's what I'm saying."

"The perfect bomb," Jake said somberly. "You don't have to worry about hiding it or someone finding it or some dog sniffing it out. You just dupe some guy into wearing it and point him in the right direction."

"And they're impossible to stop," Joanna added gloomily.

"Tell me about it," Jake said, opening the car door for her.

Neither of them paid any attention to the car that slowly passed by or to the two occupants wearing baseball caps pulled down over their foreheads.

26

A small, unmanned earthmover lumbered across a grassy field and stopped in front of a miniature white flag. The flag marked the spot where the bloodhounds had bayed and pawed at the ground, indicating the site where the remains of José Hernandez were buried.

A hundred yards away Jake, Farelli and Dan Hurley stood behind a protective metal barrier, watching a television screen. The robot claw on the earthmover was slowly digging up the earth and pushing it aside.

"You figure the bastards might have booby-trapped it just in case?" Farelli asked.

"I've seen it done before," Hurley replied. "And sometimes the booby trap is nastier than the initial bomb. The last one I saw was packed with tenpenny nails so that anyone within a block would get sliced up."

Jake shivered. "They really don't give a shit, do they?"

"They couldn't care less," Hurley said. "The more people they kill and maim the better they like it."

"But why blow up José Hernandez?" Jake asked. "What purpose would that serve?"

"I would guess it was a practice run," Hurley said. "You never know how well a bomb will work until you give it a try."

"In the great outdoors of Southern California."

Hurley nodded. "That's one of the reasons we're the bomb capital of the world. There are a hundred places in

Los Angeles County where you can set off a bomb and nobody would notice or give a damn. But I have to admit, you won't find a better spot than this."

The bomb site was in a remote northern area of the county. It was northeast of Valencia, well off the Interstate Highway 5. There were ravines and valleys and knolls nestled in the hilly terrain. Tall trees and dense shrubs blocked out aerial views of the ground.

"So they told the poor bastard he would be modeling hunting apparel," Jake said, thinking aloud. "Which of course was pure BS. Then they fitted him up with a vest filled with C-four and blew him to bits. All so they could see how well a bomb would work."

"Nice guys," Farelli commented sarcastically.

"But if these guys were really suicide bombers," Jake went on, "what did they need four of them for?"

Hurley shrugged. "Two possibilities come to mind. Either they had four different targets, or they were all going to the same place and blow it to hell and back."

Jake asked, "Which do you think it was?"

"They were all going to the same place for one big bang," Hurley said. "My guess is it's some kind of government facility they're after. And they don't want to leave one brick standing."

"Or one person living," Jake added.

"That too."

Jake's gaze went to the television screen. The little earthmover was now surrounded by mounds of freshly turned earth. Jake kept his eyes on the screen as he talked. "Have you ever heard of some group called the Ten Righteous?"

Hurley shook his head. "Not offhand. Why?"

"Because Maria Gonzalez told us that was the name her husband heard the bombers call themselves."

"Jesus," Hurley hissed under his breath. "These bastards go around blowing up people and killing cops and they call themselves the Ten Righteous. Go figure."

Jake asked, "What's the best way to check it out?"

"Through the FBI Domestic Terrorism Unit," Hurley said. "They've got a computer full of loony-toon groups. I'll run it through first thing this afternoon."

"Which reminds me," Jake said sourly. "I got another call from the FBI this morning. They want to know why we haven't made more progress."

Hurley nodded. "That's their way of telling us they're going to bring in more agents. They're catching hell from Washington on down. People want this case solved pronto."

"I got the feeling that they may try to push us aside."

Hurley shook his head. "They need local guys on this one. They'll keep us around for a while." He took out a notepad and jotted down *the Ten Righteous*. "Got anything else?"

"One more thing," Jake said. "Gonzalez's widow told us her husband once overheard the terrorists talking about *their friend at Memorial*."

Hurley squinted an eye. "You think they had somebody on the inside?"

"Had to," Jake said, nodding. "Somebody had to guide them through Memorial and show them where the body parts were stored."

"Maybe, maybe not," Hurley said, unconvinced. "They could have found out the location of the forensics laboratory by asking at the information desk. And we clued them in to where the work was actually being done. We had a cop sitting right outside the door."

"We had *two* cops sitting outside *two* doors," Jake argued. "The bombers didn't bother with the door that read 'Department of Forensic Pathology, Joanna Blalock, M.D., Director.' They went directly to the cold storage room that was unmarked. Somebody pointed it out to them. And somebody probably told them when was the best time to plant the bomb."

Hurley slowly nodded. "And they must have had some idea of the dimensions of the room, because they knew just how much C-four to use to destroy it without blowing down half the hospital."

Farelli couldn't believe what he was hearing. "So you think some doc was involved in all this?"

"It could be anyone," Jake told him. "Doctor, nurse, technician, you name it. But whatever it is, he's hooked in with these terrorists big-time."

Hurley took out a notepad. "How many people work at Memorial?"

"Over a thousand," Jake said.

Hurley grumbled. "And we'll have to put every damn one of their names through the computer."

"How long will that take?"

"Too long."

"We're home!" a bomb squad sergeant called out from the far end of the metal barrier. He deftly turned a knob on a remote-control box.

All eyes went to the television screen. The earthmover was lifting a big duffel bag from the hole in the ground. The metal claw of the machine ripped into the cloth bag, and its contents spilled out onto the grass. A television camera slowly magnified and scanned each piece of debris.

"So far so good," Hurley said quietly.

From a distance two bomb squad members in full body armor cautiously approached the earthmover. They moved with measured steps, keeping their eyes glued to the ground as they neared the heaped-up earth. Carefully they examined the torn duffel bag and its spilled contents and the hole in the ground from which it came. Using long-handled shovels, they sifted through the mounds of earth. Finally they gave the all-clear signal.

Hurley led the way around the metal barrier and across the field. The grass was soft and green and gave off a fresh springtime aroma. Above, the sky was blue, with puffs of white clouds and not a trace of smog. Jake looked up at the beautiful day, wondering if it had been this pretty when the terrorists brought José Hernandez to this spot to blow him to bits. The poor bastard probably thought he was going to make some easy money and go home to his wife. The only things going to José's home in Mexico now were his body parts in a sealed casket.

A putrid smell arose from the duffel bag and the debris around it. Jake could see what looked like a part of a chest with a rib sticking out. Next to it was a silver belt buckle and a piece of pants still attached to it.

Jake used a stick to turn the buckle right side up. On it were the initials JH. The pants beneath it appeared to be blue jeans. There were small brass studs on the lining of a pocket.

"Ain't much left of him," Farelli said, holding his hand over his nose.

"Yeah," Jake said sourly, now probing the pocket with his stick. Out came a handkerchief, then a small piece of paper stuck to it.

Hurley snapped on a pair of latex gloves and picked the paper up. It was torn and partially shredded, and he could make out only a few letters and numbers.

EV
2 FL

"What the hell does this mean?" Hurley asked, more to himself than the others.

Jake looked over Hurley's shoulder. "It's not a telephone number, that's for sure."

"Maybe the FL stands for Florida," Hurley guessed. "But if that were the case it should have the name of a city in front of it, not a number."

Farelli peeked in at the note. "Is there a city in Florida that's called by a number rather than a name? In South Carolina, for example, there's a city called Ninety Six. My wife has a cousin there."

"We'll check it out," Hurley said and placed the piece of paper in a plastic envelope. "Meanwhile we've got to sift through every mound of dirt here looking for the other part of this paper." He stared into the deep hole, watching ants and other insects making their way down. "We need a name, a person we can go after."

With the toe of his shoe, Jake moved around the remaining debris. There were large, irregularly shaped fragments of pottery scattered about. Jake studied them at length before deciding they were made of some type of tan-colored ceramic material. "What the hell would they have flowerpots out here for?"

"Beats me," Hurley answered. "Maybe they had him holding something they made out of clay. You know, like a prop to make him feel he was really modeling."

Farelli knelt down to get a closer look at an elongated piece of ceramic. It was tubular, with a thumb and part of a finger at its end. "Son of a bitch!"

"What?" Jake asked.

"It's not pottery," Farelli said, holding up the ceramic arm. "It's the arm from a mannequin."

The detectives quickly rummaged through the ceramic rubble. They found a piece of a head, a leg with its knee flexed, another arm, another piece of head with half a nose still recognizable.

"What the hell are they using mannequins for?" Jake asked.

"My guess is they wanted to determine the killing range of the blast," Hurley answered, now scanning the trees nearby for damage that could have been caused by the bomb. "You can do that by placing mannequins at various distances from the blast center. An explosion that blows a mannequin to pieces will easily kill a man."

Jake nodded at Hurley's reasoning. "Can you imagine the carnage if four suicide bombers were strategically placed in a crowded place, like a shopping mall or an athletic event?"

"Yeah, I can imagine," Hurley said darkly. "But the domestic terrorists in this country don't work that way. It's not their style. They're different from the Middle East terrorists."

"How do you mean?"

"I mean killing a lot of people is usually not their main objective," Hurley explained. "They go after government institutions, like courthouses and federal buildings."

"Like the one in Oklahoma City."

"Exactly," Hurley said. "So why the mannequins? They don't have a damn thing to do with destroying a building."

"Maybe the terrorists want to destroy the building *and* kill all the people inside," Jake suggested.

Hurley shook his head. "They usually don't go after ordinary citizens."

"They might if the ordinary citizens happen to be FBI or ATF agents."

"Good point," Hurley agreed, taking out his notepad and scribbling a note. He would recommend that all federal buildings in the Greater Los Angeles area be placed on high alert on April nineteenth, particularly those that housed large numbers of federal agents.

Farelli recovered more parts from mannequins. A hand, a foot, a half buttock with a smear of blood on it.

He put on latex gloves and placed the bloodstained buttock into a plastic bag. "Should we send this over to the doc's laboratory?"

Jake nodded, then turned his attention to the torn duffel bag. Using a stick as a probe, he extracted more mannequin fragments and a piece of clothing that appeared to be part of a T-shirt. He probed in deeper and felt his stick come up against something very firm. Carefully he removed the square-shaped, dark object. It was a leather wallet. "Well, well. Look at what we have here."

Farelli stood on his tiptoes and peeked over Jake's shoulder. "Hell! The insides are all blown away."

"Ripped away," Jake corrected him. "You can still see the threads where the inner pockets were torn out. Chances are a human hand jerked out those inner pockets."

"To make sure there weren't any papers or identification items hidden away," Hurley said dispiritedly.

"So we've got a torn-up empty wallet," Farelli said.

Jake smiled thinly. "Oh, we may have more than that. A lot more."

Farelli studied the wallet again and saw nothing new. "Show me."

"Take your wallet and let it drop to the ground." Jake stepped back and watched Farelli's wallet hit the grass. "Now pick it up and give it to me."

Farelli stooped down and handed the wallet to Jake. "Here you go."

"Look where your thumb and fingertips are."

Farelli stared at his fingers for several seconds as he turned the wallet from side to side. Suddenly his eyes widened. "Fingerprints! The guy who picked up the wallet to rip it apart left his fingerprints."

"On smooth oily leather," Jake added. "It's a perfect surface for prints."

"Lord knows I hope you're right," Hurley said. "But the guy might have been wearing gloves and left no prints."

"That's possible," Jake conceded. "But let me ask you a question. What would you do with gloves—particularly those that are bloodstained—after you'd used them?"

"I'd discard them," Hurley said at once.

"Would you take them back to your car first?"

"No. I'd—" Hurley stopped in midsentence and nodded to himself. "If he were wearing gloves he would have stripped them off and buried them."

"Where?"

"In the duffel bag."

Jake picked up the duffel bag with his stick and turned it inside out. "No gloves."

27

Jake could sense the somber mood the moment he entered the forensics laboratory. The technicians were huddled together talking in hushed voices. Lori McKay was staring at the computer screen in Joanna's office. On the desk beside her was a bunch of flowers with a card attached.

"Where's Joanna?" Jake asked.

"She left early," Lori said. "She wasn't feeling well."

"What was wrong?"

"A phone call from a guy in New York."

"And?"

"And she listened, then left her office in tears."

"How did you know she was talking to a guy in New York?"

"I went out after her and caught her in the parking lot. She told me all about it."

Jake glanced down at the bouquet of flowers. On the card he could make out the word *Love*. "Are they getting back together?"

"You'll have to ask her."

Jake hesitantly knocked on the front door of Joanna's condominium. He was now sorry he had come. The questions he had for her weren't crucial and could have been asked later. But he wanted to see her, and he wanted to know if she was getting back together with her new boyfriend. Jake knocked again.

Kate opened the door. "Hello, Jake. Come on in."

"How is she doing?" Jake asked.

"Not too bad, considering the emotional roller coaster she's been on."

"I thought it was over between them."

"So did she."

Jean-Claude came galloping into the living room on his broomstick. He was wearing a cowboy hat that was tilted badly off to one side. "Jacques!"

"Hello, Jean-Claude," Jake said warmly. He reached down and tickled the toddler's stomach, making him laugh. Then Jake carefully straightened the child's cowboy hat. "Now you look like a real cowboy. Go get those bad guys."

Jean-Claude happily rode out of the living room and into the den, where a television set was playing loudly.

Jake turned to Kate. "Where's Joanna?"

"In the library."

Jake knocked on the library door and entered. Joanna was seated at her desk, staring at the phone. A small wastebasket beside her was overflowing with used Kleenexes.

"I hear the guy called again," Jake said.

Joanna nodded. "Bad news travels fast."

"What happened?"

"He told me he loved me and that the reason he acted so badly was the pressure he was under," Joanna said unemotionally. "He had closed his deal successfully and things were great. Now we could start again."

"And what did you say?"

"That I wasn't a lightbulb he could turn off and on," Joanna continued. "That really set him off. He said some very unpleasant things and harped on the fact that I wasn't married and approaching middle age. He said I was too fixed in my ways and would never get married."

"Not as long as you keep dating horses' asses like him," Jake added.

Joanna managed a weak grin. "I'll be more selective in the future."

"Do you feel like doing some work?"

"There's no way I could even begin—" Joanna stopped and stared up at Jake, trying to read his face. "You've got some new evidence you can't figure out. Is that it? Is that why you're here?"

"Naw. I came around to make sure you were all right."

"Liar," she said, smiling faintly.

"Well, there are one or two things," Jake admitted.

Joanna sighed wearily. "Tell me what you've got."

Jake told her about the buried duffel bag that contained José Hernandez's remains and the blown-apart mannequins. As he gave her the details, he watched Joanna nod and mentally sift through the findings, separating the important from the irrelevant. Now she was asking questions about the mannequin pieces, questions that even he hadn't thought about.

"Where did they get those mannequins?" Joanna asked.

Jake shrugged. "Probably stole them."

"Or maybe bought them," Joanna speculated. "You'll have to check out all the places that sell mannequins, particularly wholesale outlets."

"Maybe there's a trademark on them," Jake said, following her line of thought.

"Or a store label or marking of some sort."

Jake winked at her. "You're not so useless after all."

Joanna took a deep breath, the sadness now returning to her face. "I wouldn't be of any real help to you, Jake. I'd be distracted. I couldn't hold my concentration, and I'd miss things and make mistakes. Believe me, I'd be a liability, not an asset."

"Maybe you're right," Jake said, not believing it for a

moment. Joanna Blalock at fifty percent efficiency was better than most investigators working at full speed on their best day. He would have to think of a way to convince her of that. "Can I show you one more piece of evidence that's got us stumped?"

"Sure," Joanna said unenthusiastically.

Jake gave her the torn piece of paper found in José Hernandez's jean pocket.

Joanna studied the paper:

EV
2 FL

"It means nothing to me," she said.

"It's obviously not a phone number, huh?" Jake asked.

"No. It's not that." Joanna tried to concentrate, but her mind refused to cooperate. She thought about Paul again and the flowers he had sent and how thoughtful he'd sounded at first. Then the anger and bitterness had spewed out and he'd shown his real self.

"I don't know," she said and pushed the scrap of paper away. Her gaze went to the calendar on her desk. She had written a note on it, reminding herself of a lunch date with Kate. It read:

KATE
THE IVY
2 P.M.

Joanna reached for the torn paper and studied it once more. She wondered if it was a reminder note of some sort. Those types of notes usually had the name of the person to be met first, the meeting place next. Her eyes suddenly narrowed. "What was the name of the street in West Hollywood where the bomb went off? Didn't it start with an *F*?"

Jake took out his notepad and hurriedly thumbed through it. "Here we go. It was Fletcher Drive. Two one two two Fletcher Drive."

"That's what the *2 FL* probably stands for."

Son of a bitch, Jake thought. It was right in front of his eyes and he missed it. "What about the *EV*?"

"I'd guess it was the first letters of a person's name."

"Maybe Evelyn or Eva or Eve," Jake guessed, thinking about the female terrorist. "We can have Hurley run it through their computer file on domestic terrorists."

"And now we know for certain that José Hernandez was a part of all this," Joanna said. "He was at that West Hollywood house—or at least was planning on being there."

Jake looked at Joanna admiringly, now wondering if they would ever have gotten the answer without her.

"What?" Joanna asked.

"Nothing," Jake said, needing her almost as much as he loved her. He thought about what his world would have been like if she had married her ex-boyfriend. Empty as hell, he decided.

Joanna reached for Jake's cigarette and absently puffed on it. "Damn, it hurts. It hurts so much, Jake."

"I know," he said. "But sitting in this room isn't going to help."

"I need to be alone for a while," Joanna said softly. "I need time to put the pieces back together."

"You'll have to do that later."

Joanna stared at Jake, her face hardening. "You're not even going to let me get my head on straight, are you?"

"Do it another time," Jake said unsympathetically.

"You go to hell!" Joanna blurted out. "And you can take your goddamn case with you."

"A lot of people are going to die, Joanna," Jake said evenly. "Those blown-apart mannequins represent human beings who are going to be ripped into pieces. And only

God knows how many will die. Ten. Twenty. A hundred. Maybe even more."

"And you think I'll be able to prevent that?"

"You just might," Jake said.

"Chances are my presence won't make a damn bit of difference, one way or the other."

Jake walked over to a hanging skeleton in the far corner of the room. He pushed it gently and watched it swing back and forth. "This I can guarantee you, Joanna. If a building filled with people is blown to smithereens while you're sitting on your ass in this library, you'll spend the rest of your life asking yourself if you could have made a difference."

"You don't give up, do you?"

"No, I don't." Jake gave the life-size skeleton another push. "And I'll tell you why. I keep seeing those body parts we found at the West Hollywood bomb site. I keep seeing that fireman walking out of the rubble carrying a dead child. I keep seeing those images, even in my dreams. Now those images may not bother you, but they bother the hell out of me."

"All you can see is this case," Joanna said and looked away.

"All I can see are a bunch of terrorists who are going to kill again unless we stop them."

"For just a few minutes, can you think about *me* and what I'm going through right now?" Joanna asked. Her lower lip began to quiver, and she bit down on it. "Is that asking too much?"

Jake stomped over to Joanna and picked her up out of her chair. "Now, you listen to me, and listen good. I care about you more than anybody on the face of the earth. And if you don't realize that by now, it's your problem. And I do know how much you're hurting, and I wish to God there was something I could do about it. Like take you to Cancún and sit on a white sand beach and hold you and tell you everything is going to be all right and that the pain will pass and life will go on. I wish I could do these things, but I can't because I have a bunch of murdering bastards I have to catch first." He held her out at arm's length. "Am I getting through to you?"

Joanna nodded and tried to sniff back the tears welling up. "Would you really do all those things for me?"

"And more." Jake brought her close and hugged her tightly. "You just hang on to me. I won't let you fall."

"Oh, Jake!"

The cellular phone in Jake's coat pocket rang. He touched Joanna's nose with his index finger, then reached for the phone and spoke briefly.

Joanna watched Jake's face tighten. His eyes went icy. "What?" she asked.

"It's Farelli," Jake said, his hand over the phone. "He's in Maria Gonzalez's apartment."

"And?"

"She's been murdered," Jake said. "And whoever did it tortured her first."

28

Farelli was waiting for them in the hall outside Maria Gonzalez's apartment. The air was warm and still and filled with a nauseating odor.

"I hope you don't have full stomachs," Farelli warned.

"Bad, huh?" Jake asked.

"Double bad," Farelli said and waved his hand, trying to stir the air. "She messed herself while they were slicing her up."

Jack reached in his pocket for a small jar and opened it. He and Joanna placed small amounts of cream on the tips of their index fingers and dabbed it under each nostril. The cream was mentholated and would block out the strongest stench.

"Tell us what you've got," Jake said.

Farelli took out his notepad and quickly flipped pages. "All morning the neighbors noticed a bad smell coming from the apartment. They contacted the building's owner, who finally got here at two-forty p.m. He's the one who found her."

"Did anyone other than the owner go into the apartment?" Jake asked.

"Not according to him. He saw the body and got the hell out of there, locking the door behind him. Then he called the police."

"How did they know to contact us?"

"A black-and-white unit was the first on the scene. They saw your card next to the body."

Farelli led the way inside. The living room looked as if a hurricane had gone through it. The sofa and chairs were turned upside down, their cushions and lining torn wide open. Cotton and foam stuffing were strewn about the floor. Even the dining table was turned on its side with its legs ripped off.

"I wonder what they were looking for," Jake said.

"Whatever it was, they must have wanted it bad," Farelli said.

They stepped back as a detective from the Crime Scene Unit turned the table right side up and began dusting for prints. Another member of the unit was carefully examining the large picture of Jesus on the wall. Someone had slashed through it, leaving a gaping hole in the canvas.

"And nobody saw a damn thing, right?" Jake asked.

"If they did they're not talking," Farelli answered. His foot came down on a wad of cotton stuffing and crushed something underneath it. He moved the cotton aside and saw a woman's gold wristwatch. "Do you think all this is connected to the terrorists?"

"Could be," Jake said, sensing that it was and still wondering what they wanted.

"Well, I'll tell you this," Farelli went on. "This wasn't some run-of-the-mill robbery. And it wasn't done by one of the local Mexican gangs either. They steal and kill, but they don't torture. That's not their style."

"It's still possible some gang did it," Joanna suggested, her voice flat and somewhat distant. "Maybe they thought she had something valuable hidden away."

Farelli studied Joanna's face for a moment. Something about her was different, but he couldn't put his finger on it. Something was off. "Are you okay, Doc?"

"I'm fine," Joanna assured him.

"Good," Farelli said, not believing her. "But this wasn't just some robbery by locals, and I'll tell you why. We found her purse emptied out on the kitchen floor. Her wallet had forty dollars and some credit cards in it. The local guys would never have left that behind."

Or the gold wristwatch on the floor, Joanna was thinking. She should have known to ask whether other things, like jewelry or money, were missing. That was the important clue in determining whether robbery was the motive. And it had gone right by her. Damn it! Get your brain in gear!

Farelli applied an additional dose of mentholated cream beneath his nostrils. He took a deep breath, readying himself. "Twenty years on the force and you think it can't get any worse. And then it does."

Joanna and Jake stopped at the kitchen door, stunned by what they saw. Maria Gonzalez's nude body was taped into a highbacked dinette chair. Her ankles and legs, hands and arms, head and neck were fastened to the chair by masking tape. She couldn't have moved an inch. Even her mouth was taped shut. Her body seemed to be covered with a thousand cuts, all of them outlined by crusted blood. But the most gruesome feature was her face, lacerated and bleeding and distorted by pure terror.

"Oh, my God!" Joanna murmured, forcing herself to look.

Jake swallowed hard. He had never seen anything like this, and he hoped to God he never would again. He wondered how long it had taken her to die.

Girish Gupta was examining the floor behind the corpse. He stood and dusted off his pants legs, then came over to Jake and Joanna. He was wearing a mask and long rubber gloves. "This is savagery beyond belief," Gupta said, shaking his head slowly. "What kind of person would do something like this?"

Some psychopathic asshole like Charlie Manson, Jake wanted to say. But he didn't see any of the usual signs that the real crazies left behind. Like notes or messages written in blood on the wall. And there was no evidence that this was some type of ritual slaying either. Jake moved in closer, now noticing a white powdery substance around many of the cuts. "What's the white stuff?"

"Salt," Gupta said grimly. "They rubbed salt into her wounds to make the pain even worse."

The stench of human excrement was breaking through the mentholated cream beneath Jake's nostrils. He applied more cream, then turned to Joanna. "Do you want to take a look?"

"I guess," she said, trying to focus her mind. Outside she heard a police helicopter coming closer and closer. It reminded her of the helicopter ride she and Paul had taken from San Francisco to Carmel. And the ride back the next evening had been so spectacular, with the lights of San Francisco twinkling in the darkness.

"Is something wrong?" Jake asked.

"No," Joanna said. "I'm just waiting for the noise to die down."

"Between the helicopter and the jackhammers outside, the noise has been almost incessant," Gupta complained. "You cannot hear your own voice. We tried closing the window, but the smell became intolerable."

Jake looked over to Farelli. "Why the helicopter?"

"A neighbor saw somebody on a rooftop. It turned out to be an old man feeding his pigeons."

Joanna snapped on a pair of latex gloves and forced herself to concentrate on the victim's body. Push your grief aside for now, she told herself, hoping her brain would listen. She slowly circled the body, paying particular attention to the cuts. They were all small—no more than an inch or two in length—and deep. No part of Maria's body had been spared. Now Joanna was studying the victim's head. There was a vertical gash over the left temporal area and a black-and-blue swelling along the jawline.

Joanna glanced at Farelli. "Whoever it was, they forced their way in."

Farelli nodded. "The door chain was ripped off."

Joanna closed her eyes and tried to reconstruct the crime. Images flashed through her mind. The broken door chain. The gash over the temple. The black-and-blue swelling on her jawline. The gold wristwatch on the floor in the living room. All of the pieces suddenly came together. Joanna opened her eyes. "Maria Gonzalez didn't know these people. She had never seen them or heard their voices."

Jake quickly scanned Maria's body, looking for the clues Joanna had seen. "How can you be sure of that?"

"It happened this way," Joanna said quietly, again visualizing the events. "There is a knock on the door. Maria comes to answer it, but there is no peephole. She asks who's there. Someone answers, but she doesn't recognize the voice. Cautiously she opens the door, leaving the chain in place. The killer slams the door into her head, breaking the door chain in the process."

Jake asked, "What's the evidence to show that actually happened?"

Joanna pointed to a deep gash on Maria's temple. "This wound is vertical and wide, not short and narrow like the others. It was made by a blunt edge, such as the side of the door. So now we have an explanation for the broken door chain and the unusual gash on her head."

"And that knocked her out," Farelli concluded.

"No. That knocked her down," Joanna went on. "She tried to get up, but he was on top of her in a flash. Then he slugged her on the jaw and knocked her out." Joanna pointed to Maria's jawline. "You can see the black-and-blue area here."

Gupta stepped in for a closer look at the traumatized area. He had missed it altogether, just as he had missed the significance of the forehead gash. He would never have related those findings to the broken door chain, never in a million years. He wondered if Joanna Blalock was really that brilliant; perhaps she had some remarkable psychic power that allowed her to see into the past. Whatever it was, she made most medical examiners look like amateurs. Gupta leaned over and carefully examined the victim's hands and arms, searching for defensive wounds. There were no bruises or abrasions. "She didn't have a chance to defend herself from the blows."

"Maybe she did," Joanna said. "We found her wrist-watch on the living room carpet. Perhaps she brought her hand up to defend herself and the killer's fist knocked the watch off her wrist."

Psychic, Gupta decided. Joanna Blalock had to be part psychic.

Joanna went back to studying the wounds on Maria's breasts. "What do you think was used to make these cuts?"

"Something very sharp," Gupta said. "Like a scalpel."

After a pause, Joanna said, "I don't think so. Scalpels would make longer and wider slashes. I'd bet on a razor."

Jake's eyes narrowed. "And the killer wouldn't have walked out of here with a bloody razor in his pocket."

Joanna nodded. "He would have chucked it."

"Into a trash can or down the garbage disposal," Jake said, thinking aloud. "And there's only one way to hold a razor."

"Between the thumb and index finger."

"That damn razor could have a wonderful set of prints on it." Jake quickly turned to Farelli. "Check out all the garbage cans, particularly those in the hall and near the elevator. Is there a Dumpster in the rear?"

"Yeah," Farelli said. "Near the back door."

"Check that too."

As Farelli hurried from the room, the jackhammers outside started up again. Joanna and Jake looked at each other and exchanged knowing glances, both thinking the same thought. Maria Gonzalez could have screamed her lungs out and nobody would have heard her above the noise of the jackhammers.

"What the hell did they want?" Jake asked again. "And why did they do this to her?"

"That I can't answer," Joanna said and began circling the corpse once more.

Jake watched Joanna as she searched for more clues, now totally immersed in the case. Good, he thought. At least for now her sadness and broken heart were set aside. But that wouldn't last. The pain would return. It always did. Particularly at night, when you were alone with your thoughts.

"Want to take a look at this?" Joanna asked after pulling back the strip of tape covering Maria's mouth. Her lower lip was almost bitten off. "The pain was so bad she bit through her lips."

Jake studied the chewed lip, then glanced down at the woman's genitalia. There were cuts there too. He looked away, disgusted.

"So vicious," Joanna said softly. "It defies description."

Farelli came back into the kitchen waving a handful of twenty-dollar bills. "Hey, Jake! Look what the boys found in the bedroom closet."

"How much is there?"

"Over two grand," Farelli said, flipping through the stack of twenties. "Maybe this is what they were after."

"Maybe," Jake said skeptically. "But I don't think so. With the pain she was going through, she would have given up her own mother."

"And the thought of being cut and disfigured," Joanna added, shivering. "She would have given up anything to avoid that."

Farelli said, "They found something else in the back of the closet."

"What?" Jake asked.

"A Latino type with a tattoo over his nipple and a bullet hole in his head."

"Her cousin," Jake commented dryly.

"Who?"

"Nothing," Jake said. "Make sure to check those bills for prints. That's probably some of the money the bombers gave her husband."

"Right. By the way, no razor blade yet."

"Keep looking."

Jake turned back to Joanna. "It was something else they wanted. Something they were willing to kill her for. What the hell could it be?"

Joanna shrugged. "Only one person in this room knows for sure, and she's dead."

Jake clasped his hands behind his back and began pacing the floor, talking to himself. "She's in excruciating pain. She'd tell them anything they wanted to know. Anything. But she doesn't. Why not? Why doesn't she answer their questions?"

Joanna thought for a moment. "In general, there are two reasons why people won't answer a question. Either they don't want to or they have no idea what the answer is."

"So you're saying she may not have known what the hell they were talking about?"

"It's a possibility."

Jake started to circle the kitchen once more, again grumbling to himself. He stopped in front of a wall cabinet to have a cigarette. As he reached for the pack, his eyes focused in on the side of the cabinet. "Where's the calendar that was up here?"

Gupta said, "It's on the dinette table next to your card."

"Did you put them there?" Jake asked at once.

Gupta shook his head. "They were there when I arrived. No one has touched them. They had some blood smudges on them, so we're going to check them carefully for prints."

"Son of a bitch! Son of a bitch!" Jake pounded a fist into his palm. "Those bastards were here."

Jake hurried over to the table and quickly examined

the calendar and the card with his name and phone number on it. There were smudges of blood on them but no obvious fingerprints. Jake's gaze went from the table to Maria's body to the chair between them. He pointed to the empty chair. "One of the terrorists sat here and showed Maria Gonzalez the calendar with the dates marked. They probably focused in on April nineteenth, which was circled in red."

Joanna nodded. "They thought she really knew what was going to happen on that date, and she didn't. They kept torturing her for information she didn't have."

Jake nodded back. "And they knew we'd been here. They wanted to know everything she had told us."

Farelli looked at Jake quizzically. "How could the terrorists be so certain you'd been here?"

"I left my calling card," Jake said hoarsely.

Farelli shook his head. "Uh-uh. That doesn't work."

"Why not?"

"Because the terrorists didn't see your card until *after* they broke in. They must have known beforehand that you two had been here." He scratched at his ear. "Hell, that's why they busted in here to begin with. Otherwise why would they bother with a young widow who's an illegal alien? She sure as hell isn't going to the police or the FBI."

"But how could they have known we interrogated Maria Gonzalez?" Jake asked. "We only got her address yesterday afternoon from the—" His face suddenly went cold as he turned to Joanna. "Did you talk with anyone about our visit here yesterday?"

"No," Joanna said promptly.

"Me neither. Except to Lou and Hurley, I haven't mentioned it to a soul." Jake lit a cigarette and spat a bit of tobacco from his lip. "Which means we've got a leak. Somebody passed that information on to the terrorists."

"And it had to be someone at the rehabilitation institute," Joanna said. "They're the ones who gave us Maria

Gonzalez's address. They were the only ones who knew we were coming here."

Jake held up a hand and began counting on his fingers. "Let's see now. There were the two doctors, Wales and Bremmer. And Lucas, the black therapist. And the gal who brought the chart in from the file room."

"And the receptionist," Joanna added.

"And anyone else at the institute who they might have talked with. We're going to have to check out the whole damn place and everybody associated with it." Jake tapped a finger against his chin, his eyes drifting back to the calendar and the notation "Friend at Memorial." It was partially obscured by a smudge of blood. "Maybe it was their so-called friend at Memorial. Maybe that was their source."

Jake took out his cell phone and called Dan Hurley. He told Hurley briefly about the new findings and asked him to concentrate his computer search on the staff and employees at the rehab institute. "And *EV* may represent the first letters of one of the terrorists' names." Jake pressed the phone to his ear. "Yeah. Like Evelyn or Eva. . . . Yeah, it could be the female terrorist. . . . I haven't seen her picture. I'll check with Farelli on that."

Jake put the cell phone away and turned to Farelli. "Have you seen the police artist's sketch of the female terrorist?"

"Yeah," Farelli said, reaching into his inner coat pocket. "I got a copy just before I came over here."

Jake studied the sketch at length. The terrorist was young, in her early thirties, with thin lips and high cheekbones. She was attractive, but there were no distinguishing features or marks. Jake visualized her as being thin and bright and middle class. And deadly as hell.

Farelli said, "There's some uncertainty about her hair. The technician who saw her says it was pulled back, like Grace Kelly used to wear hers. The cop in the lobby who thinks he saw her says it was just cut short."

Joanna stared at the sketch, her mind flashing back to an attractive woman, stepping off the elevator. "It was pulled back."

"Are you sure?" Jake asked quickly.

Joanna nodded, still studying the portrait. "I'm positive."

"How accurate is the sketch?"

"It's not bad," Joanna said. "But the lips are too thin and the cheekbones a little too high."

Jake rubbed his hands together, pleased. A really good picture was what they needed. It would give them a face to chase. "Have you got time to talk with our sketch artist today?"

"Sure."

Jake carefully folded the sketch, then glanced around the kitchen to see if he'd forgotten anything. He stared at Maria Gonzalez's tormented face before turning to Girish Gupta. "Would you mind if Dr. Blalock did the autopsy?"

"Not at all," Gupta said in a clipped British accent. "But I would very much like to assist."

"Is nine a.m. good for you?" Joanna asked.

"That would be most convenient." Gupta was about to turn away, then he looked back at Joanna. "Oh, by the way, I have the number of my friend in Montreal for you."

"What friend?" Joanna asked, caught off guard.

"Surely you remember," Gupta said. "Last month I told you about my friend who is on the pathology staff at McGill University in Montreal, and you asked me to obtain his number for you. Don't you recall?"

"Oh, yes," Joanna said weakly. She had wanted to talk with the pathologist about possible forensic openings at the Montreal medical school. In her mind's eye she saw Paul du Maurier smiling and waving to her. All of her sadness returned. "Just leave the number with my office, please."

Gupta studied the change in her expression. "Is there something wrong?"

"No," Joanna said, trying to keep her voice even. "It's just that the room is getting a little stuffy."

Jake and Joanna left the apartment and took the elevator down. It moved in a slow, jerky way and made a sound like it needed oil. A small fan above them barely stirred the air.

"I did all right for a while," Joanna said quietly.

"You did damn good," Jake said and gave her shoulder a quick squeeze. "You held up great."

"But I'm about to come undone."

"Can you keep it together until we get to the car?"

"I'll try."

The elevator door opened, and they quickly walked down a hall and out the front door. The sidewalk was blocked off in both directions with crime scene tape. Uniformed police were everywhere. Across the street a large crowd had gathered, some with binoculars hoping for a better view. The windows of the surrounding apartment buildings were all open, people peering out and talking loudly in Spanish.

"Let's get a drink," Jake said, opening the car door.

"I'm not in the mood," Joanna said as she ducked to get in.

The door window suddenly exploded and shattered into a thousand pieces. Then the rear window blew out with a loud bang. In an instant Jake pushed Joanna down onto the front seat and lay atop her.

He heard the crowd screaming as they scattered in panic. Policemen were yelling, "Get down! Get down!" Then there were more shots. It sounded like a high-powered rifle firing from above. Maybe from a rooftop, Jake thought, concentrating his hearing and waiting for the next round.

Everything went quiet. Seconds ticked off, and the silence seemed to deepen. A baby cried out briefly, then the stillness returned.

Joanna lay motionless beneath Jake, but he could hear her breathing. "Are you okay?"

"I—I think so," she whispered.

"Stay down and don't move."

In the background they heard police radios with officers trying to communicate through the static. Somewhere in the distance there were sirens and the sound of an approaching helicopter. Jake considered turning on the ignition and making a run for it. But he would still have to look through the windshield, and that would expose part of his head. He stayed put.

"There he is!" a uniformed cop yelled out. "On the rooftop across the street!"

Suddenly there was a barrage of gunshots. Police fired round after round with pistols and rifles and shotguns. The noise was deafening.

Above, the helicopter was returning. Its sound drowned out that of the gunfire. The noise was so loud and near that Jake wondered if the helicopter was going to land.

"Hold your fire! Hold your fire!" a voice commanded over the helicopter's loudspeaker. "You're firing at the old man who was feeding his pigeons."

The shooting stopped abruptly.

Policemen slowly got to their feet, weapons still drawn, their eyes still scanning the rooftops and open windows across the street.

A young cop cautiously moved to the blown-out side window of Jake's car. "Are you hurt, Lieutenant?"

"No. We're okay."

"Sir, it might be best for you to get the lady out of here. We'll have to do a house-to-house search before we can secure the area. And that's going to take a while."

"Cover us," Jake said.

The young cop signaled, and a half dozen policemen trained their weapons on the apartment houses across the street.

"I'll lift up, and you squirm toward the door," Jake told Joanna.

Joanna felt slivers of glass cut into her arms as she moved backwards. Her legs were now halfway out the door, so she curled them underneath her. She pressed her body down onto the seat, giving Jake as much room as possible.

In a fraction of a second he was behind the wheel. Keeping his head down, he turned on the ignition and pushed the gas pedal to the floor. They sped away, tires screeching.

Joanna waited until they turned at the intersection before sitting up. She took deep breaths, trying to calm herself. Her heart was pounding against her chest. "Jesus! That was so close."

"Another six inches and we would have been dead," Jake said. His voice sounded calm, but inwardly he too was shaking. Both he and Joanna had been standing in profile when the shooter opened up. The bastard was aiming for a head shot. He glanced over at Joanna's arms. "Your arms are bleeding."

"I know." She carefully picked the slivers of glass from her forearms. There were small cuts everywhere, with blood oozing out.

Her linen jacket was badly stained. She took more deep breaths and tried to swallow away her panic. "You think it was them?"

"It had to be."

"I guess," Joanna said, looking in the visor mirror for facial cuts. There weren't any. "But this is a very tough neighborhood. Maybe some gang banger decided to try his luck."

"No way," Jake said firmly. "They may shoot at one cop or one cop car, but they're not going to take on an army of police. They're not that stupid. And besides, they didn't open up until you and I stepped out. Those bullets were meant for us."

Joanna nodded slowly. She tilted her head back against the seat and took more deep breaths. "All because they think we're getting too close. They must really be worried."

Jake reached for a cigarette and lit it, inhaling deeply. He glanced over at Joanna, again thinking how close the shots had been to them. "It might be a good idea for Kate and Jean-Claude to move into a hotel."

Joanna's brow went up. "You think they're going to try again?"

"They might," Jake said. "And that could put Kate and her little boy in real danger. Remember, they kill anybody who gets in their way. Old men, young cops, sleeping babies. It doesn't bother them a damn."

"I'll move them to a small motel away from Memorial," Joanna said, wondering if it might not be best to send Kate and Jean-Claude to Disneyland for the weekend. She shivered, now thinking how easy it would be for the terrorists to wipe out the entire Blalock line. "Where should I stay?"

"At your condominium."

"Are you serious?"

"Oh, yeah."

Joanna looked at him oddly. "But won't they come after me there?"

"I hope they do," Jake said hoarsely.

"Why?"

"Because I'm going to be in your living room waiting for them."

29

In the control room of the Secret Service, senior personnel gathered around a circular table to study an enlarged map of West Los Angeles. The routes the President would take during his visit were highlighted in red.

"So most of the trip from Santa Monica will be on the freeway, right?" asked Jack Youngblood, the agent in charge of the team that traveled with the President.

"That's correct," Mary Beth Curtis said as she retraced the scheduled route with a wooden pointer. Her eyes quickly scanned the surface streets between Loew's Hotel and the freeway. There were five intersections with traffic lights. The motorcycle escorts would have them blocked off. "POTUS will leave his hotel at seven forty-five a.m.," she went on, using the Secret Service's abbreviated name for the President of the United States, "then proceed to the Santa Monica Freeway. He will travel east, exiting at Overland, then onto surface streets to Pico Boulevard, reaching Century City at eight a.m."

"The California Highway Patrol has been notified, of course."

"Of course."

"Did they bitch about closing down one of their busiest freeways during rush hour?"

"I didn't ask how they felt about it. I just told them what was required."

Youngblood smiled. He liked Mary Beth Curtis, a thin, middle-aged black woman who had worked her way up through the ranks over the past ten years. Originally with the Counterfeit Division, she was now in the protective branch of the Secret Service. Every time the President left the White House, Curtis had planned far in advance every street the limousine would take, every corner it would turn, every intersection it would pass through. And when. She also planned the escape routes in case of an attack on the presidential limousine.

Curtis tapped her pointer against a street called the Avenue of the Stars. "POTUS," she continued, "will breakfast at the Century Plaza Hotel, entering and leaving via the service entrance."

Youngblood shivered. Every time he heard the words "service entrance" he thought about Robert Kennedy walking through the kitchen area of the Ambassador Hotel in downtown Los Angeles. Security had been virtually nil. Sirhan Sirhan had had a clear shot at the senator's head. Youngblood felt his jaw tightening. His greatest fear was that the President would be assassinated on his watch. Just the thought of it caused Youngblood to sweat.

"At nine-fifteen sharp," Mary Beth Curtis was saying, "POTUS leaves the hotel and travels surface streets, Pico to Westwood Boulevard and then to the medical center. He should arrive at the John Edgar Wales Institute at nine-thirty. The dedication—"

"Whoa!" Youngblood interrupted. "POTUS decided to skip the dedication. Remember?"

"Well, POTUS has changed his mind," she said. "He now wants to attend it. We got a direct order on that an hour ago."

"Christ," Youngblood growled.

"If you want to go and try to talk him out of it, we'll wait here while you do."

Youngblood sighed heavily. He didn't like the change

in plans and he didn't like the President going anywhere near Memorial Hospital. Too damn risky. If it had been up to Youngblood, he would have canceled the entire trip to Los Angeles. He looked over at Thomas Harrington, director of the Secret Service. "Sir, with all due respect, I think the President is making a mistake."

"POTUS was informed of the advance agent's recommendation," Harrington said. "I was standing in the Oval Office when he read the report. I expressed my concern as forcefully as I could." Harrington was about to give more details of the conversation but decided not to. "The short of it is the President does not want the public to have the impression that a group of violent individuals will dictate what the President of the United States does and does not do. The President and his advisers have considered the matter carefully, and they feel the risks can be minimized."

Not when you're dealing with crazy, goddamn terrorists, Youngblood was thinking. "Sir, do they know these bombers have struck twice already?"

"They do."

"And do they know that April nineteenth is the projected date for the next terrorist act?"

"They do."

Youngblood tried to hold his temper. He was a large, broad-shouldered man with a squared-off jaw and a crew cut. His face rarely showed what he was feeling. "Our first advance agent thought Memorial Hospital was a potentially dangerous place for the President to be. And he underlined the word *dangerous* twice."

"And for that reason the President will not visit the pediatric ward at Memorial Hospital, as previously planned," Harrington said. "He will limit his brief stay to the new institute, which is two blocks away from the hospital."

"I still don't like it," Youngblood said frankly.

Nor does anyone else in the Secret Service, Harrington wanted to say. But he held his tongue. "The institute is a brand-new building and has no occupants. It will remain that way until after POTUS's visit. The building will be sealed off for forty-eight hours prior to the President's arrival. Another team of agents is on their way to Los Angeles at this moment. Their sole function is to keep that building clean. Over the weekend, nobody goes in and nobody comes out. And I mean nobody."

Youngblood took a deep breath and exhaled loudly, resigning himself to the decision the President had made. "The list of dignitaries attending the dedication will have to be carefully scrutinized."

"That's being done now."

"They'll be given a specific time to arrive," Youngblood went on. "Anyone arriving after eight-thirty a.m. will not be admitted. All limousines will be instructed to park a minimum of two blocks away."

"Good, good," Harrington said approvingly. "Of course, metal detectors will be set up, and everyone will be required to pass through them. And we should have dogs sniff out the building every six hours."

Youngblood thought back to the design of the new institute he'd seen a week ago. It had four floors, each with an area of 12,500 square feet. "Which dogs would you like us to use?"

"Our Belgian Malinois," Harrington said. "They can detect explosives a hundred yards away."

"I'll need four of them."

"They'll be on the plane tonight," Harrington said, then turned to Curtis. "I want at least two routes the President can take away from the institute."

"That won't be possible," she responded. "The institute is located on a dead-end street."

"I see," Harrington said, fuming inside but not showing it. He should have been given that piece of information earlier. "Double-check and see if there's a driveway or alley that can be used as an exit."

"Will do," she said and reached for a phone. "I'll have our advance agent fax me an aerial view of that street."

"Get back to me when you have it," Harrington said and turned to leave. "Come on, Jack. Walk me to the elevator."

At the watercooler Harrington stopped and leaned over for a paper cup. He glanced back, making sure they were out of earshot, then spoke in a low voice. "If there's even a hint of trouble, Jack—I mean just a whiff—you get POTUS's ass out of there pronto and back onto Air Force One. Got it?"

"Yes, sir."

30

Eva showed Rudy around the spacious living room of their new house. The room was bare except for a mattress shoved up against the wall.

"Keep the venetian blinds shut," she told him. "And turn the lights on for a few hours in the evening. That way nobody will get suspicious."

"What if someone rings the doorbell?"

"Ignore it."

She led the way into a narrow hallway. There were bedrooms and bathrooms and a small den off to the side. Near the kitchen was a half-opened door that had a dead bolt lock on it.

Rudy peered in. All he saw were steps down and darkness beyond. "What's in here?"

"A basement."

"Is there a way out?"

Eva shook her head. "There's a small window up high, but it's got iron bars across it."

They entered a large, freshly painted kitchen that had a refrigerator, freezer and stove. Atop a Formica counter were cans of food and soft drinks and plastic bottles of water. And next to them were detonators and wires and two bricks of C-four.

Rudy parted the venetian blinds and looked out. He saw a small, neglected garden on one side, a garage on the other. Between them were trees and a tall hedge.

"Who lives on the other side of the forest?" Rudy asked.

"An old couple that's hard of hearing."

"Any dogs?"

"A toy poodle that barks once before it runs away."

Rudy nodded, pleased with the house and its setup. The escape route through the hedge was perfect. Anyone chasing them would have to come through the tangled bushes. They'd be an easy target. "This place is perfect. How did you find it so fast?"

"Just luck," Eva said. But it wasn't luck, and she hadn't found it fast. She had rented the house and the one in West Hollywood at the same time. The second house was a backup in case things went wrong, like Rudy being stupid enough to get himself caught and deciding to talk to save his skin.

Rudy studied a mattress on the floor by the pantry and went over. He plopped down on it, testing out its softness. "You going to sleep here?"

"Yeah," Eva said and watched Rudy lie back.

"Why don't we sleep in here together?" he asked, grinning seductively.

"Because I want you to guard the front door while I'm guarding the back."

"It's not that far to the front door from here."

"What do you figure? Three, four seconds?"

"At the most."

"That's plenty time enough for someone to break down the front door and blow your head off."

Rudy stared at Eva, undressing her with his eyes. She had such a small waist and great ass. He envisioned himself fucking her until she begged him to stop. "You're not even a little interested, huh?"

"Now is not the right time." Eva glanced at the bulge in the crotch of Rudy's tight-fitting jeans. It did nothing for her. She looked away.

"Well, if you change your mind . . ."

"You'll be the first to know."

The cell phone in Eva's coat pocket rang. She reached for it quickly.

"Yes?"

"We've got trouble."

Eva instantly recognized the voice of her contact at Memorial Hospital. "Where are you?"

"My outside number."

"Stay put." Eva folded up her cell phone and looked over at Rudy. "I have to leave for a little while. I want you to remain inside the house until I get back."

Rudy studied her face, trying to read her expression. It was a blank. "Is anything wrong?"

"Lock the door after me, and don't answer it for anyone."

Eva put on a baseball cap with a ponytail wig attached to it. She adjusted the bill so that it covered most of her forehead, then picked up her sunglasses. She studied herself briefly in the bathroom mirror before walking out into a bright spring day.

The residential neighborhood was quiet. There were no joggers or strollers, only a woman tending her garden across the street. The woman waved, and Eva waved back absently as she hurried along. She knew the matter had to be urgent. Otherwise the contact wouldn't have called her on her cellular line during the day. He'd been told never to do that. Never, never. Except in cases of real emergency. What could it be? What?

She took a deep breath and considered the two worst-case scenarios. The first possibility was that the bomb plot had been uncovered. Unlikely, she quickly decided. If that had happened, the contact wouldn't be talking on the phone. He'd be under arrest. The second possibility was that the dedication plans for the institute had been changed or canceled. That would be disastrous. All of their work and effort wasted. The perfect plan gone up in smoke.

At the corner Eva turned into a small shopping mall. She went to a pay phone just past a beauty salon and picked up the phone book. As she flipped pages, her eyes scanned the mall and the intersection beyond. A black-and-white police car was stopped at the traffic light. Eva waited for the car to move on, then lifted the receiver, inserted two quarters and began dialing.

"Yes?" the contact answered.

"Is Mr. Right there?" Eva asked in code.

"He's on vacation," the contact responded correctly.

Eva glanced around the small shopping mall once more. "What is it?"

"The police know someone at the institute is involved. They're going over this place with a fine-tooth comb and questioning everyone again."

"They're just guessing."

"It's more than that," the contact said worriedly. "They know someone here leaked information on Ramón Gonzalez."

They found the body, Eva thought, wondering again if Maria Gonzalez had told them all she knew.

"And to make matters worse, the Secret Service wants to talk with all of us as well."

"They're still guessing," Eva said calmly. "If they really knew anything, they'd be making arrests, not talking."

"But they're going to dig, and they'll find out my sister was one of the people killed by the FBI at the Idaho compound. And when they do, they'll make the connection right back to me."

That will take time, Eva was thinking, and by then you'll be dead. "Alice never used her maiden name on anything. You know that."

"But they're going to check on everybody fifty ways from Sunday."

"Let them," Eva said, sounding unconcerned. "You're squeaky clean and you'll stay that way. And after the big bang all the evidence will say your colleague did it, and he won't be here to defend himself."

"But there won't be any solid proof he did it."

"Sure there will. Particularly when they find the C-four we planted in his garage at home."

"Jesus! You did that?"

"Of course. Do you think we'd leave you uncovered?"

"Never. Never for a moment," he said appreciatively.

Eva could hear him breathe a sigh of relief. Just a few more days, she thought. Just hold those idiots together for six more days. "So everything is in place, right?"

"Yes," the contact said. "But I think we have another problem. A big one."

"What?"

"Joanna Blalock."

Eva heard a loud roaring over the phone that gradually faded. "What was that?"

"A jet taking off. This pay phone is near the Santa Monica Airport."

"You were talking about Joanna Blalock. What's the problem?"

"She knows too much, and she's going to lead the cops right to us." The contact swallowed audibly. "She and the big detective are doing all the questioning, but it's Blalock who is showing him the way. I can feel her closing in on us."

"Like how?"

"Like asking me questions about Ramón Gonzalez and his prosthesis and how it was made and who fitted him for it."

"So?"

"She focused in on the prosthesis and the machinery

that made it," the contact went on. "She spent twenty minutes in that machine room, talking with me and the others. If she would have had one of those dogs that can sniff out explosives with her, the dog would have gone crazy. And that would have been the end of our plan."

"But she didn't have a dog."

"But the Secret Service will. And Joanna Blalock is scheduled to meet with them tomorrow afternoon." The contact paused as another plane roared overhead. "I'm telling you, one more good clue and Joanna Blalock will put everything together."

"Sprinkle cayenne pepper around the room," Eva said, thinking quickly. "You don't need a lot. A few grains here and there will do it."

"Will that cover the smell?"

"For a while." Eva knew that the pepper would distract the dogs and throw them off, but the well-trained ones would eventually sniff out the C-4. "What time is the meeting between Blalock and the Secret Service agents?"

"Sometime tomorrow afternoon."

"Sprinkle the pepper around the machinery tonight. And remember, use very small amounts."

"What about Joanna Blalock?"

"If necessary, I can see to it that she doesn't ask you or anyone else any more questions."

"That's easier said than done," the contact told her. "Somebody took a shot at her yesterday as she was leaving Ramón Gonzalez's apartment. Now there's a cop by her side wherever she goes."

"You know this for a fact?"

"Me and everybody else at Memorial." The contact took a deep breath. "It wasn't you, huh?"

"No, it wasn't."

"Anyhow, you'll have a tough time getting close."

"I'll keep that in mind."

"There's one more thing."

"What?"

"They've got a picture of you."

"What!" Eva's heart stopped for a moment, then began racing. "Wh-what kind of picture?"

"A sketch done by a police artist," the contact said. "Luckily, you were wearing a wig. Otherwise the sketch would have really been close."

"Could you still recognize me?"

"I could," the contact said. "But I'm not sure others would. At least not on first glance. They've got your cheekbones too high and your mouth a little too wide."

"So it's just a semblance?"

"Yeah. But somewhere, somebody saw you."

Who? Eva asked herself, her mind racing for an answer. She always wore disguises and different wigs when she went to a new place, and that should have been good enough to— Eva pressed the phone to her ear. "What kind of wig was I wearing in the sketch?"

"Your hair was pulled back in a bun."

Eva's eyes narrowed as she thought back. She had worn that wig twice, and both times were at Memorial Hospital. Once when she scouted out the Pathology Department and once when she blew it up. She now remembered passing Joanna Blalock in the corridor while checking out the forensics area. "Did Joanna Blalock have anything to do with the sketch?"

"I don't know," the contact said. "All I was told was that the person in the sketch was believed to be the individual responsible for the Memorial bombing."

It had to be Joanna Blalock, Eva thought. No one else had looked me straight in the face. But how could she have known what I was planning? Maybe Blalock had compared notes with others, like the cop in the lobby or the technician who had stuck her head out into the corridor. But it was Joanna Blalock who had gotten the best look, and it was Joanna Blalock who could pick Eva out of a lineup. "Joanna Blalock," Eva said sourly to herself.

"You think she's at the bottom of this too?"

"I think she's at the bottom of everything."

"She could screw everything up."

"If we let her."

"And there's one more thing that may or may not be a problem."

"What?" Eva asked irritably.

"I heard a rumor that the dedication of the new institute may take place on the steps," the contact said. "That's where they may present the medals as well."

"What medals?"

Eva listened carefully to the details of how the Medals of Freedom would be presented by the President to Joanna Blalock and her colleagues. "Are you saying the President may not actually go into the new building?"

"That's the rumor I heard."

"Oh, Christ," Eva said. All of their plans to assassinate the President depended on him entering and touring the new institute. "So the medal presentation will be a part of the dedication ceremony, right?"

"That's how it seems. Apparently the Secret Service is antsy about the President's visit to Los Angeles. They want to combine everything into one and get him in and out as fast as possible."

Eva tried to think through the problem. The presentation was the key. If the medals were presented on the steps, the President wouldn't be going inside. "Can you find out for sure where the medals are being presented?"

"I tried, but nobody has a clue. I don't think anybody knows."

"Well, I know one person who should know."

"Who?"

"I'll call you back when I have the information."

Eva hung up and hurried out of the shopping mall.

Damn! Damn! she cursed under her breath as she turned onto the street where her house was located. Her problems were mounting. If the President didn't enter the building, it would really complicate matters. They could probably still blow him up, but it would be messy, and there was a real chance they would miss. No, she thought, we need the President inside the building for a sure kill. *Damn! Damn!* And to make matters even worse, now there was a sketch of her being circulated to every cop within a fifty-mile radius. And they would no doubt show it on the television news programs too. The short-term consequences of the picture concerned her the most. She would have to be very, very careful with her disguises from now on. And only go out when she absolutely had to. The long-term consequences didn't bother her. After the assassination she had already planned to fly to Costa Rica and have plastic surgery done. She would have a whole new identity and all the money she would ever need. Her father, the leader of the Ten Righteous, would see to that.

Eva walked up the steps to the house and went through the door Rudy had opened for her.

"Close it," she snapped.

"What's wrong?" Rudy asked.

"Plenty." Eva stomped back to the kitchen, thinking how best to deal with Rudy. The idiot! The stupid idiot! She leaned over the sink and splashed water on her face, then dried her cheeks with a hand towel. Slowly Eva turned to Rudy, her temper now under control. "Where were you yesterday afternoon?"

Rudy was instantly on guard. "I had to pick up some stuff."

"Like what?"

"You know, cigarettes and razor blades. That sort of thing."

"That took a couple of hours, huh?"

"I drove around for a while too."

Eva threw the hand towel aside. "Did you take a shot at Joanna Blalock yesterday?"

"Not me," Rudy said at once and vigorously shook his head. "Hell, no! Why would I do that?"

Eva could tell by his body language he was lying. The brainless idiot! He could have gotten caught, and if that had happened he would have talked his head off to save his skin. "I need to know the *truth*."

"Not me," he said again, stronger this time.

"Well, whoever did it, it's too bad they missed," she said, trying a different ploy. "A dead Joanna Blalock would have been fine with me."

Rudy shrugged, thinking about confessing then deciding not to. He didn't want to do anything that might jeopardize the $500,000 he was receiving for the job. A hundred thousand was already deposited in a Mexican bank. The other $400,000 would be deposited once the President was dead. He would be on easy street forever. "That neighborhood is filled with Mexican gangs. Maybe it was some gang member."

"Maybe," Eva said.

"I could check it out."

She shook her head. "What's done is done."

"Yeah, I guess so."

Rudy went over to the counter and opened a can of soda, now wondering where Maria Gonzalez had hidden the rest of the money. They had found $2,000 tucked away behind the portrait of Jesus. There was another $3,000 somewhere, but they couldn't find it. That was why Rudy had gone back the next day—to search for the remaining cash. But the place was crawling with cops, so he went to a nearby rooftop and watched. He still wasn't sure why he'd opened fire on the cop and the woman doctor. It was like an irresistible urge, a voice inside his head telling him what to do. And it felt so good while he was doing it.

Rudy turned and saw Eva still staring at him through narrowed eyes. She knows, he thought, she knows I'm lying. A streak of fear shot through him. It wasn't just the $500,000 that was at risk. It was his life. Eva's people didn't screw around. They killed anyone that got in their way. "Is—is something wrong?"

Eva saw the fear in his eyes and instantly knew that her expression had given away what she was feeling. She smiled at Rudy, distrusting him even more. But she needed him. For now. She sighed loudly. "I was trying to decide how we should deal with Joanna Blalock."

"We should kill her," Rudy said at once. "Nice and slow."

"I'll think about it," Eva said and walked out of the kitchen.

31

Jake checked the windows in Joanna's condominium, making certain they were all locked. In the living room he cracked the drapes and looked out at the dimly lit courtyard. A steady rain was falling, the sky dark and moonless.

He closed the drapes tightly and spoke into his walkie-talkie. "Let me hear from you."

"Everything is fine outside," said the detective in a car parked near the entrance to the condo.

"Nice and quiet here." The second reply came from a vacant condominium directly across the way. The detectives stationed there had night-vision binoculars trained on Joanna's front door and the path leading up to it.

"Stay alert," Jake said.

Jake heard the shower in the bathroom turn off. He quickly scanned the room again, searching for anything he might have overlooked. The door, the drapes, the heating and air-conditioning ducts, the light fixture above. All checked and secured. His gaze went to the blazing log in the fireplace and locked in on it. Hurriedly, he spoke into the walkie-talkie. "What about the chimney?"

There was no response other than a burst of static.

"What about the chimney?" Jake repeated.

"Hurley took care of it this afternoon," the detective across the courtyard answered. "He put a wire-mesh screen across it with an alarm attached. If even a bird lands on it, all hell breaks loose."

Jake thought for a moment. "Can you punch a hole through the screen?"

"No way. It's made of titanium."

"Good," Jake said and put the walkie-talkie down.

Joanna was standing by the hallway entrance, drying her hair with a thick towel. "Jesus! It sounds like an armed camp in here."

"That's because it is," Jake said.

"Do you really think they'll shoot at us again?"

Jake shook his head. "They're crummy shooters. Otherwise we'd be dead." He thought back to the person on the rooftop who had fired at them. The slugs they found had come from a semiautomatic pistol. Had the shooter used a rifle with a telescopic sight, he could have easily killed them both and had time to spare. "Naw. They won't shoot at us again."

"Then how will they try to get to us?"

"With a bomb."

Joanna abruptly stopped drying her hair and stared at Jake. "Are you serious?"

"Oh, yeah," he said without hesitation. "C-four is what they know best. And it would be easy to do. Just break a back window and throw in a bomb. They wouldn't find enough of us to bury."

"That's a pleasant thought to go to sleep with," Joanna said.

"I just wanted you to know what we're up against."

She nodded, sighing deeply. "There's no way you can stop a determined bomber, is there?"

"Not really," Jake said. "The best you can do is make it tough as hell for them to get close."

"And most of the time you can't even do that." Joanna went back to drying her hair. "Like you just said, they could break out my bathroom window before the detectives outside could begin to react. And that's a fact."

"It would be except that your bathroom window is now crisscrossed with barbed wire," Jake told her. "There are also two canine units patrolling the outer perimeter of the building. And each of them has a big-ass rottweiler that's not afraid of C-four."

"Now it feels like we're in a prisoner-of-war camp," Joanna said.

"In some ways we are."

"Who would ever think this could happen in America?"

"Welcome to the new world," Jake said sourly.

Joanna took a large comb from her terry-cloth robe pocket and ran it through her hair. She watched Jake adjust the gun in the holster under his arm. He never wore that damn thing when he was in her place. Never. But tonight was different. He would probably sleep with it on.

She gazed around the still living room. It was so quiet with Kate and Jean-Claude no longer here. She kept expecting Jean-Claude to come galloping in on his trusty broom. But she knew he wouldn't. He was cooped up with his mother in a motel far from Memorial Hospital. And he was wondering why he couldn't be with his aunt Joanna. Joanna sighed again. How do you explain terrorists to a two-year-old?

There was a sudden thump from above.

Jake reached for his weapon, instantly on guard.

Joanna looked up and slowly backed away. Then she heard the sound of soft footsteps. "It's the woman in the unit upstairs. She's always dropping things."

Jake holstered his weapon and quickly picked up the walkie-talkie. He spoke to the team inside the condominium across the courtyard. "Did you see anything?"

There was a brief burst of static before the response came. "The woman who lives upstairs just walked in."

"Describe her," Jake said at once.

"Short and plump with a small dog."

Jake looked over at Joanna inquiringly. She nodded back.

"Call me whenever someone comes or goes in the courtyard," Jake said into the walkie-talkie.

"Will do," the detective replied. "But we were sure on this one. We saw her being checked out by the canine unit at the front entrance."

"I still want to be notified."

"You got it."

Jake put the walkie-talkie down and exhaled loudly. He gently rotated his head and relaxed the taut muscles in his neck. "You want a beer?"

"I could really use one," Joanna said.

Jake went over to the wet bar and came back with two frosted bottles of imported beer. He took the caps off and handed a bottle to Joanna.

"To happier days," he toasted.

"And a lot of them," she added.

Joanna sat on the sofa and watched Jake pacing the floor. Even he was unnerved by these bastards and their bombs, she thought. And rightly so. They were cold-blooded murderers who would have no reservations about blowing up the entire condominium complex, just to rid themselves of an obstacle to their great plan. But what great plan? What building will they blow up? What institution will they go after? How many people will die in the explosion? And will I still be around when it happens?

Joanna had no illusions about her situation. Those bullets outside the apartment house had been meant for her. Had she not ducked getting into the car, the shots would have blown her head off. The terrorists wanted her dead, and they could come after her again, with or without Jake at her side. What is it I know? What is it that concerns the terrorists so much?

Her gaze went to the fireplace as the blazing logs cracked loudly. Even the chimney was a danger, Joanna thought miserably, wondering if the terrorists could devise a way to cut through the titanium screen. That was all it would take. Then the terrorists could drop a brick of C-4 down the chimney and blow everything in the condominium to kingdom come. In her mind's eye she saw the victims being pulled out of the West Hollywood bomb site. Now she was envisioning a fireman carrying a dead little child out of the rubble. She would never forget that image. Nor would anyone else who saw it.

Joanna took a deep breath, thinking that nothing in her life had gone right since that damn explosion. Nothing. Her whole world had been turned upside down. But it wasn't the explosion that had done that.

Jake glanced over and saw the faraway look on Joanna's face. He came to the sofa and sat next to her. "Are you all right?"

She rested her head on his shoulder. "I should have told you."

"About what?"

"Paul du Maurier."

Jake shrugged. "You did what you thought was best."

"Are you angry?"

"I'm past that now."

Joanna managed a weak smile. "No, you're not."

Jake growled softly. "If you already know the answer to your question, why do you bother to ask it?"

"That means you're still angry. Right?"

"A little," Jake admitted. He lit a cigarette and blew smoke at the ceiling. "My problem is I never realize how important something is until I've damn near lost it."

"Welcome to the club." Joanna reached for his cigarette and took a puff, then handed it back. "I had almost gotten you out of my mind, Jake. Almost."

"Forgotten me altogether?"

"I wasn't trying to forget you," she said candidly. "I was trying to stop loving you."

Jake squeezed her shoulder gently. "I guess fate has thrown us together, for better or worse."

"I guess," Joanna said, staring at the fire but seeing Paul du Maurier's face. He was smiling at her. "I'm still hurting bad, Jake. The damn pain just won't let up. It's going to take time for me to get over this."

"Don't try to get over it," Jake advised. "Just accept the pain and get on with your life."

"Is that what you did when you lost Eleni?"

"Yeah."

"How did it work out?"

"I ended up with you, didn't I?"

Outside the rain was coming down harder, now pounding against the bay window. In the distance there was a loud crack of lightning followed by a rumble of thunder. The entire apartment shook for a moment.

"Are you going to sleep in here?" Joanna asked, getting to her feet.

"Yeah," Jake said. "I want to be near the door. If you hear anything, any disturbance at all, you dive for your closet and pull down everything on top of you. Got it?"

"Got it." Joanna leaned over and kissed his cheek. "Thank you for being here, Jake."

"I wouldn't want to be anywhere else."

"Good night," she said and left the room.

Jake watched the blazing logs in the fireplace crumble and turn to dead cinders. It was like life, he kept thinking. One moment everything was bright and warm and felt good. Then, in an instant, everything turned to shit. And people had no control over that. Events did it to them. Or fate. Whatever the hell it was. He thought back to his former wife, Eleni, and the pain he'd experienced when she was gone. *Christ! What a mess I was.* And it had taken forever to get over it. But Joanna was doing a lot better than he had. She was at least functioning. She'd do fine, he tried to convince himself. Hell! She'd already smiled a few times earlier that evening. She was already starting to heal.

A moment later Jake realized how wrong he was. Faintly, above the sound of the rain, he heard Joanna crying herself to sleep.

32

Jake and Lou Farelli walked past the concrete barricades outside the federal building in West Los Angeles. The area between the barricades and the building was being patrolled by armed guards with police dogs.

"Do you believe this shit?" Farelli asked disgustedly. "Look at what a few terrorists can do to a city."

"And it's going to get worse," Jake told him. "Just wait until April nineteenth. Every federal building within a fifty-mile radius is going to turn into a cement fortress."

"And you think the terrorists will still strike, huh?"

"Oh, yeah," Jake said. "You can't secure every window and every door in every building. It's just not possible. And remember, these terrorists are experts at finding weak spots and exploiting them."

Jake nodded, thinking back to the explosion at Memorial Hospital. There had been two policemen guarding two doors in a deserted corridor, and still the terrorists had detonated a bomb, killing a cop in the process. "They're going to blow up something big right in front of our eyes."

"Unless we nail them first."

"We've only got five days until the nineteenth," Jake said gloomily. "What do you think our chances of catching them are?"

Farelli shrugged. "Maybe we'll get lucky."

"Yeah. And maybe pigs will start to fly."

They came to the curb and stepped up onto the sidewalk. A row of drive-by mailboxes had been removed;

the entire area was now a red zone. No vehicles were permitted to stop, not even to let off passengers. A motorcycle cop was nearby, watching. He recognized Jake and Farelli and gave them a half salute.

They entered the twenty-story building and had their ID's checked by two armed guards. They were still required to put their shields and weapons in a plastic dish before passing through the metal detector. A German shepherd eyed them warily, then lost interest.

Taking the elevator up, Jake stared at the ceiling and the trapdoor leading out of the car. There were no screws or devices locking it in place.

Farelli asked, "What are you looking at?"

"I was just thinking," Jake said, standing on his tiptoes and reaching up to the trapdoor. It moved without resistance. "We're all assuming the terrorists are going to sneak in and plant a bomb. Right?"

"Right."

"How can we be sure the bomb isn't already in place?"

"Because the dogs would have sniffed it out."

Jake pointed to the trapdoor. "Suppose the terrorists climbed up through there and hid a bomb in the wall of the elevator shaft. Unless our guys actually put a dog into the shaft and let him sniff around, he'd never find it. And there's got to be a hundred nooks and crannies like that in every building."

"Jesus," Farelli hissed under his breath. "There's no place safe from those bastards."

"Tell me about it."

They exited the elevator and hurried into the reception area of FBI headquarters. Their ID's were checked again. Then they were escorted down a corridor to a spacious conference room. Dan Hurley, with a man they didn't recognize, was waiting for them.

"Sorry we're late," Jake apologized.

"No problem." Hurley stood and introduced them to

William Kitt, section chief of the FBI's Domestic Terrorism Unit.

"Have a seat, gentlemen," Kitt said formally. "The new information is being faxed to us now."

Jake glanced over at the fax machine, again wondering about the urgency of the meeting. He hadn't been told who or what or why, only to get over to FBI headquarters as soon as possible. The first sheet came out of the fax machine, and Kitt reached for it.

Hurley couldn't hold back the news any longer. "Jake, we know who the bastards are."

Jake's brow went up. "You got names?"

"And faces."

The lieutenant leaned over the table, his eyes fixed on Hurley. "Are you absolutely sure?"

Hurley nodded. "We lifted a partial set of fingerprints off the wallet you uncovered in the buried duffel bag. And an even better set of prints was on the razor Farelli found in the murdered woman's kitchen."

Jake looked over at Farelli and gave him a thumbs-up signal. No one had been able to find the razor that was used to slice up Maria Gonzalez. They had all but given up when Farelli decided to disassemble the garbage disposal. And there it was, twisted but still intact.

"And the prints are a match," Hurley went on. "They belonged to the same person."

Jake's mind flashed back to the woman the razor had been used on. Every part of her had been mutilated. He didn't even want to think about the pain she must have suffered. He took out his notepad. "You got a full name for this sadistic son of a bitch?"

"Rudolph Payte," Hurley said. "Known to his friends as Rudy."

"A real piece of work," Kitt added, now stacking the fax sheets together. "Let's begin with the group he belongs to."

Kitt described the extremist group in precise detail. Although he appeared to be reading from the fax sheets, it was obvious that he already knew a great deal about the group. "They call themselves the Ten Righteous. All of their members are white supremacists who are violently opposed to the federal government and its laws. A few years ago they claimed a twenty-five-square-mile area of wilderness in northern Idaho as their own nation. They built a large compound, closed off roads, refused to pay taxes and shot at anyone who entered uninvited. When a United States marshal came to serve papers on them, they killed him in cold blood for trespassing on their nation.

"That federal marshal had a wife and two children," Kitt continued, his voice noticeably lower. He took a deep breath before going on. "Within days an army of federal agents moved in and a war broke out. A real firefight. The compound was set ablaze. Most of the supremacists perished in the fire. A few were shot to death. Unfortunately, Walter George Reineke, the leader of the group, escaped. And so did his bodyguard, Rudy Payte."

Jake asked, "So this Rudy Payte wasn't a true believer?"

"If you paid him enough he was," Kitt said flatly. "Anyhow, we thought the group was done and finished and would no longer be a problem. Obviously we were wrong."

"Who's the woman we're after?" Jake asked.

"Reineke's daughter, Eva." Kitt passed them a faxed photograph of Eva Reineke. The details were hazy, but there was no doubt the woman in the photo was the same as the woman in the police artist's sketch. "She's the mastermind behind the bombings."

"How did she get so good at it?"

"We taught her," Kitt said. "Eva Reineke joined the army out of high school and became an expert in demolition. Her specialties were plastic explosives and the usual timing devices. She was so good at it she was considered a prime candidate for the Special Forces. She applied for the elite unit and was accepted. Her training performance was consistently rated as outstanding.

"A week before she was to be given her green beret," Kitt went on, "she was dishonorably discharged."

"For what?"

"For joining a paramilitary group and trying to persuade the other troops to do the same."

Jake asked, "Did any of the others join up?"

Kitt nodded. "Rudolph Payte. He was also dishonorably discharged."

Kitt handed them photographs of Walter George Reineke and Rudy Payte. "These will be given to every law enforcement officer in Los Angeles County. And of course they'll be on television as well. On April nineteenth, every guard at every federal building will check every visitor against these photographs."

Jake thought back to the first explosion, in West Hollywood. "Those photos should also be shown around the supermarkets and convenience stores on the Westside."

"And in all airports and bus and train stations," Hurley chimed in.

Farelli flipped through the photographs of the three terrorists. They looked so ordinary, like people you'd see at a baseball game. "Well, these photos should make things easier."

"Not by much," Kitt cautioned. "Homegrown terrorists are far and away the most difficult to catch. They speak our language perfectly. They look like us and act like us. They know our customs, they know the lay of the land. They fit right in because they *are* us."

There was a sharp knock on the door, and a tall, well-built FBI agent entered. He quickly walked over to Kitt and handed him a folder.

"Sir, these new pictures just arrived," the agent said. "They're of much better quality."

"Good." Kitt opened the folder and scanned the new color photographs. "Have you finished cross-matching the names of the Righteous against the employees at Memorial?"

"Yes, sir. No matches were found."

Kitt sighed wearily. "Another dry hole."

"Sir, some of the women who died in the Idaho compound had middle initials. Those may represent maiden names."

"Check it out as rapidly as you can."

"We're trying, but the going is tough," the agent said. "None of the women had social security numbers, and the courthouse that housed the records of their births and marriages was burnt to the ground."

"Shit," Kitt grumbled.

"Yes, sir."

"Keep on it." Kitt waited for the agent to leave, then passed the new photographs around for the others to see.

He tilted his chair back, now thinking about the problems in tracking down the terrorists. He needed a tip-off or an informant, otherwise nailing the terrorists before they acted would be almost impossible. That was why finding their so-called friend at Memorial was so important. Maybe he could be squeezed hard enough to talk.

Farelli growled under his breath as he looked at the photograph of Rudy Payte. "Where do vermin like this come from?"

From everywhere, Kitt wanted to say. From every part of America. They were in compounds spread from the Pacific Northwest to the desert Southwest to the Ozarks and beyond. All were zealots, all bent on destroying the country and then rebuilding it in the form they favored.

It was Kitt's view that domestic terrorists represented the single greatest threat to America. And the threat was growing. His agents were currently investigating nearly a thousand cases of potential domestic terrorism. Some were straightforward, like threatening letters sent to the IRS. Other cases were far more ominous, like the recent unsolved theft of twenty-five tons of ammonium nitrate from a West Virginia farm supply business. The amount stolen was twelve times that used in the bombing of the federal building in Oklahoma City. Kitt wondered if any of that ammonium nitrate had found its way to Los Angeles.

No, he decided promptly. Eva Reineke was an expert with C-4 and other plastic explosives. She wouldn't use something bulky like ammonium nitrate. But, then again, maybe she had a backup plan. The best terrorists always did.

Kitt checked his watch. In twenty minutes he would meet with agents from the Secret Service. "I'll have copies of the photographs made for you, along with the terrorists' other physical characteristics."

Jake was studying the photo of Walter George Reineke. The terrorist looked more like a grandfather, with his thinning gray hair and benign smile. But his eyes were small and dark and cold. They resembled BB's. "What turns a guy like this into a terrorist?"

"Having your wife and son and daughter-in-law die in a burning compound," Kitt told him. "And blaming the federal government for it."

Jake picked up the photograph of Eva Reineke and examined it. "I take it Eva wasn't in the compound at the time of the attack?"

"Oh, yes, she was," Kitt said. "According to an eyewitness, the old man led Eva and Rudy out through a secret escape tunnel that only he knew about."

"Why didn't he take the rest of the family with him?"

Kitt gathered up the photographs and stacked them together. Then he rose from the table. "That's a question you'll have to ask Walter George Reineke."

33

"There are cops with Joanna Blalock everywhere she goes," Rudy said.

"How many?"

"Two," Rudy answered. "One follows her into the hospital. The other stays in a black-and-white and watches her car."

"Which one is hers?"

Rudy pointed through the windshield. "The blue BMW next to the handicapped parking spaces."

They were sitting in a dark green Chevy van at the rear of the parking lot behind Memorial Hospital. The morning sun was bright and shining directly into their eyes. Both of them were wearing baseball caps and oversize sunglasses.

Eva studied the police car parked close to the back entrance of Memorial. It was positioned so a cop could see anyone coming or going well in advance. "Does Blalock remain in the hospital all day?"

Rudy nodded. "Just about. At lunch yesterday she went out for a little bit."

"Where to?"

"A small park a few blocks from here. I think it's used mostly by people from the hospital. I saw a lot of doctors and nurses there. And a bunch of kids were playing on the grass. It's kind of like a family park."

"Was Joanna Blalock alone?"

"No. The cop was right behind her."

Rudy was so loyal, Eva was thinking. It was a shame he was so stupid. "I meant, did she meet anyone there?"

Rudy thought back, concentrating. "Well, a little kid ran up to her and called her Aunt Joanna."

"Was the kid with anyone?"

"His mother. He called her Ma-ma, or something like that."

Eva's eyes narrowed behind her dark glasses. So Joanna Blalock had a sister and a nephew. Interesting. "Did they stay in the park?"

"Just for a little while," Rudy told her. "Then they went to a small ice cream place behind the park."

"Did the cop remain close to them?"

"He was ten or fifteen feet away."

"And what about the cop car?"

"He cruised the ice cream parlor and parked at the curb across the street," Rudy said. "I'm telling you, they've got her covered like glue."

Eva pulled down the sun visor and reached for a stick of gum. Carefully she digested all the information about Joanna Blalock and her sister and nephew and the cops watching them. Then she began searching for a weak spot. She found two immediately, both risky. Too risky.

"Maybe we should just forget about her," Rudy said, breaking into her thoughts.

Eva shook her head, trying to ignore Rudy and focus on the problem she faced. Somehow the cops guarding Joanna Blalock would have to be separated, their views of each other blocked. But how?

"I don't see why—"

"It's not your job to see why," Eva snapped, her concentration gone. "But I'll give you the reasons anyhow, so listen up." She ticked off the points on her fingers. "First, Blalock saw me well enough to give the cops a description. The police artist was able to come up with a sketch of my face."

"Oh, shit!"

"That means she can pick me out of a lineup or recognize me in some picture the FBI may have."

"Oh, shit!" Rudy said again.

"And she's leading the investigation," Eva went on. "Without her those cops would be stumbling over one another like a bunch of clowns. She keeps pointing them in the right direction."

"Yeah, but there's only four days left."

"Which is enough time for someone as smart as Joanna Blalock," Eva said. "And remember, every aspect of this case revolves around Memorial Hospital, one way or another. So the cops and the FBI and the ATF will pass all of their information through Joanna Blalock. They need her expertise."

Rudy nodded slowly, finally understanding. "She's like the cog in the wheel."

"She *is* the wheel. And anything the cops and feds know, she'll know." And Blalock would also know whether the Medals of Freedom would be presented on the steps or inside, Eva thought. That information was critical to their plans.

"Boy! Wouldn't you like to crawl inside Blalock's head and find out exactly how close the cops are?"

"Yes, I would," Eva said, thinking that on occasion Rudy wasn't so dumb. Her mind went back to Joanna Blalock and her family and the park and the nearby ice cream parlor. "Did her relatives go back to the hospital with Joanna Blalock?"

"No," Rudy said. "She hugged them and said she'd see them tomorrow."

"And that would be today, wouldn't it?"

"Yeah."

"Did they say where they were going to meet?"

"At the park, I guess."

Eva smiled. "We're going to need a baby carriage. I want one with a big bonnet."

"Now?"

"Right now."

"For what?"

"You'll see."

12:25 P.M.

Jean-Claude ran across the grass with his arms spread wide apart, waving to Joanna.

Joanna knelt down and gave the little boy a tight hug. "Do you know how handsome you are?"

Jean-Claude nodded, smiling happily.

"Did you have a nice day?"

Jean-Claude nodded again and lifted his pants leg, showing off his new cowboy boots.

"They're beautiful."

Jean-Claude kissed Joanna's cheek. "We go ice cream."

"Of course, but later. You go play now."

Joanna watched her nephew gallop away on his horse, riding into a make-believe world that only children knew. He waved to his mother, who was sitting on a park bench, then rode on, making the sound of a cowboy moving cattle.

Joanna walked over and sat next to Kate. "Does he ever rest?"

"Only when the herd is safely in."

"How did he become so infatuated with cowboys?"

"Lord knows." Kate lit a cigarette with a disposable lighter and inhaled deeply. "I think he even dreams about them."

"When did you start smoking again?"

"When I heard there were people trying to kill you."

Joanna reached for the cigarette and took a drag before handing it back. "Well, in a few days it'll all be over. The terrorists won't give a damn about me one way or the other."

"What makes you so sure of that?"

"Because on the nineteenth, they'll—" Joanna stopped in midsentence as she realized the threats against her might never end. Even after the big explosion, they might still want her dead. She again wondered what she knew that was so important to them. Joanna glanced over at the uniformed policeman standing ten feet away. "Chances are the terrorists will scatter once they've done their deed."

"And with any luck disappear forever." Kate crushed out her cigarette on the ground, then leaned back and studied Joanna's face. "You look beat."

"The nights are long."

"Even with Jake close by?"

Joanna shrugged. "I hear noises. I have dreams."

"Are you still thinking about Paul a lot?"

"Not so much," Joanna lied. The night before she had dreamt that she and Paul du Maurier were still together. She had awakened feeling so good. Then she'd realized it had been only a dream and the tears had come again.

Jean-Claude zoomed by, stopping briefly to give his mother a quick kiss. He waited for a woman pushing a baby carriage to pass, then galloped off again.

Joanna glanced at the baby carriage and the young woman behind it. The woman had long red hair and was wearing a baseball cap with its bill pulled far down to protect her face against the sun. In profile she seemed so young—no more than twenty-five. And her abdomen was beginning to bulge with another pregnancy. Joanna tried to see the baby, but the bonnet on the carriage blocked her view. She looked away, then down at her own flat stomach.

Joanna sighed deeply. She was now approaching middle age, the years slipping by too fast. There would be no pregnancies for her, no children, no family.

On the street in front of the park, a motorcycle roared past and stopped at the traffic light. The rider had a shaved head and beard. His arms were heavily tattooed. The policeman next to Joanna quickly moved in front of her, obstructing any view from the street. His hand went to his holster, unsnapping the strap. His eyes stayed on the skinhead. The cop in the black-and-white was out of his car, keeping the door open to serve as a shield. Seconds ticked by. The light changed. The motorcyclist gunned his engine and rode away.

Kate breathed a sigh of relief. "I don't know how you can stand this."

"I don't have any choice."

"Sure you do," Kate said at once. "Get on a damn plane and fly to a place ten thousand miles away."

Joanna shook her head. "If they want you, they can find you."

"But you said they'd leave you alone after they've committed their act of terror."

"I said *chances are* they would," Joanna corrected her. "They may still come after me. There are no guarantees."

"Jesus." Kate groaned softly.

"This place is as good as any."

Kate reached for her cigarettes but couldn't find her lighter. It had slipped through a small hole in her pocket into the inner lining of her jacket. With effort she worked the lighter back up into her pocket and lit her cigarette. "How can you work with all this going on around you?"

"It's not easy."

"Can you still concentrate?"

Joanna smiled faintly. "I keep thinking they're going to kill me. Believe it or not, that thought concentrates the mind wonderfully."

Kate smiled back at her sister. "You really are a package, aren't you?"

"I guess."

"Are you getting any closer to identifying these bastards?"

"We know who they are," Joanna said. "We've got names and faces now."

"Great!"

"It sounds great on paper," Joanna said tonelessly. "But knowing who they are is one thing. Catching them before they detonate their bomb is another."

Joanna told Kate about her phone conversation with Jake earlier that morning. She described in detail Eva and Walter George Reineke and Rudy Payte and the terrorist group they belonged to and how it was founded. "They call themselves the Ten Righteous."

Kate's eyes suddenly widened. "Did you say the Ten Righteous?"

"Yes," Joanna responded, seeing the startled look on her sister's face. "What's wrong?"

"Something terrible is going to happen," Kate said darkly. "It'll be like an Armageddon."

"How do you know that?"

"Because of their name," Kate explained. "It's a prediction of things to come."

Joanna moved in closer, ears pricked. "Tell me about it."

"It comes from the Book of Genesis," Kate said. "When God decided to destroy Sodom and Gomorrah, Abraham tried to convince him not to. Abraham argued that if God destroyed the cities, he would be killing innocent people along with the evil ones. God reconsidered and said he would spare the cities if Abraham could find ten righteous men living in Sodom. Just ten. Abraham couldn't, and what followed was one of the Bible's great catastrophes—the destruction of Sodom and Gomorrah."

Joanna shivered. "God! What do they have in store for us?"

"A disaster of some sort. That's for sure."

Religious zealots, Joanna thought disgustedly, all believing they were doing God's work. Even when they were blowing up babies or strangling an innocent patient. To them, it was God's will. Joanna looked over at her sister, now thinking about the biblical derivation of the group's name. She wondered if it might contain hidden clues about the terrorists. "How do you know so much about Sodom and Gomorrah?"

"I don't," Kate said. "A few years back my husband was on an archaeological dig, and they uncovered what they believed to be the remnants of Sodom. The evidence was fairly compelling, and he presented the findings at a conference in Paris. What I told you is what he told me." She ran a hand through her hair and patted it back into place. "We used to laugh about what would happen if God demanded that ten righteous people be produced from the city of Paris. It doesn't seem so funny now."

Jean-Claude zoomed past, chasing imaginary outlaws. He circled the policeman nearby, then rode off again.

Kate asked, "Do these creeps have any unusual features? Anything that makes them stand out?"

"Not in physical appearance," Joanna said. "But Walter George Reineke has severe asthma."

"So?"

"So he was last seen in San Diego and is believed to be on his way to Los Angeles," Joanna went on, her voice now clinical. "The air here is putrid, filled with smog and other pollutants. It could trigger a severe asthmatic attack that wouldn't respond to the drugs he usually takes. He would have to go to an emergency room."

"And you've got his picture plastered on the walls of every ER in Los Angeles, right?"

Joanna nodded. "And his name is in the computer file of every drugstore, just in case he tries to have his Idaho prescriptions filled down here."

Kate looked at Joanna admiringly. "Sis, I'd hate to have you tracking me down."

"Apparently the terrorists feel the same way," Joanna said as she thought about the futility of trying to track down the leader of the group through his medical problems. The ER's in Los Angeles were so busy on weekends that the personnel barely had time to glance at people's faces. All Walter George Reineke would need was thick glasses and a false mustache, and nobody would recognize him. "It's a real long shot," she muttered, more to herself than to Kate.

"But that's better than no shot."

"I guess." Joanna stood and straightened her skirt. "Do you feel like some ice cream?"

"Not really," Kate said, waving Jean-Claude over. "But I know someone who does."

1:02 P.M.

Rudy Payte lay on the floor in the rear of the Chevy van, sweating in the heat. All the windows were rolled up and the noontime sun was blazing down, raising the temperature inside to over a hundred degrees. Rudy cursed at his discomfort, hating the heat and humidity and the pools of perspiration forming beneath him. But most of all he hated the dangerous position Eva had placed him in. The van was parked in a loading zone in front of the ice cream parlor. Directly across the street was the black-and-white squad car that was watching Joanna Blalock. *Son of a bitch! Son of a bitch!* The cop is going to know something is wrong and come over and check the van. And I'll have to kill him. What the hell could Eva be thinking about? There was a cop right across from him, and there was another cop inside the ice cream shop with the Blalock family. And the street was busy. There would be no quick getaway, even if they did manage to survive. Stupid plan! Stupid! Whatever the plan was.

Eva hadn't given him the details. All she had told him was to lie flat in the van and not look out the window. When he heard two raps on the side door he was to open it, then get behind the wheel and drive off. Right! While the cops just stood there and waved to him. *Shit! She's going to get us killed.* Rudy took deep breaths, trying to calm himself. Four more days, he thought, and I'll be laying on a beach in Mexico. With a half million in the bank.

There was a soft rubbing sound on the windshield.

Rudy reached for his semiautomatic weapon, all his senses instantly on alert. It's got to be the cop, he told himself. He lay perfectly still, his heart pounding in his chest. He wondered if the cop was going to try the doors. They were all locked, except for the side door nearest Rudy. If the cop opened that door, Rudy would kill him and drive off. He'd have no choice. Eva would have to fend for herself.

Rudy heard the sound against the windshield again. Carefully he inched his body forward so he could peer through the opening between the front seats. It was a fat meter maid placing a parking ticket between the windshield and the wiper blade. Fuck you and your ticket! The guy I stole the van from can pay it.

Rudy worked his way back to his original position. The heat made it hard to breathe. The temperature seemed to be rising by the minute. Rudy reached for a small bottle of distilled water and gulped it down. He wondered how much longer it would be and how much longer he could tolerate the heat. Another fifteen minutes and his brain would be fried. He again reached for the small bottle and tilted it up, trying to suck out the last few drops of water.

Outside he heard traffic passing by, then the laughter of a small child. He wanted to take a quick look, but Eva had instructed him to stay out of sight. He heard the sound of laughter once more, this time much closer. Rudy couldn't resist the urge to look. Slowly he raised up and peeked out of the lower corner of the window. The Blalocks were entering the ice cream parlor, a cop right behind them. Coming up the street he saw Eva pushing a baby carriage.

Rudy dropped to the floor and tightened the silencer on his weapon. Then he waited.

"Chocolate," Jean-Claude announced to the man behind the ice cream counter.

"One scoop or two?" the man asked.

Jean-Claude looked up at his mother for guidance. She held up a finger. Jean-Claude nodded and held up one finger.

"He likes those tiny marshmallows too," Kate told the server.

The man prepared the ice cream cone and handed it to Jean-Claude. "Here you go, little fellow."

"Merci beaucoup," Jean-Claude said, smiling at the server. The man was wearing a red apron and had a protuberant abdomen and a fluffy white beard. Jean-Claude thought he looked like Santa Claus. Carefully Jean-Claude picked off the miniature marshmallows and ate them one by one. "More, Ma-ma."

"Coming right up." The man came from behind the counter and added a fresh layer of marshmallows.

Kate said, "You're going to spoil him."

The owner of the ice cream parlor nodded happily. "That's my job."

The small shop was crowded with lunchtime customers. All the tables and stools were occupied. There wasn't even room to stand against the wall.

"We should start back," Joanna said.

The policeman guarding them led the way out into bright sunlight. Traffic was heavy with cars and big trucks. He waited for the vehicles to pass before giving a hand signal to the black-and-white squad car across the street.

A young woman pushing a baby carriage approached.

The policeman stepped back to give her room.

Now the carriage was positioned between the policeman and the Blalocks. The cop moved back farther, almost touching the green van parked at the curb.

The red-haired woman smiled at the policeman as she reached into the carriage. He thought she was adjusting the angle of the bonnet to keep the bright sun out of the baby's face.

Eva had the gun with a silencer out before the policeman could even begin to react. The first shot went into his abdomen, the second into his shoulder. He stood stupefied for a moment, then dropped to the sidewalk.

Eva rapped twice on the van door, and it instantly opened. She grabbed Jean-Claude by the collar of his shirt and threw him inside. Quickly she turned back to Joanna and pointed the gun at her forehead. "Get in or I'll blow your head off!"

Eva shoved Joanna into the van, then Kate after her.

"Hey! Hey!" The owner of the ice cream parlor came running out of his shop. "What are you doing?"

Eva whirled and fired again at point-blank range. The rotund man dropped like a dead weight. Now Eva was inside the van, slamming the sliding door shut. "Go! Go!" she yelled at Rudy.

The policeman in the black-and-white cruiser watched the Chevy van drive off. He searched for his partner but couldn't find him. Then he saw the crowd gathering. A woman screamed.

The policeman threw open the door of the squad car and ran for the ice cream shop. He didn't see the motorcycle that ran over him.

34

Jake hurried through the automatic doors and into the ER at Memorial Hospital. The area appeared to be in a state of chaos. Nurses and orderlies rushed by, some pushing gurneys, others carrying plastic bags of fresh plasma and whole blood. A young doctor was trying to yell orders above the turmoil. Jake stepped back and waited impatiently as another gurney passed. The body on it was motionless and completely covered by a sheet.

"Jake! Over here!" Farelli called out. He was standing by the door to Trauma Room 1. At his feet was a transparent container that held a policeman's badge and weapon.

Jake waited for a wheelchair to go by, then quickly walked over. "How many dead?"

"None of ours," Farelli reported. "At least, not yet."

"I just saw a body on a stretcher. Who was that?"

"A suicide," Farelli said. "Some guy took a dive off a nearby hotel."

The door to the trauma room opened, and an EKG technician with her machine came out. Jake and Farelli moved aside as she hustled down the corridor and into another room.

Jake took out his notepad and rapidly flipped pages. "All right, tell me what you've got."

"Nada. A big zilch," Farelli said.

"Did anyone see Joanna?"

Farelli shook his head. "Nobody saw her or anything else."

"No witnesses at all?"

Farelli shook his head again.

"Jesus," Jake hissed angrily. "How the hell did that happen? How the hell did they pull it off without anybody seeing anything?"

Farelli shrugged weakly. "I got no idea."

"Somebody should have seen something," Jake snapped. "These bastards aren't invisible."

"Weathers said it happened in a flash." Farelli took out his notepad and began turning pages. "One second Joanna was there, the next she was gone. All he remembers is seeing a dark van drive away."

William Weathers was the policeman who had been stationed in the squad car adjacent to the ice cream parlor. While running across the street to aid his partner, he was hit by a passing vehicle and sustained a badly fractured leg. Farelli had spoken with him briefly in the ER.

He turned to another page in his notepad. "Weathers couldn't be sure of the van's make. Ford or Chevy, maybe."

"And I'll bet the driver didn't stop."

"Nope. He just kept on going. And, again, there were no witnesses."

Jake cursed under his breath, wondering how the terrorists could have worked out so many details in such a short time. "That hit-and-run driver was probably a part of the plan."

"Could be," Farelli said, nodding. "Everything else was so well executed. It was like a commando strike."

Jake nodded back. "That fits too. Remember, Eva Reineke was being trained as a Green Beret before they booted her ass out."

"Well, they must have trained her real good," Farelli said sourly. "Because all she left behind was a baby carriage and two shot-up bodies."

The swinging doors to Trauma Room 1 abruptly

opened, and a heavyset surgeon came out into the corridor. He was middle-aged and balding with a thick mustache. The front of his scrub suit was soaked with perspiration.

"How is he doing?" Farelli asked, holding up his shield.

"He'll live," the surgeon said. "But he's got a compound fracture of the tibia that will have to be surgically repaired."

"Can we talk to him?" Jake asked.

The surgeon hesitated before shaking his head. "We're moving him to the OR right now."

"All we need is a few minutes," Jake implored. "A person's life may depend on it."

The surgeon hesitated again, then said, "Make it quick. When the orderlies with the gurney get here, he goes."

Jake hurried into the room, Farelli a step behind. A nurse was adjusting the flow rate of the IV in Weathers's arm. Jake approached the surgical table, his eyes going to the dressing atop the jagged bone sticking out of Weathers's leg.

"How are you feeling?" Jake asked.

"Like shit," Weathers said through parched lips. "My leg is killing me."

The nurse looked over. "Do you want another shot?"

"I'm all right," Weathers said, but he was clenching his jaw against the pain.

"We have to talk fast because you're on your way to the OR," Jake said urgently.

"I know."

"Start from the moment Joanna Blalock left the hospital."

"She walked out the back entrance with Keely in front. They went through the parking lot to the park behind the hospital. That's where she met her sister and the little boy."

"Did you ever lose sight of her?"

"Not at that point."

"What happened next?"

"The women sat on the park bench while the little boy played," Weathers continued. "There wasn't anything or anybody unusual. You know, women with kids and babies. That kind of thing."

Jake's eyes narrowed. "Were there any baby carriages?"

"Yeah, there was a—" Weathers winced as a sharp pain shot up his leg. Perspiration poured off his face. He turned to the nurse. "Maybe I'll have that shot after all."

The nurse injected Demerol through the IV tubing.

Weathers felt his head floating, the pain now more of a dull ache. He forced himself to concentrate through the haze.

"You said there was a carriage," Jake prompted.

Weathers nodded. "It had a big bonnet. A young woman with red hair was pushing it."

"Which way did she go?"

Weathers thought for a moment. "She didn't come back by me, so she must have gone out the back of the park."

And then to the ice cream parlor, Jake thought. He exchanged knowing glances with Farelli. The woman pushing the carriage was probably Eva Reineke, doing a reconnaissance run to make sure everything was in place. "What happened next?"

"Nothing much," Weathers said, trying to moisten his lips with his tongue. "A motorcycle roared by and stopped at the light, then went on."

Jake leaned forward. "Did you see the rider?"

"A skinhead with tattoos on his arms."

"Old or young?"

"Older. Middle-aged. Maybe fifty-five or so."

The description fit Walter George Reineke. It had to be him, Jake thought. "Then what happened?"

"They left the park and walked over to the ice cream parlor. I—"

The door swung open with a loud bang, and an orderly came in pulling a gurney after him.

Jake looked over to the nurse. "I need another minute."

"No can do," the nurse said. "It's moving time."

As the nurse and orderly went about shifting Weathers from the table to the gurney, Jake kept asking questions. "When you reached the ice cream parlor, was the van already there?"

"It was parked right in front of the loading zone."

So damn smart, Jake was thinking. Not only did the van block Weathers's view, but it made him park the squad car across the street. "Did you notice anything about the van? Color? Make?"

"I didn't pay it much attention," Weathers said as the pain started to return. "I know I should have."

You're goddamn right you should have, Jake wanted to say, but he held his tongue.

"Then the van drove off and I heard a scream," Weathers went on. "I got out of my car and headed across the street. Then something roared by. That's the last thing I remember."

"Roared?"

Weathers nodded as the nurse and orderly rolled the gurney toward the door. "It sounded more like a motorcycle than a car."

Now the trauma room was empty and silent, the floor littered with used dressings and IV tubing and paper wrappings. The air was filled with the odor of old blood.

"He said he didn't pay the van much attention," Jake growled. "He must have had his head up his ass."

Farelli nodded. "He didn't play it too smart."

Jake began pacing the floor, kicking at the litter as he went by Farelli. "He got sloppy and he got lazy. And he just might have cost Joanna her life."

"They were up against pros, Jake. I'm not sure any of us could have done much better."

"Maybe, maybe not." But Jake knew Farelli was right. The terrorists had a perfectly designed plan that they executed with precision. They knew exactly how to take out both cops. He turned back to Farelli. "Who do you figure ran over Weathers?"

"The skinhead on the motorcycle," Farelli said at once.

"Do you know who that was?"

Farelli shook his head.

"Walter George Reineke."

"Get out of here!"

"Oh, yeah," Jake said firmly. "It was him. The FBI profile said he was in his late fifties but looked younger. He was balding fast, so he often shaved his head. And he had tattoos on his arms and was a motorcycle freak. Now, who do you think ran over Weathers?"

"Old Walter George himself."

"I guess he decided to come up and help out his little girl."

Farelli smiled crookedly. "That's what daddies are for."

Jake started pacing the floor again, still angry with Weathers for screwing up, but angrier yet with himself. He should have insisted that Joanna stay in the forensics laboratory during the day, with a cop at her side and another at the door. But the park had seemed so innocent and so easy to guard. It wasn't the park that caused the problem, though. It was the trip to the ice cream parlor that had turned out so deadly. Who could have known? Who could have even guessed?

But you knew they were coming after her, Jake berated himself, you knew it. And you weren't there when she needed you the most. And that was the story of your whole goddamn life.

Jake took a deep breath, trying to push his guilt and anger aside and focus in on the problem he faced—finding Joanna before the terrorists killed her. What was the single most important thing that could lead him to her? What questions had to be answered first? He thought again about the events outside the ice cream parlor. The cops. The shooting. The scream. The motorcycle. There were no clues, nothing to go on. He went through the events again, slower this time. "The van," he finally said.

"What?"

"Wherever the van is, that's where Joanna will be," Jake went on, now concentrating on possible ways to identify the vehicle. "First, check out all stores within a ten-mile radius that sell baby carriages."

Farelli began scribbling in his notepad. "I don't see how that's going to help us. They sure as hell wouldn't leave their license number with the store."

"No, but maybe a clerk carried the carriage out to the van. Maybe he remembers it. The make, the year. Who knows?"

"But chances are it's going to be a stolen vehicle," Farelli said thoughtfully. "Maybe they dumped it."

"They're probably still using it," Jake told him. "When you've got five or six people to move around, a van is the best way to do it."

Farelli nodded. "Particularly if you've got those tinted windows."

Jake wrinkled his brow and concentrated harder, trying to cover all possibilities. "Of course, they could have stolen yet another van to switch over to. Kind of like a backup." Jake slowly rubbed his hands together. "Get a list of all vans stolen in the greater Los Angeles area over the past ten days. Pay particular attention to the dark-colored Chevies and Fords."

Farelli looked up. "Weathers was just guessing when he said Ford or Chevy."

"I know. But first impressions are usually the best ones."

Farelli jotted down a final note. "Jake, I think our best chance to ID the vehicle is to talk with Weathers's partner and the ice cream shop owner. They were the ones closest to the van."

"I guess," Jake said, unconvinced. Sometimes the people closest saw the least. But then again, he thought, the van was parked out front for more than a few minutes. Maybe the ice cream shop owner got a good look. "How are they doing?"

Farelli shrugged. "They rushed them up to surgery before I got here."

Jake started pacing again. "We've got to find that damn van."

"And hope the doc is close by."

"Yeah." Jake sighed, knowing they were hoping against hope. He wondered why Joanna posed such a threat to the terrorists. Was it something she knew or something she was close to finding out? Maybe. But why kidnap her? Why not just kill her like they tried to do the day before? There was no rhyme or reason to it. Nothing made sense here. Nothing.

"Jake," Farelli said quietly. "You know there is a real chance the doc is already dead."

"I don't think so," Jake said as a picture of Joanna flashed through his mind. "If they'd wanted her dead they would have shot her on the spot. And they wouldn't have bothered to take Jean-Claude either."

"Why do you think they grabbed the kid?"

"Insurance," Jake said. "They'll separate the kid from Joanna and Kate and promise not to hurt him as long as

Joanna cooperates. And of course they'd never try to escape unless they had Jean-Claude with them."

"That may all be true," Farelli said somberly. "But come the nineteenth they'll kill the doc."

"I know."

"And the boy and his mother."

"I know that too."

The door to the trauma room opened, and the heavyset surgeon entered. He had on a new scrub suit but was already starting to sweat through it.

"I've got bad news," he said.

"What?" Jake asked.

"The cop who got shot died on the table," the surgeon said without emotion. "One of the bullets tore through his pulmonary artery. He didn't stand a chance."

Farelli looked away, shaking his head sadly. He had known Joe Keely for ten years. A good cop with a wife and teenage children. A daughter about to go to college whom Joe couldn't stop talking about. "Does his wife know?"

"Not yet. We're trying to contact her now."

Jake asked, "What about the ice cream shop owner?"

"He's not doing so good."

"Is he going to make it?"

"It's touch and go," the surgeon said, turning for the door. "Last I heard they were having trouble keeping his blood pressure up."

35

"No! No!" Kate yelled, holding Jean-Claude tightly. "My baby stays with me."

"It's going to be dark and damp in the cellar," Eva said calmly.

Kate turned away, placing herself between Jean-Claude and the terrorist. "He stays with me."

"If the boy starts screaming and crying, we'll gag and tie the three of you up. Understood?" Eva's voice was controlled and nonthreatening, but she kept her hand on the butt of the pistol that protruded from her coat pocket. "And once you're bound and gagged, you'll remain that way."

Kate glanced over at Joanna, uncertain what to do. She couldn't let them have Jean-Claude. She just couldn't.

"Well?" Eva asked as she reached for the door to the cellar. "Make up your mind."

There was a tense stillness in the hallway. No one moved. Outside, somewhere in the distance, a siren wailed.

"What do you want?" Joanna asked, trying not to show her fear. Her eyes darted down the hall of the house, looking for a way out. The male terrorist was standing at the entrance to the kitchen, adjusting the silencer on his weapon.

Eva followed Joanna's line of vision. "Don't even think about it."

Again Kate glanced anxiously at Joanna, silently asking for guidance. Her hold on Jean-Claude tightened even more.

Jean-Claude squirmed in his mother's arms. "Ma-ma, may I have some water?"

Eva signaled Rudy, who disappeared into the kitchen. Then she took out her pistol and slowly screwed on a silencer. Her eyes never left Joanna.

With effort Joanna pushed her panic aside and hurriedly assessed their situation. They were in a residential, middle-class neighborhood that she didn't recognize. After the shooting they'd been forced to lie on the floor of the van while it drove around for what seemed like hours. When the van finally stopped, Joanna had no idea where they were. She didn't even know if they were still in Los Angeles. But wherever they were, they were trapped and being held by terrorists who would eventually kill them. Maybe there was some way to bargain with them, Joanna thought desperately. Maybe she could trade information for their lives. But deep down she knew that would never work.

Rudy returned with a plastic cup of water for Jean-Claude. The little boy gulped it down and said, "Merci."

"Right." Rudy took the cup back, crushed it and dropped it to the floor. "Let's get on with it."

"Aunt Joanna, do they have a television?" Jean-Claude asked innocently.

"I don't think so," Joanna said.

Eva smiled, but there was no warmth to it. "We'll have one for you in a few minutes."

"May I go with the lady and watch the television?" Jean-Claude inquired.

Kate looked over at Joanna. "What do I do?"

"Let them take Jean-Claude," Joanna advised. "They won't hurt him."

"How can you be so sure?" Kate asked worriedly.

"Because it's me they want, not him," Joanna said,

surprised by the evenness in her voice. "And they know if they harm him they'll get nothing from me."

Reluctantly Kate put her son down and patted his back. "You must stay with the lady."

"Then I can watch television also?" Jean-Claude asked.

"Yes."

Eva opened the door to the cellar, her gaze still on the women. "Leave your purses and your watches on the floor before you start down."

Rudy came over and quickly searched the women's jackets for possible weapons. He felt nothing except Kate's cigarettes, which he pocketed. "They're clean."

"Move it!" Eva ordered, nudging Joanna with the barrel of her pistol.

Joanna led the way down into the darkened cellar. The light was so dim it was hard to see the steps, but she could feel them. They were narrow and made of wood and creaked loudly as weight was placed on them. The railing consisted of a length of metal tubing. It was old and rusty.

"Hold on to the railing," Joanna said. "And take the steps slowly, one at a time."

"It—it's so dark down here," Kate whispered.

"I know." Joanna was counting the steps. Eight. Nine. Ten. Eleven. Twelve. Now her feet were on the cement floor. She quickly calculated the height of the cellar. There were twelve steps down, each step approximately a foot long. That meant the ceiling was twelve feet off the floor.

The door locked behind them. They heard the lock slip into place.

Joanna sensed Kate close by in the darkness. From somewhere near the ceiling she saw a faint glimmer of light. It came and went, then came again, but Joanna couldn't locate its source. Then it was gone.

Slowly Joanna moved forward. A cobweb touched her

face, and she quickly brushed it away. She tried to orient herself, but it was impossible in the blackness. Damn it! They needed light, if only for a moment. From behind her she heard Kate crying softly. Joanna reached back for her sister. "Jean-Claude will be fine."

"But he's just a little boy." Kate sobbed. "He has no idea what's happening."

"And that's good," Joanna said reassuringly. "That way he won't cause any trouble. The last thing we want is to be gagged and tied up."

"What difference does it make?" Kate asked hopelessly.

Joanna leaned toward Kate and lowered her voice. "When we talk about important things, whisper it. They may be listening in. Got it?"

"Got it."

Joanna moved in closer. "The reason it's important not to be tied is that tied people can't escape."

"There's no way out of here," Kate said loudly. "This is a damn cellar."

"Shhh!" Joanna hushed her sister. "Keep it down."

"But there's no way out," Kate said, whispering.

"Sure there is," Joanna whispered back. "We just have to find it."

"What about Jean-Claude?"

"We don't leave without him," Joanna said, her voice calm and a thousand times braver than she felt.

Joanna sighed in the darkness, knowing she was talking nonsense. The only way out was up the steps and through the door, which was locked and probably guarded. And even if they got through the door, they could never reach Jean-Claude, who would be watched by Rudy. Joanna shivered thinking about the male terrorist. He was cold-blooded and had probably enjoyed slicing up Maria Gonzalez. Jake had told Joanna about

Rudy's fingerprints on the razor blade. The sadistic bastard. He had killed the poor woman inch by inch.

She shivered again, wondering what Rudy might do to her if she didn't deliver what they wanted.

"Are you okay?" Kate asked.

"Yeah," Joanna said as the glimmer of light flickered once more.

Joanna looked up and saw a faint streak of light coming from high above. Cautiously she moved forward, waving her hand in front of her to detect any obstacles in her path. The light intensified for a moment, and this allowed Joanna to see the outline of a small window. It was up high, at least ten feet. She could never reach it. The light faded and the darkness returned.

Joanna turned back to Kate. "Did they take your cigarettes?"

"Yes."

"What about your lighter?"

"They took that too." Kate reached down and double-checked. The lighter had slipped through the hole in her pocket again and fallen inside the lining. "No," she said, digging. "I've still got it."

"Give it to me."

Kate placed the disposable plastic lighter in Joanna's hand. "I don't know how much fuel it has left. I've had it for a while."

"I thought you just started smoking again."

"Cigarettes," Kate told her. "I have an occasional joint."

"Very nice," Joanna said sternly. "We'll have to talk about that when we get out of here."

"You mean *if* we get out of here."

Joanna flicked the lighter. The flame was small and illuminated things poorly. Joanna quickly surveyed the cellar. It was square, approximately twenty-five by twenty-five feet. The walls were bare and covered with green plaster. In the far corner were a bucket and mop, and next to them a little wooden table. The window was very small and up near the ceiling.

The flame burnt Joanna's fingers, and she jerked her hand away. The lighter fell to the cement floor and rattled around.

"Goddamn it!" Joanna cursed, licking at her fingers. "I dropped it."

"Keep your voice down," Kate reminded her. "We don't want them to know we've got a lighter."

"Right," Joanna said softly, still licking at her thumb and hoping a blister wouldn't form. "Stay put while I try to find it."

Joanna knelt down and searched the floor around her. It was cold and dirty and in places had what felt like slicks of oil. Her hand came to a balled-up rag. The lighter was atop it.

"Found it," she said and got to her feet. The light flickered in through the window again, and Joanna thought she saw a lightbulb above her. Then the cellar went dark again. "Did you see a lightbulb on the ceiling?"

"It was a light fixture," Kate said. "And it's too high for us to reach."

"The switch wouldn't be near the fixture. It would be on the wall somewhere."

"Or in the hall outside the cellar door."

"Or maybe on the wall inside the door," Joanna said, hoping against hope. The light was crucial. There was no chance of escape without it. "When they let us go upstairs, check the walls for the light switch."

"Why do you think they'll let us upstairs?"

"To use the bathroom and to pacify Jean-Claude," Joanna told her. "Eventually he'll get cranky and demand to see you. The last thing the terrorists want is a baby crying loudly. That could draw attention from the outside."

"But what if he keeps crying?" Kate asked, alarmed. "They won't hurt him, will they?"

Joanna reached for Kate's hand. "He'll stop crying the moment he sees you, and I can guarantee they won't hurt him."

"How can you be so sure?"

"Because they know if something happens to Jean-Claude, they won't get anything from us."

Kate began sobbing again. "They're going to kill us and then they're going to kill my baby."

"Only if we let them," Joanna said, trying to keep her voice firm but feeling every bit as helpless as her sister. "Now dry those tears. I can't think with you crying."

Kate sniffed back her tears and swallowed audibly. "My God! What a way to end up. We're going to die in a cellar. They'll never even find our bodies."

"Don't think about dying," Joanna said quietly. "Think about getting out."

Kate shivered. "This place is like a tomb. The darkness almost swallows you up. It makes you want to scream."

"I know," Joanna said, remembering how she had screamed and yelled and cried when she was buried in a large drainage pipe beneath six feet of earth. Jake and a bloodhound named Sniff had found her. She envisioned Jake now working around the clock to find her, pushing himself and Farelli to exhaustion and beyond. But there were no clues left behind, nothing for him to follow. It would take a miracle for Jake to locate them, but he was their only hope for survival.

"Sis," Kate said softly, breaking the silence, "did I ever tell you how much I love you?"

"A lot of times."

"You did so much for all of us," Kate went on. "You always put the family first."

"It was my pleasure."

"It was really hard for you, but you did it so well," Kate said. "And even when I was older I was always the little sister you had to look out for. That made me love you even more."

Joanna thought back to her father's death. Kate had been only eight years old and had no grasp of what had happened and how drastically their lives would be changed. Joanna tried to envision her mother and father, but their faces were indistinct. Now Joanna could see their headstones. And she knew that soon she and Kate and Jean-Claude would follow them into the grave. The Blalock line was about to be wiped out by a bunch of terrorists. "We've got to find a way out of this damn place."

"How do we do that?"

"First, you've got to push your fear aside."

"I don't think I can."

"If you can't do it for yourself, then do it for Jean-Claude."

Kate took a deep breath. "Tell me what to do."

Joanna lowered her voice even further. "When they come down for us, do everything very slowly. The longer it takes them to get what they want, the better chance we have to survive."

"What do you think they want?"

"Information," Joanna whispered. "It's something they need to know."

"Like what?"

"I can't be sure. My guess is I know something they need badly for their plans on April nineteenth." Joanna tried to swallow away the dryness in her throat. "I'll have to play it by ear and try not to give them what they want. Perhaps I can alter things just enough to keep them confused."

"That could be dangerous, Joanna. Remember, they've got my little Jean-Claude."

"How could I forget?"

"The Ten Righteous," Kate said disgustedly. "They probably believe that God approves of their kidnapping women and children."

"They don't believe in anything other than their own cause. To them, God and the Bible are just convenient excuses."

A glimmer of light came through the window again. It flickered and dimmed but didn't disappear. Carefully Joanna walked forward in the hazy darkness, her hand stretched out in front of her. She reached the far wall and felt around for the wooden table. She had to ignite the lighter briefly to find it. Quietly she slid the table across the floor until it was directly under the small window. She climbed up on the table and, standing on her tiptoes, looked out.

The window was very small and covered with a thick layer of dirt, both inside and out. There were heavy metal bars across it. In front of the window was a pile of leaves or trash or maybe a thick bush. Joanna couldn't be sure, but whatever it was it seemed to sway with the breeze.

Joanna tried to wipe away the dirt and grime on the window with her sleeve. Outside it looked like early evening with shadows everywhere. For a moment Joanna thought she saw something move. Was it a person? An animal? She strained for a better look.

The door to the cellar suddenly opened, and light flooded in from above. Something bounced down the steps and hit the floor with a dull thud.

Joanna and Kate stared into the dimness and, holding their breaths, listened for the sound of a baby's cry.

The door above them slammed shut, and the darkness returned.

36

"I feel like a vulture waiting around to see if this guy is still alive," Farelli said.

"He'd better be," Jake said gruffly. "He's the only chance we've got to identify that van."

They were pacing the floor outside the surgical ICU. It was almost noon and Sol Fischer, the owner of the ice cream shop, had just returned from his second operation in the past twenty-four hours. The first surgery was to remove a bullet as well as the spleen and a large segment of intestines it had ripped apart. The second surgery was needed to find the source of Fischer's internal bleeding and stem it before he hemorrhaged to death.

"How old is this guy?" Jake asked.

Farelli referred to his notepad. "Seventy-two."

"Shit."

"But the doc said his general health was pretty good."

"Seventy-two is still seventy-two," Jake said hoarsely. "And he caught one right in the gut."

"Yeah."

They continued pacing, both looking haggard and fighting the deep fatigue that came from working through the night without sleep. Despite their efforts, they still had no information on the van. A careful check of all the vehicles recently stolen in the Los Angeles area listed sixteen vans. Six of these were dark-colored, and all had been recovered before the shooting at the ice cream shop.

The witnesses to the crime had been thoroughly reques-
tioned. Nobody remembered the van.

The door to the ICU opened, and a middle-aged nurse
walked out. The front of her scrub suit was splattered
with blood.

Jake hurried over and showed his shield. "How is Mr.
Fischer doing?"

"He's still with us," the nurse said wearily. She sighed
deeply and shook her head. "Do you know how long Sol
Fischer has had that ice cream parlor?"

"A long time, huh?"

"Try forty years," the nurse said sadly. "Everybody
from Memorial goes there and takes their children so Sol
can dote on the kids and give them extra sprinkles for
their ice cream and make them smile and laugh. He's a
wonderful, generous man, and look what they've done to
him." She shook her head again and wiped her nose with
the back of her hand. "The world is really fucked up."

"Tell me about it," Jake said and watched the nurse head
for a nearby lounge. His eyes went to the wall clock overhead. It was noon. April nineteenth was sixty hours away.

Turning to Farelli, Jake said, "It sounds like the guy is
barely holding on."

Farelli nodded. "We need to get lucky here and real
soon. We'd better hope somebody sees the pictures of the
terrorists on television and remembers seeing those bastards somewhere."

"That won't happen," Jake said. "They'll go underground now until Monday."

"Sometimes it's not so easy hiding two women and a
kid."

"Sure it is. Just tie them up and pull the drapes."

And kill them after they've served their purpose,
Farelli thought grimly. "Maybe somebody will spot the
van somewhere it shouldn't be."

"Chances are it's in a garage," Jake said, hoping

against hope that their ongoing search of new house rentals on the Westside might turn up something. The terrorists had to have established a new base of operations after the West Hollywood bomb destroyed their old one. But there were so many houses. It was like looking for a needle in a haystack.

"We must be missing something," Farelli grumbled. "They can't be this good."

"Oh, yes, they can," Jake said frankly. "They are pros at this. And they're always one step ahead of us because they know where they're going and we don't."

Jake went over to a drinking fountain and took a swallow, then splashed cool water on his forehead. All through the night he had gone over every detail of the case, looking for a clue or lead but finding nothing. The van was the key to the terrorist group. Jake was certain of that, and so was Dan Hurley. It was Hurley's idea to check the tire marks left by the van as it screeched away from the crime scene. An automotive expert had been called in in an effort to identify the tire manufacturer, which might lead them to the make and model of the van. But the tire mark was incomplete. The expert guessed it was made by a tire from a General Motors van, but he couldn't be sure. And while we're looking at tire marks, Jake thought miserably, a sadistic son of a bitch with a razor could be working over Joanna. The van. The goddamn van. He had to find it.

The door to the ICU opened abruptly. A surgeon wearing a long white coat came over to the detectives. He was tall and lanky, his hair gray and crew cut. The name tag on his coat read ROBERT KANE, M.D.

"How's our man?" Jake asked hurriedly.

"Not good," Kane said. "He should have been dead five times over. But he's a real fighter."

"I need to talk with him," Jake said urgently. "Three people's lives are at stake."

The surgeon hesitated. "I doubt that he'll be able to answer your questions. His vital signs are still shaky, and he's heavily sedated to boot."

"It's life and death," Jake said gravely.

Kane took a deep breath, not wanting to subject his patient to any additional stress. "Keep your questions simple, and don't push him. If he starts to go sour, you move out pronto."

"Right," Jake agreed quickly.

The surgeon led the way back into the surgical ICU. The room was much smaller than Jake thought it would be. There were five beds lined up in a row against the wall, all occupied. The patients lay motionless, but some were groaning above the sound of the ventilators. Over the head of each bed was an electronic monitor that showed the patient's pulse, blood pressure and respiratory rate.

The surgeon went to the middle bed, where he leaned over the patient and called out, "Mr. Fischer! Can you hear me?"

Sol showed no response.

"Sol! If you can hear me, open your eyes."

Sol's eyelids fluttered briefly, then opened a little.

"Sol, the police are here. They need to ask you a few questions."

Sol's head moved in what seemed to be a nod. He wet his lips with his tongue.

Kane glanced at the monitors above the bed. The blood pressure was 100/70, the pulse rate 96 per minute. He hoped again that he had found and tied off all the bleeders in Sol Fischer's abdomen. The surgeon gestured to Jake with his head.

Jake moved in and bent over, close to the patient's ear. "Mr. Fischer, I'm Lieutenant Sinclair. Do you remember the shooting yesterday?"

Sol licked at his parched lips. "They grabbed the little boy. I ran out to help. That's all I remember."

"Do you remember the shots?"

"Jus-just the sound." Fischer slowly exhaled, then closed his eyes.

The surgeon quickly looked up at the electronic monitors. The vital signs were stable. Kane gently shook the old man's shoulder. "Sol, are you still awake?"

Sol swallowed with effort, keeping his eyes shut. "When can I have a little water?"

"We'll give you some ice chips to suck on in a few minutes."

Sol nodded appreciatively.

Jake asked, "Do you recall the vehicle outside your shop? The one that drove away?"

"They parked in the loading zone and stayed there until the shooting."

"What kind of vehicle was it?"

"A van."

Jake moved in closer. "What was the make?"

"Don't know."

"Do you remember anything about it?"

Fischer's eyes blinked briefly, then shut again. "I think it had a dark color."

Jake straightened up, realizing that he had come to another dead end. He looked across at Farelli. "We've got to find that damn van."

"We ain't going to do it without a license number," Farelli said. "No way."

"Ask the meter maid," Sol muttered, his voice barely above a whisper.

"What?" Jake quickly leaned over the patient. "What about the meter maid?"

"She gave him a ticket for parking in the loading zone." Jake ran for the door, Farelli a half step behind him.

37

Joanna awakened stiff and groggy. Everything was black and dead quiet, and for a moment she didn't know where she was. Then she heard Kate stirring beside her and felt the hard mattress beneath her.

With effort Joanna pushed herself up and waited for her head to clear. The mattress, she thought, now remembering how the terrorists had thrown it down the stairs. In the darkness it had landed with a thud. At first she and Kate had believed it was little Jean-Claude's body that had bounced down the steps and slammed onto the cement floor. It had frightened them out of their wits. Then they saw the mattress, which had ended up in a standing position against the wall. Thank God for the lighter. Without it they could have spent an hour crawling on the floor, frantically searching for a body that wasn't there.

Above Joanna heard people walking. First came very soft footsteps, then loud ones. Two people, she surmised. Probably Jean-Claude and Rudy, whose job it was to follow the little boy around. The footsteps gradually faded, and Joanna envisioned Jean-Claude galloping away on his imaginary horse, having no idea how close to death he was. Maybe it was best that way.

She again thought about their predicament and about possible ways out. There was no chance of escape even if Jean-Claude was in the cellar with them. He was small enough to crawl through the narrow window, but not through the iron bars across it. She wondered whether the bars were bolted in. If not, maybe they could be pried loose. But then what?

Joanna's gaze went to the place on the wall where the window should have been. There was no light, not even a glimmer. There was no sunlight, which meant it must be night. She shifted around on the mattress, trying to guess what time it was and how long they'd been asleep. Hours for sure, if the stiffness in her joints and muscles was any sign. But how many hours? Joanna wished she still had her watch. At least that would have kept her oriented to time.

There was a loud thud on the floor upstairs. Then another, even louder.

Kate awoke with a start. "What? What was that?"

"Something fell on the floor above us," Joanna said.

"Was it Jean-Claude?" Kate asked, her head clearing quickly.

"I doubt it," Joanna said. "I heard him running into another room a moment ago. He's fine."

"When do you think they'll let me see him?"

"In a little while. It won't be much longer."

"How can you be so certain?"

"Because Jean-Claude will get cranky and start crying if he doesn't see you soon, and they don't want that," Joanna told her. "Now, I want you to flex your arms and legs and get the circulation going."

Kate stood and tried to stretch the soreness from her muscles. "Jesus! I'm so stiff."

"It'll pass." Joanna flicked the disposable lighter. The flame seemed even smaller than before and illuminated things poorly. She quickly reached for the oily cloth on the floor, then turned the lighter off.

"What are you doing with the rag?" Kate asked quietly.

"I'm going to wrap the lighter in it and place it against the wall," Joanna whispered. "They might search us again when we go back upstairs."

"Why not just put it under the mattress?" Kate whispered back.

"Because they might search down here while we're up there."

Upstairs a faucet was turned on, and they could hear water running through the pipes. The blackness around them intensified the noise, which went on and on. Then there were heavy footsteps and the noise stopped.

Kate reached out her hand, trying to locate Joanna. "Where are you, Sis?"

"On the other side of the mattress."

"Damn! It's so dark down here."

"I know."

The darkness seemed more intense to Joanna as well. And the air was so still it was almost suffocating. She now wished she hadn't flicked the lighter on to find the rag that was right at her feet. The brief light had only made the blackness seem more enveloping. And more important, she had used up another flick of the lighter, which was already low on fuel. Stupid! Stupid! Use your damn brains!

The door to the cellar suddenly opened. It took a moment for them to acclimate to the blinding light. Then they saw a long shadow coming from the top of the stairs.

"Get up here!" Eva barked out.

Joanna quickly turned to Kate. "If they ask you anything, keep your answers short. The longer you talk, the more likely you are to make mistakes."

"I'll just tell them I don't know," Kate whispered.

"Be careful," Joanna cautioned. "Remember, they're not stupid."

Joanna started up the steps, taking them slowly. The bright light was still hurting her eyes, and she had trouble focusing her vision. She stumbled briefly, grasping the metal pipe railing to steady herself. As she neared the top of the stairs, she slowed even more, searching for a light switch on the wall. She saw only cracked plaster.

"Hurry it up," Eva said impatiently. "You're wasting time."

Joanna came through the doorway. She turned her head away, as if the bright light was still painful to her eyes. She used the extra seconds to scan the wall behind her. Then she saw the light switch. It was in the hall *out-side* the cellar door. Shit!

Joanna turned back to face Eva and Rudy. Jean-Claude was standing between them.

"Ma-ma?" Jean-Claude asked, looking up at Joanna.

"She's right here," Joanna said and stepped aside.

"Ma-ma!" Jean-Claude cried out happily and threw himself into his mother's arms.

Kate hugged and kissed Jean-Claude again and again. She tickled the secret spot on his neck and watched him laugh, loving him more than life itself. Then she hugged him again. "How are you doing, my little man? Are you okay?"

Jean-Claude nodded to his mother.

"Have they fed you?"

Jean-Claude nodded hesitantly.

"Is the food not good?"

Jean-Claude made a face.

"You must still eat it," Kate said. "That is very important. You must promise me."

Jean-Claude nodded unenthusiastically and took his mother's hand. "Come to television."

"Perhaps later," Kate said and hugged her son once more.

Joanna glanced down the hall and saw bright light flooding in through the kitchen window. She had been wrong. It was day, not night. Probably late morning or early afternoon. They had slept for over twelve hours.

Eva watched Joanna, who continued to stare down the hall toward the kitchen. "I hope you're not going to try anything dumb."

"I was looking for the bathroom," Joanna lied easily.

"It's the next door down," Eva said, then motioned to Rudy with her head.

Joanna walked across the hall and into the small bathroom. Rudy was right behind her. She tried to close the door, but he blocked it with his foot.

"Do you mind?" Joanna asked.

"Mind what?" Rudy smiled humorlessly.

"I can't go if you're watching me."

Rudy considered the situation, now pulling at his crotch. He wondered if he could persuade Eva to let him fuck the two women before he killed them. And he could screw them without a struggle too. All he had to do was promise to free them afterwards. They'd go for it. He stared at Joanna's bust, thinking she'd be a much better piece of ass than her sister.

"Well?" Joanna asked.

"Leave the door open," Rudy said and stepped outside.

Joanna sat on the toilet and began urinating. She quickly surveyed the bathroom. It was small and windowless, with a tub, basin and medicine chest. There was no soap or towels, nothing on the countertop. To her side was a small cabinet beneath the basin. She leaned over and peeked in. It was empty. There were no utensils or tools, nothing that could be used as a weapon.

She wiped herself and flushed the toilet. With the sound of rushing water she hurried over to the medicine chest and opened it.

Rudy stepped in behind her and slammed the mirrored door shut. He gave her a hard stare. "Looking for something?"

"Toothpaste," Joanna said, thinking quickly.

"I'll bet," Rudy said. "Get your ass out into the hall."

Eva was waiting for them at the entrance to the kitchen. Kate was sitting on the floor in the hall, Jean-

Claude in her arms. The little boy was sucking content-
edly on his thumb, his eyes half closed.

Eva said to Rudy, "Take the mother and child to the
television room and keep them there."

"What if she's got to pee?"

"Watch her."

Rudy grinned malevolently. "I'll stay real close."

"If anything happens to her, you'll get nothing from
me," Joanna warned.

"I'll keep that in mind," Eva said tonelessly. She signaled to Rudy and watched him usher the mother and
child into the front room. Then she turned to Joanna.
"You. Into the kitchen."

Joanna entered the bright kitchen. The windows were
all closed, their venetian blinds down but opened. Outside the sky was clear and blue, the sun blazing. The
backyard was large, with a garage and trees and hedges.
Joanna couldn't see any other houses.

"Sit," Eva commanded, pointing to a dinette chair.

Joanna pulled up the chair and tried to collect herself.
Think! she told herself. Think before you answer the
questions. And talk slowly. You set the pace, not her.
Make her wait. It'll give you more time to think.

Eva sat across from Joanna and leaned forward, her elbows on the dinette table. "I'm going to ask you some
questions, which I hope you'll answer truthfully. I really
do. Because for every lie I catch you telling, I'll have
Rudy break a finger on your sister's hand." Eva grimaced
theatrically. "And you know how much that will hurt."

Joanna swallowed hard. "You'll get the truth."

"Good." Eva stood and began circling slowly around
the table. "I need to know who is in charge of the rehabilitation institute. I want his name."

A test question, Joanna thought. "If you're talking
about the director, his name is Josiah Wales," she said de-
liberately.

"Have you ever visited the institute?"

"On several occasions."

"How many times?"

Joanna furrowed her forehead, as if she were searching for the correct answer. "Two, I think."

"Recently?"

"Within the past month."

"And what was the purpose of these visits?"

Joanna hesitated, wanting to keep the answers as general as possible. "To track you down."

"Well, all you tracked down were a bunch of stupid Mexicans."

"Which led directly to you."

"Yes, you were very clever." Eva took out her pistol and pointed it at Joanna's forehead. "You were so clever that you're now looking into the barrel of a gun I'm holding."

Joanna nodded, realizing how foolish her response had been. Don't be confrontational. Be submissive. And think one step ahead. "I'm not in a very good position, am I?"

"And it'll get worse if you lie." Eva returned the gun to her coat pocket and began circling the table again. She waved away a flying insect and continued to pace.

Joanna kept her eyes on the terrorist and quickly organized her thoughts. One of the test questions was bothering her. The terrorist had readily accepted Joanna's answer that she'd been to the institute twice. How did she know that was the correct answer? Someone must have told her, and that someone had to be in the institute. But who? And why?

"I need some information about the new institute," Eva said, breaking into Joanna's thoughts. "What do you know about it?"

Joanna shrugged. "Not much. I've never been inside."

Eva stopped abruptly and gave Joanna a long stare. "Never?"

"Never," Joanna said firmly. "I've passed by it a few times, but I've never been inside."

Eva started circling again. "Do you know when the new institute will open?"

"The dedication is set for April nineteenth."

"And who will be there?"

"A lot of dignitaries, I guess."

"I need names," Eva said sharply.

The test questions were over, Joanna told herself. The invitation list was known only to Simon Murdock and the Secret Service. No one in the institute, not even Josiah Wales, knew the entire list. "I don't have that information."

"Do you think the mayor of Los Angeles will be there?"

"I guess so."

"What about the governor?"

"Maybe."

"And, of course, you'll be there."

Joanna looked at the terrorist oddly. "Why would I be invited?"

Eva took a deep breath and sighed loudly. "What a shame! You've just cost your sister a broken little finger."

"Why?" Joanna asked, suddenly shaken. Her heart was in her throat, thumping away. "I've told you the truth."

"No, you haven't," Eva said. "We know you'll be there to receive the Medal of Freedom from the President of the United States. If you deny it, we'll break another finger on your sister's hand."

Joanna felt a sudden surge of nausea and ran for the sink, where she threw up. There was no real vomitus, just a mouthful of foul-tasting bile. She retched once more and waited for the nausea to pass, her head still over the sink. Desperately she tried to push her fear aside and think. She had told the truth, yet the terrorist didn't believe her. Why? Why? Joanna thought about the question and her answer again. Then it came to her. At the request of the Secret Service, the ceremony for the medal presentation had been shifted from the hospital to the new institute. The medals would be presented before the dedication ceremony. Joanna had only learned of the change yesterday morning. How could the terrorists be aware of that? She splashed water on her face and turned to Eva. "Please let me explain."

"It'd better be the truth," Eva said menacingly. "Remember your sister's fingers. And keep in mind we already know certain things."

Joanna nodded submissively, detecting a change in the terrorist's voice and manner. She had become more threatening, more demanding. And this told Joanna they were talking about the information the terrorists really wanted. What the hell did they need to know?

Joanna pointed to the cans of soda on the countertop. "May I have some soda? Maybe that will settle my stomach."

"Go ahead," Eva said and took out her weapon, just in case Joanna decided to try something stupid.

Joanna opened a can of soda and slowly sipped it, her mind racing ahead. Be careful here, she warned herself, be very careful. Don't lie, but don't give them the information they want. Because once they have it, they'll kill you and Kate and little Jean-Claude.

"Why did you lie to me about being invited to the dedication ceremony?" Eva asked, staring at Joanna and watching her body language.

"I didn't lie," Joanna said, picking her words carefully. "I wasn't invited to the dedication ceremony. I was going there to receive a medal from the President. Nothing more."

"And then you were to leave?"

"I would think so," Joanna said. "I have no connection at all to the institute."

"So," Eva said, thinking out loud, "you were only there because the President would be there?"

"That was my understanding."

"Where were you to meet the President?"

"They didn't say."

Eva's lips curled into a snarl. "I think you're lying again."

"I'm telling the truth," Joanna said as sincerely as she could.

"So you were just going to walk over and hope you ran into the President, huh?"

Joanna shook her head. "I was told to call the dean's office Monday morning for instructions."

Eva's eyes narrowed. "You were to call them?"

"That's correct." Joanna saw the change in the terrorist's expression. Something was wrong. Something hadn't gone down well. "I'm telling you the truth."

"Ah-huh," Eva muttered neutrally, giving no indication that she believed Joanna's story. "Did they mention whether the presentation would be on the steps of the institute or indoors?"

"I think I was to be told about that in the phone call."

"Ah-huh," Eva said again, studying Joanna's face, looking for a twitch or nervous tic that would tell her if her captive was lying.

Joanna looked away, intimidated by the terrorist's stare. She felt fear flooding through her once more and tried to push it away and concentrate. All of the questions now centered on the President's visit to the institute. Why? Why was that so important to the terrorists? What possible— Oh, God! The dedication was set for April nineteenth, the date on which the terrorist act was to occur. They were going to blow up the building with the President and the other dignitaries in it. That had to be it. And they need more information to make sure they can carry it out. But what information is so critical? Joanna sipped the can of soda, her mind now racing. Find out what information they need and don't give it to them. Stall. Use up time. Make them wait.

"I could call the dean's office now and ask them about the presentation," Joanna suggested, knowing the offer would be immediately refused. "They might give me the information."

"Oh, sure," Eva said nastily. "And what would you tell them? That you'd just escaped from your captors and you're on your way over right now? They wouldn't buy that, never in a million years. And they might have enough sense to contact the police, who could track your phone call down. Is that what you have in mind?"

"No," Joanna said softly. "I'm just trying to save my family's lives."

"Well, you're not doing a very good job so far."

Desperately Joanna tried to think of a way out of her dilemma. She had to string them along and give them a reason to keep her alive. She had to make them believe that she could eventually get the information for them. But how? She thought about the medal presentation and who else would be there. A picture of Joe Wells flashed into her mind. "There's another possibility that might work."

"Tell me about it."

"I have a colleague who is also receiving the Medal of Freedom," Joanna said. "His name is Dr. Joe Wells, and he's flying into Los Angeles from Montana late Sunday night."

"So?"

"So he'd have to contact the dean's office Monday morning and get instructions too," Joanna said. "I could call him at his hotel after he's talked with the dean's office."

"What time were you supposed to call the dean's office on Monday morning?" Eva asked quickly.

"Eight a.m."

"And where is this Dr. Wells staying?"

"At the Hilton near Memorial. It's a ten-minute walk to the institute."

"So you could call him at five minutes after eight and get the information on where the medal presentation would take place. Right?"

"I would think so," Joanna said, her heart beating so violently she thought it would jump out of her chest.

Eva weighed the matter carefully before saying, "Where is this Hilton Hotel located?"

"On Wilshire."

Eva took out her cell phone and dialed 411. After obtaining the phone number from information, she called the hotel. She spoke to the hotel operator.

"Good afternoon," Eva said sweetly into the phone. "Could you tell me if Dr. Joe Wells has checked in? . . . Oh, he hasn't. I have to leave a message for him. Could you connect me to the front desk? . . . Thank you."

Joanna held her breath, hoping the medal presentation hadn't been canceled altogether in view of her being kidnapped. If it had Joe would have canceled his reservation. Without Joe Wells, she was doomed. She had no backup plan. Her eyes went to the butt of the pistol protruding from the terrorist's coat. There was no way Joanna could get to the weapon. And even if she could, she didn't know how to work it.

"Yes," Eva said into the phone. "This is the dean's office at Memorial Hospital. You have a reservation for a Dr. Joe Wells, and it's very important we reach him. Could you tell me if he's scheduled to check in tonight or sometime tomorrow? . . . You can't give out that information. I see." Eva squinted an eye, concentrating. "Could I leave a message for you to give him as soon as he arrives? . . . Good. Will you see to it personally that the message is delivered? . . . Oh, I see. You can't. You're not on duty tomorrow." Eva grinned broadly. She had the confirmation she wanted. "Well, that will be fine. Just make certain the message gets to him. It should read: 'Call the dean's office at seven forty-five a.m. on April nineteenth. . . .' That's correct. Thank you."

Eva put the cell phone down on the countertop and looked over at Joanna. "We'll do it your way. We'll wait."

Joanna breathed a sigh of relief. She had bought more time.

"Unless we find another way to get the information," Eva added ominously. She walked over to the door and yelled down the hall. "Rudy! Bring them in here."

Joanna's gaze went to the cellular phone on the countertop. Lord! If she could only get her hands on that. Not only could she call Jake but he could trace the signal and pinpoint her location.

Kate came into the kitchen, carrying Jean-Claude. The little boy was so sleepy he could barely keep his eyes open. "Sis, I think there's something wrong with Jean-Claude."

Joanna walked over quickly. "Is he sick?"

"He says he feels all right," Kate said. "But he's so drowsy and lethargic. And he's usually very active at this time of day."

Joanna placed her hand on Jean-Claude's forehead. There was no fever or blush. His pulse and respiration were steady and slow. "Hi, Jean-Claude," she said softly. "Do you feel bad?"

"I am fine," Jean-Claude said sleepily, his eyes now closed.

"I think he's okay." Joanna touched the boy's forehead again, making sure there was no fever. "It's probably all the excitement. And remember, they've let him run wild and do whatever he wants to. He may have just tired himself out."

Kate rocked the little boy in her arms as he drifted off

to sleep. "He never gets tired like this during the day. Something isn't right."

"We'll keep an eye on him," Eva said.

"Like hell you will!" Kate snapped and held her son close. "You go play your goddamn games somewhere else."

Eva came over to Kate and stared at her, nose to nose. "Don't push it, or you'll never see your son again."

The color left Kate's face. "I—I was just worried about my little boy."

Eva continued to stare at her. "Don't push me again. Do you understand?"

"I'm sorry," Kate said submissively, resisting the urge to scream and run.

"Do what we tell you and no harm will come to the boy," Eva said. "Now, give the child to Rudy."

Kate hesitated for a moment, looking at the window and wondering if she could break through it with Jean-Claude in her arms.

"Now!" Eva commanded.

Kate did as she was told, making certain Rudy had a firm hold on Jean-Claude. The sleeping child didn't notice the transfer.

Eva went to the refrigerator and returned with two half-pint cartons of milk and two slices of white bread. "Eat and drink quickly. You've already taken up too much time."

"I hate milk," Kate said.

"You'd better drink it," Eva said sternly. "Because that's all you'll get today. But if you want to sit in the cellar dying of thirst, that's your business."

"Drink the milk," Joanna advised. "You don't want to let yourself become dehydrated."

"Yeah," Eva said mockingly. "You don't want to become dehydrated."

Joanna gulped the milk down and watched Kate do the same.

The milk was ice cold and went down easily. There was a slightly sour aftertaste, but the bread took that away.

Joanna's gaze returned to the cell phone on the countertop near the sink. "Could we have some water?"

"Make it quick," Eva said tersely.

Joanna walked over to the sink, gently pushing Kate in front of her. "Drink at least two cupfuls."

At the sink Joanna positioned herself so that she blocked the terrorist's view of the countertop. She filled the cups from the faucet and handed one to Kate. Joanna's left elbow was less than a foot away from the phone. As she drank from the cup she inched her arm closer to the phone.

"This water looks rusty," Kate complained.

"Drink it," Joanna said, edging her arm over so that it was now touching the phone. "It won't hurt you."

Kate took a mouthful and immediately spat it into the sink. "Ugh! It tastes like metal."

"Just sip it."

Kate tried again and again spat the water out. "It won't go down. Maybe we should let the water run for a minute," she said and reached for the faucet.

Eva came over and jerked the women away from the sink. "You've had enough water. Now move out."

In the hall Joanna and Kate looked for Jean-Claude and Rudy. There was no sign of them. A television set was on low volume in one of the front rooms. Outside a heavy truck passed by, causing the house to rattle. Joanna heard a crying sound and stopped abruptly, then realized it was coming from the television set.

"Get into the cellar," Eva ordered, nudging them forward with her gun.

Joanna went down the steps slowly, using the light behind her as long as she could. Everything in the cellar was the same. The mattress was still on the floor, the oily rag concealing the lighter beside it. The mop and bucket were in the corner, the table still against the wall beneath the small window.

The door behind them slammed shut, and the cellar went black. The darkness was so sudden and so intense it was disorienting. For a moment Joanna felt light-headed. She took some deep breaths and waited for the sensation to pass.

"My God! It's even darker than before," Kate said softly. "It's like a tomb."

"Give yourself a few minutes to acclimate to it," Joanna said, her head swimming again. She looked up to where the window should have been and saw no light, not even a glimmer. Why? Had something moved in front of the window, blocking out the light altogether? She thought about climbing up on the table to check it out, but her legs seemed so tired.

"Sis," Kate said. "I don't feel so good."

"What's wrong?"

"I feel like I'm going to pass out."

Joanna searched the floor with her foot until she found the mattress. She reached back and guided Kate down. "Just sit and rest for a minute."

"I've got to lie down," Kate said drowsily.

Joanna felt the swimming sensation in her head returning, more intense now. She tried to keep her eyes open but couldn't. What's happening to us? Why are we so tired and feel so— The milk! The milk with its peculiar aftertaste! They doctored the milk. It was the last thought she had before drifting off into a deep and dreamless sleep.

38

"What the hell is taking so long?" Jake demanded.

"Do you know how many parking tickets we write every day?" asked Molly Anderson, a senior supervisor in the Parking Enforcement Division.

"I don't know and I don't care," Jake said irritably. "Just find the ticket."

"I'm talking thousands and—"

"Just find the damn ticket," Jake cut her off.

Anderson took a deep breath and tried to hold her temper. "And this couldn't wait until Monday, huh? What's so important that I had to drag in four of my people on a Saturday?"

"A kidnapping," Jake said, a picture of Joanna now flashing into his mind.

"A kidnapping! Jesus H. Christ! Why the hell didn't you tell me?"

Jake watched the woman rush out of the office and into a large ticket-sorting area. Through a glass window he saw the plump supervisor spreading the word and urging her co-workers on. They were searching through mountains of parking tickets, looking for the one given to the van outside the ice cream shop. Under ordinary circumstances, locating the ticket wouldn't have been a problem. All that should have been required was to identify the meter maid and examine the pads of tickets she had written. But that was where the problem was. The meter maid originally assigned to the area had become ill while on duty Thursday morning, and a replacement had been called in. It was the replacement who had written the ticket, and no one knew who she was. The supervisor responsible for making the switch was on his way to a vacation in Mexico. Without the meter maid's name, every pad of tickets would have to be examined.

Jake looked up at the wall clock. It was 7:45 P.M. They had been at it for over twenty-five hours with no luck. Jake lit a cigarette despite the no smoking sign and again went through every aspect of the case, trying to uncover some clue that might help locate the terrorists. And again it came down to the parking ticket, which would lead them to the van. But even that was a long shot. They'd still have to find the van, and by now it had probably been dumped and, if not dumped, certainly well hidden. A real long shot, Jake thought miserably, but it was the only shot he had. He took a deep drag on his cigarette, now thinking about Joanna and Kate and Jean-Claude and wondering if they had been harmed or injured. Or maybe they were dead, their bodies thrown into roadside bushes somewhere. A chill went through Jake as he envisioned Joanna lying in a coffin. He pushed the image from his mind and glanced up at the wall clock. 7:50 P.M. Just over twenty-eight hours until April 19th.

Jake leaned back against the wall and took the weight off his feet. His deep fatigue was coming on strong now, the urge to sleep almost irresistible. Jake willed himself to stay awake, knowing that if he closed his eyes he would instantly doze off and waste valuable hours. Again he thought about Joanna and wondered if she was still alive. The elevator door down the hall opened, and Jake heard approaching footsteps. With an effort he pushed himself away from the wall.

Lou Farelli trudged into the office and sat down wearily in a swivel chair. "I got bad news."

"What?"

"The guy from the ice cream parlor died."

Another one gone, Jake thought, the number of people killed by the terrorists now twenty-nine. "Did you get a chance to talk with him before he bought it?"

Farelli shook his head. "They rushed him to the OR because he started bleeding again. He died on the table."

Jake grumbled, wishing the man had lived, wishing even more that Farelli had gotten the opportunity to talk to him again. Maybe the old guy would have remembered something else after his mind cleared from the surgery and sedatives.

"You should have seen the mood on the surgery ward when the word came down that the old man was gone," Farelli went on. "Nurses were crying, doctors were trying to swallow back their emotions. I'm telling you, Jake, it was like they'd lost somebody in the family."

"In a way I guess they did," Jake said somberly. He extinguished his cigarette in a styrofoam cup half-filled with cold coffee. "What else you got?"

Farelli began flipping pages in his notepad. "The bullet in the old guy's gut matched the one in Maria Gonzalez's boyfriend. They were both shot by the same weapon and probably the same person." Farelli turned to another page and studied it briefly. "And we may have found the motorcycle that was used to run down the cop outside the ice cream parlor. It was a stolen Harley-Davidson that was parked in an alley a couple of miles south of the crime scene."

"Does it have any prints on it?"

"A bunch," Farelli answered. "They're checking now to see if any of those fingerprints belong to George Walter Reineke."

"It was him," Jake said with certainty.

"Got to be."

"Make sure they check the front wheel for bits of skin

or clothing that might have come from the officer who was run down."

Farelli jotted down the instructions before turning to a new page. "And one more thing. We came up with a slug from the rooftop shooting. The damn thing was embedded in the trunk of your car. Anyhow, it was a nine-millimeter slug, the same caliber bullet that killed the old man. But it came from a different weapon."

"Two different shooters," Jake said.

"Had to be."

And both terrorists had come from the same group, Jake thought, now pacing. Something was screwed up. The sequence of events just didn't fit right. One day they tried to kill Joanna, a few days later they risked everything to kidnap her. It didn't make sense, except maybe to terrorists. Something must have happened to cause them to change their minds. For some reason, they now needed Joanna alive. At least for a while. But why?

Molly Anderson burst into the office holding up a thick pad of tickets. "We got it!"

"Hallelujah!" Jake shouted out.

Anderson read from the ticket. "It was written on Thursday at one-fifteen p.m. on Broxton Avenue. The vehicle was a Chevy van. The license plate number is 3 VDM 593."

Jake rubbed his hands together. "Can anyone here access the computer at the Department of Motor Vehicles?"

"You're looking at her." Anderson hurried over to the computer on her desk and began punching in a code. "Who did they kidnap?"

"A little boy," Jake said vaguely.

"When you catch the bastard who did it, you should shoot him."

"That's against the law," Jake said.

"Not in my book." Anderson punched a final key and sat back while numbers flashed across the computer screen faster than the eye could follow. Finally the license number 3 VDM 593 came up.

Jake and Farelli leaned forward to read the information off the screen. The Chevy van was registered to

LEWIS KOPPELMAN
2524 SIERRA MADRE DRIVE
BEVERLY HILLS, CA 90210

"I know the neighborhood," Farelli said. "It's upper-middle-class with big homes. Mostly doctors, lawyers, movie people. Not exactly your terrorist type, huh?"

"In today's world, who the hell knows?" Jake nodded his appreciation to Anderson, then left the office. The workers who had spent hours sorting through tickets were slumped in their chairs, exhausted. Jake gave them a strong thumbs-up signal. They smiled back.

At the elevator Farelli asked, "How do you want to handle it?"

"With a SWAT team and a bomb squad."

Sunday, April 18, 12:21 A.M.

It was past midnight, and the neighborhood was quiet and dark. Only the house next to the Koppelmans' had a light on. Because of a local ordinance, there was no street parking. All vehicles were either in driveways or in garages.

A block away Jake was peering through night-vision binoculars. He adjusted the intensity, and everything took on a bright phosphorescent glow. Now he could see the SWAT team moving into position around the house.

Dan Hurley was next to Jake, listening intently through a device in his ear. "They're checking the house out with infrared scopes, looking for any signs of life. Everything is negative so far."

Jake watched members of the SWAT team, now crouching under windows to the house. They were being covered by marksmen who were lying prone across the street. "That damn house is going to be empty," he grumbled.

"Yeah," Hurley agreed. "Except maybe for two dead bodies."

Earlier they had called the Koppelman home and gotten the answering machine. Then they'd contacted the security company that was responsible for guarding the house. The Koppelmans had informed the security company that they would be leaving Wednesday for a vacation and would be returning late Sunday. No phone or address was given where they could be reached.

Three explanations could fit the situation. First, the story was true. The Koppelmans were on vacation. Second, the Koppelmans were somehow connected to the terrorists. And, third, the terrorists had invaded the Koppelmans' house to use as a base. They had forced the Koppelmans to call the security company, then killed them. The police favored the third explanation.

"The infrared is negative, and there's absolutely no sound within the house," Hurley reported. "It looks like nobody is home."

"But they could have left a present behind for us."

"Yeah," Hurley said hoarsely. "One that goes boom in the night."

Hurley knew the most common place for the first bomb was at the door, front or back. The backup devices were harder to find. They were usually in the kitchen or bathroom or den. For some reason they were almost never placed in bedrooms.

Hurley listened to a message before speaking into a small microphone. "Go through a bedroom window." He heard glass breaking, then a dog barked, then another and another. Lights in the surrounding homes went on.

Jake saw men crawling into the house through an open window. One. Two. Three. All were dressed in black and white and wore night-vision goggles. The Koppelman house stayed dark.

Hurley pressed the earpiece in further and listened, hoping to God he wouldn't have to hear the sound of a bomb exploding. The booby trap could be anywhere. All it took was one small mistake, and you'd be dead and so would the people around you. Hurley could still remember the sound of the bomb that had taken off a part of his hand. It resembled a muffled thud, and in an instant two of his fingers were gone. The lights suddenly came on in the Koppelman house. "Nobody is home," Hurley reported.

"How long will it take to search the place for bombs?" Jake asked, putting down his binoculars.

"It depends," Hurley answered. "If the house is orderly, we can do it quickly. If it's been trashed, we could be here for hours."

A police loudspeaker suddenly came on with a high-pitched squeal. "This is the police! Please stay in your homes! I repeat—this is the police! Stay in your homes!"

The neighbors who had come out on their lawns scurried back into their houses. Doors slammed. Dogs started barking again.

Minutes dragged by as Jake smoked one cigarette after another. He repeatedly glanced at his watch, wanting time to slow, but it only seemed to go by faster. It was already 12:30 A.M., less than twenty-four hours until the nineteenth of April. He wondered again what the terrorists planned to blow up and how many people would die. It had to be something big, he guessed, and it had to be filled with people. Like the federal building in Oklahoma

City. One bomb. One building. A hundred and sixty-nine people dead.

"The first sweep is clean," Hurley said. "Now they'll bring in the dogs to sniff out hidden explosives. It won't take long."

"Did they see any signs of a struggle?" Jake asked.

"No. Everything is nice and neat. There's nothing to indicate the terrorists were ever there."

Which meant they hadn't invaded the house, Jake thought quickly. Then how did they get the van? Either Koppelman gave it to them or they stole it. But that didn't bring Jake any closer to the terrorists.

He lit another cigarette and again considered whether the Koppelmans were somehow involved. They were obviously successful and well-to-do, and Beverly Hills was a million miles away from some paramilitary compound in Idaho. But then again, who the hell knew? There was a time when only the downtrodden and disillusioned committed acts of terrorism. Those days were long gone.

Jake leaned back against his car and blew smoke into the cool night air. They were standing behind a police car, just in case an explosion occurred. And behind them was a police barricade that sealed off the dead-end street. Two blocks away ambulances, paramedics and backup police units waited. And a police helicopter was circling less than a mile away. All for two goddamn terrorists, Jake thought sourly. And the terrorists weren't even there. But they still could have left explosives behind, just as they had done in West Hollywood.

Jake heard someone crossing the street and turned. It was Farelli. "Anything new on Koppelman?"

"Nothing," Farelli said. "Nada. Zilch. He's got no sheet with us, so I gave his name to the FBI. They can dig a lot deeper than we can."

"And take a lot longer."

"That too."

The lights in the Koppelman house suddenly went on. The front door opened. In the distance they could hear the *putt-putt* of an approaching helicopter. A squad car behind them started up.

"The house is secured," Hurley told them and removed the listening device from his ear.

The detectives walked briskly down the street past the large, well-manicured lawns. With the exception of the homes that had been evacuated by the police, every house was now lighted up. Curious neighbors were peeking out of windows and doors. Dogs were barking loudly. A car alarm went off but lasted only a few seconds. Ahead they saw SWAT team members assembling on the sidewalk, their night goggles now sitting atop their heads.

Jake pointed to a lighted house on the far side of the Koppelmans'. "Lou, check them out. See what they know about the Koppelmans."

"Right." Farelli took out his weapon and carefully inspected the chamber.

"You know something I don't?"

"Not really. I just don't like surprises at the front door," Farelli said and placed the gun in a belt holster.

Jake nodded, remembering back. "You be careful."

As Farelli walked away, Hurley asked, "What's that all about?"

"A couple of years ago we had a similar situation involving a suspected murderer," Jake told him. "When Farelli knocked on the door, the neighbor answered it and aimed a shotgun at Farelli's head. You see, it wasn't the neighbor. It was the murderer."

Hurley sucked air through his teeth. "I take it the guy didn't fire."

"Oh, he tried," Jake said. "He pulled the trigger, but it misfired."

"What'd Farelli do then?"

"I'm not sure," Jake said evasively. "But the guy

ended up with a broken jaw and split lips and cracked ribs. I think he hurt himself trying to get away."

"Yeah, sometimes that happens if the guy trips and falls." Hurley checked his weapon and made certain the safety was off. "You know, if he lands wrong."

Jake headed up a brick path that led to a lighted house near the Koppelmans'. A small, thin man in his midsixties with fluffy gray hair was waiting for them at the door. He was wearing a silk smoking jacket.

Jake flashed his shield. "I'm Lieutenant Sinclair and this is Lieutenant Hurley. We need to ask you some questions about the Koppelmans."

"Sure, sure," the neighbor said quickly. "Do you want to come inside?"

"That'd be fine."

The man led them through a marble foyer and into a large, expensively decorated living room. The furniture was mahogany that was upholstered in a rich, light blue fabric. On the walls were paintings by French Impressionists. One looked like a Renoir. Jake wondered if it was real.

"My name is Marshall Quinn," the man said. "And this is my wife, Vicki."

Jake nodded to the woman standing by the old brick fireplace. She was blond and beautiful and looked at least thirty years younger than her husband. She also looked very bored.

"Did something happen to the Koppelmans?" Quinn asked, his concern genuine.

"We don't know," Jake said and took out his notepad. "All we know for certain is that a vehicle belonging to them was used in the commission of a crime."

"What kind of crime?"

"A shooting."

Quinn stared at Jake incredulously. "And you think Lewis was involved?"

"We've got to check it out."

"Then you're checking out the wrong man." Quinn went over to a small writing desk and picked up a highly polished pipe. "I've known Lewis Koppelman for over twenty years, and he's as solid as they come."

Jake waited for the man to light his pipe. Behind Quinn was a large door that opened into a library. Jake could see framed movie posters on the wall, and on a shelf he noticed a small golden statue. An Oscar. Then the name Marshall Quinn rang a bell. He was a big-time movie producer. "Did Mr. Koppelman belong to any crazy, far-out group?"

Quinn gave Jake a suspicious glance. "Is that against the law?"

"It is when the group kills a police officer."

Quinn nodded his agreement. "The answer to your question is no. Lewis Koppelman is a rock-hard Republican. He and Ronald Reagan were on a first-name basis until the President got sick. I can tell you with no hesitation that Lewis has no use for people on the far right or far left."

"When did you see him last?"

"Tuesday night. They stopped in for drinks." Quinn looked over to his wife. "It was about seven o'clock. Right, babe?"

"Yeah, I guess," Vicki Quinn said, still bored. Now she was examining the bright red polish on her fingernails.

Jake asked, "And they were okay?"

"They seemed fine to me," Quinn said. "They were looking forward to the trip to the desert."

"Did they tell you where they could be reached?"

Quinn shook his head. "They never do. They like to roam around. Sometimes they go to Palm Springs, sometimes to the Mojave to see the wildflowers."

"Did they take their Chevy van?"

Quinn shrugged. "I don't know. They left real early."

"They have another car?"

"A Mercedes."

"Do you know when they're supposed to return?"

"They didn't say."

"Do the Koppelmans have any close relatives?"

Quinn shook his head again. "None living."

Jake closed his notepad and sighed. A big nothing. Not one damn clue to help them. He turned to Hurley. "Do you have any questions?"

"Just a few," Hurley said, watching Quinn relight his pipe. "Can you tell us what kind of business Mr. Koppelman is in?"

"Army-Navy surplus," Quinn answered promptly.

Hurley's eyes narrowed. "Weapons? Grenades? Stuff like that?"

Quinn hesitated, thinking. "I believe it's mainly tents and blankets and clothing. You know, things that can be used in civilian life."

"Does he own a gun?"

"Nope. He hates them. His only brother died in a hunting accident."

Hurley and Jake exchanged glances and put away their notepads.

"Thank you for your time, Mr. Quinn," Jake said.

Outside the night air was growing colder and a heavy mist was forming. The SWAT team were packing their gear away in a truck. The neighborhood dogs were barking loudly at the bomb-sniffing dogs, who sat, unperturbed, waiting for their next command.

"We got nothing," Jake said miserably. "A big nothing."

"Maybe the Koppelmans can help," Hurley said.

"Don't bet on it," Jake grumbled. "And remember, they don't return until sometime tonight."

"Well, if they get back early enough, that'll still leave

us some time to work with. You never know, they just might have some information we can use."

"Christ! We're grabbing at straws!"

"That's all we've got for now."

They turned as Farelli hurried across the damp lawn, coughing into the chilly air.

Jake asked, "What did you find out?"

"That Lewis Koppelman is red, white and blue, and gives to every charity in Los Angeles." Farelli coughed again and spat out phlegm. "And his wife gives even more than he does."

"Do the neighbors know where the Koppelmans went?"

"Nope."

"Or when they'll get back?"

"Sometime late tonight."

"How late?"

"Around nine or ten. They like to wait until the freeway traffic slacks off." Farelli coughed again and cleared his throat. "And if the traffic is real bad, they don't come back until Monday morning."

Jake walked away, shaking his head dejectedly. Time was running out. And they were standing still.

39

Joanna drifted in and out of her nightmarish sleep. One moment she was in total darkness, the next she was in bright light being forced to drink orange juice with a gun to her head. She jerked her head away and kept her jaws clenched together. Then the darkness returned, and Joanna couldn't tell whether she was awake or asleep. Again there was light, and again there was a gun aimed at her and somebody was pulling the trigger. Now everything was in slow motion. The flash. The bang. The bullet coming directly at her. She threw up her hands and tried to move away, but something cold and hard stopped her. She desperately pushed against it, but it wouldn't budge. *Oh, God! Oh, God! Oh—!*

Joanna was suddenly awake. Her heart was pounding, her mind disordered and still half-asleep. She took deep breaths, gathering herself and trying to get her bearings. She reached out and felt the cold cement floor and the mattress beside her. Then she realized she was still in the cellar.

She rolled back onto the mattress and lay next to Kate. She rubbed at her eyes and waited for her head to clear. Slowly, recent events began to come back. She remembered the milk. The goddamn milk! They had been drugged. Joanna cursed at herself in the darkness. If she had been half as smart as people thought she was, she would have seen it coming and prevented it. The signs were all there. Little Jean-Claude was so sleepy he couldn't keep his eyes open when normally he would have been chasing outlaws nonstop at full steam. Kate had told her something was wrong with Jean-Claude, but Joanna had ignored it. *Stupid! Stupid!* And the milk had tasted peculiar. She had ignored that too.

Joanna's mouth was so parched that it was difficult to swallow, and her limbs were stiff and aching. She wondered how long they'd been asleep. Probably for hours and hours, she guessed. But there was no easy way to know, not with the window totally blocked. Joanna couldn't even tell if it was day or night.

She stood and took a few careful steps in the darkness, trying to stretch her sore muscles. Her foot touched something on the floor, and she reached down for it. It was small and square and hollow and had a waxy feel. And it had a spout. A carton! But she remembered that they had left the milk cartons upstairs. Quickly she brought the spout of the empty carton to her nose and sniffed. Orange juice!

So what she thought she'd seen in her nightmare had actually happened. They had been awakened and, in their drugged state, forced to drink orange juice that probably contained more drug. That would explain why she was so stiff and groggy and her throat so parched. With all those drugs in them, they could have slept an entire day. It might already be Sunday.

Joanna leaned over Kate and felt around for the oily rag containing the cigarette lighter. At first she couldn't find it, and she wondered if the terrorists had discovered the rag and lighter while they were pushing more drugs into their prisoners. Without the lighter they had no chance at all. Joanna cursed at herself again, wishing she had hidden it better. Then her hand swept over the floor near the wall and made contact with the oily rag. The lighter was still in it.

Kate was now moving about, groaning in the darkness but still asleep.

Joanna gently shook her sister's shoulder, then whispered loudly into her ear. "Kate! Kate!"

"Wh-what?" Kate asked groggily.

"Time to get up," Joanna said.

"Just a little more sleep," Kate muttered and dozed off.

Joanna shook Kate's shoulder harder. "Get up!"

"Wh-what's wrong?"

"Do you remember where we are?"

Kate's eyelids started to droop, but she forced them to stay open. "What?"

"Do you know where we are?" Joanna asked again.

"How could I forget?" Kate tried to prop herself up, then dropped back onto the mattress. "My head feels so heavy."

"That's because we were both drugged," Joanna said. "They put something in the milk we drank."

"Bastards," Kate said, then pushed herself up again and waited for the dizziness to pass. She tried to orient herself in the blackness but couldn't. She had no idea where the window or the stairs were. She couldn't even see Joanna. "Sis, where are you?"

"Over here."

"What time do you think it is?"

"I have no idea."

Up above they heard heavy footsteps passing by. Then silence returned.

Kate listened intently and waited for the sound of tiny footsteps. There weren't any. "Have you heard Jean-Claude running around?"

"I think he's still asleep," Joanna said in a low voice. "Remember how drowsy he was when we saw him last? They probably drugged him too."

"Real bastards," Kate hissed loudly.

"Keep it down," Joanna whispered. "If they hear us

talking they'll give us more drugs and we'll never find a way out."

"We're never going to get out of here, Sis. We're hopelessly trapped and you know it."

"Maybe, maybe not," Joanna said, although deep down she knew her sister was right. It was only a matter of hours before they would be killed, Jean-Claude along with them.

Her gaze went to the wall where she thought the window was. There was still no light, not even a glimmer. She reached over and touched Kate's arm. "I want you to help me get up on the table."

"For what?"

"So I can determine why there's no light at all coming in now."

"Maybe it's nighttime."

"And maybe it's not."

"So what?" Kate asked gloomily. "A glimmer of light isn't going to help us any."

Joanna tightened her grip on Kate's arm. "Listen to me, and listen good. The next time those bastards come down the stairs will probably be the last time. And I won't just sit here and wait for them. I'm going to look for a way out, and you're going to help me. Now that window is our only connection to the outside world. Let's see where it leads us."

"To nowhere," Kate said dismally. "It's got bars across it. Remember? We're as good as dead."

"Goddamn it!" Joanna snapped. "If you don't want to fight for yourself, at least fight for Jean-Claude."

Kate glared at her sister, angry with Joanna for bossing her, angrier yet with herself for not being stronger. "Let's get to it."

Joanna flicked the lighter, and it gave off a very small flame. The table was now off to the left of the window. Joanna tried to recall whether she had pushed the table to its new place before going up the steps. She thought she had, but she wasn't sure. The lighter went out by itself. "Help me lift the table over to the window. Don't drag it on the floor. We don't want to make any noise."

They lifted the table and placed it under the window.

Joanna climbed up and steadied herself, her legs still weak and rubbery. She looked out the window and saw only blackness. Her eyes went to the upper part of the windowpane, and she noticed a faint, thin line of light to the left of the glass. It took her a moment to realize she was looking at the edge of something that was blocking the window.

Joanna looked down at Kate. "Keep your hand on the wall and move to the corner on your left. You'll find the mop there. Bring it to me."

Kate found the mop in the darkness and brought it back to the table. She handed the mop up to Joanna, wooden handle first.

Joanna placed the mop over her shoulder, pointing the handle forward. With a quick punch she knocked out the left upper corner of the windowpane. She slowly advanced the mop through the broken pane, and the object in front of the window gave way. A bright stream of light flooded into the cellar. Joanna turned away and waited for her eyes to adjust, then looked out the window. She saw a large piece of cardboard, now tilted back and resting atop a dried-out bush and some trash.

Joanna eased herself down and leaned wearily against the table. Her legs felt shaky and ached with fatigue. She reached down and gently massaged her calf muscles. In the light she could see Kate, and beyond her the stairs leading up. On the floor was the mattress, which looked dirty and slimy.

"What was blocking the window?" Kate asked.

"A big piece of cardboard, probably put there by Rudy."

"Won't he see it's been moved?"

"Maybe he'll think it just fell backwards."

"But then he'll see the broken window and figure out what we did and he'll really get pissed."

"Maybe not," Joanna said, thinking quickly. "The entire window isn't broken, only a corner. If we hear anyone coming we'll stuff the oily rag in the cracked pane and move the table back to where it was. With any luck, they won't make too much of it."

Kate shook her head. "They're too smart for that."

"We'll see."

Kate glanced up at the shaft of light. It was bright and circular, like that given off by a flashlight. "It must be morning."

Joanna nodded. "Or early afternoon."

"You think we slept for twenty-four hours?"

"Maybe more."

"Well, I'm going to stay awake from here on," Kate vowed. "I don't want any more of those damn nightmares."

"You had them too, huh?"

"They were the worst," Kate said. "And they seemed so real. It was almost kinky."

"How so?"

Kate hesitated before saying, "I think I was in a bathroom somewhere, pulling down my panties. And Rudy was there. He kept smiling at me and laughing, watching my every move. Then he tried to touch me and a voice screamed out. And Rudy laughed even harder. It was scary as hell, even for a nightmare."

Joanna nodded, but she knew what her sister had experienced hadn't been a nightmare. In all likelihood it had actually happened. While they were drugged and heavily sedated, they were probably taken upstairs and made to urinate. That way they wouldn't have to be brought upstairs again. And that also explained why neither she nor

.

Kate had the urge to pee now although they had just awakened. Their bladders had been emptied only a few hours before. With Rudy watching them. Joanna shivered, wondering if Rudy had touched her too.

Outside the window a car pulled up. Its door opened and closed quickly.

In an instant Joanna was standing atop the table on her tiptoes, looking through the crack in the window. The cardboard still partially blocked her line of vision, but she saw the back of a man with blond hair walking away. He was holding something under his arm. A small box or package, Joanna couldn't be sure. A moment later he was gone. Her eyes went back to the car, but she couldn't make out the make or model. The only parts of the car that were clearly visible were the top of the hood and the windshield. Then she saw the blue parking decal on the windshield. A sudden shiver went through Joanna. The decal looked like the ones given to the faculty members at Memorial. It allowed them to park in the lots closest to the hospital.

Joanna heard the doorbell ringing, then footsteps hurrying to the front of the house. Quickly she climbed down from the table.

"Who was that?" Kate asked excitedly.

"One of them," Joanna said and handed Kate the oily rag. "I'm going up the stairs and try to listen to what they say. I want you to climb onto the table and watch for my signal. If I hear them coming to the cellar, I'll snap my fingers. That means plug the hole in the window with the rag and get back on the mattress like you're asleep. Got it?"

"Got it."

Joanna hurried up the steps and pressed her ear against the door. She heard loud voices coming from the kitchen area. A man and a woman. The female terrorist was obviously upset.

"Are you crazy coming here?" Eva screeched. "Are you out of your mind?"

"I had no choice," the man said. "I tried your cell phone number fifty times, but it was always busy."

"Nobody has been on the phone."

"Then you'd better check it."

"Rudy!"

Joanna heard Rudy coming down the hall with loud, thumping footsteps. Suddenly the doorknob to the cellar turned. Joanna held her breath and waited for the sound of the lock opening. Rudy tried the door again, apparently making certain it was still secured. Then he walked on. Joanna breathed a sigh of relief and pressed her ear back to the door. Now they were arguing, everybody talking at once.

Eva asked angrily, "You gave the phone to the kid to play with?"

"He was starting to cry," Rudy explained. "So I gave it to him to play with. He doesn't know how to use it."

"Give me the phone," Eva said.

There was a pause. Joanna heard what sounded like a can of soda being opened. She licked at her parched lips, now even more aware of her thirst.

"Well," Eva was saying, "the kid might not have known how to use the phone, but he somehow turned it off and disconnected us from the outside world."

"Sorry," Rudy said weakly.

"Sorry doesn't get it done," Eva snapped. "Now go back and watch the kid."

Heavy footsteps came past the door again. Rudy didn't bother to check the doorknob this time.

"What's so important that you had to come here?" Eva demanded.

"I've got to know whether the dedication ceremony at the new institute will be held on the steps or inside," the man said.

"I told you we won't find that out until tomorrow morning."

"But we may not even find out then," the man said. "This arriving doctor might not be told a damn thing until he gets to the ceremony."

"I know, I know," Eva said worriedly.

Joanna listened intently, trying to place the man's voice. She thought she had heard it before but couldn't be sure. The thick door and the distance to the kitchen gave the voice a muffled quality.

"There might be a way to get to our target whether the ceremony is on the steps or inside," the man said.

"How?"

"Put the prosthesis on Wales before the ceremony starts."

"Can you talk Wales into it?"

"I think so," the man said. "The original plan was for him to have his new prosthesis fitted with the President and everybody else looking on. If the ceremony is held on the steps, obviously that can't happen. And Wales isn't going to like that at all. So when I see him tonight at the cocktail party, I could suggest he be prepared to put the prosthesis on before we go to the ceremony. If it's on the steps, he could be seen lifting up his pants leg and showing the prosthesis to the President. If it's inside, we could just reenact the fitting. Either way Wales gets his picture taken with the President."

"You think he'll go for it?"

"Probably. But there's a risk if the ceremony is held outside. If it's held inside, we'll know exactly where everyone will be. If it's held on the steps, there could be a lot of distance and people between Wales and the President."

"Inside is better," Eva agreed. "Much better. Your backup plan has too many problems. Too many things could go wrong."

"I'm aware of that," the man said. "And I'm also aware that if I push too hard for a change in plans, Wales may become suspicious. And that's the last thing we want. He's edgy enough as it is."

"Has something happened to tip him off?"

"Not so far. But he's a perfectionist, and he'll want to know everything that's going on and why."

"But he has absolutely no idea you're involved, right?"

"Right. He still thinks I'm his little underling who does what he's told and makes all of the computerized prostheses for him."

Timothy Bremmer! Joanna thought bitterly, the terrorists' friend at Memorial who was feeding them vital information so they'd always be one step ahead of the police. A doctor! A doctor who was responsible for killing dozens of people—children, widows, policemen, even his own patients. And, unless some miracle happened, he would also be responsible for the deaths of Joanna and her family.

Joanna pressed her ear firmly against the door, silently cursing Bremmer and the terror he was involved in. And they were going to assassinate the President. But how were they going to do it? And why was fitting the prosthesis on Wales such an important part of their plans?

Bremmer asked, "Do you want me to implement the backup plan or not?"

"Yeah. Just in case we need it."

"It's too bad our first plan didn't work out. It would have been beautiful. And it was so simple. Four Mexicans strategically spread out in the crowd as the presidential limousine pulled up. And each Mexican with two bricks of C-four incorporated in his protective vest. The President would have come over to the crowd to touch people and shake hands. Then, at the right moment, the C-four would have been detonated and everybody, including the

President, would have been vaporized. And with any luck it would have been recorded on television and shown to the whole world."

"Our current plan is almost as good," Eva said. "Just let them hold the ceremony inside so the President can bend over and get a close look at Josiah Wales's new prosthesis. Then, from a distance, you can detonate the C-four that's packed into the prosthesis."

Oh, my God! Oh, my God! Joanna pressed her ear even closer to the door, trying to overhear more details.

Bremmer was asking, "And you're double sure that the explosive-sniffing dogs can't detect the C-four in the prosthesis?"

"I'm positive," Eva said. "We did two test runs. As long as the C-four is incorporated between the layers of laminated plastic, no aroma gets out. Not even a trace. The dogs gave the plastic a quick sniff and moved on."

"Excellent."

Joanna heard footsteps passing the door, the voices now low and muffled. Then the front door opened and closed.

Joanna hurried down the steps and signaled to Kate, waving her down from the table.

Kate scrambled off the table and came over. "What did you hear?"

"You're not going to believe it."

"Try me."

"They're going to assassinate the President of the United States," Joanna said darkly. "They're going to blow him up."

"Oh, my lord!"

"And they've got a perfect plan to carry it out."

40

Agent Jack Youngblood leaned over in his seat and looked down at the golden plains of Kansas, thirty-five thousand feet below. It was where he had been born and raised and lived until he left to join the Marines. He could still remember standing in the cornfields of his father's farm, watching planes fly overhead, wondering where they were going and wishing that one day he would be riding in them. Never in his wildest dreams did he imagine himself aboard Air Force One, the lead agent in charge of protecting the President of the United States.

Youngblood leaned back in his seat and closed his eyes, listening to the steady hum of the jet engines. For the next two hours he would have no worries or concerns, because everyone and everything aboard had been carefully screened and controlled. There was no threat from within or without. On Air Force One the Secret Service agents guarding the President could relax.

Youngblood heard someone approaching and opened his eyes. In an instant he was on his feet.

The President waved him down. "Keep your seat, Jack."

"Yes, sir," Youngblood said, but he continued standing. He couldn't sit while the President stood. He just couldn't.

"You don't listen to me anymore, Jack," the President jested. "I tell you to sit and you keep standing."

"Yes, sir," Youngblood said and remained standing.

The President moved about the cabin, limping noticeably on his left leg. He was a tall, good-looking man in his midfifties, with sharp patrician features and thick gray hair that was turning white at the temples. He was now well into his second term of office, and his approval rating in the polls was an astonishing 78 percent.

The President walked around in a circle, trying to shake the stiffness from his knee. He had injured it while playing football for Stanford in the big game against California, which they'd won. At the time he thought it was worth it. But now he didn't. The knee bothered him just about every day. He glanced over at the Secret Service agent. "Jack, did you ever do something in your youth that you later wished to hell had never happened?"

"Yes, sir," Youngblood answered.

"But you'd rather not talk about it, right?"

"Yes, sir."

"Jack, you really must do something with your vocabulary. You seem to be stuck on 'yes, sir.' "

"Yes, sir."

"Jesus." The President chuckled. "Jack, I'm going to give you a direct order. Don't say 'yes, sir' again."

Youngblood hesitated. "Okay, sir."

The President laughed aloud, his knee less bothersome now. "I understand you'll be leaving us soon."

"In another month, sir."

"We're going to miss you, Jack. You've done a solid job for us."

"Thank you, sir."

"You sound like you're kind of anxious to leave us."

"No, sir," Youngblood said truthfully. He considered guarding the President an honor and a privilege, and if it had been left up to him, he would have done it forever. But the Secret Service would not allow that. Agents were assigned to guard the President for only six months. The reason was the Secret Service didn't want them to become too familiar or too accustomed to guarding the President. They didn't want the agents to lose their focus.

The President gave Youngblood a long look. "You're still unhappy about me going to Los Angeles, aren't you?"

"No, sir."

The President held up an index finger and waved it at the agent. "I don't want your standard answer. I want the truth."

"It could be dangerous, sir."

The President shook his head. "That's not the real danger, Jack. The real danger is running scared because of a bunch of goddamn terrorists. The minute you let them dictate is the minute we begin to lose all of our freedoms." The President took a deep breath and firmly set his jaw. "Now tell me, Jack, how does this sound to you? There are some terrorists blowing up people and buildings in Los Angeles. Accordingly, the President of the United States will cancel his visit to the country's second largest city." The President's jaw tightened even further. "Let me tell you what message that sends to the people of Los Angeles. You stay put and hope for the best and, by the way, the President isn't coming here because he might get hurt. You and your children may get blown up, but don't worry. The President will be watching from a safe distance. How does that sound, Jack?"

Youngblood said nothing.

"Answer me."

"But, sir, you're the commander in chief."

"You're goddamn right I am," the President said stonily. "And I'm not about to let some terrorists tell me what to do and when to do it."

Youngblood watched the President leave the cabin, then slumped back into his seat, hoping he had all the bases covered. The usual number of agents for a presidential visit had been doubled. The new institute was now secure, all agents in place and no one except the bomb-sniffing dogs and their handlers allowed in or out. The metal detectors had been set up and their sensitivity raised to a level that would detect car keys.

In his mind's eye, Youngblood quickly went over the details of the visit to the institute. They would enter through the front door and spend a few minutes in the atrium, where the President would greet the invited dignitaries, all of whom had been carefully screened. Then the President would take a brief tour of the institute, accompanied by five people: the governor of California, the mayor of Los Angeles, the senior senator from California, the director of the institute, and the dean of the medical center. They would be in and out in less than thirty minutes.

Everything seemed secure.

But Youngblood knew it took only one mistake and the President was gone. Like in Dallas when President Kennedy ordered the Secret Service agents not to stand on the rear bumper of his limousine. He wanted everybody to see him. And everybody did, including Lee Harvey Oswald, who would have never gotten a shot off had the agents been on the rear bumper.

Youngblood envisioned the famous frame on the Zapruder film, the one showing JFK's head exploding with blood and bone flying into the air and onto Mrs. Kennedy. It was the Secret Service's biggest failure and worst nightmare. And every agent guarding the President dreaded even the thought of it happening again.

Youngblood closed his eyes and silently said the prayer he'd said a hundred times before.

Dear God! Don't let it happen on my watch.

41

Monday, April 19, 6:20 A.M.

From the front seat of his car Jake watched the dawn breaking. Red streaks were spreading across the dark gray sky, the full moon overhead fading fast. Again he glanced at his watch. Only five minutes had passed since he checked it last. It was 6:20 A.M. He looked over at Farelli, who had his head resting back against the seat, eyes closed.

"Are you awake?" Jake asked.

"Some," Farelli said. "You got anything?"

"I got nothing."

Farelli curled up against the morning chill, his head now down on his chest.

They were parked at the curb outside the Koppelman home, waiting for the family to return. Despite an intensive search, no trace of the Koppelmans could be found. An all-points bulletin for the entire state had failed to turn up their Chevy van. And every hotel and motel in Palm Springs and the surrounding desert had been checked. And again there was nothing. The Koppelmans had vanished.

Jake lit a cigarette, now wondering if the Koppelmans had been killed and dumped somewhere out in the desert. That was the most likely scenario. If it was true, any chance of finding Joanna had died with them. Jake inhaled deeply on his cigarette and began coughing loudly, phlegm rattling in his lungs.

"You're going to kill yourself with those damn cigarettes," Farelli said.

"I know," Jake rasped, his throat raw from the pack he'd smoked since midnight. "But the nicotine is the only thing keeping me awake." He took another drag and said, more to himself than to Farelli, "Got to stay awake. Got to find her."

Farelli opened an eye. "The doc is dead, Jake. You may as well face up to it."

"There's still a chance," Jake persisted.

Farelli shook his head. "Forget it. Even if the Koppelmans lead us right to her, all we're going to find is dead bodies."

Jake nodded somberly, knowing that Farelli was right. The chance that Joanna was still alive was one in a thousand at best. And the odds were even greater against the Koppelmans being somehow involved with the terrorists and able to lead the police to them. A background check on Lewis Koppelman revealed that he was a Holocaust survivor who had come to America as a boy, worked his way through college and become a self-made millionaire. And he was a staunch Republican. His profile was exactly opposite that of a terrorist.

The car radio suddenly came to life. "Lights coming your way!"

In an instant Jake and Farelli were out of their car, crouched down behind the open car doors. They watched a pair of headlights approaching in the dawn. The vehicle was moving very slowly, at times almost coming to a stop. There was an intermittent, soft thudlike sound that neither Jake nor Farelli could identify. Then they saw the vehicle. It was a pickup truck with men standing in the back throwing newspapers.

Jake put his weapon away as Farelli picked up the car microphone to talk with the officers in the black-and-white that was parked a block away. Jake lit another cigarette and watched the pickup truck make a U-turn to deliver newspapers on the other side of the street. Darkly, he wondered what the headlines in tomorrow's newspapers would be. In big, bold letters they would tell what was blown up and how many were killed and who might be responsible. And the death of Joanna Blalock would be a side story, buried somewhere deep inside the newspaper. And since she had no family, Jake would have to handle the funeral arrangements. He had no idea how to do it. Just call the mortuary and give them your credit card, he guessed.

"Another car coming!" the car radio blurted out.

Farelli quickly picked up the car phone. "You got a make?"

"Mercedes. Sedan. Two people in the front seat."

Again Jake and Farelli crouched behind open car doors and waited. The headlights came into view, moving slowly but without stops.

"Remember," Jake called over, "there could be an asshole in the backseat with a gun."

"Uh-huh," Farelli said and made certain the safety on his weapon was off.

The black Mercedes pulled into the Koppelmans' driveway and stopped. Its lights stayed on.

Jake stayed behind the car door, his weapon drawn. "Mr. Koppelman! This is the police," he yelled. "I want you and your wife to step out and move away from the car."

Neither of the figures in the Mercedes moved. The lights remained on.

"If there's anyone in the backseat," Jake went on, "listen and listen good. You've got two guns trained on you and two black-and-white squad cars waiting for you to do something stupid."

The front door of the Mercedes on the driver's side opened, and a man got out, holding his hands above his head. He was short and well-built and balding, with thin gray hair.

"Open the back door and step away," Jake ordered. "Then have your wife do the same."

The Koppelmans did as they were told. Now they were well away from the car, which had all of its doors open.

Jake and Farelli advanced slowly, their weapons in front of them. At the rear fender they stopped and exchanged silent hand signals.

"There's no one in there," Koppelman said.

Farelli waited another second, then threw himself on the lawn and rolled over into a prone position, his weapon pointing directly into the backseat. It was empty. Slowly he got to his feet. "All clear."

Jake placed his gun in its holster and went over to the Koppelmans.

Lewis Koppelman lowered his hands and stepped in front of his wife, glaring at Jake. "What the hell is that all about?" he demanded.

"Murder and kidnapping," Jake said.

"Someone from around here?"

Jake ignored the question. "Where's your Chevy van?"

"At the back of the driveway," Koppelman said at once. "Here, I'll show you."

They walked over to the Mercedes, and Koppelman turned on its bright lights. The high beams shined on the garage door at the end of the driveway.

"Son of a bitch!" Koppelman hissed angrily. "Somebody's stolen it again."

Jake's shoulders sagged. His last and only chance to find Joanna and the terrorists had just gone out the window. "When was the last time you saw it?"

"Wednesday morning a little after eight. That's when we left on our trip."

"Do you have any idea who stole it?"

"None," Koppelman said, taking his wife's hand and drawing her closer to him. "Do you know if they broke into our house?"

"They didn't," Jake assured him. "We checked it out."

"How did you get inside?"

"We broke a window," Jake said, starting to cough again. "We'll have it repaired for you."

"I'll take care of it." Koppelman looked down the empty driveway and shook his head. "And they used my van to do a kidnapping, huh?"

"Yeah."

"Do I know the victim?"

"No."

"Are you certain they used my van?"

"Positive," Jake said, not wanting to go into details. He turned to leave. "Sorry to have disturbed you."

"Officer," Koppelman's wife called after Jake. "Could you notify the police so they can track down our van and have it returned?"

Jake sighed wearily. "Ma'am, it might be best for you to make the call. You can provide them with all the details they'll need. You can describe the van better than we can."

"Oh, they don't need a description," the woman said. "We just give them our number and they activate the Lo-Jack system."

Jake moved in closer to the woman, his ears pricked. "The what system?"

"The LoJack system," Koppelman explained. "After our van was stolen for the second time, we had the device installed under the hood. Now all we have to do is call the police and they'll activate the system. The device under the hood gives off a radio signal that the police can track down. They can usually find the vehicle pronto, before it's been damaged or cut up into parts."

"It's a wonderful system," his wife added. "They even use a helicopter to zero in on—"

"I need the number you're supposed to call." Jake cut her off.

Koppelman took out a small address book and began thumbing through it.

42

"Should I go ahead and kill the boy?" Rudy asked.

"No," Eva said at once. "Blalock will want to see the kid before she makes the phone call."

"How much longer do we have to wait?"

"About an hour."

Joanna pressed her ear to the cellar door and listened to the voices coming from the kitchen. Another hour, she thought, which meant it was now seven o'clock. In sixty minutes the Blalock family would be wiped out forever unless she could come up with a way to delay things. Maybe she could give the terrorists a phony message after talking with Joe Wells. No, she quickly decided. That would never work. The female terrorist was too smart for that. She'd have her ear next to Joanna's while the phone call was being made.

The voices in the kitchen became muffled for a few minutes before clearing again.

"So you want me to kill the woman doctor first," Rudy was asking, "then the boy and then the boy's mother?"

"Right," Eva said. "And I want them all to be head shots."

"There's going to be blood everywhere. On the floor, on the walls, everywhere."

"Exactly." Eva's voice faded briefly then came back. ". . . drag the bodies to the cellar door and throw them down the stairs."

"Why bother with all that? We're not going to be here."

"But the police will," Eva told him. "After we leave here we'll walk to the shopping mall on the corner. From there we'll call the police and give them the address of the house and tell them we heard screams inside. Then we'll describe the green van sitting in the driveway, put the phone down and drive away in the rental car that you parked in the shopping center."

"I don't see how all that does us any good."

"Sure it does," Eva went on. "First, it will bring every cop and federal agent in Los Angeles to an empty house. They'll think we're inside, and that will keep them distracted while we get away. Eventually, though, they'll storm the house and see blood everywhere. When they don't find the bodies upstairs, some idiot will turn the knob to open the cellar door."

"What happens then?"

"The C-four in the ceiling of the cellar will be detonated and everything will go boom. It will be just like West Hollywood again, except it'll be cops and federal agents who die."

"Beautiful," Rudy cooed.

"Yes," Eva agreed, wondering when would be the best time to kill Rudy. While he was killing the boy's mother, she decided. A head shot from behind.

"Then we pick up Bremmer. Right?"

"Bremmer stays behind."

"But they'll catch him and he'll squeal everything."

"Not if he's dead."

There was a long silence.

Joanna listened intently, concentrating, wondering if they had lowered their voices or moved outside.

"How will you do it?" Rudy asked finally.

"After the assassination, Bremmer will drive away and call us on his car phone for instructions," Eva said.

"When he puts the receiver down, I'll dial the number of his car phone. As he picks up the receiver, a detonator will be activated, and the C-four under his hood will go off. There'll be just enough left of him to identify."

"Screw him." Rudy shrugged, but he was thinking how dangerous Eva was and how she might kill him to avoid paying him the $400,000.

Eva watched Rudy's expression change and immediately regretted telling him about her plans for Bremmer. Now he would be more cautious. "Let me tell you why Bremmer has to go," she said. "It won't take the feds long to figure out the C-four was in the prosthesis. They'll know it had to be Bremmer who placed it there, and they'll come after him and they'll catch him. And before they're finished with him he'll tell them everything he knows. Now, do you want that to happen?"

"I guess not."

"Okay. Let's go check . . . before . . . the . . ."

The voices were now muffled, but Joanna could hear footsteps approaching. Quickly she tiptoed down the steps and sat next to Kate on the mattress. In a whisper she said, "If the door opens, lie down and pretend you're asleep."

They waited in silence. Above them the floor creaked, then went quiet again. Joanna looked up and wondered where the C-four had been placed. Probably in the space between the ceiling and the floor above. She searched the ceiling for wiring, but the morning light coming through the window was too dim to let her see anything clearly.

"Is Jean-Claude all right?" Kate asked softly.

"He's playing," Joanna lied. "I heard him running around."

"I haven't heard his little footsteps."

"He's in the kitchen."

Kate eyed the unopened cartons of milk on the floor,

which had been left sometime during the night. "We shouldn't drink the milk, huh?"

Joanna shook her head. "It's probably been doctored."

Kate sighed deeply and tried to swallow her thirst away. "Do you have any idea what time it is?"

"Seven o'clock."

"Only an hour left for us."

"Yeah."

"They're not going to find us, are they?"

Joanna said nothing because at this point it didn't really matter. Even if they were found, there would be a shoot-out, and with their last breaths the terrorists would somehow manage to detonate the C-four. And she and Kate and Jean-Claude would still end up dead. Unless, during the shoot-out, they could get out through the window. But it was barred and impossible to squeeze through.

Joanna tried to think of ways to escape or to attract attention to their imprisonment. But she kept coming to dead ends. There was no avenue of escape, and just trying to draw attention from the outside could be very dangerous for Jean-Claude. It could only be done safely if the terrorists remained unaware she was doing it. But how could she accomplish that? Joanna concentrated, trying to find answers, but there weren't any. She stared up at the window she couldn't fit through and shook her head dejectedly.

"Do you believe in an afterlife?" Kate asked, breaking the silence.

"Yes," Joanna said.

"Do you think we'll see Mom and Daddy again?"

"I hope so."

"Me too."

Joanna wondered if her vision of the afterlife was the true one. A heaven and a hell, a good and a bad. And where would she end up? In heaven maybe, close to her mother and father, with Kate and Jean-Claude. All the Blalocks together again.

"Do you really think hell is full of fire and brimstone?" Kate asked. "You know, like Dante's *Inferno*?"

"Maybe."

"I hate fire," Kate said weakly. "It's always frightened me." She shivered, rubbing her hands together against the morning chill. "Although I wouldn't mind a little fire right now. You know, just enough to warm my fingers."

"All you've got to do is flick—" Joanna jumped to her feet and stared up at the window. "There may be a way to attract someone on the outside."

"How?"

"You'll see," Joanna said, reaching for the oily rag and the lighter it held. "Get the mop."

Joanna hurried over to the table and repositioned it beneath the window. She climbed up on it and took the mop from Kate. Using the mop end, she pushed out the remaining glass pane. It made a soft cracking sound. The pieces of glass fell silently onto the bush and cardboard outside the window.

"What are you doing?" Kate was on her tiptoes, straining to see.

"Shh!" Joanna hushed, now wrapping the oily rag around the mop and tying it in place with mop strands. She flicked the lighter, but it didn't ignite. Then again, and again it didn't light. On the third try a tiny flame appeared. Carefully she held it to the oily rag wrapped around the end of the mop and waited. Sparks came, then smoke, then a small tongue of flame. Joanna slowly pushed the mop through the window and let it drop on the cardboard and dried-out bush.

The cardboard smoldered briefly, becoming black and scorched in the center. Then it went out. A moment later the flame at the end of the mop died. Quickly Joanna brought the mop head back inside and tried to reignite it. She flicked the lighter, but it gave off only sparks. Again and again she flicked the lighter, and every time she saw only sparks, fewer with each flick.

Joanna sank down on the table and sighed dejectedly.

"What's wrong?" Kate asked.

"The lighter is dead," she said gloomily. "And so are we."

43

From a block away Jake studied the terrorists' house through high-powered binoculars. There were no lights on. Everything was quiet. His eyes went to the Chevy van parked in the driveway, then to its license plate, which read 3 VDM 593.

"Are they detecting any signs of life?" Jake asked.

Hurley held up a hand as he pushed the listening device deeper into his ear. "They're securing the last of the surrounding homes now. They'll be in position in a minute."

Jake watched the front door of the home next to the terrorists' hideout open and close. A couple dressed in pajamas and bathrobes hurried down the steps. A SWAT team member kept them close to the house, quickly escorting them out of sight. The surrounding homes were now empty except for police marksmen with infrared scopes and acoustics experts with equipment so sensitive it could pick up a soft voice a hundred yards away. Everything was still again. A dog barked briefly, then stopped. Jake glanced at his watch. It was 8:02 A.M.

"You figure they've got the house wired with explosives?" Jake asked.

"Probably," Hurley said.

"Shit," Jake muttered under his breath, growing impatient and hoping against hope that Joanna was still alive.

"But that's not the worst-case scenario," Hurley went on. "Sometimes they wrap explosives around their

hostages. You make one wrong move and a bunch of innocent people get blown up."

"Well, at least the terrorists die too."

"Not always. The really smart ones construct a thin
necklace of C-four and put it around the hostage's neck.
It's got just enough explosive power to blow the victim's
head off."

Jake winced. "Have you ever seen that done?"

"Once. The head came off and bounced down the
street. I swear to God it actually bounced, like a baseball."

"Christ," Jake said, trying not to envision the gruesome sight.

Abruptly Hurley held up his hand again. "We've got
an infrared image in the front room of the house." He
tilted his head, listening intently to the communication
between SWAT team members. "There's one and a half
people in the living room."

"What's a half person?" Jake asked quickly.

"A child."

Jake breathed a sigh of relief. It had to be Jean-Claude.
And if the boy was still alive, there was a good chance
Joanna and Kate were as well. "Who's with the child?"

"Can't tell for sure," Hurley said. "And the voice detectors can't help us because they've got a television set
on."

"It's probably one of the terrorists."

"Probably isn't good enough. We've got to know for
sure." Hurley concentrated his hearing as another SWAT
team member reported in. "There are two more infrared
images in a rear room, probably the kitchen. And they
hear two voices, both female."

"Are the people in the kitchen calling each other by
name?" Jake asked anxiously.

Hurley waved away Jake's question. "Now they're
picking up a man's voice. There are three voices but only

two images. Where the hell is—" Hurley stopped in mid-sentence, listening carefully and nodding at what he heard. "It's a telephone call. A man and a woman . . . The woman is asking, 'Where are you supposed to go? On the steps or inside?' . . . The man says, 'Don't know yet. I called and the secretary said I'd have to talk with—'" There was a brief burst of static, and Hurley waited for it to pass. "The man is still talking. He's saying, 'They want me to call back at eight forty-five.'"

There was more static, lasting several seconds. Then it cleared.

The phone conversation was over.

Hurley looked over at Jake. "Can you make anything of that?"

"Not a damn thing."

"Me neither."

"Maybe the eight forty-five phone call will tell us more," Hurley said and readjusted the listening device in his ear. Suddenly his eyes narrowed. "The two images are leaving the kitchen. A door is opening and closing. Now they hear footsteps walking downstairs. Into a cellar, they think."

"Good," Jake said, thinking that was where the terrorists would keep Joanna and Kate.

"Bad," Hurley told him. "The outer walls of the cellar are covered with thick stucco. They can't get infrared readings through it."

Jake focused his binoculars on the base of the house, just in front of the Chevy van. "What about the window at ground level? It looks like it goes into the cellar."

"It does, but it's too small and too high up."

"Shit," Jake grumbled, now watching a SWAT team member crawl up to the near side of the van and slash its tires in case the terrorists decided to make a break for it.

"We're picking up a conversation in the cellar," Hurley reported. "Two female voices. One is called Kay or Kate."

They're alive! Jake thought. *Oh, sweet God in heaven, they're alive!*

"One of them is talking about trying to get a lighter to work," Hurley continued. "And now they're saying something about a mop and a rag of some sort." He glanced over at Jake. "I hope they're not stupid enough to start a fire down there."

Jake swallowed worriedly. "That whole place could explode, huh?"

"That's not the problem," Hurley explained. "You can light C-four and cook on it and it won't explode. It requires an electrical charge to detonate. My concern is that they could suffocate if they start a blaze down there."

"They could break the window," Jake suggested.

"That would only make it worse. Air would be sucked in and feed the fire even more."

"They're desperate," Jake said somberly. "And that may be their only chance."

"I know," Hurley said, wondering if he should take the risk of having a SWAT team member crawl up to the window and transmit a message. The man would be exposed, and if he were seen by the terrorists he'd be dead. And the terrorists would be alerted. Too risky, Hurley decided.

Jake trained his binoculars on the small, barred window of the cellar. Something was being pushed out of it. He focused in and saw the burning mop head dropping onto the litter outside the window. The trash caught fire and sent black smoke upwards. "Smart move. Beautiful. So damn smart."

Hurley heard the news of the fire from the SWAT team member in the adjacent house. "We'd better hope that fire doesn't spread to the walls of the house. If it does, we're going to have dead people."

Jake hurriedly put down the binoculars. "Call the nearest fire station and have them send one engine, siren blasting. Tell them to stop one block south of here so I can speak with them. And tell them to bring along an extra fireman's outfit."

Hurley hesitated briefly before saying, "Jake, it might be best to let the SWAT team handle this."

"Will they be able to distinguish Joanna and Kate from the terrorist bitch in a split second?"

Hurley nodded slowly. "You've got a point."

"Make the call."

44

"See? I told you the ceremony would be held inside," Josiah Wales said, leading the way out of the old rehabilitation institute.

Timothy Bremmer was a step behind, hurrying to keep up. Under his arm was a box containing the new prosthesis Wales would put on in front of the President.

"You've got to remember," Wales went on, "the President loves to shake hands with wealthy donors, and he can do that better inside. That will also give the photographers and television people time to get plenty of pictures."

"Yeah. Plenty of pictures," Bremmer said absently, wondering if he should contact Eva and tell her he had the information they needed. There was no reason to keep the Blalocks alive any longer. It would be best to kill them now. That would save time later. But things were moving too fast, and Bremmer couldn't call from the new institute. He didn't trust the phones there, not with all the Secret Service agents around.

"Do you have any idea how many votes this dedication can get the President?" Wales asked.

"A lot, I guess," Bremmer answered, wishing Wales would shut up so he could think. There were still details to be ironed out.

"Try a couple of million," Wales said. "Every disabled person who sees me putting on that prosthesis in front of the President will vote for him. And then there's all the veterans who will be reminded that the institute is named after a fighter pilot who fought in Vietnam."

Bremmer saw the opening to obtain the last piece of information he needed. "Are you sure the President will want to actually watch you put the prosthesis on?"

"I'm positive," Wales said at once. "I suggested it to Simon Murdock, and he told me to set it up."

"Will I be involved in that?"

"I'm afraid not. There will only be five people accompanying the President on his tour of the new institute. I tried my best to have you included, but they wouldn't go for it."

Bremmer sagged his shoulders in mock disappointment. "I know you did your best."

"But you and the other dignitaries will be able to see everything," Wales said consolingly. "Remember, all the corridors and rooms are scanned by closed-circuit television cameras."

"Great," Bremmer said as the last piece of the assassination plan fell into place. Wales would put the new prosthesis on, probably in the fitting section of the workshop. With Wales's first step the pressure on the heel of the prosthesis would prime the detonator. Then Bremmer would push the switch that would detonate the C-four, killing Wales and the President and everyone around them. In the chaos and confusion that followed, Bremmer would slip away unnoticed.

They picked up the pace as they approached the new institute. The street was barricaded, and there was no traffic except for a single limousine dropping off a late-arriving dignitary. A very old man who was bent at the waist and walked with a cane slowly made his way up the ramp for the handicapped.

"I thought all the dignitaries were supposed to be here by eight-thirty," Bremmer said.

"That's Mortimer Rhodes," Wales informed him.

"The billionaire?"

Wales nodded. "And the most powerful man in the state of California. He comes and goes when he wants to."

Bremmer watched Rhodes struggle up the incline, thinking the old man had lived too long. His gaze went to the steps of the new institute, then to the sidewalk across the street. Secret Service agents were everywhere, their eyes constantly searching for anything suspicious. Atop the Bank of America building were two figures dressed in black, scanning the area with binoculars. Sharpshooters, Bremmer guessed.

At the bottom of the steps they were stopped by Secret Service agents. Their invitation cards were examined, their faces matched against twelve-by-twelve glossy photographs.

"Please place your thumb here," an agent instructed Wales and pointed to an illuminated square in the center of a flat computer screen.

Wales placed his thumb on the square. His thumbprint was electronically transmitted to a computer bank and compared with those known to belong to Josiah Wales. Seconds later the computer screen flashed the message ACCESS CLEARED.

"Thank you, sir," the agent said. "Please proceed directly up the steps."

Bremmer placed his hand on the screen and tried to remain calm, but his heart was pounding and sweat was rolling down his back. He could get through the thumbprint test without a problem. But the explosives-sniffing dogs were another matter. They could detect the barest trace of C-four. And although Eva had assured him that C-four sealed between layers of plastic gave off no odor, Bremmer was still nervous about it. If they caught him with C-four, he'd spend the rest of his life in a maximum-security prison, locked up in a small cell twenty-three hours a day. That would be worse than death. It would be a lifetime of torture. If they discovered the C-four in the prosthesis, Bremmer had decided to detonate it and kill himself.

ACCESS CLEARED flashed on the computer screen.

"Thank you, sir," the agent said. "Please proceed directly up the steps."

Bremmer followed Wales up to the entrance and through the door. Another agent stopped them.

"Please open your box," the agent asked Bremmer.

Bremmer removed the top of the cardboard box and showed its contents to the agent.

"What are these devices?" the agent asked.

"Prostheses," Bremmer said. "Would you like to examine them?"

"Yes. One at a time, please."

Bremmer took out a highly advanced prosthetic hand. He willed his own hand not to shake, but he knew it was trembling. "This is a prosthetic hand. Would you like to see how it works?"

"Yes, sir."

Bremmer held the hand up. Its outer surface was whitish pink and closely resembled human skin. Uncovered wires and slender titanium rods projected from the wrist area. "When you push this button, the hand grips. Shall I demonstrate?"

"Please."

Bremmer pushed a button on the hand, and the fingers slowly flexed.

The agent moved in closer, fascinated. Another agent came over for a look.

"And if you press the other button it opens," Bremmer told them. He pressed a second button, and the fingers slowly extended.

"Incredible," the agent said, now thinking about a

friend who had lost both hands in Vietnam. "Too bad it wouldn't work in a double amputee."

"Oh, but it would," Bremmer said. "The final product won't have buttons. It'll be activated by a shrug of the shoulder."

The agent made a mental note to call his friend and tell him about the highly advanced prosthesis. "Very impressive," he said.

Not as impressive as when the two buttons are pressed simultaneously to detonate the C-4, Bremmer thought. He reached back into the box. "And this is a foot prosthesis."

The agent examined it carefully and placed it back in the box. "The metal rods on that hand will probably activate the metal detector."

"They shouldn't," Bremmer said. "They're made of titanium."

"Proceed through the metal detector, please."

Bremmer walked on, holding the cardboard box securely under his arm. He kept his pace slow and even and tried not to show any nervousness. But his heart was racing wildly and his throat was dry as sand.

At the entrance to the metal detector, a bomb-sniffing dog eyed Bremmer warily, sensing his fear. The Belgian Malinois tilted his nose up and sampled the air.

Bremmer forced himself to walk slowly and not look at the dog. The Malinois came over and sniffed at Bremmer's ankles and shoes, making a low-pitched sound before it lost interest and went back to the side of its handler.

Bremmer was almost through the metal detector when he heard loud murmurs and saw people moving toward the door. He turned and looked back.

The presidential limousine was pulling up to the curb.

45

Eva heard the siren coming closer and closer. Quickly she primed the detonating device on the cellar door, then hurried into the living room. Rudy was peering through a crack in the venetian blinds, holding Jean-Claude by the nape of his neck.

"What is it?" Eva asked.

"A fire engine, and it's right in front of our house," Rudy answered. "I thought I smelled smoke a little while ago."

Eva turned and sniffed the air, but she detected nothing. "Where do you think it came from?"

"I don't know." Rudy hastily let go of the venetian blind and stepped away. "But two firemen are walking across our front lawn."

All of Eva's senses suddenly heightened, her mind now racing. What was on fire and where was it? It couldn't be very big. Otherwise they would have sent more than one engine. And the firemen were walking, not running. Maybe it was just a check of some sort. No, it couldn't be that. They had used their sirens, and minutes earlier Rudy had smelled smoke.

The doorbell rang.

Eva ignored it and thought on. It couldn't be coming from the cellar. The smoke would have seeped up under and around the cellar door. And besides, the Blalock women didn't have anything to start a fire. They had both been carefully searched while they slept. But then again, it would be a mistake to underestimate—

The doorbell rang once more, followed by a loud knock.

"Well?" Rudy asked, reaching for his weapon. "What do we do?"

"Play it by ear." Eva tucked her gun into the back of her jeans so that only the handle was visible. Then she picked up Jean-Claude, who was still lethargic from the sedatives given to him the night before. "I'll open the door and be the concerned mother with her child. You cover me from the kitchen."

"What if they want to check out the cellar?"

"Then we kill them," Eva said tonelessly. "Now go!"

Eva waited for Rudy to disappear into the kitchen before opening the front door.

She faced two firemen clad in heavy fire-resistant gear and wearing large plastic helmets.

"Sorry to bother you, ma'am," the SWAT team member said. "But there's a small fire smoldering near the side of your house."

"Oh, goodness!" Eva said, feigning alarm. She held Jean-Claude closer, and he tried to wriggle out of her grasp. "Wh-what caught on fire?"

"Some trash," the SWAT team member said. He glanced over the woman's shoulder and looked for more terrorists, but saw only an empty room.

"I told my husband to clear that away," Eva said. "I know how dangerous that can be."

"Yes, ma'am. Your whole house could have gone up in flames."

"Well, I really appreciate your putting it out for me."

"Yes, ma'am. Now we'd like to inspect your cellar to make sure no sparks got in there."

"Is it really necessary to check out the cellar?" Eva asked, raising her voice to alert Rudy.

"Yes, ma'am."

Eva stepped aside.

As the SWAT team member in the fireman's gear entered the house, Eva reached back for her gun. Now she was holding Jean-Claude with only one arm.

Jean-Claude leaned forward and grabbed the brim of the other fireman's helmet, pulling it up. "Jacques!" he cried out happily.

In an instant Jake slammed his fist into the terrorist's face, splitting her lips and breaking her nose. She crumpled to the floor, her head bouncing on the hardwood.

Jake picked up Jean-Claude and dove out the front door. He landed on the grass and rolled over, using his body to protect the little boy. From inside he heard two dull, popping sounds and knew they came from a silenced weapon.

A moment later the SWAT team member staggered out of the house, holding a bleeding shoulder. He collapsed on the lawn.

Jake was now in a prone position on the grass, Jean-Claude beneath him. He had his weapon pointed at the door, as did the SWAT team marksman standing behind the fire engine.

Eva was groaning loudly, and Jake could see her hand starting to move.

"Jacques! I cannot breathe," Jean-Claude complained.

"Shhh!" Jake hushed him. "The outlaws are inside."

"You will catch them?"

"Yeah."

"Good."

Rudy came to the door, crouched low and tried to pull Eva inside the living room.

Jake's shot missed, but those from the SWAT team marksman didn't. Rudy's head exploded, brain and bone and blood flying into the air.

Eva tried to stand. As she got to one knee, Jake fired

again. She grabbed at her chest and fell back onto the floor.

Two SWAT team members dashed across the lawn and up to the side of the house. One smashed the front bay window and tore out the venetian blinds. They waited for their spotters with high-powered scopes and binoculars to give the all-clear signal. Then they disappeared into the house.

Jake sent Jean-Claude back to the fire truck, where a genuine fireman waited for the boy with open arms.

Jake stayed in a prone position with his weapon trained on the door until Jean-Claude was out of harm's way. Then he got up and slowly moved toward the house, his gun still pointed at the door. Inside he saw Rudy on the hardwood floor. Except for the chin and mouth, there was nothing left of the terrorist's head. Beside him was Eva Reineke, close to death. A bloody froth was bubbling up through the hole in her chest.

"No more bad guys," a SWAT team member called out.

Jake put his weapon away and hurried into the hallway. "The people we're here to rescue are in the cellar," he said and reached for the doorknob.

The SWAT team member grabbed Jake's wrist and jerked it back from the knob. "Don't touch!" He pointed to the wiring atop the door that came down to a small metal box next to the light switch.

"Christ!" Jake shivered. "Should we get the bomb squad in here?"

The SWAT team member shook his head. "There may not be time. They might have put a timer in it as a backup."

"Then we'll go through the basement window."

"That may be wired too."

"Well, then, we'll just have to take our chances, won't

we?" Jake moved close to the door, careful not to touch it. "Joanna! Joanna!"

There was a silence that lasted several seconds.

"Joanna!" Jake yelled out again.

"Jake?" came the reply from within.

Jake smiled, recognizing Joanna's voice. "It's me," he shouted. "We're going to get you out. But for now the most important thing is for you not to touch the door. It's wired to explosives."

"I know," Joanna called back. "How is Jean-Claude?"

"He's playing in the fire truck." Jake thought he heard someone crying, but he couldn't be sure. "You stay put. We'll get you out the side window. Can you tell if it's wired?"

"I don't think it is," Joanna said. "I broke the window out and pulled on the bars and nothing happened."

"Good."

"Jake, there's something you have to do immed——"

"We've got to move," the SWAT team member interrupted impatiently. "If there's a timer on that bomb, it could go off any time."

"Stay put," Jake yelled down to Joanna and ran out of the house, a step behind the SWAT team member. On the lawn he quickly pulled off his fireman's gear. "We'll need a pickax to break out that window."

"It could still be wired, you know," the SWAT team member warned.

"You want to argue or you want to help me?"

The SWAT team member hesitated for a brief second. "I'll get the pickaxes."

It was pure luck, Jake was thinking, that Joanna and Kate and Jean-Claude were still alive. Pure luck that the terrorists had stolen a van that gave off a radio signal. Pure luck. Just let it last a little longer.

The SWAT team member came back with two pickaxes and handed one to Jake. "Let's get to it."

They hurried to the side of the house.

From the loft above the garage, George Walter Reineke looked through the wooden slats of a small window and watched two policemen swinging pickaxes. Carefully he aimed his high-powered rifle at the cop closest to him and pulled the trigger.

The cop straightened up, then collapsed, facedown.

Reineke took his time lining up the second target in his telescopic sight. The man was running away, but there was no rush. The cop had nowhere to hide. He was as good as dead.

46

The President was nearing the end of the reception line, now talking with Mortimer Rhodes. The old man, leaning heavily on his cane, had refused to sit although a chair had been provided for him.

"Mortimer, I really appreciate all the support you've given me," the President said.

"I didn't do it for you," Rhodes said bluntly. "I did it for the country. I thought you were the best man to lead us, and I was right."

"I take that as high praise."

"Take it as straight truth."

The President smiled broadly and patted Rhodes on the shoulder, liking the old man and his directness. "Stay well, Mortimer."

"You do the same, Mr. President."

Agent Jack Youngblood was right behind the President, moving with him as he went down the row of dignitaries. Youngblood watched the people's heads and eyes. That was how he read them. When a person was about to do harm, the head moved first, then the hands. That instant was enough for Youngblood to throw himself between the attacker and the President.

Youngblood adjusted his earpiece and listened to the communications between the agents outside. Everything was secure. The armor-plated limousine was running and waiting. And the backup car, a Chevy Suburban with enough firepower to wipe out a platoon, was nearby.

Youngblood glanced at his watch. They were on schedule, and with a little luck they'd be out in less than thirty minutes. A quick tour of the institute. The medal presentation. Another round of handshaking. Then back to Air Force One.

Youngblood's eyes went back to the President, who was now being introduced to the last two people in line. They were doctors wearing long white coats. One of them held a cardboard box under his arm. It had been carefully checked and contained only new prostheses.

"Mr. President," Simon Murdock was saying, "I'd like you to meet Dr. Josiah Wales, the director of the institute."

The President shook Wales's hand firmly. "I've heard nothing but good things about you, Dr. Wales."

"Thank you, sir. It's an honor to have you here."

"It's my privilege."

Wales pointed to Timothy Bremmer. "Mr. President, this is my associate, Dr. Bremmer."

Bremmer bowed awkwardly and shook hands with the President. "I'll remember this day for the rest of my life, Mr. President."

The President nodded and smiled. "It's a good day for all of us. What have you got in the box?"

"Some of our newest prostheses," Bremmer said. "May I show them to you?"

"Please."

Bremmer took out the lifelike artificial hand and demonstrated its ability to grasp. "It can pick up a nickel from a table."

"Remarkable," the President said, obviously impressed. He reached out and touched the surface of the prosthesis, which resembled human skin, then turned to Murdock. "This is exactly how I like to see federal research dollars spent."

Murdock and Wales exchanged delighted glances. The

President had signaled that even more research money would be coming their way.

The President asked, "What else do you have in the box?"

"A foot, Mr. President." Wales removed the newly made prosthesis and held it up. "As you may know, Mr. President, I require one of these. If you'd like, I can show you how it's made and fitted."

"I'd like that very much."

The group headed for the door at the far end of the reception area.

Youngblood spoke into the microphone on his lapel. "Liberty is moving. We're going inside."

Bremmer stepped back and watched the small television screen overhead. The group was now in the inner corridor, walking briskly toward the fitting room.

Bremmer placed the artificial hand back in the box, but he kept his fingers on the detonating buttons.

9:40 A.M.

George Walter Reineke was now on the ground level of the garage. He lay as close to the floor as possible, a wet handkerchief over his face to prevent the tear gas from seeping through. But his eyes and nose were still burning, and he was having trouble breathing. Desperately he kicked at the wall and felt it give. He kicked again, and the wood split apart. A cool draft of air came through the crack, and Reineke eagerly sucked it in. His eyes began to clear, and he could see a small fire truck now being parked at an angle in the driveway. It blocked his view of the street and of the small cellar window.

Reineke took the telescopic sight off his rifle and used it to study the ground beneath the fire truck. There were no feet or people visible, and that told him they were no longer trying to break through the cellar window. At least for now.

Reineke took long breaths of the fresh air and tried to think things through. He still wasn't sure what was going on. But one thing was certain. Those weren't firemen and ordinary cops out there. They had to be a SWAT team. When he shot the first cop, they'd responded with a volley of rapid fire that had blown the loft apart. And the response was so quick he didn't have time to shoot the second cop. The big guy wearing a fireman's uniform. But he got the other devil, the one in black.

Reineke reattached the telescopic sight to his rifle, now wondering if his daughter was all right. Probably, he decided. She and Rudy were still in control of the house, otherwise the cops wouldn't be trying to gain entrance through the cellar window. All the police were interested in now was rescuing the hostages. Good. Let them keep at it and be distracted. The Blalock woman was no longer of use anyhow. Just let the President go inside the institute so we can blow him to smithereens and send him to the hell he so richly deserves.

Reineke peered through the crack again and saw feet on the other side of the fire truck. They were going after the hostages again. Reineke reached for his rifle, careful not to put the barrel through the crack in the wall, then focused in with his telescopic sight. Abruptly he placed the rifle down. The SWAT team probably thinks you're dead, he told himself. Let them continue to think that, and let them leave the fire truck where it is, so it will block their view and let me get to my daughter.

Reineke crawled to the rear of the garage and kicked out two large wooden boards from the back wall. He eased his way out, staying low in the thick bushes that separated the two adjoining properties. He looked over into the neighbor's yard and saw no one. His escape route was still intact. A car was parked and waiting for them on the next street over.

His gaze went to the houses on each side. Tall trees in the backyard partially obstructed the views from both houses. From the second floors snipers could see nothing but branches and leaves. Reineke studied the distance to the back door of the house. Thirty feet. Maybe a little more. He took a deep breath and dashed across the grass, smashing into the door with his shoulder and rolling onto the kitchen floor.

There was no sound except for the pickaxes working on the window and outer wall of the cellar.

Reineke crawled across the kitchen and into the hallway. The front door was open, and he could see two bodies lying close to it. Now he could smell the stink of blood and death, and he hoped against hope that his daughter was still alive. He came to Rudy's headless body and pushed it aside. Then he saw his daughter. She was barely breathing, her chest covered with blood and froth.

"Eva! Eva!" Reineke whispered urgently into his daughter's ear. "Can you hear me?"

Eva's eyelids twitched before they opened slightly. "Father?" she asked weakly.

"You just hold on," Reineke said, dragging her away from the door and into the hallway. "I'll get you out of here."

Eva shook her head and coughed up blood. "No way. Cops ev—everywhere. They . . . kill us."

"No, they won't." Reineke took the semiautomatic weapon from Eva's jeans and checked to make certain it was loaded. "Because I'm going to carry you out of here with two hostages in front of us."

"But the—"

"You just rest here," Reineke said, reaching for the door to the cellar.

Eva's eyes opened widely. "No! It's wire—!"

Reineke turned the doorknob and pulled on it.

He saw a bright flash of light coming at him. For a fraction of a second he was engulfed in a sea of red and orange. Then everything went black.

Bremmer kept his eyes on the closed-circuit television screen, watching the group move into the room where the prostheses were manufactured. The prosthesis loaded with C-4 had been placed on a table near the door. A Secret Service agent was standing directly in front of it.

Bremmer took a very deep breath and tried to calm himself, but his pulse continued to race, and now his hands were starting to sweat. He dried his right hand with a handkerchief, then reached back into the cardboard box. His gaze stayed on the television screen as his fingers again rested on the detonating buttons.

"And the fitting room is right across the corridor, Mr. President," Wales was saying. "We have specially designed chairs to make it more comfortable for our patients."

The President asked, "What's special about them?"

"They can be automatically raised and lowered and tilted back by either the doctor or the patient."

"I'd like to see them," the President said, genuinely interested.

"Of course. And with your permission, I'll serve as the patient and show you how the prosthesis is actually fitted on."

"Excellent."

Wales led the way across the corridor, the prosthetic foot tucked under his arm.

The fitting room was small and compact, with no furniture except two large chairs that were bound in leather. Between them was a metal cabinet, its drawers opened.

The President moved in for a closer look. The drawers contained tools and screws and thick elastic strips. "So the final fitting is done in here, and the patient walks out on a new foot?"

"Exactly," Wales said. "Now, sir, if you'll give me a little room, I'll climb up and put on my new prosthesis."

The President stepped back, bumping into Agent Youngblood. "Sorry, Jack."

"My fault, Mr. President."

Wales plopped down in the chair and shifted around until he was comfortably seated. "You can move in a little closer, Mr. President, and I'll show you how the prosthesis is attached to my stump."

The President stepped forward.

Wales removed his old prosthesis and let it drop to the floor. Then he picked up his new one. "Now, these straps are critically important to a good fit. They—"

Youngblood jerked the President away as the message came through his earpiece. "Bomb! Bomb!"

In an instant Youngblood shoved the President out the door and hurried him down the corridor. Two more agents appeared, guns drawn, and ran alongside, covering the hunched-over President. Then another agent appeared and another, completely surrounding the President. They burst through the door into the reception area, knocking people down and out of the way.

There were screams and shouts as the dignitaries tried to reach the front entrance. Some stumbled and fell, others tripped over them. At the door people were bumping and shoving, desperate to get out. The Secret Service agents formed a phalanx and headed straight for the door, bowling over anybody in their path. They ran out into bright sunlight and down the steps, keeping the President low and completely covered. Then they shoved him into the limousine, facedown, Jack Young-blood atop him.

The limousine sped away, tires screeching.

There was chaos in the reception area. Some of the dignitaries were on the floor, stunned by their falls. One old man was unconscious, another was clutching his chest and gasping for air. Mortimer Rhodes was groaning, holding his fractured wrist.

Rhodes looked up at the doctor in the long white coat. "I think I broke my arm."

Bremmer ignored the old man and frantically tried to organize his thoughts. They knew! They knew about the bomb! But how? Somebody must have talked. Or maybe one of the dogs sniffed it out. Yes! That was probably it. The dog! And that means they don't know who's involved. But they'll figure it out as soon as they examine the prosthesis and find the C-4. They'll know it's me! I've got to get that prosthesis and destroy it. Without it they can't prove a damn thing.

Bremmer looked up at the television screen. Wales was still in the inner corridor, attempting to skip along on one leg and making little progress. The prosthesis was under his arm.

"My wrist." Mortimer Rhodes groaned in obvious pain.

Bremmer stepped around him and went through the door that led to the inner corridor. He wondered what to do if the arrogant bastard refused to give up the prosthesis. Just take it, Bremmer thought, and if necessary kill him. Crush his skull from behind and make it appear that he tripped on his one leg and hit his head on the floor.

"Tim!" Wales called out. "I need a hand."

Bremmer hurried over. "What's wrong?"

"One of the straps came off, and the damn prosthesis

won't stay on my stump." Wales handed the prosthesis to Bremmer. "Can you fix it?"

Brernmer quickly examined the prosthesis. A screw was loose. "Sure. But I'll need a screwdriver and a new strap."

"Then let's go back and get—"

"They're evacuating the building," Bremmer interrupted. "You limp your way out to the front. I'll grab a screwdriver and new strap and be right behind you."

"Good," Wales said and struggled away, using the wall as a support.

Bremmer waited for Wales to disappear, then hurried down the corridor and out the rear door. Screw Wales! he thought. Get in your car and drive and conveniently lose the prosthesis. Without it, nobody could prove a damn thing.

Joanna stood behind a black-and-white squad car a block away from the site of the explosion. She slowly scanned the devastation, again thinking it was a miracle that none of the neighbors had been killed. The terrorists' house had been demolished; only a fireplace and the back of the kitchen were still standing. The surrounding homes were badly damaged, with blown-out walls and windows. And the small fire truck that had been parked close to the cellar window was now on its side on the next-door neighbor's front lawn. Lucky, she thought. Lucky to be alive.

Joanna slumped down to the curb and sat beside Kate. "How are you doing?"

"Pretty good," Kate said, gently rocking the sleeping Jean-Claude. "And my little cowboy has decided to rest now that all the bad guys are gone."

"He's a tough little critter, isn't he?"

"He's a Blalock," Kate said and kissed the little boy's head.

Joanna looked over at Jake, who was sitting next to them smoking a cigarette. His hands were bloody from pulling on the iron bars and digging them out of the cement around the cellar window. Even when a SWAT team member saw a terrorist dash from the garage into the house, Jake kept digging and pulling and scratching. He was ordered to leave, to get out while the getting was good. Jake stayed.

Joanna moved closer to him. "I owe you."

"Next time leave more clues. Okay?"

"What makes you so sure there'll be a next time?"

Jake smiled thinly. "With you, there always is."

"I guess," Joanna said wearily, wanting to find a bed and sleep for a week. She glanced up as Hurley walked over. His earpiece was now in his hand. "Did the warning get through in time?"

Hurley nodded. "The President is on his way to LAX, and they're warming up Air Force One."

"Good," Joanna said, then rested her head on Jake's shoulder. "Jake?"

"What?"

"Thanks."

Timothy Bremmer was on the Santa Monica Freeway heading west and wondering what he should do next. Get rid of the prosthesis, he decided. Break it into small pieces with a hammer and dump them into the ocean off the end of the Santa Monica Pier. Good! But first, call Eva and tell her what happened and get instructions.

Bremmer used his car phone. He dialed Eva's number and waited. It rang a dozen times. There was no answer.

"Where the hell is Bremmer with my prosthesis?" Wales demanded. He was back in his office at the old institute, his stump resting on his desk. "He was supposed to fix the damn thing and give it back to me."

Lucas, the black therapist, shrugged. "I saw him get into his car and drive away like a bat out of hell."

"With my prosthesis next to him, no doubt."

"He was probably scared of the bomb."

"Shit! We're all scared," Wales said angrily. He flipped through the Rolodex on his desk and picked up the phone. "Let's see if we can reach him in his car."

Bremmer's car phone rang. He smiled. It was Eva. It had to be. He lifted the receiver, and that sent an electrical charge to the C-4 under the hood.

Bremmer saw a brilliant ball of fire through the windshield. In the instant before he died, he thought the sun was falling from the sky.

Epilogue

Joanna had never seen or been to a rodeo. It was not what she expected. There was something majestic and courageous about the cowboys as they came out of their chutes riding angry bulls that twisted and turned and did everything possible to throw the rider off.

A bell rang. A chute opened and out came a mean bull named Terminator. The bull bucked and jerked ferociously, but the cowboy managed to hang on for a full eight seconds.

"God," Joanna said in wonderment. "How do they stay on?"

"The cowboys call it grit," Jake told her.

"What does that mean?"

"It means they will themselves to do it."

Another cowboy on a bull came out of the chute and held on for dear life. But the bull was too strong. The rider lasted only a few seconds before hitting the ground hard. Joanna winced. "It's amazing they don't get killed."

"Some of them do."

"Why do they do it? For the money?"

Jake shook his head. "For the trip."

"A trip to where?"

"To a place only cowboys know."

The crowd applauded the cowboy, now limping out of the Long Beach Arena. Jean-Claude applauded with them. The little boy was standing up in his seat, mesmerized by the rodeo. He was wearing boots and a white cowboy hat. The hat was autographed by Webb Stevenson, a champion bull rider, whom Jake had arranged for Jean-Claude to meet before the start of the rodeo.

Joanna moved in closer to Jake and asked, "How do you know Webb Stevenson?"

"I don't," Jake answered. "Webb is related to a desk sergeant in the Rampart Division. He's the guy who set it up."

"With a big nudge from you."

"All it took was one phone call."

"Well, you've made Jean-Claude a very happy little boy."

"I just didn't want him to go back to France thinking America is full of goddamn terrorists."

"We've still got our share of them," Joanna said disgustedly.

"But there's four less now."

"Can you believe that damn Timothy Bremmer?" Joanna asked angrily. "A doctor, for chrissakes!"

"They go bad too."

"But not as bad as George Walter Reineke. Can you imagine sending your daughter out to kill the President?"

"He probably thought it was a good idea," Jake said flatly. "He had some fatherly instincts, though. I'd guess he went back into that house to try to save his daughter."

"Why didn't the sharpshooters get him?"

"Their views were partially blocked by the trees in the backyard. They couldn't get a clear shot."

"In a way, I'm glad they didn't," Joanna said. "It's kind of poetic justice that they all got blown up by a bomb."

"I guess," Jake muttered, his attention now on the next cowboy coming out of the chute.

Joanna stretched her back, which was still sore from her ordeal in the cellar. She waited for the ride to end, then said, "Jake, I've got to get away for a while."

"You want to go by yourself?"

"Yeah." Joanna took Jake's hand and held it. "I'm going to fly to Washington to receive my medal from the President. Then I'm going on to Paris with Kate and Jean-Claude." She sighed before continuing. "I still haven't gotten Paul du Maurier completely out of my mind. I guess I need a little time alone to get over it altogether. Does that bother you?"

"Nope," Jake said evenly. "It's something you've got to do, and you've got to do it alone. It's what the shrinks call closure."

Joanna nodded slowly. "Now I know why you had to go back to Eleni's funeral in Greece."

Jake nodded back as a picture of his former wife flashed into his mind. They were at an outdoor restaurant near Athens, the wind blowing through her hair. She was smiling at him.

"Does it help?" Joanna asked, breaking into his thoughts. "This closure thing?"

"Some."

The PA system squealed loudly. "And now, ladies and gentlemen, the final bull rider of the night, Webb Stevenson. He needs an eighty-six to walk away with first prize."

The crowd applauded, then became silent.

"Is eighty-six points a lot?" Joanna asked.

"It takes a hell of a ride to score that much."

The gate to the chute flew open. Stevenson was atop a big black bull that twisted and turned and threw its head back fiercely.

Stevenson seemed to be floating, as if he were one with the bull. He kept one hand high, balancing himself, while he held on to a leather strap with the other. With one mighty jump, the bull leaped off the ground, its body almost twisting on itself. Stevenson stayed on.

The buzzer sounded, signaling he'd made his eight seconds.

"Jesus," Joanna said breathlessly. "That was unbelievable. No man could stay on a bull like that."

"Unless he's a world champion."

The score was announced.

Eighty-eight.

The crowd roared, up on their feet, cheering the cowboy and his ride. Jean-Claude was yelling at the top of his little voice.

The ovation went on for a full minute. It finally quieted when the bull rider was handed his first-place check and given the microphone to say a few words.

"Thank you, folks," Stevenson said in a soft Texas drawl. "Thanks for coming out and being with us tonight."

The female announcer next to Stevenson asked, "That bull gave you a plenty tough ride, didn't he?"

"They don't come much tougher. He had some really good moves, and I was lucky to stay on."

"Webb, I know you've got a message for a special friend of yours."

"I sure do," Stevenson said and pointed up to the seats where Jake and the Blalocks were sitting. "I want to give a big hello to my partner and friend who comes all the way from Paris, France. He's a real cowboy, folks. Let's hear it for my buddy, Jean-Claude."

The crowd applauded politely.

Then the spotlight was put on Jean-Claude. He stood on his tiptoes and took off his hat and waved it cowboy style.

The crowd went wild.

Jake chuckled and shook his head. "He's all Blalock, isn't he?"

Joanna laughed at him and snuggled up close to Jake,

her chin on his shoulder. "I have one more question for you?"

"What?"

"When you were shot and in the ambulance and thought you were dying, you told Farelli to tell me something if you didn't make it. What was the message?"

Jake hesitated, thinking back. After a pause he said, "That I loved you. That I always had and always would."

Joanna studied his face, staring into his eyes. "There's more, isn't there?"

Jake nodded. "I told him to tell you that I'd wait for you in the next world. Even if it took you a thousand years to get there."

Joanna smiled. "Why is it so difficult for you to tell me sweet and tender things?"

Jake put his arm around her shoulder and drew her closer. "If I said it easy and often, it wouldn't mean as much. Now, would it?"

Joanna nestled her head against his chest and sighed softly. "Oh, Jake."